CENTYR DOMINANCE

By

Michael G. Manning

For more information about the Mageborn series check
out the author's Facebook page:

https://www.facebook.com/MagebornAuthor

or visit the website:

http://www.magebornbooks.com/

 CHAPTER 1

Moira Illeniel studied her companions. They stood close to her in the near darkness of the castle courtyard. It was still some hours until first light.

"Are you sure this is wise?" asked Gram. His new dragon, Grace, rode on his armored shoulders. She was still small, having hatched only a few days previously, but she already weighed close to fifty pounds. The young warrior gave no sign of noticing her weight.

Mordecai's creations, the dragons of Lothion, grew quickly. Grace would probably be larger than a horse within a couple of weeks, and she would be large enough to ride soon after that. Today though, the two of them would ride with Moira, atop her dragon, Cassandra's wide back.

Matthew stood next to him, looking upward with his natural sight, although it was too dark for them to see anything. Instead his magesight roamed outward, hoping to detect the approach of his dragon, Desacus.

The Countess will be angry once she realizes we have gone, noted Grace, broadcasting her thoughts to all of them. *And I can't say that I blame her.*

"Someone has to find Father, and the people need her," said Moira, repeating her earlier argument. "We have to go."

Chad Grayson spoke, "And she'll be rightly pissed when she discovers ye've tied her hands. Once the two of ye have left, she'll be forced to stay close to home."

"We are much better equipped for this search," pronounced Matthew. "She's better suited to handling the task of ruling here." He turned his face toward the hunter, "No one is asking you to come."

Chad's features grew irritated, "Might as well sign my arrest warrant if ye leave me here."

"No one knows you had any part in this," observed Moira.

"Heh!" chuffed the ranger. "That dark witch will suss it out before the day is done, and they'll have me before the Countess soon after. Ye might as well put me in chains yerself."

"Mother wouldn't put you in chains…," began Moira, but Gram interrupted.

"Dark witch?" said the broad-shouldered knight.

"Yer mother, Lady Hightower," clarified the woodsman. Lady Rose Thornbear had inherited her father's title, and while Elise Thornbear still lived she was properly called Lady Hightower rather than Lady Thornbear.

Gram and Chad had worked together long enough that the hunter's rough words rarely bothered him anymore, but he was still puzzled. "Witch? My mother doesn't have any magical ability."

Chad squinted in the dim light, "I ain't so sure o' that. She always kens more than any person has a right to know. It makes a man nervous when she looks into his eyes."

Moira smirked at that, but only her brother could discern the expression in the dim light. Matthew was nodding in agreement.

"It could be that she conspires with dark powers," suggested Matthew with an air of mock seriousness.

Gram was agape at that. "Really? I'm surrounded by wizards, and you're suggesting *my* mother's a witch?"

Moira laughed softly, keeping her voice low, "You have to admit it's uncanny what she figures out, Gram. I have magesight, and she still knows more than me about what's going on in people's heads."

Gram knew they were teasing him by then, and he certainly understood how frightening his mother's powers of discernment could be. "She wouldn't have you locked up," he stated firmly, directing his remark toward the hunter. "She's not vindictive."

"That's as may be," said Chad, "and I ain't so sure of it, but the Countess is most certainly temperamental. Once Lady Hightower outs me, Her Excellency might well put me in chains for letting her young cubs run off on their own."

"It still might be wiser for you to take your chances here rather than come with us," said Moira.

"And that's exactly why I'm comin'," responded Chad. "None of ye are old enough to have the sense of a goat."

I hope you aren't including me in that assessment, Master Grayson, responded Grace mentally.

His reply was drowned out by the sound of beating wings, Cassandra and Desacus were descending. Once the massive creatures had landed the group split up. Moira, Gram, and Grace climbed aboard Cassandra, while Matthew and Chad took spots on Desacus' back. Soon they were winging their way carefully to the east, heading in the direction of the mountains where Mordecai Illeniel had disappeared.

As they flew the sun slowly appeared on the horizon in front of them, setting the sky aglow with red and orange hues. Gram and Chad were white knuckled, clinging desperately to the rough scales of their respective dragons as they rode behind Moira and Matthew. Grace was considerably more relaxed; even if she were dislodged, she could fly on her own.

Several hours later they landed on the southern slope of one of the smaller mountains.

"This doesn't look promising," said Gram, studying the stony ground. It would be hard to track anything there, assuming they found any sign of the lost Count to begin with.

"You're sure this is it?" asked Matthew.

Moira nodded. "This is the area. All of my spell-beasts returned except the one assigned to this region."

"Bitchin' about it ain't gonna help," remarked Chad. "Let's spread out and start lookin'."

The dragons took to the air once more, circling to study the terrain below. The humans did likewise, albeit much more slowly since they were now on foot. Matthew and Moira studied the terrain with their magesight, while Gram and Chad looked for more mundane signs.

The day dragged on slowly, while the dry mountain air grew steadily hotter. It was shortly after noon when Gram spotted the cracked granite stones that indicated a place where something had struck the mountainside with tremendous force.

There was no discoloration of the rocks, but the shear lines were fresh and sharp, a subtle contrast to the more softly weathered stones around them. He was too far from the others for them to hear him, so he sent his thoughts skyward, calling to his dragon. *Grace, I think I've found something.*

The small dragon passed the word along to the others, and in less than a quarter of an hour they had gathered around his find.

"I don't see anything," said Matthew.

Moira felt similarly, but her brother's confidence annoyed her, "I'm not a tracker so I wouldn't presume to make assumptions."

Matthew glared at her, but Master Grayson spoke first, "No, the lad has found somethin' here. Look at the edges, do ye see that?" The older man ran his finger along the sharp granite.

"They're more jagged," said Matthew, rubbing his chin.

As if he hadn't just said he didn't see anything, thought Moira. "Can you tell what happened?" she asked, keeping her irritation to herself.

Gram and the huntsman exchanged glances. "We're on a mountainside, and it's been over a week now. Anything more subtle than this is probably long gone," admitted Gram.

"Still, it gives us a place to work around," suggested Chad.

Moira closed her eyes, expanding her senses outward. Beside her, she could feel her brother doing likewise. At first she felt nothing unusual, but after a minute she found something. Using her aythar, she invisibly highlighted the spot to draw her brother's attention to the area. "Do you see it?" she asked aloud.

"The start of a cave," he mumbled in agreement. He pointed downslope for the benefit of the two non-mages.

Moving carefully, they made their way downward, studying the rocks as they went.

"I can't see shit," complained Chad, looking at the area around his feet. They were near a large boulder which, along with a sturdy bush mostly concealed what appeared to be a small recess in the mountainside. "If he went in there is anyone's guess."

"He isn't there now," stated Moira, "unless it goes farther in than I can sense. Hopefully, we can find something to tell us where to go from here."

"An' what if we don't? What if we find whatever put yer almighty father down? How're we gonna handle somethin' like that?" said the hunter.

Moira glared at the dour ranger, biting her tongue rather than respond immediately. She already wished he hadn't come with them.

"There's nothing in there," observed Matthew. "Nothing powerful at least, although I can feel something odd." His eyes held a distant look.

"Some sort of trace aythar," agreed Moira, "but it smells strange."

"Smells?" asked Gram.

"We don't really have proper words for what we sense with magesight, so I just borrow whatever seems to fit," she explained. "This has an unusual flavor, like some sort of magic I haven't seen before."

"Then it's probably a trap," advised Chad.

"You think everything is a trap," said Gram, hoping to lighten the mood.

"An' I'm never disappointed," replied the hunter, "only pleasantly surprised when I'm mistaken. Better that than the other way 'round."

"It isn't a trap," pronounced Matthew.

"Ye can't know that," argued Chad.

The young wizard gave him a flat stare, "I know. I'm familiar with this magic."

Moira's brow wrinkled as she listened.

Matthew understood her question, and in response he pointed at his upper arm, tracing a line across the area just below the shoulder. "Remember?"

That's where I had to reattach his arm, she thought to herself, *after he practically amputated it.* The reminder brought with it the memory of the strange aythar that had lingered in Matthew's workshop that day. Moira nodded before adding, "That isn't reassuring."

Her brother sighed. He should have known she wouldn't understand. "I need to examine whatever is in there if I'm going to figure this out."

"It'd be more prudent to tell yer lady mother first..." suggested the hunter. "We probably ain't ready fer whatever's in there."

"He's already fought one god and won," noted Gram, and with another word he activated his sword. Scales of shining steel appeared in a cloud around the hilt and rapidly began covering his body. Within moments he was covered in glimmering armor.

Moira felt a hint of recognition as the scales began winking into existence. The aythar was similar to what lay within the cave.

"An' his father fought more'n that and look what good..." began Chad, but Gram wasn't listening. With his armor on, the young man was already making his way into the cave. The twin wizards filed in behind him. *Feckin' kids,* groused the hunter silently.

The back of the niche held a tall but narrow passage. The dark crack was perhaps ten feet from top to bottom, but it was only two foot wide at its broadest point. The bottom was narrow and awkward to step on, threatening to trap their feet or twist an ankle. There were places on either side where the stone was scorched. Ragged grooves indicated the claw marks of something impossibly strong.

"I don't think the opening was originally this wide," suggested Gram.

Ye think?! quipped the hunter mentally. He kept his mouth shut, however. He was too busy trying to figure out how he would use his bow if something came at them from the darkness. It was on his back, with the string across his chest to allow his hands the freedom he needed to clamber through the awkward passage. If anything happened, he would be hard pressed to respond in any meaningful way. Worse, the entry was so difficult it would make any sudden retreat impossible.

Ten feet in, the floor widened and they were able to walk again, rather than scrabble along.

"It goes farther back than I thought," said Matthew.

"Hold on," said Moira. Lifting her hand, she focused her will, producing a small insect-like creature of pure aythar on her palm. Once the shape had formed, her mind twisted the strands of aythar that composed it until they began to pulse and thrum with life. Thousands of complex connections formed within the tiny beast in no more than the span of a minute, guided by the young woman's instinct.

Matthew watched her manipulating the aythar with undisguised curiosity, and perhaps a touch of jealousy, although he would never have admitted it. His sister's Centyr heritage gave her the ability to do some things that seemed patently absurd to his rational mind. After a moment, he felt the tiny beast's mind awaken and begin to communicate with Moira's.

She held her arm out, and the creature leapt away, taking flight on delicate wings. It flew into the darkness and was almost immediately lost to sight. It remained quite visible to magesight, though. It sent a steady stream of descriptions and mental impressions back to her as it ranged outward to the limits of her senses, using its perception to extend her range.

"There's nothing else here," she told them after a few minutes. "Or if there is, it's nothing my pet can discern."

"Anything new in the area where the traces are?" asked Matthew.

That place was less than a hundred yards from their current location and well within both of their perceptual ranges. Moira's pet had revealed nothing new about that area.

"No," she responded. "But there are no other traces deeper in. Whatever happened here, that's probably the extent of it."

"Let's go have a look for ourselves then," said Gram, his voice oddly muted by the metal armor that covered his face. It was easy to forget it was there. The enchantment made the parts that covered his face transparent to the point of invisibility, but they still altered the resonance of sounds coming and going.

Maybe I should fix that, pondered Matthew, *but if I do, the armor might completely ignore sonic attacks. It might be possible to selectively ignore the sounds produced by his voice while filtering non-native sounds, but then he'd be effectively deaf.* Someone punched his shoulder then.

"Hey, dumbass, let's move," said Moira. "You're blocking the way."

"I was thinking about something," he answered angrily.

9

Moira leaned closer, already incensed, "It would be nice if you did your thinking when you weren't standing in front of everybody."

"You're such a jerk, Moira," he spat out reflexively.

The words were nothing unusual, but she felt a familiar pain at their utterance. *I've always tried to look out for you, and you do nothing but attack me as soon as you're the least bit inconvenienced,* she thought. "I'm a jerk?!" were the words that actually came out of her mouth. "You're the idiot who cut off his own arm! Maybe I was being a jerk when I put it back on for you?"

Gram separated them and moved into the space between them, "Let's argue about stupid shit after we find the Count."

"Perhaps one of ye would be so kind as to make a light?" asked the hunter from the rear of the group. "I can't see a gods-damned thing back here."

Matthew closed his mouth even as he created a light on the end of his staff. Moira created two small firefly-like creatures, each carrying a similar light. They buzzed ahead and illuminated the caverns in front of them.

"Show off," said Matthew with some irritation.

The hunter ground his teeth in annoyance at their continued bickering. "Worst feckin' twins I've ever known," he said softly to himself.

"She's adopted," said Matthew.

Moira gave her brother a look that promised future retribution even as Chad wondered to himself, *How did he hear me?*

Gram answered his unspoken question, "The dragons give all of us unbelievably good hearing."

"Now, if they would just make the lot of ye smarter too, I'd be eternally grateful," responded the hunter.

Gram responded by pushing past the twin wizards and moving forward into the passageway. They followed him, saving their argument for later, while the hunter brought up the rear.

Two offshoots led to dead ends, but Moira warned Gram away from them, and they continued until they came to the chamber that held the strange traces of aythar. It was a larger cavern, some twenty yards across and nearly forty in length. Water lay in a shallow pool to one side, but it was a flattened area in the center that drew their attention.

The floor appeared to have been melted there, and it was readily apparent that it hadn't been from some natural geologic process. Moira and Matthew both moved to the spot, their faces rapt with concentration.

Damned magic, thought Chad, but then his eyes spotted something off to one side, a ripped and torn tabard. Gram followed his eyes and picked it up before he could say anything.

Moira considered the traces of aythar with curiosity. The cave was full of them. Something momentous had occurred there. The feeling they carried was indeed similar to the magic that lay behind Gram's sword and the magic she had felt the day Matthew had accidentally severed his own arm. Even so, she could make no sense of it. She turned her attention to Gram and the ranger. "What's that?" she asked.

"Someone's discarded livery," offered Gram, holding up the ragged cloth.

Chad frowned. Something seemed off to him.

"I don't recognize it," admitted Moira.

"It represents the Earl of Berlagen, in western Dunbar," explained Gram.

Moira gave him a surprised look, "How did you know that?"

"I may not be as bright as some, but Mother made me memorize the crests of every known house in Lothion, Gododdin, and Dunbar," answered the young knight.

"This didn't come from Dunbar," interrupted Matthew. "It came from someplace—*else*."

"Those soldiers that came with T'lar crossed over the northern wastes from Dunbar," asserted Gram, "and this tabard came from there as well. I don't see that there's any reason to doubt that."

Chad spoke up, "Why would they leave something as obvious as a tabard here, unless they're trying to lay the blame on someone else…"

Matthew shook his head, "Not the tabard, *this*." He gestured at the empty area in the middle of the room.

Neither Gram nor Chad could see anything there other than the partially melted floor, but Moira knew he was referring to the otherworldly aythar that lingered in the area.

"Could Celior have crossed over here, or re-entered here?" she wondered aloud. As far as either of them knew, he had remained in the world since his first entry when Elaine Prathion had summoned him, the year before they had been born.

"No, but something did," said her brother. "I think the boundary has been changing since Mal'goroth tore his way through. It's weaker. I think something new has come."

Moira shrugged, "Well whatever it is, it's here now. We need to find it, and Father."

"Celior flew when I saw him leave after his fight," Gram reminded them, "and whatever was here hasn't left any significant trace of its departure."

"We need to go to Dunbar," stated Moira firmly. "Someone there was part of this. Once we find them, we may be able to find their unnatural allies."

"We don't know that your father was taken back there," said Chad. "Yer best chance is to widen yer search here. Not that it's a good chance."

"We'll do both," she answered decisively. Her eyes went to her brother, looking for his inevitable argument. She was surprised when he nodded in agreement.

"She's right," said Matthew.

"Chad can stay with you," she continued without skipping a beat. "I'll take Gram with me to Dunbar."

"Take them both," said her brother. "I won't need help searching and Chad can't track from dragon back. I'd feel better if you had two people watching out for you in a strange place."

It was uncustomary for her brother to show such concern, and she bristled at his suggestion that she might need protecting. They argued over it for several minutes before she gave in. Matthew was unreasonably stubborn. It wasn't worth the energy.

"Tell Mother what we're doing when you get back home this evening," she told him at last. It gave her some small pleasure knowing that he would face their mother's disapproval alone.

"You should send one of your little minions," he replied. "I might not go back for a day or two."

Something in his words didn't quite ring true. Moira wondered what he might be planning, but then she decided he was just covering up his fear of facing the Countess by himself. *He's going to use his search as an excuse to avoid facing her for a few days,* she guessed.

She used her aythar and a few quick words to lighten Gram and Chad, so they wouldn't present too much of a burden for Cassandra. As they took to the air, she looked down, watching Matthew wave goodbye. She couldn't help but think she had gotten the better of their bargain.

CHAPTER 2

Cassandra's back was crowded with three passengers. Moira rode in front, with Gram behind her and Chad behind him. She had used a temporary spell to lighten their weight and another to cause them to stick to the dragon's back.

Knowing they couldn't fall off helped with their anxieties, but she could tell they were still uncomfortable. She smiled to herself as she listened to the hunter swearing quietly to himself. Gram on the other hand remained silent, but his hands were clenched into fists.

It's going to be a long and tiring flight, said Cassandra's voice in her mind.

We shouldn't be too heavy, answered Moira. *I lightened the load for you.*

It's more than that, responded her dragon, *the three of you disrupt the airflow around me, so I have to spend more energy using my wings to keep us aloft.*

Let me know if you get tired, said Moira. *There's no reason we can't take breaks if necessary.*

Grace flew beside them, her slender form keeping up with ease. She was still too small to help by carrying Gram, but she had been growing rapidly. In another month or so she might be able to carry a rider, judging by the rate at which the other dragons had grown after hatching.

The wind made normal conversation difficult, and they lapsed into silence. Moira wasn't bored, though. Her mind was preoccupied with the ever changing vista around her. Despite their speed, the mountains seemed to pass by slowly beneath them. The sun might have been hot on their shoulders, but the frigid air did more than compensate for that. In fact, they were becoming increasingly cold.

Moira created a shield around the humans in a sloping dome-like shape to divert the rushing wind, and then she used a word to adjust the temperature within.

That's better, noted Cassandra.

Were you cold? she asked the dragon, somewhat surprised.

I meant the strain of staying airborne. It isn't perfect, but you aren't creating as much drag now, explained Cassandra.

That wasn't what I was aiming for, but it's good to know, thought Moira. She was still relatively new to flying, but she was learning that it was more complicated than she had originally realized.

They only had to stop twice before nightfall. After their second break, they flew until dusk had deepened to the point that they could barely see. Magesight was a poor substitute for normal vision when flying, given its range limitations. Without moonlight, they were resigned to finding a place to stop in the mountains.

The eastern edge of the Elentirs was still more than an hour's flight away, and although the mountains were getting smaller there were still no towns. They were saved from a rough camp when they spotted a sturdy cabin in one of the valleys.

It had smoke coming from the chimney, so it was definitely inhabited. They landed several hundred yards away and hoped that the dragons hadn't been seen. Moira could only imagine what sort of panic the sight of a beast as large as Cassandra might cause.

I will sleep here, the massive dragon told her.

She nodded, *Thank you, Cassandra. I wish you could stay with us.*

It is no hardship. Morning will arrive soon enough.

Grace wasn't quite as content. She knew she was small enough to accompany them within, but her form was still a problem. She was tempted to suggest using an illusion so that she could accompany them, but in the end she kept her thoughts to herself. It would be cold on the mountainside, but she would be warm enough if she stayed beside the larger dragon.

Chad took the lead as they approached the wooden building. "Let me do the talkin'."

"I can speak for myself, thank you," said Moira immediately.

Gram winced at her remark. He already knew better than to argue with the ranger on most matters.

"Yeah? An' what do ye plan to tell 'em when they come to the door?" replied the hunter wryly.

"The truth," she answered. "We have nothing to hide."

"I'm the daughter of the Count di'Cameron. Would you mind putting us up for the night? I'm just out searching for my lord father in the mountains. We won't be any trouble. Do you think you could spare some tea?" responded the ranger pitching his voice higher to imitate hers.

She glared at him, "I do *not* sound like that."

"Don't be so sure o' that, princess," said Chad.

"Nor am I a princess..."

"That ain't the point," he interrupted. "Ye may not sound like that to yer own ears, or even to mine, but to people who're livin' out here in the wilderness, that's how ye'll come off. They'll be scared half to death at the thought of someone like you bein' here. Worsen' that if you tell 'em yer the daughter of the Count."

Moira graced him with an angry stare but held her tongue for a moment as she considered his words. Chad Grayson never failed to irritate her, but she couldn't deny his logic. Finally she spoke again, "What would you have us do then?"

"Let me talk. Yer my daughter, Gertie, an' he's my son-in-law, Gram," explained Chad.

"Why does he get to keep his own name?" she protested.

"Fer one, it ain't that uncommon a name, but yer's is a dead giveaway."

"Son-in-law? You want them to think we're married?" added Gram.

Chad laughed, "Ain't no one gonna believe a great brute like you is my son, an' there's no way ye could be brother an' sister." He looked at Moira then, "Oh, an' we're gonna have to tell them ye're slow. Try not to talk. Stick to grunts if ye can."

Moira's eyes went wide, "What?!"

Gram began chuckling at that.

"This isn't funny," she told him angrily, before turning on Chad. "Shouldn't he be silent too? We both grew up in the castle."

"Yeah, if he talks too much it'll be a problem, but I think he can get by if he sticks to short sentences. Gram's spent a lot of time hangin' around the barracks an' talkin' with yer father's soldiers," said the ranger. "Ain't that right, Son?"

"That's right, Pa," answered Gram, snickering.

She looked back and forth between the two laughing men, growing more annoyed as they continued to laugh. "Mebbe ye should consider that this big lout ain't the only one who kin act differ'nt if needs be," she said suddenly, using a thick accent.

The two of them began to laugh harder, until Gram had to gasp for air.

"What's so funny?" she asked, puzzled.

"Please stop!" begged Gram. "You're killing me here."

Chad smiled at her, "I'm convinced now. Don' say a word girl, from here on yer a mute. Gram, can stick to short sentences, otherwise stay quiet. Yer a very shy boy. Ye ken me?"

"Okay, Pa," said the young warrior.

"This really isn't fair," said Moira, shaking her head.

"Can you disguise us?" asked the hunter. "Our clothes will give us away sooner'n our voices will."

She had already thought of that. Anyone could tell by the fine leather and linen of their outfits that they were far from peasant folk. "Don't worry, *Father*," she told him with a sarcastic grin. "I know just the thing."

A few minutes later, they were inspecting each other. Moira had gone over them with a light touch, altering their appearances with several minor illusions. Their clothes were now scuffed and worn, while their skin looked to be smudged here and there. Chad was notably missing one of his front teeth, and Gram had acquired a bad case of acne with pimples dotting his cheeks and forehead.

"I don't think all this was strictly necessary," said the hunter as he looked at himself in a small mirror she had with her.

Gram chuckled until he looked over the other man's shoulder and saw his pocked cheeks reflected there. He gave Moira a sour look. "You don't look any different, other than your clothes," he told her indignantly.

"You had to have some reason to marry a poor girl who couldn't talk," she shot back, tossing her hair over one shoulder with a look of innocence.

"Some would say a woman who couldn't talk was a bonus, not a drawback," muttered Chad.

Moira's eyes twinkled with amusement, "Would you like to be bald and hunchbacked as well?"

Gram laughed, "Good one, Gertie!"

"Let's go," said Chad gruffly, "before she gets any more nasty notions in that head of hers."

The man who answered their knock stepped into the front yard, closing his door behind him. He studied them suspiciously, and his eyes frequently lit on Gram's broad shoulders. The young man's size clearly made him nervous.

"What do you want?" he asked.

"Pardon us fer intrudin'," began Chad. "We won't be botherin' ye much. It's cold out, an' we were hopin' we could impose on ye fer a place to shelter fer the night, even the barn would be fine. The wind gets to bitin' somethin' fierce at night."

"You're a long way from civilized country," replied the man. His words held a strange accent which Moira supposed must be because they were already on the Dunbar side of the mountains. "Who are you?" added the cabin owner.

"Chad Grayson," answered the hunter truthfully, "an' this here's my daughter Gertie an her husband Gram." He held out his hand, "Pleased to make yer acquaintance."

The other man ignored his proffered hand, "What are you and your kin doing out here?"

"We're lookin' to find a place in Dunbar," answered Chad. "Drought last year ruined our farm, an' the tax man wasn't so understandin'... *if* ye take my meanin'."

"You crossed the mountains?" replied the stranger incredulously. "Damn stupid thing to do. You're lucky to have gotten this far. There're smarter ways to get there."

Chad scratched the back of his head while projecting an air of embarrassment, "Well, we was in a bit of a hurry."

The silence stretched awkwardly for a minute before the man spoke, "You must be strong to have made it this far. The Iron-God bids us to honor strength. You can sleep in the barn tonight. There's a small stream that's safe to drink running about thirty yards to the west. You can find water there. I can't afford to offer you food."

"We appreciate it," said Chad gratefully, ducking his head.

"Steal from me, and you'll regret it," added the stranger. "We don't abide thieves here." He turned away, as if to return to the house.

"Thank ye, sir," said Chad quickly. "We won't cause ye no trouble. I didn't catch yer name..."

"Clarence," said the man, stepping inside. "Stay away from the house," he added as he shut the door. They could hear the heavy sound of a bar being dropped into place.

The barn wasn't particularly spacious, having only one empty stall and a small hayloft that held little hay. Moira guessed that the rocky mountain valley didn't provide much in the way of summer hay to be stored. The stall probably belonged to the big boned mule she sensed in the distance. Clarence must have left it out to forage since the weather wasn't too cold yet.

Aside from the loft and the stall, there was only a small storage area that held a variety of tools. Chad led them up a ladder into the loft.

"You surprised me," Moira told the ranger once they had settled in.

"How's that?" asked Chad.

"I've never seen you so polite before."

Gram laughed at that.

"Hah," said Chad. "I show respect when it's due. These folk live a hard life, an' they're helpin' us out."

Comparing his current behavior to his normal surliness back home, she wondered what that meant for his opinion of her family.

Her thoughts must have been written on her face, for he addressed them directly. "Nobles get more respect than they deserve," he added. "Yer father knows that, which is why he lets me speak as I please. An' it's why I continue to live there."

"So you don't respect my family?" she challenged.

The hunter grinned, "Nah, I'm sayin' yer father is a wise man, an' I honor his wisdom by bein' my normal asshole self."

Moira frowned, not quite sure what to make of that remark.

"Even a nobleman needs an asshole now and again," added the hunter.

Gram chuckled, "Every man needs an asshole—at least once a day."

She looked from one face to the other, "You are definitely a bad influence on Gram." Her tone was serious, but her smile let them know the humor wasn't lost on her. "By the way," she added, "there were two other people in the house."

"Family?" asked Gram.

"I presume so," she replied, "an older woman and a younger one, probably close to my age."

"That explains why he kept his door closed," observed Chad.

"He did seem unusually fearful," she agreed.

"You're probably the only reason he let us use the barn," noted the hunter.

"Me?" she questioned. She also observed that the hunter's accent had become less noticeable now that they were alone. It seemed to vary with his mood and the situation.

"Way out here men get lonely. With you along, he wouldn't be as worried that we'd be desperate," explained the ranger.

Moira's brows furrowed, "Desperate?"

"Yeah," said Chad, "You know—to get…"

"Don't finish that sentence!" interrupted Gram, blushing furiously.

Moira felt her own face growing hot as his meaning sank in.

CHAPTER 3

Moira sat up. She had been drowsing. They had been in the barn for over an hour, and without light, the best option had been sleep.

She could have created a light, but they didn't want to worry their host. They could have lit a lantern too, but there wasn't much point. The best way to get through the night was simply to sleep and rise early.

Besides, the dried meat and hard crackers they had brought hadn't done much for her hunger. She hoped that they would reach a town soon, for living rough didn't really agree with her.

"Someone's coming," she announced for her companions' benefit. "It's the two women from the house."

The two people approaching carried a lantern and a basket between them. Chad coughed before answering when they knocked at the barn door, "Come on in. It's yer own barn after all."

The older woman was dark skinned, and the younger woman who followed her was of a shade somewhere between that of her mother and the pale man they had met earlier.

"I'm Sarah," said the older one before gesturing at the other. "This is my daughter, Laura. We thought we'd offer you some bread and the beans left over from our supper."

"That's a kindness," replied Chad. "You didn't have to do that."

The mother nodded, "We don't see many visitors out here, and when Laura heard there was a girl near her own age, she wanted to meet her."

Laura's eyes went to the floor when she heard her name. The girl seemed intensely shy. Moira started to introduce herself, but Chad spoke quickly.

"My daughter don't talk much. Her mother had trouble while giving birth, an' it did somethin' funny to her. She can manage a word or two now an' then, but she stammers so badly she tends to avoid conversation."

Moira gave the hunter a look that held the promise of future retribution before suppressing her irritation and offering her hand to the younger woman. "I'm M—G—Gertie," she said, narrowly avoiding giving her own name. The stammer made it easy to cover her mistake.

Laura took her hand eagerly, flashing a nervous smile and warm brown eyes as she did. She lifted a small wooden box with her other hand. Her face conveyed an unspoken question.

Sarah appeared slightly embarrassed, "She can't talk. There was an accident when she was younger, before we moved out here. She wants to know if you would like to play a game."

Moira nodded and watched as Laura placed her box on the ground and opened it. The others split the hard loaf of bread that was in the basket. The beans were in a small pot, and there were no bowls and only one spoon, so they were forced to take turns eating. The silent girl unpacked her playing pieces as they did.

It was a simple checkered board, and the chess pieces were hand carved. One of the knights was missing, and a dark colored stone had been substituted for it. Moira sat across from the girl and began setting up the pieces on her side. Chess was a common pastime in her own home, and she guessed that it was probably the only entertainment these people had out here.

It must get boring, playing the same two other people all the time, she thought to herself.

The other girl, Laura, looked at her expectantly once the board was ready, excitement in her eyes. She had given Moira the white pieces, so it was her turn first.

Moira grinned at her. *The poor thing doesn't know what's coming.* She relished the game. Her father was possibly the best player in Castle Cameron, and she had grown up playing from a young age. She hadn't encountered many people who could give her a good game outside of her own family, other than Gram's mother, Rose.

The next quarter of an hour proved educational. After a slow start, she found herself being hemmed in as her defense was systematically picked apart. She had drastically underestimated her opponent. Her defeat came as an inevitable consequence.

Laura gave her a shy glance as she placed her in checkmate. Her expression showed clearly that she worried she might have offended her.

Moira smiled, "Y—you're g—g—good!" Being forced to pretend to stammer was more annoying than losing the game.

Laura smiled in return and held out a piece toward Chad, silently asking if he might like to play.

"Nah lass, I can see ye have me outmatched already," he demurred.

Moira took up the challenge once more, and this time she played carefully from the beginning. The game lasted longer, and she put up a hard fight, but the result was the same. *Damn! She's really good,* she thought to herself.

It was clear that the girl she was playing was far more intelligent than she had initially assumed, and Moira began to divide her attention, using her magesight to study the girl who was forcing her to thoroughly reassess her opinion of her own chess skills.

Back at home she normally couldn't study people's minds. Her father's enchanted pendants effectively shielded the minds of everyone she had grown up around, so it was a relatively rare occasion for her to be able to watch the inner workings of other human beings.

Laura's aythar was normal in most regards, but the working of her mind was unusually sophisticated. Moira could readily see the damaged areas of her brain, but it was the undamaged portions that fascinated her. She couldn't read the girl's thoughts, not without more direct contact, but just by watching, she could tell that Laura's mind was exceptionally capable. The peasant girl's mind moved rapidly as she considered the chessboard, examining and discarding possibilities with brutal efficiency.

She's brilliant, noted Moira. *I wonder if this is what Lady Rose's mind looks like when she's not wearing one of the pendants.* She suppressed a sudden urge to reach out and touch the other girl more directly, mind to mind.

That was something she was not supposed to do, her mother had warned her about it previously.

Not her real mother, of course, but Moira Centyr, the shade left behind by her original mother, who had died over a thousand years past. She had cautioned her about such contact years ago, before she had been given a new body and become human.

You must never allow yourself to touch the minds of normal humans, the Stone-Lady had warned her.

"Why not?" she had asked. She had been only ten at the time.

You are a Centyr mage. We perceive the mind in a different way.

"But I talk to Dad and my brother that way all the time," Moira had protested.

They are wizards. Their minds are not so delicate.

"And Mother and Father talk mind to mind sometimes…"

Your father is not a Centyr. We must be more careful.

Why? asked Moira silently.

We can change things. We have a special affinity for the aythar of the mind, but without sufficient skill even the slightest touch could alter or damage a human's mind.

"Is that why everyone wears those necklaces Father makes?" she had asked.

No. Your father made those for a different reason, but it is for the best that they wear them. In my day, Centyr children were kept away from non-mages until they were old enough to control their impulses.

"I would never hurt someone," she had insisted.

Have you ever built a house of cards? the Stone-Lady had asked. *What happens when your younger brother finds it? Now imagine if everyone's mind were a complex house of cards, one touch can bring the entire thing tumbling down. That's why young Centyr mages were kept isolated. Even after you are grown, you must avoid contact with normal minds. The tiniest mistake can destroy someone's life, and if ever they suspect what you can do, they will fear you.*

"I should return," said Sarah, breaking Moira's train of thought.

Her daughter shook her head negatively. She wanted to play more, and it was obvious that her new friend was willing to continue for a while.

Sarah held her breath for a moment before answering, "Fine. Stay if you wish, but come in as soon as they get tired. I don't want you making a nuisance of yourself."

Moira smiled at that, and Laura nodded in agreement. The two of them played for another couple of hours, while Gram and Chad both gave up and fell asleep. In all that time Moira never won a game, though she came close at one point when Sarah began to drowse.

The other girl closed her eyes while Moira set up the pieces once more. When she finished she realized that Laura had fallen soundly asleep. Moira pushed the board aside and studied the other girl intently. Now that she had some quiet, she could devote herself to studying damage to Laura's mind.

The part of Laura's brain that was responsible for speech in normal people was dark. At a physical level Moira could see that some of the tissue there had died, leaving a disconnect that prevented the girl from speaking, even though she could still understand others' speech.

She had no idea how to restore lost brain tissue, but being a Centyr she knew that wasn't strictly necessary. The sentient intelligences she regularly created had no physical brain whatsoever, their minds were constructed from a web of pure aythar. It would be easy to create something similar and attach it to Laura's mind. Her natural aythar would support it, and it could perform the necessary function of bridging the gap between Laura's intentions and the motor centers that controlled her tongue and voice box.

If I'm really careful, it shouldn't disturb anything else, thought Moira.

Reaching out mentally she crossed the boundary of Laura's mind. She felt slightly guilty, breaking the rule her mother had warned her about, but she knew it was for a good purpose. Deftly she constructed the necessary pattern to enable speech, and using the lightest of touches she connected it to Laura's psyche, allowing it to bypass the areas that no longer worked. So gentle was her work that the other girl never even woke, although she did begin to babble in her sleep, but just for a moment.

Moira withdrew and studied her handiwork. The patterns in Laura's mind had shifted ever so slightly, but otherwise she seemed unchanged. Everything was still balanced and she doubted that the girl would notice a difference. *She'll be able to talk when she wakes. I wonder what she will think.*

She touched Laura's shoulder, "It's late. You should go to bed so your mother doesn't worry."

Laura stirred, opening sleepy eyes, "Mmm, yeah." The sound of her own voice startled her, and she sat up suddenly, staring at Moira in surprise. "What's happening?" she said, with a note of alarm in her tone.

"You can talk now," stated Moira plainly.

"What happened to your stutter?" asked Laura. She clapped one hand over her mouth in surprise. "I'm talking!" she added through her fingers.

"Actually, I need to apologize," explained Moira. "I was only pretending to stutter. We were afraid my accent would give away our origin, and we didn't want to alarm your father."

"You don't sound like him," observed Laura, indicating Chad. The sound of her own voice continued to startle her, and her eyes began to water. "My voice!" she exclaimed. "I can't believe it. I must be dreaming. Who are you?"

"There isn't much point in hiding it now," said Moira. "I'm Moira Illeniel."

Laura stared at her in surprise, almost taking a step back, "You're the Blood-Lord's daughter?" She looked at Chad Grayson who had awoken and was quietly watching them talk. "He's the Blood-Lord?!"

Chad was irritated already by the fact that Moira had revealed her identity, but this new pronouncement made him groan, "Ahh, for fuck's sake."

Moira was none too pleased herself at hearing the name 'Blood-Lord'. It was an appellation that people had begun using for her father after he had slain Duke Tremont and his men in Albamarl. Technically it hadn't even been her father who had done it, but no one believed that. "That's not my father," she corrected, "and I really don't like the term 'Blood-Lord'. My father is a good man, and he's far too kind to deserve that name."

Laura's thoughts were moving several times faster than her newly restored speech could keep up with, "But he...!" She was staring at Chad. "He's not? But then, who is he? Why are you...? What have you done to me?!" She punctuated each question by clapping her hand over her mouth, only to remove it to ask the next one. It was almost comical.

"I just made it so you could talk again," said Moira simply. "I saw a way to help, and it didn't feel right to do nothing."

"You're a witch!"

32

Moira winced at that remark. Most witches were simply older women with some knowledge about medicine and herbal lore. Some even possessed weak abilities to manipulate aythar, but in general they were just ordinary people who had been badly misunderstood. "I prefer 'mage', or 'wizard'."

Laura was backing away now. "I don't believe in demons. Doron protects us. You have no power over me!" Fear was written plainly in her features.

"Stop, Laura," said Moira. "I'm not a demon worshipper. I don't think they even exist, unless you are talking about the dark gods."

Laura darted for the door suddenly, but Moira erected a quick shield over it to keep her from reaching the latch. The girl looked at her hand in horror when she discovered the unseen barrier. "Please, don't hurt me!" she begged. "I never did anything to you."

"I warned ye not to reveal us," commented Chad. "Now she's goin' ta make a terrible ruckus."

Laura's eyes went wide, "Are you going to...? Please, I won't tell anyone. Don't hurt my parents!"

Moira sighed, "This is ridiculous. Doron doesn't even exist anymore."

The other girl's face registered shock at that pronouncement, and her lip began to quiver. "That's blasphemy," she whispered to herself.

"Yer not goin' to get through to her," remarked Chad. "An' now we're goin' ta have to leave. Do somethin' about her."

Laura's mouth opened wide as she prepared to scream.

"Shibal," said Moira, sending the girl into a deep slumber. She caught Laura as her limp form began to fall

and eased her awkwardly to the ground. "Now what?" she asked.

"How long will she sleep for?" asked the ranger.

"At least an hour or two," said Moira, "probably a lot longer since she's still tired."

"Put a little more juice in it, then an' let's go back to sleep. We'll leave before dawn and let them sort it out after we're gone."

"Why did she react like that?" asked Moira.

"People in Dunbar don't have much to do with Lothion. They get most of their news from folk in Gododdin. They don't have a high opinion of magic. After what happened with Mal'goroth an' his sacrifices there, they tend to take a dim view of wizards," explained the older man.

"But wizards had nothing to do with that," argued Moira.

"They don't know that," responded Chad. "Priests, wizards, an' magic, they're all the same to them. She was raised to believe that Doron is good, an' that the people of Gododdin suffered because they turned away from the true gods. To them, there's no difference between yer dad an' Mal'goroth."

Moira's mouth tightened. She didn't like what she was hearing, but she couldn't deny that Laura had reacted badly to learning her identity.

Chad rolled over, pulling his blanket tight.

"Are you just going to lie there?" she asked him.

"Nah, I'm goin' to sleep." His eyes were already closed.

She stared at him for several minutes before sitting back down. Gram's soft snores became more noticeable as silence returned. He had never awoken at all, and now Chad showed every sign of being asleep as well.

Eventually Moira lay down as well, but it seemed like hours before sleep found her. Her thoughts kept running in circles. When Chad woke her before dawn, it felt as though she hadn't rested at all.

Quietly they packed up their things and left, taking care not to wake the girl sleeping near the door. They found the dragons and resumed their journey, but Moira's mind kept going back to the night before. She couldn't get over the sight of Laura's terrified face.

CHAPTER 4

The land began to gradually flatten out as it rolled by beneath them, slowly changing to a rolling plain covered with soft grasses and dotted by trees. There were a surprising number of farms to be seen. While the shiggreth and the war between Lothion and Gododdin had greatly reduced the population of Gododdin, and to some small extent Lothion, Dunbar had grown from an influx of refugees.

Moira watched the scenery slide by, but her mind's eye was turned inward, recalling an old conversation with the shade of her mother. *"No one must ever know the true depths of the Centyr gift, otherwise you will have no peace. Men will fear you, and none will trust you,"* Moira Centyr had told her.

Laura had feared her for nothing more than her wizard parentage and that she had given her the gift of speech. If people feared magic that much, how much more would they hate her for being a Centyr mage? *It isn't fair,* thought Moira, but she knew it was true. She had seen enough unshielded minds to understand that the differences between normal folk and the artificial sentiences she could create were purely technical. Last night had merely brought the lesson home to her in a more direct way.

If you can change one, you can change the other. That thought left her feeling alone, more alone than ever before.

"What do you think we should do once we get to Halam?" asked Gram, yelling into her ear to be heard over the rushing wind. The words startled her from her dark reverie.

She turned her head, leaning back to respond in kind, putting her mouth close to his ear, "Obviously we need to find the Earl of Berlagen, since that's our only clue." Without intending to, she found herself once more inhaling the smell of Gram's hair. It was a comforting scent, masculine and familiar. She resisted a sudden impulse to press her face closer.

"Well, yeah, I knew that," he replied. "I meant, how do you think we should go about it? Are you going to present yourself to King Darogen?"

Moira hadn't really considered that option. "Don't you know where Berlagen's estate is located?" *Why does he smell so good?* She turned her head away so he could respond. *And why am I thinking about that? I'm not interested in Gram. He's like my brother.* She suppressed a shiver when she felt his breath on her ear.

"No, I just know it's somewhere in western Dunbar. I don't even know who the current earl is," answered Gram.

Moira was irritated with her strange reaction to Gram's closeness, and she let it show in her voice, "I don't really want to turn this into a formal visit until we know more about what's going on." Gram began to respond, but she waved him away when he leaned in. "We can talk after we land!" she told him.

He is rather attractive, suggested Cassandra mentally, *for a human.*

Moira blushed, she hadn't realized she was broadcasting her thoughts. *It isn't like that,* she responded silently. *Are you eavesdropping on me somehow?*

No, replied Cassandra, *but I can sense your feelings.*
There are no 'feelings', insisted Moira.
Whatever you say, responded Cassandra demurely.

Moira caught herself growling to herself before she made a conscious effort to stop. Cassandra simply didn't understand. She and Gram had grown up together. They were more like siblings than anything else. Not to mention the fact that Gram had fallen in love with someone else. Tragic as his relationship with Alyssa had turned out to be, it was still someone else he was pining for.

And she's far more beautiful, thought Moira, remembering Alyssa's grace and charm. *If there were some way I could help him find her, I would. He deserves to be happy.*

Halam had appeared on the horizon, and they were drawing rapidly closer, so Moira forced her thoughts back to more productive channels. At her urging Cassandra descended, finding a place to rest in a small copse of trees several miles from the capital city. Gram and Chad stretched their legs once they were back on their own feet again.

"What now, princess?" asked the hunter.

Moira frowned at him, "Don't call me that."

Chad grinned, "What now, milady?" He gave a small bow to punctuate his rephrased question.

"We can enter the city on foot to avoid drawing attention to ourselves. Once there, perhaps we can find out where the Earl's lands are situated. When we know that, we can return and move on," she told him.

"And the King?" asked Gram, referencing his question from before.

"We'll avoid letting him know of our presence, unless it becomes clear that we need his help," Moira answered.

"I don't like the thought of you entering a strange city without me," observed Grace from where she sat beside Gram.

Moira smiled reassuringly, "I'll have the world's most fearsome warrior and a legendary archer with me, not to mention my own magic. I doubt we have anything to fear. Besides, if anything goes wrong Cassandra will feel it, just as you would with Gram."

"Not if you're too far for us to sense you," countered Grace.

Gram was still processing her last remark, "Fearsome? Legendary archer?"

Chad put a hand on his shoulder, "Don't interrupt the girl when she starts makin' sense."

"The city is at the limit of my magical perception," noted Cassandra in her deeper rumbling tones. "Once you're inside I doubt I will be able to feel you."

"It may take us a few days to learn what we need," added the hunter.

"You can fly over the city once night falls," suggested Moira, addressing her dragon. "No one will see you or Grace once it's dark. You can check on us then."

In the end, they went along with Moira's plan. Before they moved on she made two small spellbeasts. The first she sent flying homeward, to inform her mother of their location. She had been worried about her mother for a while now. Hopefully, keeping her informed would help when she had to eventually face the music. The second she kept with her, naming the tiny sprite-like creature 'Pippin'. She could use him to send her next update.

Gram watched Pippin tuck himself away in the collar of her jacket with a raised eyebrow, and then the three humans made their way to Halam on foot, while the dragons once again waited. As they approached the main gate they were stopped by guards. A shabby man with tattered clothes stepped forward, holding his hand out.

They stopped, staring at the stranger. He appeared to be little more than a common beggar, but his hand wasn't held as if he was expecting charity. The guards watched him with disinterest, though it was clear he was acting on their behalf.

"Hello...?" said Moira uncertainly, not quite sure what to make of the stranger's outstretched hand. Gram moved forward to stand between her and the beggar.

"What's this about?" asked Chad.

The guards tensed, losing their bored expressions and making sure their hands were free. Two of them lowered spears. Whatever reaction they had been expecting, a question was clearly not it. "Take his hand!" barked one of them.

Moira could see their unease, not just in their faces and body language, but in the flickering network of aythar that represented their minds. The beggar was some sort of test, a reassurance, and by ignoring his offered hand they were presenting themselves as a danger. *Shiggreth,* she realized. *They're testing everyone who enters to make sure they're still human.* The tattered beggar made perfect sense when seen in that light. Obviously none of the guards would be expected to put themselves at risk touching strangers.

"Let's not get testy, sirs," said Chad. "If ye'll explain what ye want..."

She could sense the muscles tightening in the hunter's shoulders and torso, even as his legs relaxed. His tone was calm, but she knew he was preparing to fight if discussion failed. "It's ok," she told her two companions. Slipping past Gram, she took the poor man's hand in her own. "We're human."

The level of tension dropped noticeably. The guard captain nodded at Gram and Chad, "Them too."

Gram followed Moira's example, and then Chad did the same. Now that they understood the reason, the actions of the guards made perfect sense.

"I thought the shiggreth were all gone," said the hunter.

"Where are you from?" asked the guard captain, ignoring his remark.

"What are 'shiggerth'?" asked one of the guards in the back, mangling the pronunciation.

One of his companions answered in a mutter, "I think he means the night-walkers."

"We're from Gododdin," replied Chad quickly. "Hoping to find work. Things aren't so good back home."

The guard captain squinted at them suspiciously, "She don't sound like she's from Gododdin."

"She's my niece. The two of them lived south of Surencia, before things got bad," explained the hunter.

"That doesn't look like a farmer's weapon," observed the captain, looking at Gram's sword. Thorn was currently in its 'broken' form, but the large hilt still made it conspicuous.

Chad spoke quickly, before Gram could respond, "That's cuz he ain't a farmer. He was a guard in Dalensa. That's all he's got left of his father's."

"Let's see it," said the captain, and one of the guards reached out to pull Thorn from Gram's belt. Instinctively, the younger man knocked the soldier's grasping hand away, stepping to one side.

Everyone tensed.

"Let's not be hasty," said the ranger. "The lad's touchy about his father's sword."

"It's alright, Gram," reassured Moira, but he had already drawn the broken blade, showing it to the guards.

"It's just a broken sword," he offered quietly.

Their eyes widened, and one man whistled in appreciation. "Damn thing looks like it's worth a fortune. You see that stone?"

"There's still enough blade left on it to do someone a serious hurt too," remarked another.

Moira could see the greed flashing in the captain's mind as he stared at Thorn. "We're going to have to confiscate that—for the public good...," began the guard.

Chad reached out and placed a few coins in the captain's palm, "Surely that won't be necessary."

The captain might have refused, for the sword was clearly worth far more than any small bribe, but Moira touched his mind softly, dimming his avarice and teasing his more generous side to the forefront.

"Fine," said the guard-captain. "Don't let me hear of you three causing any trouble." Stepping back he waved them forward. The others cleared the way for them.

"Thank ye, sir," said the hunter.

As they walked on Moira could hear them muttering behind them, "That was odd. Why'd the captain let them pass?"

"...sword must have been worth a fortune."

"Shut up, Simmons!"

When they had gotten out of sight of the gate, Chad let out a lungful of air. He had been holding his breath. "I didn't think he'd let us go so easy."

Gram had already twisted his sword belt around to hide Thorn's hilt behind his cloak.

"Let's find something to eat," suggested Moira, hoping to divert the conversation. She felt a small amount of guilt over altering the guard's mind, and she wanted to put the moment behind them.

Gram gave her a broad smile, "I won't argue with that. I feel like I could eat enough for two men." The sunlight caught his hair as he spoke, creating the illusion of a golden halo around his features.

Moira let the view sink in for a second before replying, "Now we just need to find a decent inn." *When did he get so handsome?* She couldn't help but admire the breadth of his shoulders as he walked ahead of her.

"There ought to be a tavern or somethin' similar around the corner there," said Chad.

"Have you been here before?" Moira asked him in surprise. In point of fact, her magesight had already revealed an establishment that was probably an inn ahead of them to the right, just out of sight.

"Nah," answered the hunter, "but I know pubs, an' we just left the main gate. There'll be several nearby."

CHAPTER 5

The Dusty Doxy was anything but dusty. They had just stepped inside, and Moira's eyes revealed a main room that was meticulously clean. Patrons sat quietly at tables scattered around the room, watching the newcomers curiously. The bar looked relatively new, compared to the old wood paneling that decorated the rest of the taproom.

Chad coughed before muttering, "This don't look good. Let's look a little further down."

Gram shrugged and then looked at Moira.

"It's lovely," she ventured. "Why don't you like it?"

The hunter grimaced, "Who could be comfortable in a place like this? It's too clean. The place gives me the creeps. I can't trust a bar that looks like a woman's boudoir."

"Hello," said a new voice. An attractive woman in her middle years was approaching. Her hair was a dark auburn, but it was heavily interspersed with gray streaks. There was an air of authority about her that enhanced rather than detracted from her welcoming smile. She gave the impression of being well accustomed to dealing with men, a friendly confidence; her large bust did nothing to distract from that feeling.

"Hello," said Moira promptly, smiling in return. "Do you serve food here?" From the corner of her eye, she could see Gram had frozen, his eyes drawn to their hostess' proudly displayed bosom. *Oh, for goodness sake!*

"In a little while, if you're patient," said the newcomer. "Cook just arrived, but he should have the evening fare ready in an hour or so. You look like you've traveled far." Her eyes moved between them, noting their clothing.

"Yeah, this is my dau...," began Chad, but Moira interrupted him.

"I'm Moira, and these are my servants. We've come from southern Gododdin," she said quickly, determined not to be caged again by one of the hunter's stories. While their hostess's overly exposed chest, and Gram's reaction to it, irritated her, she still felt a certain warmth from the woman. Observing her aythar, Moira could tell that she was easy going and straightforward compared to most.

The redhead smiled, "I'm Tamara. Nice to meet you, Moira. Would you and your companions like to sit at the bar, or perhaps you'd prefer a private table?"

Moira would definitely have preferred a private table. The eyes of the room were still on them, making her uncomfortable, but Chad spoke first.

"The bar would be fine," he put in. Seeing the dark look Moira shot him, he leaned over and whispered to her, "We won't learn anything sitting alone."

Tamara's eyes lit on him in curiosity, no doubt wondering at a servant who made so bold as to make such decisions. After a second, they switched to Gram, and she smiled. "Where were you twenty years ago young man, before I retired?" She gestured to the bar, indicating they should sit.

They made their way over, while Gram struggled to answer her question, "I wasn't born yet."

Tamara laughed, enjoying his discomfort.

Gram and Chad sat on either side of Moira, protectively situating her between them. After a moment Tamara sat beside Gram. Leaning forward she placed her hand casually on his shoulder while addressing Moira, "Would you and your companions like something to drink while you wait?"

"Tea would be lovely, please," she answered, hiding her annoyance at the woman's excessive familiarity with Gram. It didn't help that she could easily tell what sort of effect Tamara was having on him. The young warrior was blushing furiously.

"An ale for me," announced Chad. "Somethin' that doesn't taste like dog piss if ye have it."

"M—me too," agreed Gram, stammering slightly.

"Perhaps you'd rather have small beer, don't you think?" suggested Moira. Small beer was half water, half beer, a drink meant mainly to quench thirst rather than to inebriate.

He glared at her, "I'd rather have ale."

Tamara waved at the man behind the counter. He had been listening, letting her do the talking rather than interrupt. He put a kettle on the stove in the back and then began pouring the ale.

"Tamara, if it's permissible for me to ask, are you the manager here?" asked Moira.

"Oh no, that would be Lars, the fellow pouring the ale. I just hang around because I enjoy meeting people, and to annoy him. I'm the owner," explained the older woman.

Chad watched Lars pulling ale with professional interest. He seemed to approve of the man's technique as the heavy mugs were filled. "How did this place get its name?" he asked Tamara idly.

The owner smiled, "I renamed it after I stopped working and bought out Madame Brengir. It was called the 'Red Lady' before that."

"That explains the look then," he said, sipping his ale carefully. "I bet you were one of the top ladies here, if you could afford to do that."

Tamara wondered if she had misjudged the hard-faced ranger; he was definitely more perceptive than she had realized. Grinning she replied, "I was very popular, and I was no fool when it came to saving. Thankfully, Madame Brengir wasn't the kind to steal from her girls."

Moira was the one blushing now. *This was a brothel?* She found herself even more embarrassed as the older woman met her eyes boldly. The other woman's expression told her that she knew exactly what Moira was thinking. Dropping her gaze, she found herself looking at Tamara's ample bosom, which only made her feel more awkward. *She's a...*

"I was a pleasure girl," said Tamara, without any hint of shame. "I named the place after myself in a way."

"Ye don't look so 'dusty' to me," laughed Chad.

"Thank you," she answered, accepting the compliment. "I thought dusty sounded better than 'grey' or 'decrepit'."

"I'd think ye'd make more money if ye had kept it as a whorehouse," commented the hunter without the slightest hesitation.

"That's true," agreed Tamara, "but I want to leave my daughter something more respectable someday. Plus, I was worried she might take up the same profession."

Moira's mouth chose that moment to start working, "Daughter?"

"Yes dear, my daughter," said Tamara. "Children are one of those things that happen in my old line of work. No matter how careful you are, sooner or later you make a mistake. Not that I regret it, of course. Amy is the best thing that ever happened to me."

"Sort of like my dad," said Gram quietly to himself.

"What was that?" asked the proprietress.

"Old story," said Chad, waving his hand, "his father was a whoreson."

Gram's face tightened and Tamara glared at the ranger. "That was unnecessary," she told him, "not to mention rude." She turned to the others, "Is he always so unpleasant?"

Moira shrugged in embarrassment, but Chad answered first, "Ye caught me on a good day, darlin'. That was a compliment. My favorite people are bastards an' whoresons." He raised his mug as if in a toast before taking a long draught.

"And what was your parentage like, to produce such a prickly personality?" wondered the proprietress.

Chad smirked, "Actually, it was surprisingly average. My dad was a farmer an' my mother a gentle soul. I can't really lay any of the blame at their feet. I was just born an asshole."

Gram shook his head. He was already well acquainted with the hunter's strange humors, but Moira began to laugh. The stress she had been holding onto had kept her tightly wound for days, but for some reason Chad's remark tipped her over the edge and she began chuckling in spite of herself.

"At least he's honest," remarked Moira, once her laughter had stopped.

"Speaking of which," began Tamara, "what brings you and your friends to Halam?"

Moira was ready for the question, "We're hoping to find the Earl of Berlagen. He knew my father, and I was hoping he might take us into his service..."

Tamara held up her hand, "Let me stop you there. If you don't want to talk about it, don't, but I've been serving people for too long to listen to tall tales."

Moira's mouth was still open, but her mind was working overtime. She could see an honest concern in the other woman's face, and her magesight revealed the truth of it in Tamara's mind. She decided to take a chance, "You're right. What gave me away?"

"I've got an ear for lies," said Tamara. "Besides, I could see too many holes in your story from the start. These two men aren't servants or farmers. The old one bears the calluses and scars of a lifetime with a bow, and your young gentleman here carries himself like a warrior-born. I'd think he was a mercenary, but his smooth skin and shy politeness point to a noble birth. Am I wrong, milady?"

Moira sighed, "I can't contradict you."

"So what brings you from Lothion?"

"Is it that obvious?" asked Moira.

"Your accent isn't that different than that of southern Gododdin, but I've been with men from both countries. I can tell the difference," said the auburn haired woman. "Don't worry, though. I doubt many around here would notice. Now, back to my question...," she added.

Moira hesitated, trying to decide how much to share, "I can't tell you the whole truth, but I am looking for my father. I think Berlagen might have information regarding his current whereabouts."

Tamara's brows shot up in surprise, "A Lothion nobleman has gone missing, and you suspect the Earl of foul play? How rare, how unusual!"

"I didn't say that exactly…," minced Moira.

"But that's the only reasonable conclusion, milady," stated Tamara calmly. "I don't involve myself in politics, so I'm afraid I won't be of much use to you. Nor am I sure I should be, since it might be treason. I don't think our good King Darogen has done much to create enmity between our nations, but the Earl is a strange one. Who knows what he might do, or have done?"

Chad's eyes were sternly on his mug, but his ears were at full attention. Gram, by comparison was watching the two women with unabashed concern. Both of them worried what the outcome might be if their new acquaintance decided to betray them.

Tamara winked at Gram before speaking to Moira once again, "Tell your bodyguards to relax. I have no intention of reporting you to anyone. In fact, I might know someone who would consider helping you."

Moira nodded, "I wouldn't expect anything from you that goes against your conscience. I harbor no ill intentions toward Dunbar. In the main, I just need help finding the Earl of Berlagen."

The proprietress smiled, "I believe you. Look over your shoulder. Do you see the man in the corner over there? The one watching you?"

Moira tensed, looking furtively across the room. While most of the patrons were talking quietly amongst themselves again, she could sense their eyes on her. "I think they're all watching us," she replied.

The older woman laughed, "That's true. We don't see many strangers in Dunbar. I mean the dark haired one in the corner, not much older than you. He's a nobleman, easy on the eyes."

Moira spotted him then, before quickly turning her gaze back to the bar. The man was well dressed and looked to be in his early twenties, with aquiline features and sharp eyes. "I think I saw the one you mean."

"That's the Baron Ingerhold," said Tamara. "He's a smart young man, and no friend of Berlagen. He's also still unmarried, if you're looking for a husband."

Moira turned a deep red, "I had no intention…"

The older woman chuckled, putting a hand on her arm, "Relax, I was only teasing. He is the most sought after bachelor in the kingdom, though. Just something to keep in mind."

"I'm not here to think about such things," protested Moira.

"He's young, and you are beautiful. If you're looking for a co-conspirator, then you should be thinking about such things," admonished Tamara. "Men are fools once their smaller brain takes over."

Moira stared at her, but her magesight could plainly see the amusement in the older woman's aythar. "Please stop teasing me," she said seriously.

Tamara sighed dramatically, "You're taking all the fun out of it. At my age I have so few pleasures. Wait here, I'll speak with him and bring him over for an introduction."

She nodded and as soon as the owner had left, Chad leaned over, "Are you sure this is wise? We just met that woman."

Gram stayed silent, but his look as he gazed at the man Tamara was talking to, was one of disapproval.

"I'm not sure of anything else here," admitted Moira, "but I get a sense of honesty from our hostess."

"Ye can't know that," argued the hunter.

She noticed that his bow was settled innocuously against his leg, and while it was unstrung, he had the string over the lower end and was holding the rest in his hand. She wondered how quickly he could ready it. It seemed an awkward weapon for a bar, but she knew better than to underestimate the ranger. "I *do* know it," she insisted. "Besides, I'm sure if something goes wrong you'll be more than ready to murder everyone in here," she added sarcastically.

The hunter sniffed indignantly before taking another drink, then he answered, "I had no such intention, but I could enjoy my ale more if ye'd stop tellin' our business to every person five minutes after ye meet 'em."

Moira saw the man rising from his table and heading toward her, following Tamara. Standing, she moved to meet them halfway across the room, leaving her tense companions behind. The stranger started to bow, but she held up her hand to stay him. "Is there somewhere more private we could talk?" she asked Tamara. She could feel Gram and Chad's unhappy eyes on her back.

"Let me show you one of our private alcoves," said the proprietress, giving her a look of approval. She led the two of them to one of the curtained rooms on one side of the main floor. Holding the curtain back, she motioned them within. "I'll be back in a few minutes with your tea."

"Thank you," said Moira, before turning her attention to her guest. The stranger motioned for her to take a seat before moving to place himself across from her. She couldn't fault his manners.

"Mistress Tamara said you might need my advice, Miss…?" He let his sentence trail off into a question.

She gave him a gentle smile as she replied, "I don't think it would be wise to share my name with you yet. I hope you don't find that offensive."

The Baron dipped his head, "I find it intriguing, and coupled with your foreign accent—beguiling. My name is Gerold Ingerhold, and I am pleased to make your 'enigmatic' acquaintance."

"Thank you, Lord Ingerhold. I appreciate your patience with my reticence," said Moira, sitting a little straighter.

"Please, just 'Gerold' if you will. Using titles makes me uncomfortable, especially since I don't know yours," he answered, flashing a smile that was probably meant to put her at ease.

She couldn't help but study his aythar, particularly the parts that revealed his intentions. She could see interest there, but it was more than intellectual. His mind was disciplined, but it was clear that he found her attractive. She shifted uncomfortably at the observation. "With your permission then, Gerold it is. I'm interested in Earl Berlagen," she said, hoping to put his thoughts onto a more practical track.

"The younger or the older?"

Moira paused, "Pardon?"

Gerold pulled at his ear, absently toying with a gold earring. "We have two Earl's, although only the younger properly holds the title. His father, the elder, handed the title down to his son when he became too ill to attend to courtly duties. I assume you mean the younger, but I thought I should make certain."

"Oh," she responded awkwardly, "you don't say?"

"But I just did," said the Baron with a confused look on his face.

"No, I meant that I understood, but I was a little surprised," she explained.

He frowned, "Then why didn't you just say that?"

Now she was a little flustered, "It's an expression we use in Lothion." She caught herself too late, and she saw his aythar flicker with a sense of victory at hearing her name her homeland.

"I see," he replied gracefully, "an idiom then, one of acknowledgement while also connoting surprise. Is that correct?"

"Uhh, yes," she answered. It was quickly becoming apparent that she was outmatched when it came to crossing words with the Baron.

He patted her hand, "Thank you for telling me your home. I know it was an accident, but I feel more comfortable knowing it nonetheless."

The touch seemed overly familiar, but she didn't withdraw her hand immediately, "I hope my nationality isn't a problem." She tilted her head down slightly, so that she looked upward at him with her eyes. *What am I doing?*

He withdrew his hand, studying her thoughtfully. "To the contrary, I find foreign women exotic. Why are you interested in Lawrence Berlagen?"

"I think he may have information regarding my father's disappearance," she said forthrightly.

Gerold's eyes widened slightly. "I would be lying if I didn't tell you that the Earl has been rather strange of late, but it might be easier to help you if I knew who your father was."

She ignored the latter part of his response, "Strange? How so?"

With a sigh he went on, "The young earl has always been a gregarious man, given to socializing, but over the past two years he has secluded himself. He almost seems misanthropic these days."

"Misanthropic?"

"It means that he seems to dislike people," explained the Baron.

"I know what it means," said Moira with some irritation. "I was curious what you meant specifically. Is he just becoming a hermit, or has he shown some actual signs of actively disliking people?"

Gerold continued, "He fired much of his staff last year, and just over a month ago, he sent more than half of his men at arms away. None of them have returned."

"They crossed the Northern Wastes," commented Moira. "We found some of his livery."

The Baron stared at her, and she could actually see a storm of activity around his brain. At last he spoke again, "Then you must be the daughter of either the Baron of Arundel or the Count di'Cameron." He paused, following his thoughts to their conclusion, "Are you a wizard then? Or is the proper term 'witch'?"

There was a faint hint of fear in his aura, but it was clear that he was keeping it under control. Moira chose her words carefully, "Witch is a superstitious term, generally used for people with very little ability, and commonly used for those disliked by their peers. I am a wizard, but I have found that people here react badly when they discover that fact."

"Can you see my thoughts? Are you reading my mind now?"

Moira almost winced, but she suppressed her reaction, "I would have to touch you to do something like that, but I can speak mind to mind with other wizards, or with someone with whom I have a special bond." She didn't bother explaining the fact that mages could sense emotions without direct contact, or the fact that her own senses could reveal far more about someone than even most mages realized. For the most part her answer was truth; she *couldn't* actually read his overt thoughts.

"Your father is the Blood-Lord isn't he?" asked the Baron directly.

She ground her teeth, "I *really* dislike that term. My father is the kindest man you could ever hope to meet. He's done nothing but sacrifice and suffer for the people of our realm. Anything you've heard to the contrary is a damn lie."

"Did he really face the gods themselves?" Gerold's voice was a whisper now, as if he feared someone hearing the question might suspect him of heresy.

"They weren't gods, merely supernatural creations given power by men of old, and yes, he did in fact face them," she answered. "None of this helps me. I need to see this Earl and find out if he knows anything about my father's disappearance."

The Baron caught himself for a moment then, before lowering his head in a gesture of contrition, "I am sorry. Realizing your identity has made me rude. You must understand that magic is distrusted here. We count ourselves as faithful devotees of Celior."

"What will you do then?" challenged Moira. "Run out and summon a mob to hunt me down? I am only here to find my father."

"No," he said after a moment. "I think you too beautiful for that, though it may damn me. Besides, you don't fear a mob do you?"

"No."

"What would you do?" he asked curiously. "I won't do it of course, but I find myself unable to help wondering. Would you fight them off? Could you hurl fire at them?"

"I would just leave. There's no need to hurt anyone. I can defend myself from most attacks," she insisted. "Why do men always think of violence first?"

"What of your companions?"

Moira laughed a little at that. "I would restrain them. To protect your people—of course."

"They are wizards too?"

"No," she said, waving her hands. "The younger one is the son of Dorian Thornbear, and the older one is just a grumpy old man, although he's fought in many battles. He's probably killed more people than any ten men you've ever met—combined."

"That those two are your only companions leads me to believe you didn't plan to find your father through diplomatic entreaties," commented Gerold. "You might find more help than you suspect, if you enlist the King's aid."

Moira pursed her lips, "I don't think your king would take kindly to accusations that one of his vassals had kidnapped my father. Besides, I thought your people distrusted wizards."

"Wizards yes," agreed the Baron, "but an ambassador from Lothion is a different matter. Allow me to present you to the King. Greet him openly, and then make your needs known in private. He is a wise man, and a fair one. He will appreciate your discretion, and given the Earl of Berlagen's odd behavior of late, I have no doubt that he will be open to helping you discover the truth of the matter."

"I'm not actually an ambassador," Moira informed him, "I came here on my own."

"Aren't you related to Queen Ariadne?"

"She's a cousin, yes," answered Moira. *My first cousin, twice removed,* she noted mentally, *though we aren't actually related by blood.*

"That's enough," said Gerold. "Present yourself as an informal representative. King Darogen is an intelligent man. He will understand your reasons. Small political fictions are a matter of convenience."

"You seem to have a lot of faith in your king. Are you close to him?" she asked.

The Baron straightened slightly, "I am, and I am sincere in my desire to help you."

She could read the earnestness in both his posture and his aythar. "If he decides not to help, it will make my options more limited."

"Options?" Gerold raised one brow, "Do you mean breaking into his home, or storming the castle at his ancestral estate? I thought it was my gender that always thought of using violence first?"

"I think I could manage something subtler than that. My intentions are peaceful, but don't mistake me, I will use force if it becomes necessary to free my father," said Moira, trying to put steel into her words.

Gerold glanced down, examining his well-trimmed nails, "You don't seem the type."

"I'm not," she admitted, "but I have seen blood. I won't shy from it if I can save my father."

"So what course will you choose?"

"I would take your advice, but I brought no attire suitable for meeting royalty," said Moira, challenging him with her eyes.

Gerold smiled, taking her hand in his, "Then we shall have to remedy that."

CHAPTER 6

"I don't like this," said Gram for perhaps the fourth time.

Moira patted his shoulder sympathetically, "That's too bad."

"I don't trust that greasy lordling," he added for emphasis.

"You're very wise," she agreed.

"Stop patronizing me," he complained.

"Then stop whining," she shot back. "We've been over this several times now."

"I don't understand why we are waiting here. You should have an escort."

"Baron Ingerhold will be escorting me. You don't have any clothes suitable for the occasion," she explained patiently—again.

"You didn't either," grumbled Gram.

"Gerold didn't have any clothes to fit you," she returned.

"And yet he had a dress that would fit you, doesn't that seem a little odd? What sort of man keeps a house full of women's clothing?"

"It was his sister's dress, and it's much easier to take in a little fabric than it is to try and create extra where none exists. You're twice the size of any man we've seen. His tailor would have to be a mage to make one of his shirts fit you," chuckled Moira.

"As your knight, I could wear my armor, then my clothing wouldn't matter," suggested Gram.

She frowned at him, "You can't bear arms when meeting a king, and you can't wear your armor without having Thorn out. Besides, do you realize what you look like in that armor? It's unworldly. You'd scare the daylights out of everyone who saw you. That's not the sort of impression I'm hoping to make."

"Don't you have anything to say?!" asked Gram, looking at Chad in exasperation. "Surely you can't agree with this plan?"

The older man took a slow sip of his brandy. Lowering the glass, he held it casually in one hand before replying, "I made meself a promise a long time ago, boy. I don't argue with stupid."

Moira glared at the ranger, but Gram pounced on the remark, "See! Even he thinks this is a dumb idea."

Chad held up a hand, "Let me clarify that. She's goin' ta do what she wants. That's clear enough. She's not exactly defenseless either, but if somethin' happens an' she don't return, we'll go straighten things out with His Royal Majesty."

"What does that mean, precisely?" asked Moira.

Chad smiled, "It means ye best be careful. Dunbar wouldn't do very well without a king."

"That would start a war," she countered.

"Assumin' there was enough of 'em left to make an army," noted the hunter. "The boy here might take a while, but he could probably slice his way from one end of this backwater nation to the other. An that ain't even considerin' the two pissed off dragons waitin' outside of the city. You might mention that to His 'Majesty' if the negotiations get rough."

A few minutes later, a carriage pulled up in front of the Dusty Doxy and Moira stepped out. The Baron's footman held the door for her as she climbed in. She didn't have to turn her head, her magesight confirmed Gram and Chad's stares on her back.

Gerold offered her a choice of seats before glancing out the window, "Your companions don't seem too pleased with your decision."

"They'll be fine," she assured him, "so long as I return by nightfall."

"You won't stay at the palace?" asked the Baron. "The King is almost certain to offer hospitality."

She smiled, "Best not to tempt fate. My friends are very protective. You don't want to see what those two are like when they get cranky. I'll be polite in my refusal—I'm sure King Darogen will understand."

Gerold nodded, "You're right, of course, about the King I mean." He put a finger across his lips, while a thoughtful look crossed his features. "Still, I cannot help but wonder. I have heard many stories about Sir Dorian, but philosophers generally advise that sons of great men rarely match their father's renown. Is the young lad really such a great warrior?"

"Let us pray that Dunbar never has to learn the truth of it," she answered mysteriously. *Ooh, that was a good line,* she thought, pleased with herself. *Father would be proud.*

The Baron let the topic pass, but after a minute he spoke again, "Before we arrive, there is some news I need to share with you."

Moira kept her features smooth, doing her best to seem as poised and polished as she hoped that he perceived her to be. "Do tell."

"The Earl of Berlagen is currently at the palace attending the King," began Gerold. "I had not known that the King summoned him, but he arrived yester eve, when I met you. This may be a highly propitious time to uncover the information you seek."

That surprised her, "Is he staying at the palace?"

"He has a house in the city, and he left his retainers there, but he stayed at the palace last night," the Baron informed her.

"Do you think I'll get a chance to talk to him?"

"It is quite likely, if you wish it, though I would advise you to discuss your situation with King Darogen first," said Gerold. "You will need his foreknowledge and support if Berlagen reacts badly to your inquiry."

"And you think he would give it?"

The Baron of Ingerhold shrugged, "That is only for the King to decide, but I hope so."

She thought for a moment, *what would mother say? No, what would Rose say?* Eventually she replied, "Then I will be guided by your experience and wisdom." *And if I find that the Earl is hiding something from me I will take him apart piece by piece until he tells me where my father is.*

Since leaving home Moira had been fascinated by the constant variety she discovered in the aythar of the people around her. In Castle Cameron and even in Lancaster, almost everyone was shielded by one of her father's amulets. She had occasionally encountered unshielded people, usually children or busy folk who had simply forgotten to put on their pendant, but since coming to Dunbar she had been surrounded by them.

It was distracting.

She had told her escort the truth, she couldn't read their thoughts, but she hardly needed to. As they rode they passed a multitude of vibrant worlds; a woman carrying water, her back aching and her mind consumed with worry, probably for her children; a man angry and frustrated, with what she couldn't be sure, but it most likely involved his employer; a child fascinated by a bird flying overhead, even while his stomach complained of its hunger. A thousand different worlds shouting at her, some bright and some dour, but all of them beautiful.

I have to focus, she told herself, pulling her attention inward. The carriage had come to a stop, and Gerold was exiting, holding a hand toward her to help her down. She didn't need his assistance, but she thought the gesture kind. Behind his actions lay a generous spirit, she could see that easily enough, despite his polished demeanor. He suffered from some of the same flaws that most men did, but she could see his mind working hard to discipline his thoughts. From what she had seen of unshielded humans thus far, it was a rare trait.

By contrast, the guards who watched them pass through the main entrance to the palace exhibited far less inner self-control. Their faces were cool and their exteriors calm, but their thoughts were lewd. One glanced away, ignoring a mild interest in the shape of her body beneath the dress, while the other seemed to be actively creating a highly descriptive narrative that probably featured her in demeaning poses and little to no clothing.

She suppressed a shudder as they passed. *Why can't more of them be like Gerold?* she wondered. She was beginning to appreciate the benefits of growing up in a place where everyone's mind was shielded.

"Is everything alright? You haven't spoken in a while."

Gerold's voice jolted her from her reverie. Nodding, she answered, "Yes, sorry. I was just trying to figure out how to explain my problem to King Darogen."

"Don't worry," said the Baron, smiling, "he's a decent man, as men go, and an excellent king, as kings go."

"Where are we going first?" she asked.

"A short audience with the King," he responded. "I sent a letter in advance this morning. After that, I suspect he will request you join him in the main hall for the noon meal."

They made their way to a small waiting room and sat on comfortable chairs while they waited for the chamberlain to call them in for their turn before the king. Several ladies entered shortly afterward, and their eyes kept moving to watch her. Their minds were fairly glowing with envy and petty thoughts. Moira began to wonder what bothered her more, lewd men or jealous women. *Will I have to get old and ugly before it gets better?*

"Don't mind them," said the Baron, as if he too could sense their hostility. "They're just sizing up the competition."

A minute later, the large double doors opened and the chamberlain, a tidy fellow named Bernard, ushered them into the audience chamber.

The room itself was similar in layout to the audience chamber that Queen Ariadne used in Lothion, but the style and ornamentation were different. Deep red and maroon tapestries dominated the walls and the furniture was all built of a dark-hued cherry wood. Most of the fittings and hardware in the room were gold, which made a brilliant counterpoint to the reds and dark wood.

Rows of cushioned benches separated by a long aisle were occupied with a smattering of people, nobles apparently. Men at arms lined the walls and three men stood to one side of what must be King Darogen himself. A tall man with light brown hair and a simple gold circlet sat upon a carved wooden throne.

Moira had sensed the people within long before they had entered, but she hadn't given them more than a cursory appraisal with her magesight before the doors had opened.

Now that she looked more closely, she was shocked. A sudden gasp escaped her.

Gerold's hand was on her shoulder as he urged her forward, "Try to keep your composure."

She turned her head toward the Baron, eyes wide. "He's dead," she whispered.

The Baron didn't know quite what to make of her remark, leading her on, he responded to her quietly, "Don't be ridiculous. What are you talking about?"

"Your king," she mumbled, pulling up short. She resisted his efforts to lead her any farther. The man staring at her from the throne was a living corpse. His heart was beating, his lungs were still moving, but there was no mind, and his aythar was almost non-existent. King Darogen might as well have been a lump of dead meat, for his body held no more aythar than the chair he sat upon.

But there was *something* within his skull. Where she would have expected to find a brain, surrounded by a vibrant and living web of thoughts built of gossamer aythar, she found instead dead metal. It was as if some twisted smith or surgeon had emptied his skull and filled it with iron. *No, not iron, it's some other metal, and it's far too complex for cast metal.* She could sense other energies moving within it too, but nothing resembling aythar and certainly nothing indicating life.

Gerold had stopped beside her, his face reddening, "You are embarrassing us. What's wrong with you?"

"Not me...," she said, her voice tremulous, "...it's him. What are you?" She pointed one hand directly at the dead king.

People were muttering on either side of the room, uncertain what to make of her actions, but the king spoke firmly, "Is the witch afraid to approach us?"

The words struck her as odd. It was like watching a statue talk, at least from her perspective. Although Darogen's face showed the normal expressions, and his voice was properly inflected, she could plainly see that there was no mind behind the words. Her eyes and magesight roamed a room that suddenly seemed filled with enemies. The others there were human, with emotions and aythar reflecting the looks of annoyance and hostility that the king's label of 'witch' had evoked.

The only others who seemed slightly different were the three standing to the left of the king. Their aythar flickered slightly, as if in anticipation of something pleasurable. The starburst symbol of Celior lay proudly displayed on their chests. *Channelers,* she realized. *This is a trap!*

The King's lip curled in disdain, "You will surrender yourself for arrest." Holding up a strange set of milky white manacles, he directed the nearest guard to approach him and handed them over to the man. "Put these on her."

Moira's eyes flashed in anger a sudden breeze kicked her hair up as she took control of the previously still air around her. Her shield grew stronger, and she turned toward the doors. "I'm leaving," she declared.

"You do not fear to defy a king?" asked Darogen, his tone strangely emotionless.

"I was raised to fear neither men nor monsters," she replied, her voice taut with restrained power. "I saw my first battle while still a child. My father fought the gods themselves and won. I will not fear you—whatever you are." Raising her fist she spoke a word and hurled the air swirling around her against the doors, flinging them open. People gasped, and some yelped in fear. "Stand back, I don't want to hurt anyone," she commanded, striding toward the exit.

The guards managed to keep their nerve, and five of them moved to stand in front of the now open doors, while the others approached her slowly, spears down and pointed menacingly in her direction.

"Shibal," she pronounced and all of them collapsed slowly to the floor, their minds slipping into unconsciousness. For a moment she was tempted to do something else, to reach out and touch them more directly, to turn them against their dead king, but she restrained herself.

"My king!" shouted Gerold, finally aroused from his shock. "What is the meaning of this? She is your guest." To his credit he moved to stand between her and the king.

King Darogen's face was devoid of expression. "Take her," he ordered the priests standing next to him. Aythar flared around the men as Celior's power flowed into them.

Moira had expected that. Her hands had already gone to her waist, pulling her upper, presumably decorative, belt free. At a touch, it separated into two smaller strips of braided metal, and her will sent power flowing through them. The buckle came apart, forming two handles, one in each hand while the metal straightened into glowing swords. Runes along their lengths flared to life as the weapons began to glow with dangerous energies.

The belt had been inspired by the enchanted blades that Elaine had made for her mother years before, but while those were simple weapons, these were designed for a wizard's use. Rune channels made them effective for augmenting her ranged attacks, while a secondary enchantment simultaneously turned them into deadly swords.

She used them to slice away the offending bands of aythar that the channelers were using to try and ensnare her as she marched implacably toward the doors.

What she hadn't expected was the sudden arousal of the sleeping guards. Eyes opening, they took to their feet again to block her path. The part that shocked her was that she could clearly see that their minds were still deeply asleep. The noble guests also rose from their seats, moving to surround her.

The noblemen's minds were a picture of terror and fear, but their faces were placid, and their bodies moved with calm precision.

They are prisoners inside their own bodies, she realized. *How is he doing that?* Her magesight revealed no extraneous aythar, and she was sure it wasn't something being done by the channelers.

Gerold, like the other guests in the audience chamber, was unarmed, and he wrestled with several of the men trying to reach Moira. She would have told him it was pointless, they couldn't touch her anyway, but there was not time for explanations. The way to the exit was momentarily clear, and while the channelers continued to harass her, the three of them together didn't have enough capacity to really be a significant problem. She had been engaging in mock battles with her brother for years, and he was far stronger than these three put together.

She paused and then turned back. She couldn't leave the Baron behind and he was already so entangled with the other guests that he couldn't possibly hope to extricate himself. Unfortunately, before she could use her power to create a shield around him and force the others back, one of the guards stepped forward and expressionlessly stuck a spear through him.

"No!" she yelled, horrified by what she saw. Blood stained his shirt where the spear head protruded from his back. Without thinking, she raised her hand and still having the wind bound to her will, she sent the offending guard flying backward. She could almost feel it when she heard his skull crack as his body struck the hard stone wall, and it made her stomach lurch. *I killed him,* her inner voice noted as a wave of guilt and shame swept over her.

"Run, Moira," said the wounded lord. "Get out while you can."

"Shut up," she told him, gritting her teeth and fighting down her rising bile. "I'm saving you. I've seen worse than that." Extending her aythar, she started to envelop him in a protective shield, but once more the channelers interfered, attacking her from three separate directions. Her shield shuddered under the assault, and she knew that she couldn't afford to play nicely any longer.

Pointing her right hand sword at the nearest channeler, a man some twenty feet away, she sent a line of incandescent power sizzling through his mid-section. The rune-channeled energy tore through his flimsy shield and ripped a fist sized hole through his abdomen. For a split second, before he collapsed, she could see through his torso to the damaged wall behind him. Aiming her left hand sword at one of the other channelers, she warned him, "You're next if you don't rethink your participation here." Her hand was visibly shaking.

While making her threat, she created a defensive shield around Gerold. The guests, as well as the guardsmen, were still trying to get to her, despite the ineffectiveness of their hands and weapons against her personal shield. Their dead expressions, combined with the terror that lay within their trapped minds, was almost enough to drive her to insanity.

With a surge of adrenaline she pulled the wind around her, turning it into a violent cyclone of air, flinging them back and creating more space for herself.

More guards entered from the hall, and these she could see were still operating normally, that is, their native minds seemed to still be in control. They gaped at the scene within.

King Darogen's face changed, resuming its previous liveliness as he yelled at them, "Shut the doors! Don't let her escape!" The effect was profoundly disturbing for Moira, like watching a dead man being controlled by a puppeteer.

The guards leapt to obey, closing the double doors and dropping a heavy bar across them to keep her in.

Things had gotten thoroughly and completely out of hand. Staring around the room, Moira tried to figure a way out of her situation that wouldn't result in the death or injury of so many bystanders. Anger and frustration warred within her, but she couldn't lash out without considering the consequences. Most of the people facing her were being controlled against their will; 'how' they were being controlled she was uncertain of, but she could see the panic and terror hidden behind their calm faces. The wind roared around her, and the simplest option would have been to expand her cyclone, destroying the room and its occupants. *I should have brought a spellbeast,* she thought. *I'd have had more options.*

She did have one magical servant with her, a tiny sprite-like creature named Pippin, but it held little power. She had meant for it to serve as a messenger later, to let Gram and Chad know that things were going well, but it was increasingly looking like it would have nothing good to report.

Moira considered channeling power into the tiny spellbeast. It would be quicker than creating one from scratch, but doing so in the middle of an ongoing battle would leave her weakened and vulnerable. She made her decision. *When fighting a snake, remove the head, and the body will die.*

The wind died abruptly, dropping broken pieces of furniture and tattered upholstery to the floor as Moira withdrew her aythar. Turning one of her swords in King Darogen's direction, she channeled along the blade again, directing a powerful stroke at the monster that appeared to be orchestrating the chaos around her.

With uncanny coordination, every person near the line of fire threw themselves into the path of her attack. The powerful beam tore through them like tissue, and twelve people died in the space of a heartbeat. The beam continued on and still struck Darogen, but its power had been somewhat diminished. The king had dodged as well, and it tore a small hole through his right arm near the shoulder, rather than piercing his heart.

Moira saw the noblemen and guards collapsing in front of her, their minds registering shock and pain as their bodies died. Darkness enveloped each in turn as their terrified minds dimmed and went out. "No!" she cried, aghast at what had happened.

That was when the remaining channelers struck.

Focusing their power they sent twin bolts of pure force, not at the young wizard, but at Gerold. Moira hadn't put the same amount of power in his shield, thinking it only necessary to protect him from their non-magical adversaries, and it collapsed before she could reinforce it. Pain blinded her as the feedback sent her to her knees, struggling to retain consciousness.

They killed Gerold, she realized, *just to capture me.* She could taste iron in her mouth, but Moira's anger was rising fast. Shaking her head she started to stand, ignoring the pain in her skull as she prepared to incinerate the channelers, and possibly everyone else left in the room.

The milky white bracelet clicked as one of the guardsmen snapped it into place around her right wrist, sending a tingling numbness up her arm. She swept her left arm across, and the blazing sword she held tore through the man as though he were made of warm butter. Before she could recover from her swing, someone else struck her head from behind, sending her tumbling to the floor. She dropped her sword as she fell, but she rolled with the blow to gain some space. Lifting the remaining sword in her right hand, she discovered it had gone limp, reverting to its inactive form as a metal belt. *That's odd.*

Men fell over her, wrestling to hold her arms even as a strange lethargy came over her. Focusing her will she burned two of them, but a second blow to her face ruined her concentration. A wrenching pain shot through her shoulder as her arms were pulled together behind her, and a second click sounded as the manacles were locked around her other wrist.

She shrieked with fury, but her aythar hardly responded to her will now. It was fading fast, draining into the strange shackles that bound her. "Get off me!" Moira kicked and twisted, but she couldn't escape the hands of her captors.

An unseen blow sent the air exploding out of her lungs, and her resistance evaporated. Choking and gasping, she collapsed and in the relative silence she heard King Darogen's chilling voice, "Kill her."

"Go Pippin," she gasped in little more than a whisper. "Find Gram, find Cassandra—tell them." A makeshift club struck her then, and darkness found her.

CHAPTER 7

"I don't like it," Gram muttered, watching the carriage carrying Moira rumble away.

"Quit yer bitchin'," responded Chad. "Today might actually be a good day."

"How do you figure that?"

"With our little princess gone, we can do whatever we like." The ranger gave him a rare smile. "Why don't we take a stroll about town?"

Gram frowned. He could sense an undercurrent of extra meaning behind the older man's words, but he wasn't sure where he was leading. "Aren't you worried about her?"

"Nah," said the hunter. "Despite what you think, that fellow she left with seemed pretty decent. Besides, she's probably safer with the King than anywhere else in this benighted city. This is a perfect opportunity fer us."

"Opportunity?"

"To see what we can find out about the Earl Berlagen."

Gram crossed his arms and waited, his posture indicating that he was anticipating a complete explanation.

"While you were wastin' yer youth an' *not* takin' a roll with our most attractive hostess, I was takin' care of business."

"'Wasting my youth?' I was sleeping, which is what *you* should have been doing, instead of spending all evening drinking," argued the young knight. What he couldn't say, what was too difficult, was that his heart was still broken. There was no way he could even consider lying with another woman after losing Alyssa. Gram wasn't sure if he'd ever be able to think of another woman that way, although he could perfectly understand why the hunter thought the proprietress was so attractive.

"Hah!" exclaimed Chad. "If I had a woman like that after me, I'd probably still be recoverin' this mornin'. I could get over a hangover quicker'n that woman! What you ain't realized yet, is that Chad here was workin' hard last night, an' while you were restin' that big wooden knob you call a skull—*I* was gatherin' valuable information."

Gram looked at the woodsman skeptically, "You don't say?"

"I do say, an' you, me boy, would be wise to listen," said Chad, giving him a conspiratorial wink. "Our dear Earl is in town, visitin' the King. He arrived yesterday, an' he's stayin' at the palace. All of his people are at his house here in the city. We could take a walk over that way an' see what we can discover while their lord an' master is out an' away."

The young knight stared at the hunter, thinking carefully. After a moment he said, "Moira won't be back until this evening anyway…"

Chad gave him a wicked grin.

"But what if she needs us before then?"

"Do ye really think that? That girl's more dangerous than both you an me put together, *an'* she's got magic too!" Chad laughed a bit at his own joke.

Gram made up his mind, "Alright, let's do it." He made a point of not laughing.

"Why am I carrying this again?" asked Gram. He shifted his hand to indicate the bow stave it held. "This doesn't exactly make us inconspicuous. Normal people don't walk around town with such weapons."

"Speak fer yerself," snapped Chad. "Our story is that we're bowmen, lookin' for employment. If ya don't have a bow, that'll spoil the tale."

Gram sighed, but didn't argue further.

"See, that fellow has a crossbow," said Chad, nodding his head toward a man on the other side of the street.

"He's a town guard," answered Gram dryly.

Chad shoved him slightly, "Don't stop an' stare, he's already lookin' at us."

Gram growled, "Then you shouldn't have pointed him out!"

They kept walking. They were on the west side of the city now, and while they hadn't yet reached the more affluent section where the Earl of Berlagen kept his city home, something felt distinctly out of place. Gram couldn't put his finger on exactly what it was, but it made him itch between his shoulder blades.

"Cut to the left there," said Chad quietly as they were about to pass the corner of one building.

Gram did, but his eyes looked a question at the other man. They were now in a narrow alley between two shops.

"We got a stalker," Chad informed him quietly. "If he turns the corner, be ready. If he keeps walkin', just stay silent."

Gram waited, letting his mind go still in the particular way that Cyhan had taught him. It was second nature to him now. Seconds crawled by until a man passed the entry to their alley. The stranger stopped, looking ahead and then turning into the darkened passage. The man's eyes widened in surprise as he spotted the two men he had been following crouching on either side of the alley.

Time froze as Gram flowed forward, his speed seeming almost secondary to the perfect grace of his movements. His right hand stretched out, and his palm caught the newcomer under the chin, slamming his head back with such force that the man fell senseless to the ground. His skull echoed loudly as it struck the cobblestones; he had been completely unconscious before he hit the ground.

"Damnitt," swore Chad. "How'm I 'sposed to question him now?!"

The young knight grimaced, "Oh…"

The hunter was already kneeling over their would-be follower. "Shit, I think ye killed him."

"What?!"

"No, wait—he's still got a pulse, but his eyes are all out o' kilter. How hard did you hit him?"

"Hard enough…," said Gram somewhat sheepishly. Cyhan had once had him train with regular soldiers to teach him to moderate his blows, but since he had received the dragon-bond he still hadn't quite adjusted to his strength.

"Anomaly detected," said the stranger quite audibly. Opening his eyes, the man began to sit up.

Gram hit him again.

"Gods-be-damned! What were we just talkin' about? Why'd ya hit him again?" cursed Chad.

"He startled me."

The stranger began to twitch and spasm as he lay between them.

Chad gave the younger man a hard stare of disapproval.

"It was an accident," said Gram, but he felt terrible already.

"There's somethin' not right about this fellow," observed Chad. "He was actin' odd, and talkin' odd besides. Do you know what an 'anonomy' is?"

"I think he said anomaly," replied Gram. "It means something strange or unusual."

"I know what it *means*," growled the hunter. "I just misheard him."

Gram wrinkled his nose, "He smells terrible. Why is a tanner following us?" He held up one of the stranger's brown stained hands to highlight his observation. That combined with the strong odor of urine was all the proof of the man's profession anyone would need.

"Good point," agreed Chad. "He's a weird choice for a spy." The ranger glanced down the alley and then back toward the street. "Let's go. We'll draw more suspicion if we're seen hoverin' over an injured body."

Gram didn't like leaving the man there, but he couldn't argue with the hunter's logic. The two of them made their way out of the alley and back down the street, doing their best to walk normally. There were a few people along the road, and each of them seemed to take far too long staring at them as they passed, heightening Gram's paranoia.

Their road intersected two others a hundred yards farther on, and the crowd grew dense. The open space there became a makeshift market, filled with people selling a variety of vegetables and other foods. It seemed ordinary enough, but Gram noticed several people openly watching them.

You're letting your imagination get the better of you, Gram told himself. *This is just a regular market. Nobody has any reason to suspect us of anything.* Chad's hand on his arm drew his attention.

Twenty feet away a fish seller stared at them from his stall. After a moment, the man's face changed, going strangely slack as he stood and began to walk in their direction. Most of the people in the crowd ignored the man, but a few others stopped and began doing likewise.

At least eight or nine different people were approaching them from different directions within the crowd. It might have seemed less unusual if they had all had something in common, like being guardsmen, but these townsfolk were seemingly unrelated. Two were women, still carrying their purchases, while another was a dried fruit merchant.

"This way," urged Chad, heading to their left. It was the shortest distance out of the crowd and to one of the roads that led away from the congested area.

They made it ten feet before another stranger, one whom Gram hadn't spotted yet, put his hand on his shoulder, tugging hard to arrest his forward motion. Already filled with adrenaline, he turned to loosen the man's grip and planted his left elbow in the stranger's belly. Without stopping, they continued forward, ignoring the gasps of surprise as some people noticed the sudden altercation.

Chad stopped suddenly in front of him. Someone else had grabbed him without warning, and the two men struggled briefly. It was impossible for Gram to see precisely what happened, but then the newcomer fell away, and the ranger began moving again, a flash of steel in his hand and blood marking the ground.

He just stabbed someone in front of everyone, thought Gram. *The town guard will be after us in a minute.* Despite the worry that thought evoked, it paled beside the mystery of why they were being followed and assaulted by perfect strangers. Two more people grabbed at Gram's sleeves, and he struck out, knocking one sideways and sending the second one flying. He felt the distinct crunch of bone as his fist connected with one of their cheeks. *That was a woman!* Guilt and fear fought for dominance within him.

People were screaming now as others within the crowd noticed the unexpected violence. The man Chad had stabbed was bleeding on the ground behind them, and several others were struggling to rise after falling back from Gram's reflexive blows. The most eerie part was that the injured made no sound at all. The only ones yelling were onlookers.

The hunter shoved a stunned farmer out of his path and broke into open air, his feet moving into a run. Gram stayed close behind him, and the two sprinted from the square and into a narrow road. Most of the people in the market watched them with expressions of either outrage or surprise, but a select few followed with blank stares.

"What's going on?" Gram said loudly as they ran.

"I dunno, but it's damn weird!" shouted the ranger.

"Which way?" asked Gram as they approached a new crossroad.

"Right, that should take us to the gate."

"We can't leave without Moira!" said Gram, already turning in that direction.

"She ain't wanted for murder an' assault," responded Chad.

"They attacked us," argued Gram.

"Tell that to the judge an' see if he believes ya," said Chad, but then he stopped. "What the fuck?"

A line of people stretched across the road in front of them. None of them were guardsmen, they appeared to be simple townsfolk, all with blank faces and glazed expressions.

Gram paused beside him, using the opportunity to summon Thorn and his armor. "I'll break through; stay close behind me."

"There're too many," countered the older man. "They'll drag you down."

"They'll shy away from the sword," said Gram. "None of them even have weapons."

"How did they even get in front of us?" wondered Chad, but he followed the young knight as they ran at the line of townspeople.

Nothing happened as Gram had expected, however. The people in front of him showed no fear of the sword at all and instead threw themselves at him. He twisted and pulled, using his elbows and shoulders to tear himself free, reluctant to strike down unarmed civilians, but the ranger's prediction proved accurate. Within moments he found himself mired in a throng of grasping hands, and their sheer weight began to bear him down.

Chad was showing less restraint, using two long knives to cut at any who approached him, but several bleeding opponents were already dragging him down to the cobblestone pavement.

Forgive me, thought Gram, desperate now. Despite the weight of those tugging at him, he ripped his arms free and swept Thorn outward, cutting two men down with one stroke. Blood flowed, and within seconds the roadway was slick with sanguineous fluids and dying men. Cutting fiercely, he cleared the area around himself and then moved to free his companion. Thorn rose and fell, and arms and legs came away from their owners as the great sword sundered flesh and bone.

More people were emerging from homes and shops that bordered the bloody street. Some cried out in dismay at the sight that greeted them. Men and women lay scattered and bleeding in the road around the metal clad knight. A loud whistle in the distance signaled the approach of the town watch.

Gram took in the scene around him with no less horror than the spectators did. *I didn't have a choice!* his heart cried within him. *Did I?*

Doubt assailed him as he heard a young boy's cry, "Mother!" Across the street a man was restraining the child who sought desperately to rush to his dying mother's side.

I don't even know which one she is. He stared at Chad in shock as the man yelled at him once more. He hadn't even heard him the first time. "Let's go, boy! The town guard is comin'."

"Why is this happening?" he asked the woodsman.

"I don't know, but if we don't get moving we'll be wondering it from a jail cell."

They ran, continuing down the road and hoping to find a clear indication that the path they followed did indeed lead toward one of the city gates. Before they got such a sign however, they encountered another group of blank faced residents blocking the road ahead of them. Without thinking, they turned left, ducking down a blind alley and hoping to find a route to escape.

Fifty feet in they discovered their mistake. The alley ended in a stone wall. They were trapped, and people were filing into the only way out. Chad strung his bow and loosened the arrows in his quiver.

"How many arrows do ye have, boy?" the ranger asked him.

Gram stared blankly at him before his mouth answered for him, "Five."

"Give me your quiver," said the older man.

"I have a bow as well," he argued. Men were running toward them already.

"No time, an' no sense wasting arrows," said the archer. His bow was up already and two arrows were in the air before he finished his sentence.

Gram's heart wasn't in it anyway. The thought of shooting people now, after he had killed so many, made him sick, but there seemed to be no alternative. Chad Grayson's bow thrummed with a steady beat as he drew and released, the man's arms working a deadly rhythm. In the span of less than a minute his arrows were gone, and seconds later he had emptied Gram's quiver as well. Seventeen people lay stretched across the road, most of them dead already, though one or two still clung to life with arrows sticking out from their bellies.

"I'm out, lad," said the archer. "It's gonna get ugly from here."

It's already ugly, it's horrific, thought Gram. "No," he said suddenly. Glancing upward he pointed for his companion's benefit.

"It's twenty feet to the roof. Even in my youth I couldn'ta climbed that, even if'n we had the time," said the archer.

Rather than explain, Gram knelt and linked his hands, clearly indicating the other man should step onto them.

"It's too far!" protested Chad. "Even with help, I couldn't jump that far."

"Just keep your leg stiff," said Gram. "I'll do the work."

More people and a few guardsmen were appearing at the opening of the alley. Shaking his head in denial, Chad nonetheless picked his bow up and slung it over his shoulders. Stepping onto Gram's hands, he locked his leg into place, balancing himself with his hands on the young man's broad shoulders.

Standing abruptly Gram heaved upward with incredible force, launching his friend skyward. Chad yelled obscenities throughout his ascent until landing at last on the slate rooftop. Miraculously, he kept his balance, although he was clearly shaken by the experience. Looking down he called out, "Now what?"

Gram looked up as he bent his knees, trying to judge the distance. With little time to contemplate, he leapt as hard as he dared. For a moment he felt as though he was flying, and then he was past the edge of the roof. He continued on for another ten feet before falling back to crash onto the hard slate tiles. They cracked and crumbled around him as he fell on the far side and began tumbling down the sloped roof.

He flailed as he rolled, trying to arrest his fall, but it was hopeless; his armored hands could find no purchase. His only consolation was that when he eventually tumbled off the roof it was on the other side of the building. His armor, cunningly crafted, stiffened when he struck the cobblestones, saving him from broken bones or worse, but he still felt bruised inside it. Chad leaned over the edge, then turned and lowered himself carefully before dropping the last ten feet to join him.

The young warrior found his feet quickly, but as he was about to set off at a jog Chad tapped his shoulder. "There's no one on this side to see us." The hunter finished by pointing at a cellar door close to where they were. An iron padlock secured the door.

Gram understood him immediately. Gripping the lock in two hands he set his shoulders and twisted. The lock hasp proved stronger than the metal band it passed through, with a pop the mounting tore loose, leaving the cellar door without a lock or a place to put one. Hurriedly they opened the doors and descended the stairs, pulling the doors closed over them.

"I don't think anyone saw us entering," muttered Gram softly.

"Hell, I can't even see us," observed the ranger. "It's darker than an old lady's…"

Gram placed a hand over the other man's mouth before he could finish the sentence. "There are people moving on the street above," he whispered. In point of fact, there weren't, but he truly didn't want to hear the end of the saying. Some phrases could not be unheard. He waited an appropriate interval before speaking again, "It looks like we're in someone's root cellar."

"Smells like it anyway," agreed Chad. "I don't know how you can see anything in here with the doors shut. It's as black as pitch in here." He paused for a moment and then continued rapidly, "Blacker'n the inside of a cow's ass." The hunter snickered as he finished his addition.

"You just had to say something like that, didn't you?"

"I was just testin' to see if cow parts bothered you as much as women's naughty bits. Now I know, all I need to do is say somethin' about c—mblrlph!" The older man's voice became garbled as Gram's hand covered his mouth. He chuckled lightly when the hand was removed.

"Next time I'll stuff a moldy turnip in that cesspit you call a mouth," grumbled Gram.

The hunter grinned at him, "Yer a terrible liar, lad."

"I wasn't lying. There are turnips everywhere."

"Nah, not that. I meant about the people above a minute ago. How can you see so well in here?"

"Grace—the dragon bond, it does more than make me stronger. My senses are all keener."

"Now that's interestin'," said Chad, rubbing his chin thoughtfully in the dark. "How about yer nose?"

"Well, yeah…," answered Gram, but then he stopped as a rank odor rose to fill his nostrils. "Damn, that's bad!" he hissed, trying to keep his voice down while still emphasizing his dismay at the awful stench. Despite himself, he began giggling and his laughter held an almost hysterical note.

Chad laughed along with him, until at last he worried that Gram was losing control. "That's enough, you're goin' to give us away."

"More likely they'll notice the foul odor emanating from the cellar," countered Gram. "What did you *eat* anyway?"

"I think it was that trollop's beer—or maybe the turnip soup…"

"I take back what I said about the moldy turnip then," said Gram, choking on another short laugh. "That might be the death of both of us." He went silent for a while after that, and the somberness of their situation settled over him once more. "How can we be laughing like this, after what just happened?"

"This ain't yer first time killin' people," observed the hunter.

"It was different before. They were assassins, and it was about protecting someone else. This was butchery. Those people never had a chance, but they just wouldn't stop…" Gram didn't go further, his throat had a large lump in it. When he spoke again it was a question, "How can you be so calm?"

"Everyone's different. Some laugh, an' some cry after a battle, but it's the nighttime that's the worst, when you're lyin' alone in your bed."

Gram could hear the old pain in the other man's voice. He knew the archer had killed hundreds in the war with Gododdin and probably others even before that. "How do you deal with it?"

Chad gave him a false smile, "I don't. In the daytime I live, I laugh, an' I go on without thinkin' on it. At night, well, I drink—a lot."

They didn't talk for a while after that, but eventually Gram broke the silence with his most awful question, "How many do you think I killed in the street back there?"

"It looked worse than it was…" said Chad, "…eight, nine, maybe."

"That's pretty bad," said Gram despondently. "Some of them were women too."

"I killed eighteen."

Gram lifted his face from his hands, "You only had seventeen arrows."

"The guy in the market," reminded the ranger. "I gutted him. He won't make it."

"Some of the arrows might not have been fatal," remarked Gram. He winced internally as he said it, realizing that whether two or three survived, it was still a slaughter.

"Nah, none of them are goin' home today. I didn't wing any of 'em. I learned that lesson the hard way a long time ago. I put every fuckin' one of those shafts through somethin' vital." Chad's words were filled with bitterness and perhaps a sense of self-loathing, but he wasn't finished, "I'm a murderin' bastard maybe, but I ain't leavin' this world without takin' as many with me as I can. When I die, it won't be while I'm holdin' a bow, more likely it'll be a knife in the dark, probably from a woman I was drunk enough to think loved me."

Gram wasn't sure how to respond, so he settled for, "Now you're just getting morbid and tragic."

"It's only tragic if they stick you before you get what you paid for…"

"I think I liked it better when it stunk in here, and we were laughing like fools."

Chad grinned, "Careful what you wish for lad."

Gram tried not to gag.

CHAPTER 8

Moira's head was yanked roughly back, while another one of the king's guests prepared to open her throat with a feast knife. It wasn't an implement normally used for murder, but since those attending the king weren't allowed to carry weapons, it was all the man had. Her eyes rolled in stark fear as he turned the sharp edge inward to do the job. She knew it would be more than adequate.

"Stop," said another voice out of her current range of vision. "Celior needs the knowledge she has. Killing her will violate our bargain."

The knife stopped, lying cold against the skin of her neck. King Darogen answered whoever had spoken, "Explain his reasoning, we were told her progenitor already had the information required."

"The wizard still resists your attempts to deconstruct his brain," said the channeler.

"His physical form continues to shift; eventually he will tire. You will have your information then," said Darogen.

"You cannot be certain of that. Even if he does falter, your attempt to absorb the information in his head may fail," countered the channeler.

"There is no reason to think his offspring has the knowledge Celior desires."

"You do not understand humans then," argued the channeler. "Even if she doesn't, she can be used as a bargaining tool to weaken his resolve."

"Our consciousness comprises a billion such minds," said Darogen, "we know far more about humanity than a creature like your master could ever dream to understand."

"Then consult them! *They* may understand, but clearly *you* do not."

A short pause followed, and then Darogen spoke once more, "It appears you are correct. The female seems to lack her father's ability to transmute himself, therefore we will take her mind. If the information is there, we will no longer need the sire, if it is not, we may still use her body as leverage against him." The king stepped forward, giving no appearance of feeling the terrible pain his shoulder must be causing him.

The knife vanished and two other men gripped her head fiercely, using their fingers to force her mouth open. Moira's jaws were strong, but their combined strength overcame her, and slowly they pried her teeth apart. Darogen's face loomed close, and his lips opened. Something metallic glinted as he pressed his mouth against hers.

No! Moira's mind was screaming as she felt something cold and hard crawling over her tongue. Sharp legs cut as the strange metallic insect pulled itself forward, seeking the back of her throat. Thrashing violently against the men who were holding her, she had no hope of escape. Panic obliterated her reason, but the fear brought her remaining power into sharp focus. With little thought she created a shield within her mouth, encasing the strange monster there and crushing it. A terrible taste made her want to retch as the shield vanished. The men holding her relaxed, and she managed to spit the strange metal thing out.

"She still retains too much strength," said the channeler. "The moon-shackles are not sufficient for this."

"Lock her away," commanded Darogen. "We will try again later. Once she is unconscious the process will be easier."

One of the guards who had entered after the start of the confrontation spoke up, the tremor in his voice indicating that he was not under the same control as most of the others, "Y—yes, Your Majesty. What about the Baron?"

"Will you take him?" asked the channeler.

"He knows nothing, and his body is dying already. Lock him away for now. We can dispose of his body later, once we have a suitable explanation for his death," pronounced Darogen. The king's dead eyes locked on the guard who had spoken, "You and the others from outside, wait for me in the next chamber. I would speak with you privately."

It doesn't control all of them, thought Moira. *It's going to do the same thing to them, to keep them from talking about what they've seen. What was that thing?* She spat as they dragged her limp body from the room, trying to clear the awful taste from her mouth.

Glancing down, she idly noticed that the dress the Baron had loaned her was ruined. One of the men that had been holding her had been badly wounded by her sword before she had been shackled. His blood had left huge stains on the fabric. Her magesight, which thankfully still functioned, showed her that the men coming behind her were carrying Gerold's unconscious body with them. *Poor Gerold.*

Exhaustion had her full in its grip now, as the adrenaline of her battle faded away, leaving her cold and shaking. Even so, her mind worked furiously, trying to understand what had happened, and more importantly, *why* it had happened. She couldn't come to any reasonable conclusion, but one thought stood out to her, *my father is definitely still alive, and they have him.*

Down they went, until at last she was brought to what must be the dungeon. Moira had read of such places before, but never seen one. Her father hadn't seen the need to build one, and no one had ever wanted to let her see the one in Lancaster, even though it was mostly empty. The one here in Halam had evidently seen good use, however. The smell of mold and old refuse perfectly matched with what she had always thought a dungeon would be like.

Each cell was a stone room cut from the bedrock beneath King Darogen's castle. While the interior walls were stone, the front wall consisted of nothing but iron bars and a door. Gerold's unconscious form was dumped in one cell, and she was shoved into the one next to it. The click of the iron lock held a terrible finality as the door closed.

Moira wondered if she had the strength to foil the lock. She knew already that she was incredibly weak now. The shackles had robbed her of most of her strength. Her magesight still worked, and obviously she maintained a certain amount of power within her own body, but the shackles seemed to bleed away any aythar that she tried to manipulate outside of her own person.

Her hopes were dashed when two of the men remained behind, standing guard outside her cell. She knew that even if she had the strength to manipulate the lock, she wouldn't have enough to fight the guards. *Shit.*

That wasn't very ladylike. She could almost imagine Grace chiding her for her language. Gram's dragon had been her first spellbeast, living as a teddy bear and playmate for years before taking on her new role. Grace had never approved of Moira's occasional lapses into foul language. *But she isn't here right now, and I'm damn well screwed if I don't figure out a way to get out of this.*

I need to be clever. She spent several minutes trying to do just that, but her mind came up blank. *It always seems so easy in the books.* She changed tactics, *What would Lady Rose do?*

That was no help either. She couldn't imagine Gram's mother being locked in a dungeon. The image refused to come to her. Imagining her mother in a prison cell was easier for some reason, but then her mother's solutions to such a situation were of no use to her either. *I can't just rip the bars apart with my bare hands.*

"Mom wouldn't have been captured anyway," she muttered to herself. "She'd have fought her way free."

A vision of her sword cutting through the man in the audience chamber flashed in her mind, and a sick feeling swept over her. Worse, it was followed by the memory of the people who had thrown themselves in front of the King. Despite the many bizarre experiences of her childhood, she had never killed anyone before.

Tears welled in her eyes, and she began to cry. The nervousness and anxiety of the past few days had worn on her, even as she had worked hard to put forward her best face. Her father had always been strong, and her mother stronger still, and yet she knew she was just a child. No matter how she had tried, it had all been a façade, and now she was out of her depth. She wept long and hard, hating herself for doing so but helpless to stop herself.

After a time, her tears stopped and her head felt clearer. *Stop feeling sorry for yourself and think about what you have.* That was easy, not very much, but now that she was calmer she realized she did still have some assets. *The dragons will be looking for me, and Gram and Chad will know exactly where I've gone.* Gram or either of the dragons alone would be enough to put an end to King Darogen and any number of his soldiers. Chad was not to be discounted either; the ranger was deadly with a bow.

I just have to survive until they rescue me. The thought reassured her, but it wasn't satisfying. She was a wizard, and the daughter of a man who had almost single handedly rewritten the course of history for Lothion. She couldn't sit idle. *I have more than just allies.* She still had her magesight, and obviously some of her abilities still worked. Her brother came to mind then, and she wondered what he would do.

Thinking of Matthew annoyed her. He would have chided her for letting herself get into the situation to begin with, not that he would have done any better. *He'd probably be trying to devise some overly complicated enchantment to get himself out of this.* Simultaneously, she found herself worrying about him. She had left him alone, back in Lothion. *What if he's gotten himself into trouble?* It wasn't long ago that she had had to reattach one of his arms after an experiment of his had gone wrong.

Thoughts of her brother did lead to one good idea, however. Lifting her manacles in front of her, she examined the subtle runes engraved on the milky white stone they were made of. She might not be quite the enchanter her father and brother were, but she still knew a lot about enchanting.

A few minutes' careful study told her a lot. The method used to produce the effects of the shackles on her aythar, was overly complicated and inefficient. If the designer had done the job properly, the shackles would have completely sealed her abilities. Instead, they merely drained away the majority of any aythar she tried to project beyond herself. On a weaker mage that might be enough to entirely stop them from using magic, but for a stronger one, it didn't quite do enough.

They were probably made a long time ago, by someone who wasn't very good at it. Despite the flaws in it, she couldn't see any way that she could break the enchantment while the shackles were around her wrists. She considered attempting to shatter them by banging them against the stone floor, but she couldn't be sure how much aythar they were storing. The reaction produced by their destruction might well end her life.

She noticed one of the guards staring at her then. Her magesight told her that he was back in control of his own mind again, though he seemed somewhat confused about what had happened earlier. If he remembered losing control of his body, there was no sign of it, he would have been more fearful. Instead, she was guessing that he had a blank place in his memories.

At the moment he was having some decidedly unvirtuous thoughts as he watched her. She tried not to shudder. *He's at least ten years older than I am, how could he even consider something like that?* Of course, she had learned quite well over the past week that many men had no qualms when it came to fantasizing about girls much younger than themselves.

Moira turned her attention to Gerold. She could see with her magesight that he was still breathing in the cell next door, but he was slowly bleeding to death. Focusing her perceptions carefully, she could tell that he was lucky to be alive at all. The spear had slid through his midsection without nicking his stomach or intestines, but his liver had been torn, most of the bleeding was from the veins there. If it had cut the artery, he'd have been dead already.

He might live if I could seal his wound and stop the rest of the bleeding. There was no way she could do that at the moment, though. Even if he had been in the same cell, she couldn't muster enough aythar to do much of anything physical.

Her mind froze then, as another idea came to her. *I can't do much on a physical level, but what about mentally?* Her eyes went to the guard once more. He was still watching her, and his aythar had a distinctly lewd cast to it. *If he were closer...*

She knew he would love to be closer, if it weren't against the rules. She fought down a feeling of disgust. *I can't believe I'm even considering this.*

But Gerold was dying, and she was his only hope.

Moira stood and approached the bars, her gaze meeting the guard's in an open challenge.

The man stared back at her in silence, not sure what to make of her sudden change in behavior.

Don't talk, you'll screw it up, she told herself. Instead, she licked her lips.

That got his attention. The guard straightened and walked closer, "What do you want?"

Her eyes went to his companion, who stood across the hall showing little interest in either of them, then they returned to the guard before her. "I'm thirsty," she said.

"You aren't allowed to have water," said the guard firmly, letting his gaze travel downward. He was separated from her by only three feet now.

Moira sent a delicate line of aythar outward, touching his mind. It would have been easy if it weren't for the manacles, but now it took everything she had. A quick pulse turned his mild lust into a burning fire. The guard's pupils dilated, and his lips parted slightly as his breathing became shallow and husky. "Maybe if we were alone, you'd be able to quench my thirst," she told him. *I can't believe I just said that.*

The man leaned closer, his face almost against the bars, and she could smell his sour breath, "You'd like that wouldn't you?"

She wanted to vomit, but instead she turned her gaze downward, toward the supposed object of her desire. Meeting his eyes again, she answered, "I think we both would."

Unable to control his lust any longer, the guard reached through and pulled her harshly against the bars with one hand before using his other hand to grope roughly at her chest. Moira gasped in pain as he pinched her. Of course, the guard was too besotted to hear her cry as one of pain, instead he took it as further confirmation of her desire.

"Not like this," she protested, as her eyes watered. "We need privacy to do this right."

"Yeah," said the man. Turning back, he looked at the other guard, who was watching them with some interest now. He walked over to him, and the two of them talked in quiet whispers for a moment. The other man smiled, leering at her.

With her magesight, she could see that the other man was growing excited as well. *No, that's not what I meant, you dolt!* Fear and adrenaline shot through her as the other guard unlocked her cell, and the two of them entered together. *Focus,* she told herself. Her plan wouldn't work if she let herself be rattled. One she thought she could handle, but she wouldn't be able to do anything if she let her fear overwhelm her. She needed precision. Self-control was paramount to her ability to manipulate others minds.

Watching the two of them, she could see that the first guard, the one she had started with, was a blazing pyre of passion, while the second was merely moderately aroused. The second one spoke then, "You go first, Lenny. I'll just watch, unless she puts up a fight."

Lenny grinned, "You sure?"

"Yeah, I ain't quite ready yet, so try to make a show of it." Looking at her, he addressed her directly, "Take the dress off, wench."

She held her wrists up to remind them of the manacles, "Why don't you help me, Lenny?" She attempted a smile to put the guard at ease, but her nervousness twisted it into a strange parody of a genuine smile.

Lenny needed no urging. Stepping forward, he brought one hand up, intending to grab her neckline and rip downward, but Moira had already seen his rough intentions. Fighting down her fear, she stepped into him before he could get a firm grip and lifted her chin as though she meant to kiss him.

Mildly surprised, Lenny let his hand slide downward to pull her hips against him as he lowered his head toward hers. As soon as their bodies came close Moira struck. A fine thread of aythar lanced outward, driving into the guard's lust addled mind. In spite of the manacles, her desperation made the initial mind touch a little rougher than it ought to have been. Lenny jerked slightly as her mind caught his firmly in its grip.

Beyond that, however, he continued on his quest for satisfaction. Lenny's hands roamed across her back and derriere.

Moira felt as though she were drowning. The manacles sapped her strength, making each moment a trial to maintain the mental contact. At first she tried to dampen Lenny's passion, to turn it from its course, but his basic instinct was too strong for that. Without even being aware of what he was doing, he fought her.

A rising sense of panic threatened to overwhelm her inner calm, but Moira refused to let go. Strengthening her resolve, she clamped down harder on Lenny's mind. *No, this isn't what you want. Protect me, help me!*

For a moment it seemed an impossible task until with a final twist of will she felt his mind snap. Lenny sagged against her, and she felt the candle that was the wellspring of his life wink out. *No! That's not what was supposed to happen.* He was dead.

His heart still beat, and his lungs still moved, but he was as dead as the king she had met in the throne room—and she had killed him as surely as she had the people fighting in the audience chamber earlier. This time, though, it had been entirely her decisions that had led to the guard's death. This time she felt his passing directly, and now she was holding his limp form upright.

She also confirmed the source of the control the guards and others had been under earlier. During her battle to control Lenny's mind, she had seen it, a small metallic creature embedded in the back of his throat. Fine metal filaments extended upward from the bizarre abomination, weaving themselves into the small apple-like part of the brain that topped the spine.

Moira already knew that that area was a sort of control center for the physical body, the place where commands were sent to enable conscious control of the limbs. If that was how the thing worked, it made sense that the earlier victims had been trapped within their minds. They had been partly awake, but direct control of their bodies had been overridden.

Thus far the strange thing seemed to still be dormant.

"Are you alright, Lenny?" questioned the guard watching them. It was obvious that something was wrong.

Moira wasn't sure how long Lenny's body would survive his passing. According to her mother, it might be days before the brain began to die, but once it did, everything else would follow in short order. Without knowing what else to do, she did what came instinctively, she created a simple spellmind. It was a matter of half a minute's work, during which she slumped, letting the guard's body fall over her own.

The second guard would want answers soon. She intended to make sure Lenny was ready to give them. Having so little time, she imbued the mind with only one directive. *Protect me.* With that she released him; she had no energy left to do more anyway.

Lenny stiffened as the new mind took over. He gazed down at her with an expression of adoration as he used his arms to lever himself upward. As he stood he placed himself between her and the other man, but things began to go wrong from there.

The beast within his throat had awoken.

The second guard had gone blank as well. Staring at Lenny, he spoke in a flat voice, "Anomaly detected."

Lenny was twitching. His new spellmind was struggling with the metal insect for control of his body. "A—a—greed," he replied.

The other guard strode from the cell, moving to snatch up one of the heavy truncheons they had left in the hall. He returned seconds later, raising the weapon and preparing to dash poor Lenny's brains out.

"No!" shouted Moira. Launching herself from the floor, she dashed at the second man, catching his arm and knocking him sideways. Lenny still stood motionless, but she knew that if she let the other guard kill him, she would lose her only ally. Well, kill what was left of him. Lenny wasn't precisely a living person anymore, but he was hers.

The other man was too strong for her. She fought tooth and nail, but he pinned her arms within his own. The manacles didn't help, of course, but he was so much stronger it wouldn't have mattered, even had she been entirely free. He held her still while Lenny approached from behind, making each step as though it were an accomplishment as his body twitched and jerked. He had produced a small knife, and it was clear that he meant to drive it into her back.

The irony of her situation didn't escape her. *I'm about to be the first Centyr to be murdered by her own spellbeast.* Frantically, she sought to use her remaining aythar to take control of the guard holding her, but she had no time and too little energy left.

She felt the knife pass by her right ear, so closely that if she had turned her head it might have done her serious harm. The blade sank into the chest of the guard holding her. Her spellbeast was still fighting for control of Lenny's body.

The arms holding her fell away as the guard grabbed at Lenny's knife arm, struggling to pull the blade from his chest. The guard grappled with Lenny, or he would have, if Lenny had been capable of resisting, but the thing in his throat had her spellbeast in a stalemate again. He convulsed as he fought the creature controlling him, while his compatriot took the knife from his hand and turned it around.

Moira had relaxed her legs, falling to the ground when the guard's grip had slackened. There she saw his fallen truncheon. Snatching it up, she lurched to her feet and brought it two-handed down on the back of the man's unguarded head. She was rewarded with a sickening crunch, and her jailor crumpled to the floor.

Lenny watched her with desperate eyes, locked in his own internal battle, his body shuddering and trembling. Eventually he lost his balance and collapsed. Moira moved to help him, kneeling beside his semi-rigid form.

Her magesight could see the struggle within him. The metal thing was sending a steady stream of commands to his brain, while the spell-beast was attempting to resist them by sending its own commands directly to the spinal column. The resulting discord created a sort of tug-of-war, and neither could gain the upper hand.

"Hang on. I'll try to help you," she told him, but his eyes showed no sign of comprehension. The spellmind was too simple. She hadn't had the time to include proper language when she had created it.

Putting that thought aside for a moment, she turned her attention to the struggle inside Lenny's twitching body. She had little strength, so she did the only thing available to her. Extending her limited aythar once more, she dampened the section of the brain that the metal filaments connected to. It was a poor solution, she knew that. Without that part of the brain, her spellbeast would be clumsy and poorly coordinated, but if it worked, he would at least have sole control of the body.

The twitching subsided, and Lenny's body took a slow deliberate breath. The look of relief in his eyes was enough confirmation for her. It had worked. He sat up and gave her a lopsided smile accompanied by a satisfied grunt, "Oohn!"

She nodded, although she doubted he understood even that gesture. *Now what do I do?*

CHAPTER 9

Gram and Chad waited a long while before emerging from the cellar. They couldn't be sure how long it had been, but Gram would have guessed it was at least a half an hour, possibly longer. It had certainly seemed like an eternity since he had been trapped in a small space with the fetid stench.

He had listened carefully for several minutes, letting his ears assure him that there was no one nearby, when they opened the doors and climbed out. After that they began walking. They had given up on the city gate for the time being, it was sure to be watched after the incidents they had been involved in.

Gram was careful to think of it that way. They had been 'involved', rather than they had 'started a mass slaughter'. It was the truth, they hadn't forced the fight, it had been forced on them, but it had most certainly become a slaughter once their hand had been forced. *What happens if they find us again? Will I kill more ordinary men and women?* He couldn't think of them as opponents, or soldiers. Their behavior had definitely been abnormal, but they had been regular townsfolk. *What if the next ones are children?*

"Keep moving," urged Chad. "A nice casual walk is all we need. If we move too quickly, we'll draw attention."

"We didn't do anything to draw attention last time," said Gram.

"Well, until we understand what the hell is goin' on, that's the best we can do," growled the ranger.

Gram's sharp hearing picked up the sounds of a group of people ahead. "There's a large group near the next intersection," he warned.

"Let's stop in here then," said Chad, indicating a bakery they had just passed.

"There's at least one person in there," said Gram nervously.

"Better one than fifteen," returned the older man, and without waiting to continue the discussion, he moved toward the door. Gram reluctantly followed him.

"Thank the gods that ye're open," said the ranger boisterously as they entered.

The baker was a fat balding man who looked at them with some surprise as they stepped in the door. "Good day. I hadn't expected to have any more business today, what with crazed madmen on the loose." His eyes took in their appearance as he spoke, and his voice grew tighter before he finished his sentence. Gram had dismissed his armor and hidden Thorn, this time sending it to its extradimensional pocket. Even so, they were both clearly foreigners. That combined with the recent events was enough to cast them in a light of heavy suspicion.

One other person stood in the shop, taking possession of a small sack of fresh bread that the baker had just handed her. The woman turned and stared at them.

Gram froze, his jaw going slack. Light olive skin and dark hair framed a pair of deep brown eyes, eyes that had haunted his dreams. It was Alyssa.

Her expression went through several rapid shifts, shock, sadness, and finally alarm. "What are you doing here?" she said softly, taking one uncertain step forward, before stopping. "You shouldn't be here. It's too dangerous."

Gram walked toward her slowly, stammering, "Alyssa—Jasmine, I feared you were dead…" His vision blurred as he blinked away unbidden tears.

"Ahh fuck it all," muttered Chad under his breath. "This ain't good." The baker had already left the counter, heading for the back. Whatever he had surmised about the situation, it probably involved finding the town guard.

"Stay back," warned Alyssa as Gram approached. She would have retreated, but she was cornered in the small shop with nowhere to go. "You don't understand. I'm dangerous."

Gram ignored her, closing the space between them. "I don't care. Why didn't you come back?"

Alyssa's face changed then, relaxing, her fear gone. Reaching out she slid one hand behind his head and pulled his face toward hers. Confused, Gram didn't fight it. He had dreamt of kissing her once more every night since he had thought she died. His lips met hers, and for a moment his world brightened again.

Until he felt the strange metal thing clawing its way into his mouth.

Chad watched them anxiously, "We need to go, boy. Bring her with us if you must, but we can't dawdle. That baker's gone to warn someone."

Gram let out a garbled cry as he pushed Alyssa away and stumbled back. He clawed at his mouth with his hands, but whatever had gotten in was too far back and it was boring into the back of his throat.

"That's what love will get ya," observed Chad, thinking to make a joke, but he quickly realized that something was seriously wrong. "What did you do to him!?" he demanded of the young woman.

Alyssa ignored his question even as she advanced on the hunter, a familiar dead expression in her eyes.

Several things passed through Chad's mind in an instant. He knew from the past that Alyssa was a deadly fighter. Facing her head on would probably be a mistake, even for him. He also knew that killing her would be the last thing Gram would want, no matter what she had just done. If he had had an arrow, he might still have done it, though, Gram's wishes be damned.

Whipping his bow-stave across, he sought to drive her back long enough to get his long knife out, but the girl didn't even dodge. The wood caught her solidly in the cheek, sending her sprawling to the floor. Never one to waste an opportunity, he pounced, grappling with her and twisting her head painfully to one side as he brought his knife to bear. He hesitated after that only for Gram's sake.

"What did you do to him bitch?!" he spat, pressing the sharp edge against her bare throat.

She didn't answer, however, instead she continued to struggle, heedless of the mortal threat his knife represented. His superior strength and weight made it a losing proposition for her, not that it mattered, for she fought like an amateur, her movements clumsy and lacking any finesse.

"Gram, are you alright? Talk to me!" he shouted.

The young warrior didn't respond, and his thrashing movements became more frantic and less deliberate. He appeared to be having a seizure.

That bizarre scene continued for several minutes. Chad hung on desperately to the still fighting woman, while calling out to his younger companion. Eventually, Gram's seizure stopped, and his body became still, but when he pushed himself up from the floor, the look in his eyes sent a chilling jolt down the ranger's spine.

They were dead eyes, set in a flat, expressionless face.

"That ain't funny, boy," said Chad, but he knew it was no joke. His fight with Alyssa had changed. No longer was he fighting to keep her under control until Gram could recover, now he was trying to disentangle himself from her, before the two of them could bear him down together. If Gram's fighting skills were similar to hers, he could probably kill them both, but that wasn't the solution he was hoping for.

Shoving her away he jumped to his feet before she could grapple him once more. A swift kick to the head sent her flying back when she lunged at him. He felt a little bad about that, but he had no time for games as he backed rapidly toward the door. Clumsy or not, Gram was far too strong to get away from, if the lad got his hands on him.

A whistle in the distance told him that the baker had found the watchmen. Ducking out the door he ran for the corner. He was alone now.

Moira let out her breath slowly, relaxing finally. The keys had let her into Gerold's cell, but it had been a tense quarter of an hour while she tried to stop his internal bleeding. Trying to affect material things with her magic while wearing the moon-shackles was frustrating, rather like trying to sew while wearing winter gloves. *No, not just heavy gloves, metal gauntlets,* she mentally corrected herself. It took enormous concentration and effort to make even the tiniest changes.

Thus far she had only managed to seal the largest vein. Several small veins were still bleeding, but she thought he might have more time now—if she could get the manacles off and finish the task.

Communicating with Lenny was futile, and she couldn't reasonably expect to improve his mental faculties in her present position. Even if he could be made more functional, the spellmind might not be able to access the information stored in the dead man's brain. Assuming that Lenny had even known where the key to her manacles was kept.

That key was her current goal.

Sneaking along the corridor turned out to be unrealistic. Some of the other cells held prisoners, many of whom felt the need to speak to her as she passed. She worried that they might make so much noise that the other jailors would come, a few were already yelling obscenities at her, although she got the impression that was normal down in King Darogen's dungeon.

If I can't sneak to the guard station, or whatever they call it, what do I do? She thought for a moment, and then an idea came to her. *Just as Dad always said, every problem is an opportunity.* She turned her attention to the other prisoners.

Being a Centyr mage had certain advantages. She went back to the first two cells she had passed but dismissed the occupants immediately. *Insane and violently insane,* she noted silently, studying them with her magesight. The third cell held more promise, *intelligent and antisocial, but at least he seems rational.*

"You," she said addressing the thin and nearly naked man within. "What's your name?"

"What's it to you?" he responded belligerently.

"If you want out of that cell, it's rather important," she held up the key ring in the air and gave it a small shake.

The man looked at her 'guard' a second time, finally realizing that despite her shackles and her escort, she seemed to be the one in charge of their situation. "What's wrong with him?" he asked, suddenly fearful.

"His comrade hit him in the head with one of those clubs a few minutes ago," she lied. "He killed the other guard, and now I have these." She shook the keys again for emphasis. Lenny contributed by smiling idiotically while shaking his head.

"You can't get past the guard station at the entrance to this place," said the prisoner. "As soon as they realize he's off his noggin they'll lock you up again, if not worse."

"That's why I need help..." she said agreeably, "Mister...?"

"Perkins," said the skinny prisoner. "Wat Perkins."

"Excellent, Mister Perkins, do you think you would like to help me escape?"

"You're mad, girl," he responded. "There are at least five men up there, and maybe more. Look at me. Do I look like I could take down a guard?"

She took a moment to reassess the dungeon with her magesight before addressing his question, "There are at least, thirty-five, or no—closer to forty men locked up down here. Surely we can muster a group large enough to handle a few guards."

"Half of them are mad, and some of them may not even be men!" said Wat, his voice dropping in volume even as it rose to a hiss filled with fear. "I've seen them, out there," he whispered. "There are demons walking in men's bodies. They could be anywhere."

"I'm sure you're much safer in here, until they come to make you one of them," she intoned ominously. "I've seen them too, and I can spot them. Would you rather wait to die or try to do something about it?"

"What do you mean, 'you can spot them'?"

"Why do you think they put these on me," she said confidently, raising her manacled wrists for his inspection. "I'm a wizard. Help me get the key, and we can stop what's happening here." She could see his doubt and fear threatening to eclipse what small hope her words brought, so she reached out with her aythar and fed what strength she could to his hope. *Trust me,* she thought.

Wat's eyes brightened slightly, but then he looked down, "Even if you can find the ones who aren't demons, half of these men would just as soon rape you as help."

"I can spot courage, Wat, and I can see decency," she declared. "That's why I came to your cell first. I will only release the ones we can trust." She sent another pulse along the delicate line of aythar that was now touching his mind, *believe me.* Sweat was beginning to break out on her brow. She couldn't do much more.

He made up his mind, "Fine. Let's do this. It's better than rotting down here."

It got easier after that. They moved from cell to cell while she inspected each prisoner, those who were plainly mad she passed by, but there were many who were sane. Some of the sane ones were definitely criminals, but most were simply people who had been locked up for convenience. As long as they were rational and able to cooperate, she released them.

What she didn't find was anyone with one of those strange metal creatures within them. She checked for that very carefully. It made sense. Whatever the purpose of the creatures was, if they had implanted someone, there was no need for them to lock them up, and King Darogen was most likely at the top of their hierarchy.

When they came to the end of the cells, they had eighteen somewhat reliable men—well, at the least they were sane and not overtly hostile to her. She had spent more than a half an hour picking them out, and she was worried that the Baron might not have much more time. She needed to get the key and get back to him.

"Remember…," she told them, "…after we take the guardroom, we wait. I have to help my companion. Our best chance of escaping the palace is if we stay together. If anyone runs off alone they're liable to get caught, and then we'll all have a castle full of alert guards to deal with."

Most of them nodded, but she could see defiance in some of them. More than a few had no intention of honoring their commitment any further than escaping the dungeon. *I will have to deal with that once we've beaten the guards.* She only hoped the key would be in the guardroom, otherwise she might be in trouble.

One guard was just leaving the guardroom as they approached. He instantly knew there was trouble and tried to retreat into the room before they reached him. If he had managed to close the door and alert the others, their plan might have failed right then, but fortunately one of the men was quick enough to get there in time to get his foot in the door.

He yelled in pain as the slamming door broke his instep, but the others got their hands around the edge and pried the door back. Bloody mayhem erupted after that as they swarmed in and took on the men on duty.

Seven guards died within a short span of minutes, mostly in brutal and horrifying fashion. There was nothing noble or glorifying about the battle. It was made even worse by the fact that whatever was controlling the guards took over, and consequently none of them made even the most normal cries of fear or pain as they died. They fought and died silently, like strange puppets made to look human.

Moira's new friends received a number of injuries, mostly bruises, but the first man still had a broken foot and another had taken a solid blow to the skull. That one lay on the floor, twisted and contorted into a tight knot, even though he was unconscious. Moira could tell that the injury to his brain would most likely prove fatal, and even if the manacles were removed, she doubted she could do much for him.

"Quick! Let's be gone before the others come and find them," declared one of the men.

"Wait. We need to find the key to these manacles," reminded Moira. "We agreed we would leave together."

He wavered, as did some of the others, but in the end they were willing to wait a few minutes while they searched the bodies of the guards, and the room itself.

The key, when it was found, turned out to be stored within a locked box that held a variety of keys. They never found the key to the box itself, but the man who had found it solved that problem by beating the box with a truncheon until the locking mechanism was bent enough for him to pry it open.

The key to her manacles was easily distinguished from the others since it was the only one made of silver.

"Alright, let's get out of here!" said the man who handed her the key.

"We're supposed to go back and get her friend," said Wat.

"He's dying already. What's the point?" said another.

A heavyset dockworker voiced what the majority were already thinking, "Fuck that, let's get out of here now. The bitch can go back for her popinjay by herself if she wants."

Moira fumbled with the key, trying to reach the manacle lock with her hands, "Help me, Wat." It was an awkward task, and although she could probably manage given enough time, she didn't think she had enough time to waste trying.

A sigh escaped her lips as the shackles were opened, and her aythar blossomed around her once more, stretching outward from her body as it normally did. She rebuilt her personal shield immediately.

Three of them were already heading for the exit when she spoke, "*Grethak!*" Everyone froze, except Wat, who she deliberately excluded from the spell.

He stared at her in confusion and fear, "What happened to them?"

Moira smiled at him reassuringly, "I told you I am a wizard, Wat. I'm just making sure none of them go back on our bargain. I won't hurt them."

Wat's eyes were wide as he stared at each of them in turn, "They're frozen solid." One of the men fell while Wat was speaking.

"Help me get them to the ground," she told him, rushing to catch another who was already toppling. "They can't balance while their muscles are immobile. A fall could hurt them."

Several fell before they could lower them, but she cushioned their falls with her aythar to prevent any serious injuries.

"What are you going to do to them?" asked Wat, trying in vain to conceal his fear of her.

Moira sighed, she had hoped that Wat would be reasonable enough to stay calm after witnessing her magic. The frenetic activity within his mind told her clearly that he was on the edge of snapping. "I just don't want them to make a break for it before we're ready. If they go charging out now, some of them will get caught, some might not, but either way, we'll have the entire palace alerted, and everyone will be looking for us. This way they stay together until I—until *we* are ready to run together. It will improve our chances."

"Magic only comes from the gods, light or dark...," began Wat, "...are you in league with the dark gods?"

The dark gods are dead you idiot! Well, most of them anyway. That was what she thought, but she kept a tight rein on her mouth. "I don't know what you were taught, Wat, but wizards make their own magic. It isn't good or bad by itself; it depends on the person using it."

There was a strong impulse to run in Wat. His eyes were darting to the sides as he wondered if he could make it out one of the doors before she caught him. Moira considered paralyzing him as she had the others, but she needed help, *willing* help. Rather than take the simple route she once again broke the ancient rule of the Centyr mages, she touched his mind directly.

She was in full control of herself now, so it was easier to be delicate. She smoothed away his fear and instilled a deeper trust in him. As she worked she found the heart of his fear rooted in memories of his childhood. She caught flashes of them, an older man, probably a priest lecturing him about wizards, practitioners of dark arts, and witches. Even his mother had spent considerable time warning him about such things. *Rubbish,* she thought, and then she removed the memories. It was easier than trying to alter them.

The process took slightly longer than she anticipated, but she figured it was better to do a good job than to mess things up. After what might have been five or ten minutes she finished, and mentally dusting off her hands, she released him. Wat was now a less fearful man, more courageous, more noble, and without a trace of fear regarding magic and wizards. She felt a faint sense of pride looking at her handiwork.

Wat blinked as his mind snapped back into motion.

"Well, Wat, what's it going to be? Will you help me, or did I misjudge you?" Moira asked him.

"Never worry on my behalf, milady," he answered solidly. "Old Wat would never abandon a woman in need. What do you want me to do?"

"Stay and watch them. If anyone comes, keep the door locked and try to delay them. I should be back in less than half an hour," she told him authoritatively. She definitely liked the new Wat better.

Standing taller, Moira strode back down the cell corridor, followed by her other companion, the 'spellbeast' made flesh, Lenny. Lenny still hobbled awkwardly. She would have to figure out some way to remove the metal thing in him, if she wanted him to have better motor control, but that would have to wait for now. Baron Ingerhold needed attention, and quickly, if he were to live.

CHAPTER 10

It took Moira less than half an hour to patch Gerold back together. *If Matthew had done this, he'd be lucky to still have his arms and legs in the right places,* she thought sarcastically. She had sealed the smallest bleeders and reattached the moderate sized and larger veins. Gerold's liver would have a scar, but it should function properly.

The biggest problem now was that the man had lost a considerable amount of blood. He needed rest and lots of liquids to help him replenish his blood volume. The Baron's heart beat at an uncomfortably fast rate as it struggled to compensate. Despite her solving the mechanical problems relating to his spear wound, he would need days to recover even a moderate amount of his former strength.

Now, how do I get him out of here? Moira considered simply levitating him, but that would require attention, and if they got into a confrontation, she might not be able to afford to divide her concentration. Fortunately, being a Centyr mage, she had never lacked for helpers.

Lenny might have carried him, but it would have been awkward, and given Lenny's lack of good muscular control, accidents would have been likely. Instead, she spent several minutes creating a spellbeast, endowing it with a bizarre configuration of arms and legs. It was four-legged, standing much like a horse, but it also had two oddly angled arms that could reach over its back to steady and retain its passenger, the unconscious Baron. She added a manlike torso and two arms in the front in case it needed to fight or hold things for her.

In the end, it wound up looking something like a mythical centaur, if centaurs had had an extra set of arms sprouting from their back, and if their backs had been slightly concave on top to accommodate prone people.

"Ok, this would have scared poor Wat to death, if he had seen it before...," her voice trailed off. *Before what?* She didn't know quite what to call what she had done. *His 'adjustment'?*

She put that aside. "Now, what to call you," she said, talking to herself. "Pal? Short for 'palanquin'? No, that won't do." After a moment's thought she decided on 'Stretch', which was short for stretcher. She had kept Stretch's mind simple to save time, but he was still probably a little smarter than Lenny. At least Stretch could talk.

Standing up, she and Lenny helped Stretch load the unconscious nobleman onto his soft dimpled back. Although Stretch was a proper spellbeast, meaning he was made entirely of aythar, he was quite physical, and he felt soft and warm to the touch. She had invested him with perhaps a quarter of her aythar, which should have been enough to last for half a week, if it had been used in something like a doll, but in this case would probably only last a day. Large creatures made purely of magic used it up very quickly.

A wave of dizziness passed over her as she stepped back from Stretch. Moira was tempted to create a second spellbeast, one meant purely as a guardian, but she worried that she might be forced to fight soon. Her aythar would recover quickly, meaning a pre-made spellbeast could be a large advantage, but if she was forced to fight while still tired, it might just as well be a hindrance. She decided to play it safe. Once she felt recovered from making Stretch, she would consider making a guardian, until then she would rely on Lenny and her prisoner friends for support.

Returning to the guardroom, she found that things were still much as she had left them. Wat seemed glad to see her again, but his eyes widened when he saw Stretch, "What is that?"

"My new friend, Stretch. Don't worry about him, he's just a bit of magic created to help me carry the Baron," she explained.

"Oh," said Wat simply, though his eyes still expressed a degree of fascination.

An hour ago Stretch would have had him running for the hills, now he's merely curious, she thought smugly. Examining the others, she realized she had made a mistake using a spell to paralyze them. Still conscious, her newly released prisoner friends were in a state of extreme terror, if not outright panic. *And that's why Father usually puts people to sleep instead of freezing them in place.*

Moira couldn't be sure of how long they had, but she was growing increasingly confident of her ability to handle people. She started with the man who'd had his foot broken when they rushed the guard room. Damping his pain, she quickly fused the broken bone in his right foot. There would still be some swelling and discomfort, but he would be able to walk. Before she released him, she touched his mind, calming him and removing his memory of the past half an hour. She was mildly surprised at how easy it was to do.

Increasing familiarity was improving her ability to manipulate memories. After a second of hesitation she altered some of his early memories as well, to make him less afraid of magic and the unusual things he was about to witness. Stretch was a special case, though. Her centaur-like creation was too odd to trust that simply removing their fear of magic would allow them to accept him.

Instead, she formulated a false memory, a simple one that she could insert into any of their minds without much tailoring to suit their individual differences. She moved to the next man and altered his memories as well, removing his fear of magic and adding her new memory of Stretch.

Once she started, it proved far easier than she would have once believed. Three or four minutes with each man, and none of them were afraid of magic. They also now had a fond memory of a strange childhood playmate who looked remarkably like Stretch.

Given some more time, I could make these men into almost anything. The thought was strangely comforting and disturbing at the same time. *What does that make me?* In her mind's eye she saw a vision of herself, surrounded by a sea of dolls, puppets that could eat and drink, walk and talk, but under the surface were little more than marionettes. *If anyone can be changed to suit my whim, then what is real?*

She closed her eyes, scrunching her face up as she willed the mental image away. *That's not true. I can't alter another wizard's mind, not without a fight anyway.* What did that imply? Did it mean that only mages were truly independent beings? Was the rest of humanity just cattle, a resource waiting to be exploited by those with power? How was she any different than the metal things that were controlling King Darogen's subjects?

"I'm not like them," she told herself. "People are not playthings." But a tiny voice in the back of her mind was still whispering, *They could be.* Moira shook her head—that way lay madness.

"Are you ready to go?" asked Wat.

She focused on his face, willing the unwelcome thoughts away, "Yes." Expanding her senses once more, she examined the area beyond the door that led out of the guardroom and back to the rest of the palace.

Past the door was a short corridor ending in stairs that led back up to the ground level of the castle. The entrance to the barracks was there and another hall that led toward the kitchens and laundry. Farther on was the entry hall, and depending on which way one went after that, it led either to the main yard or back to the formal audience hall.

The barracks held perhaps twenty men, and the kitchens were busy with perhaps ten or twelve workers. The halls themselves were almost empty, but the main entrance had a detachment of ten men. If they could get past them, there would be nothing to stop them making it into the main city, other than the final gate from the castle yard.

If we walk straight out, and I put the few we meet immediately to sleep, we might get out with almost no violence, she thought. The main gate might be a small challenge if someone managed to drop the portcullis before they got through. *But a little stone and steel aren't enough to stop me.*

She nodded, and Wat opened the door, cautiously peeking into the hall beyond it. Of course, he didn't know that she knew the way was clear already. Moira smiled to herself at that thought. "Just keep walking until I tell you to stop. Act natural, no one knows we're free yet," she told him and the other men.

"They might guess something's a little odd if they see Stretch," said one of the other men.

"I'll deal with that when the time comes," she reassured.

Moving quickly up the stairs, they passed along the first corridor until they reached the entry hall and turned toward the main entrance. Along the way they met one servant, but Moira put him to sleep before the man's eyes even had time to register the strange nature of her entourage.

So far so good.

The guards at the front reacted as expected, and Moira didn't waste any time, *"Shibal."* They collapsed without protest, but then things began to get complicated.

The men opened their eyes and began retaking their feet, even though she could clearly see that their minds were thoroughly asleep. The metal creatures in their throats could care less about whether their hosts were awake or not. Worse, her magesight showed her that the guards in the barracks were now rushing out, moving to take them from behind, while the portcullis at the main gate was beginning to descend.

So not only are they now aware of our escape, but they are somehow communicating—without aythar. The metal things that resided in them showed no signs of using magic at all. *"Grethak!"* she pronounced, putting some emphasis on it and making sure to exclude the men with her. A sleeping mind might not be an obstacle for the little metal parasites, but paralyzed muscles should be a different matter, although it took more effort for her to do it that way. "Keep moving!" she urged her companions. "They can't hurt us."

They began to run, leaving the palace and crossing the yard. Behind them came the men from the barracks. Some of the prisoners turned as if to face them, but Moira shouted at them, "Don't stop, run for the gate, you have to take the men there! I'll deal with this."

She said the words confidently, but as soon as she turned she felt her heart clench. It was the 'how' that made her fearful. Paralysis wasn't a good option, in fact she was already feeling the strain of the first men who were still fighting the spell she had put on them. Doing so with twenty more would be foolish. The easiest solution would be to kill them, but despite her experience in the throne room, she wasn't comfortable with that. *I don't want to be comfortable with that. I'm not a killer.*

The guards were only ten yards away, and her time had almost run out. Acting on instinct Moira created a small shield low to the ground. It was invisible, and seconds later the guards were tumbling over it, falling in spectacular fashion, but unlike the romance stories she loved, they didn't stay down for long. They were clambering up and running again almost as quickly as they fell.

The thought of fire flashed through her mind, but she still remembered the smell of the burning bodies after Karenth and Doron had attacked her home years before. *Not that, please.* Instead, she did what just seemed most natural. Lashing out with a fine tendril of aythar she seized control of the lead runner's mind, and before the metal thing in his neck realized it was in a fight for dominance, she turned his body and made him fall sideways. She repeated her tactic with three more in quick succession, and soon the guards were falling over one another.

Actively controlling another human being wasn't taxing, not in terms of aythar, but it did require a lot of concentration and managing more than one or two at a time was a frustrating exercise. Now that the metal things in them knew what she was doing, they were taking a firmer grip of their hosts, and she knew it would be impossible to struggle with more than one at a time.

Let me help.

The voice in her mind was her own, familiar and yet foreign at one and the same time. *How?*

Like this. Part of her reached out and took a firm grasp of one of the soldiers, and then she felt a fracture within her mind, as though she had broken in to pieces. Each piece took hold of a different man, and within seconds she had taken control of ten men, each as solidly as if she were focusing her entire attention on that individual.

The metal parasites fought, but her fragmented selves shut down the part of the brain that the parasites used, and soon 'her' guardsmen were fighting the others, clumsily, haltingly, and without skill, but they were fighting.

It should have been a disorienting experience, but somehow it felt almost natural. The part of her that she still considered her 'self' watched in amazement, taking in the overall picture, while her fragments operated individual soldiers like marionettes. She found herself overseeing the entire thing, keeping an eye on the larger battle and giving instructions to her smaller selves to coordinate their actions.

Even more incredible, she realized there was no need for her to stand watching. She could follow her companions, which would probably be the wiser course. But 'her' guards were losing, slowly being defeated by the superior motor skills of the others. Some of them were wounded already, and two were dying. *Making them fight each other is cruel,* she thought, *I should take them all.*

But could she?

Of course you can, said one of her new selves. With the thought came an instinctive act of will, and a second later there were ten more of her, each taking control of one of the remaining guardsmen. Moira felt a rising sense of exaltation as her mind expanded. She was no longer bound by the rules of a single mind, she was *more.*

Even the gods could not do this. She could hear laughter and then she was startled to realize it was her own. Behind her, the prisoners were fighting with the gate guards, and losing. Turning, she began to run toward the gate, and her new puppets followed behind her.

Her companions grew frightened, alarmed by the guards who came with her, not understanding that they were now allies as well. Since there was no time to explain she took them as well, and seconds after that she took the gate guards too. The portcullis began to rise once more, and the fighting had stopped. Moira only had one question now. *How many am I?* It was an odd question, but it made perfect sense in that moment.

It took a couple of minutes to finish counting and find the answer. *I am forty-seven people.*

The number boggled her. It was incomprehensible. No mind could do that many things at once. It beggared belief, and yet she felt no strain. The amount of aythar required to do it was still small, and her primary personality was still free to oversee all her other selves. *I should be going insane. Why am I still sane?*

She wanted to panic. None of it made sense. Moira needed to think, she needed solitude, but she felt as though she were surrounded by a crowd of people. *Correction, a crowd of me…*

Time to simplify. Moira sent the guards marching back to the barracks. She would release them once they were too far away to catch up. At the same time she set the parts of her that were controlling her prison companions to editing their memories. *Don't let them remember the escape, they'd never forgive me for doing that to them,* she commanded.

She and her companions marched into the city, with Stretch following close behind them. After a few blocks her other selves had finished their work, and she released the men who had escaped with her. Soon after that, she released the guards in the barracks, and then her smaller selves began to collapse, falling into one another and becoming a single mind once more, but it still was not *her* mind.

Who are you? She asked her other self.

I am you, but I think it's going to take some time to figure out what all of this means.

You don't know?

I know what you know.

I don't know a damn thing!

Excellent, so now you're twice as ignorant.

That isn't funny.

Yes it is.

Yeah, you're right. I think I'm going mad.

You mean, 'we' are going mad.

"Are you alright?" That was Wat. He was staring at her with a worried look on his face.

"Yes, why?" answered Moira rather hurriedly.

"You were just standing there staring into empty air and mumbling," he replied. "Some of the other men have left."

Their group was considerably smaller than it had been. There were only two other men with her now, along with Wat and of course, Stretch. "I'm sorry," she told him. "We need a place to hide. I was trying to think of where we could go."

Wat grinned, "I think I know a place. Follow me." He glanced at the other two, "There's room for you two as well, if you want to come."

Chapter 11

Chad had gotten away. That was his only consolation.

Gram was standing in the street now with Alyssa beside him. The last hour had been one of the most bizarre and terrifying of his life. Locked in his own body, he had watched himself walking the streets searching for someone, he assumed it was Chad, but he hadn't really been given any definite information. It didn't matter, he had merely been a passenger.

Watching his body betray him had been a surreal experience. He imagined it was something like what warriors paralyzed on the battlefield must experience, with one notable difference, while they also lost the ability to control their limbs, they weren't forced to watch themselves move and act while being controlled by some bizarre external force.

He couldn't even be sure if it *was* an external agent controlling him. Something had definitely lodged itself within his neck, and it was obvious that it was the means of his internal imprisonment, but he didn't know whether *it* was the real authority or whether it was merely taking commands from someone or something else.

There was certainly some sort of coordination taking place, though. Alyssa was close by, and now and then he was able to catch a glimpse of her eyes. He could see no hint of what might be going on behind them, but he guessed that she was suffering in the same helpless way that he was.

His mouth tasted of blood. Whatever it was, it had cut his tongue on its way in, and he could only imagine what it might have done to the back of his throat. The pain there was minimal, but a steady burning sensation was a sure sign that it had done him some harm farther back.

And then, just as suddenly as it had begun, it was over, and his body was his own again.

Gram began to tremble and his hands went immediately to his mouth. He had to get it out!

A warm hand landed atop his, pulling it gently away from his face, "Don't. It won't help, and if you try too hard you'll be punished." The expression on her face was tired, weary, and devoid of hope, but there was something more. Sorrow.

He seized her hands in his own, "What's happening to me, to us?!"

Alyssa's eyes darted sideways, a hint of alarm on her features, before coming back to rest on his own, "Don't speak. If you ask certain things, if you say certain things, or try to—you'll lose control. Let me talk for a while." She tugged at his arm, walking back in the direction they had come. "Follow me."

He let her lead him, "Where are we going?"

"To my home."

"Why?"

"Because it's private, not that that word really applies to us anymore," she said flatly. After a second she added, "…and because I'm selfish."

Selfish? That puzzled him for a moment, but he couldn't afford to think about it too long. "I can't. I have to find Chad. I have to warn M…mmph!"

"Stop!" said Alyssa urgently, clapping her hands over his lips, her eyes desperate with warning. "Whatever you came to do, don't talk about it, don't even thin…" Her words cut off abruptly as her eyes rolled back in her head and her body began to twitch.

He caught her as she started to fall, but as suddenly as it began, her seizure ended. Alyssa's eyes came back into focus and locked on his own. Pain and resignation were written on her face. Her lip trembled faintly and without thinking about it he lifted her, cradling her in his arms.

"It's alright. I can walk now," she told him.

Gram blinked, hard. "Let me do this," he answered. "Which way do we go now?"

"People are going to stare."

He started to laugh, but the action brought a sharp pain from his damaged throat, "Does it matter? How many of them are…?" He stopped, unsure how to phrase his question.

Alyssa leaned her head against his chest, "Fewer than you might think, for now at least. Straight down the street, then take a left when you pass the Drunken Goat."

"Drunken Goat?"

"It's a tavern," she explained.

He nodded and began walking. She was lighter than he remembered, but the last time he had carried her had been before he took the dragon-bond, so he couldn't be sure. Despite her slight figure, her body was still solid. She carried an impressive amount of muscle beneath the smooth fabric of her dress. Gram's mind recalled the details of her body all too well.

Alyssa remained silent as they progressed down the street, keeping her cheek against his broad chest. She felt like a child in his arms, an unusual sensation for her, but she was beyond caring. She looked up as he turned at the tavern, pointing at a nondescript doorway, "Over there, that's my door. You'll have to put me down to open it."

Gram ignored her advice, bending his knees slightly as he reached the door, to put one hand close to the handle. With hardly a bobble he tripped the latch and used his foot to push the door back before stepping inside. A quick turn and his foot closed the door behind them.

"Now what? You can't carry me forever," she informed him.

"Try me," he replied. It wasn't the worst thing he could imagine. His eyes took in the dim room. Light entered from a small window to the right of the door showing him a small bed near the far wall and a rough table in the center of the room. A wooden chair and a heavy trunk completed the room's spare furnishings. "Quaint," he pronounced, hearing his mother's voice as he said the word.

"I know it's meagre compared to what you're used to..." said Alyssa, embarrassment in her voice.

Gram tried to laugh once more, but the pain in his throat cut that short once again. "Damn that hurts," he told her as he set her on her feet.

Moving to one side, she lifted a pitcher and a small cup from the table, "Have some water. It will help a little."

He finished it in a single, long swallow, "Do you have anything stronger?" For the first time in his life, he felt a positive need for alcohol. The events of the day had left his nerves raw and frazzled.

"I can't afford it," she admitted. "Besides, it would burn like fire. The wound in your throat will take a few days to heal."

That made sense, now that he thought about it. A million other questions ran through his mind immediately after, but he took his time choosing one, "How long...?"

She lifted her hand to her own throat, "A week ago, just after I asked to be released from the Earl's service. As soon as I was recovered enough to walk on my own..."

"Your wounds," he interrupted, "let me see."

The dress she wore was of a single piece. Without the slightest hesitation Alyssa stood and lifted it overhead. She was naked beneath it.

Gram had seen her bare form many times, but he still blushed at the sight of her flesh. Putting that aside, he examined her ribs. A red puffy scar marked the place where one arrow had pierced her. A similar mark showed next to one of her shoulder blades, but both appeared to be healing well. "Obviously you didn't stitch these," he remarked.

Alyssa smiled, "The men who carried me would not have received your grandmother's approval, but they kept me alive."

"That's more than I could do," he said bitterly.

"Shhh," she rebuked him, putting a finger across his lips. "This was not your fault. It was T'Lar's and mine. I betrayed you and your trust. I should have died for that. This is far better than I deserve."

"I have forgiven that already," he said quickly, "and you redeemed yourself when you saved Irene."

"That is not enough," said Alyssa, looking at the ground.

"Then you will have to live your life making it up to me," he growled, pulling her closer. She lifted her lips toward his, but the recent memory of their last kiss made him turn his head aside.

Her eyes registered disappointment.

"What happened before…," he began.

"That won't happen again," she told him. "Now that they have you, I doubt they care what we do."

"What was it? I don't understand."

"None of us do," she admitted. "We aren't allowed to talk about it. You saw what happened to me a while ago."

"Aren't the questions driving you mad?"

"Yes, and until I saw you I had given in to despair. I had thought to put myself out of this misery, but even that is not allowed. I am ashamed of my joy at seeing you, for now you are trapped with me."

In spite of himself, he found his hands tracing lines along the curve of her back. "There are worse things," he told her.

"No," she said, "I don't think so."

"Then let me help you forget for a little while."

They made love then, with a desperate urgency that only those without hope could understand, and after they had finished they lay quietly on her small bed in the darkened room. Gram stroked her hair and tried to pretend that the events of the past day hadn't happened, even though he knew he couldn't forget.

As the sun dropped lower and dusk fell Alyssa rose from his side, "I have to go to work."

"Work?"

"I wait tables at the Drunken Goat. Bran rents me this room in exchange for that," she explained. "We commoners have to work, or we don't eat."

Gram felt a hot knot of jealousy in his chest as another question rose within him, "Is he the one?"

She frowned, "The one what?"

"The one you kissed."

"What?!"

"Don't play dumb. You must have kissed someone. Otherwise how did you get this?" He pointed at his neck.

Her eyes narrowed angrily. "Oh, you stupid, stupid man! You think I came back to Dunbar and found a lover, even before my wounds were fully healed?"

Gram shrugged, "Not exactly, but you could have had one before you knew me…"

"No," she said flatly. "I did only as my master commanded. I had no lovers, only targets. I had no life before I met you. 'Jasmine' was a slave. My existence was blind obedience. You ended that when you killed T'Lar."

"Then how did…?"

"One of the physicians, after I was brought back to Halam," she explained. "I was barely conscious when he forced my jaws open and dropped it in my mouth."

"Oh."

An awkward silence ensued, until eventually Gram spoke once more, "I didn't mean to imply…"

Alyssa put a finger over his lips, "Yes, your thought irritated me, but I have no right to expect you to trust me, not after all that I have done. You should not apologize." She stood and began dressing.

"What do I do while you are gone? I need to find my friends."

"You cannot," she cautioned. "You are a danger to them now. Anything you do will only make things worse, for them as well as for yourself."

He grimaced, "I can't accept this."

"Slavery isn't about acceptance, it's about survival." She turned away and stepped through the door, glancing back once. "I'll be back when the tavern closes. Please be here." Her eyes were silently pleading, and then she was gone.

CHAPTER 12

Chad held perfectly still as he watched Alyssa leave. He sat on an empty door stoop, an empty pipe dangling loosely from the fingers of one hand. Many people made the mistake of ducking or looking away when their quarry came into sight, but he knew better. Any sudden movement would draw eyes to the hunter. Better to remain still. Alyssa probably noted his presence, but she instinctively avoided looking directly at him to prevent an awkward meeting of the eyes. Consequently, she had no chance of identifying him.

Not that she would have recognized him anyway. Gone were his hunting leathers, covered by a rough tunic and loose trousers. His bow was stashed in a trash pile nearby, and a broad brimmed hat covered his head. The ranger's eyes followed her as she walked a short distance down the road before turning to enter the Drunken Goat.

Didn't go very far, did she? he noted mentally. He kept his place. Patience was his only remaining ally.

After escaping from Gram and Alyssa it had been surprisingly easy to avoid the other people of the town who had been hunting them. Before it had seemed as though no matter how he and Gram had hidden they were eventually discovered. The only conclusion he could draw from that was that somehow they had been able to track or follow Gram. Now that he was alone, there was little to differentiate him from the other citizens of Halam.

An' it was somethin' other than just our looks. At a guess, he figured it must have been Gram's magical sword, either that, or they simply didn't care about a middle-aged bowman.

Chad couldn't disagree with that assessment, though. He had no arrows and no magic, and he preferred it that way. Better to be in the background than to draw notice or be seen as important. Being underestimated had always been to his benefit, and while he wasn't proud of it, he had probably killed more people than anyone he had ever met, except the Count di'Cameron, of course. It was rather hard to compete with *that* man's body count.

Moira will just have to take care of herself for a day or two, he told himself. *Once I know what these two are up to, I can find her or the dragons an' we can decide what needs doin'.*

A rumble drew his attention, and he glanced at the sky. Storm clouds were gathering, indicating an impending downpour, which suited him just fine. He would watch until Alyssa returned home before catching a few hours of sleep for himself. Looking back at the doorway, he knew that no one would be bothering him. The owner of the small house was no longer in any position to complain.

"An' he was kind enough to lend me these fine clothes," muttered the hunter. He checked his tunic once more to make sure there were no visible blood stains. *I should check to see where he keeps his tobacco. Long as I'm holdin' this fine pipe, I might as well have a smoke.*

It was close to midnight when Cassandra and Grace began their flyover. There should have been a half-moon that night, but the clouds had solved that problem for them. They flew barely a thousand feet above the town, confident that no one could spot them in the gloom. Grace was the first to find her partner.

Gram!

Grace, came his somewhat hesitant reply.

She sensed something off in his response, *What's wrong?*

I've been captured, sort of...

What?! she asked in alarm.

You have to stay away from me, I'm not in control of myself anymore, he replied quickly.

Not in control? What does that mean?

It's hard to explain. There's something inside me. I'm not sure if it can hear my thoughts. This isn't safe, he told her.

Grace was confused and frustrated by his statements. She needed to know more. *None of that makes sense. You need to tell me more. I can help you,* she returned.

Gram's answer was quick and emphatic, *Stay away, Grace! Warn the others...* His thoughts stopped abruptly as she felt a surge of pain rip through his mind, pain that passed straight to her through their link. For a second, her nerves felt as if they had been set on fire, and then darkness overwhelmed her. Her wings twitched and folded. She was falling.

She came to herself a short time later. She lay in a dim alley, but that was no obstacle for her keen eyes. The wall beside her was made of timber, cracked and bowing inward, as though it had been struck by something moving at high speed. That probably explained the pain she felt when she began untangling her wings. Something had broken in one of them, one of the long bones.

If I had known bodies could hurt so much, I might have rethought my decision to become a dragon, thought Grace. She could feel Gram nearby. He was walking toward her, and focusing her vision in his direction she saw him turn the corner.

She felt a sense of relief at the sight of him, but only for a moment. As she got her legs under her she could sense the wrongness in him. His eyes were open as he approached, but Gram's mind was silent, as though he had fallen into a deep slumber. *No, not even slumber,* she realized, *more like a coma.*

Gram stopped ten yards away, and his lips opened, "Destroy the other dragon."

Grace's eyes widened, "What's wrong with you? You know I won't do that!"

"I command it, and you will obey." The words fell from lips empty of all emotion.

Despite herself, Grace sank her clawed feet into the timbered wall beside her and began to climb. She would have flown, but her damaged wing made that impossible. *Gram! Wake up!* she shouted at him with her mind, but she couldn't reach him.

Cassandra was flying closer, having circled to return after seeing Grace fall from the sky beside her. *Grace are you alright? What happened?*

Grace had reached the roof now, and she knew Cassandra would spot her momentarily. She couldn't fly, but she expected that her companion would likely fly down to help her. Inside she was screaming, raging at herself, but her body refused to obey, and her mind quietly calculated a plan of attack. She felt as though her heart and soul had been split into two separate entities. One blindly following orders, while the other watched in horror.

She could see the chain of events forming already. Once she was close she would make a surprise attack. Cassandra was more than twice her size, but Grace had grown considerably over the past week. If she could get her jaws around the soft part of the other dragon's neck, just below the head, she might well succeed.

Cassandra was landing now, her heavy body making the roof beams groan as her weight came to bear on them.

Grace had no choice, but rather than let the surprise scenario her mind had provided play out, she threw herself voluntarily at the other dragon, shrieking a roar of challenge and baring her teeth as she charged.

That at least gave Cassandra a brief warning, and she turned her head to meet the unexpected attack. She caught the smaller dragon's initial assault with the bony crest that protected the upper portion of her head before sweeping Grace aside with a heavy blow from one forelimb. Grace rolled and scrabbled along the slate roof tiles before slipping off and hitting the ground with a heavy thud.

What are you doing?! shouted Cassandra in Grace's head, but she couldn't answer. All her desired responses were warnings, and the enchantment that bound her to obedience had clamped down even more strongly after her subtle attempt to undermine Gram's command a moment before.

Grace began clawing her way up the side of the building once more, her sharp claws tearing heavy splinters and shards of wood away as she struggled to reach her designated foe. Cassandra watched her for a moment before spreading her wings and launching herself skyward once more.

Rising quickly, the larger dragon spotted Gram in the alleyway and understanding dawned as she realized the source of Grace's sudden change in behavior, although it still made little sense. Cassandra began flying away.

Faced with a target she couldn't hope to reach, Grace dropped back to the ground and began running through the streets, following as closely as she could from her earthbound position. She knew she couldn't catch the flying dragon, but inwardly she was glad, not only of that, but also that she was now out of earshot. Gram couldn't give her any further orders if she couldn't hear him.

Fortunately, there were very few people on the streets that late, but the few she encountered got the fright of their lives. Grace had grown and was now slightly larger than the average horse. One man turned and saw her racing toward him in the dim light, and once she was close enough for his eyes to resolve her reptilian features he screamed and threw himself sideways.

She hoped he wasn't injured as he fell against a building in his haste. Grace ran past without pausing. She could still sense Cassandra in the air above, and she couldn't stop.

Did he order this? asked Cassandra.

Nothing in her order prevented honesty, especially now that the element of surprise was lost. *Yes,* answered Grace. *Something has happened to him. When he first spoke to me, before he started acting oddly, he told me he was no longer in control.*

If it wasn't him, shouldn't the enchantment allow you to ignore the command?

It was a verbal order. Apparently the enchantment doesn't discriminate very well, she replied.

What if Moira has also fallen prey to whatever has Gram? wondered Cassandra.

That hadn't occurred to Grace yet, but it was a terrible thought. *Then you must avoid her, otherwise she might give you a similar command.*

You said it was a verbal command, noted Cassandra, *but he warned you mentally beforehand. Correct?*

Grace gave the mental equivalent of a nod.

Then I will lead you on a futile chase until I locate her. Once I have found her, I will fly beyond your range, which should leave you free to help her.

That was a clever plan, and Grace had to admire the other dragon's forethought. She had another question though, and despite her better judgement the enchantment forced her to ask, *What will you do after that?*

A brief pause came then, as Cassandra considered her response. *Nothing. I will fly higher for a while.*

Grace smiled inwardly, grateful that her friend had realized the trap. If she had told her what her plans were, Grace would have been forced to try and follow her. Leaving her in the dark would allow her the freedom to actually help Moira.

Gram found himself standing alone in an alley, not far from Alyssa's apartment. He remembered warning Grace, but his memories turned black after that. He had lost control.

The last time, while hunting Chad, he had been able to remember most of what had happened, but this time he was left wondering. There had been a flash of pain, and then—nothing. He couldn't be sure why he had been able to remember the time before, but not this time. It might have to do with the duration, or the method of transition, but such things were beyond him.

He waited quietly for several minutes, considering his options. He didn't know where Grace had gone, or where any of his other companions were, nor did he really want to meet them—not in his current condition. There was only one practical option left to him. Turning back, he headed for Alyssa's door.

As he began to move he heard a faint sound. His ears automatically focused, and then he could hear the sound of breathing, along with a heartbeat. He might have missed it in the ordinary noise of the city, but at this time of night it was quiet enough to pick out from the background noise. Someone lurked, hidden half a block away around a corner. Whether it was a stranger or someone deliberately watching him, he had no way of knowing.

He kept those observations in the silence of his unspoken awareness, the place that Cyhan had taught him, the darkness of raw sensation where the unconscious worked beneath formalized thought. As his perception worked its way into the light of his conscious he gave it a verbal form, *probably just a late night drunk out wandering.* But somewhere deeper, he doubted the truth of that statement.

Gram walked on, returning to the room where Alyssa lived.

CHAPTER 13

Moira watched the rain from a small window. The house that held the window was situated in one of the most squalid parts of Halam. It belonged to Wat's mother, his father had died years earlier.

His mother, Lana Perkins, was elderly to say the very least. In fact, Moira thought she might be the most decrepit example of womankind that she had ever met. The crone had no teeth that she could discern, not that she had wanted to get close enough to count them. The smell had been enough to discourage close proximity.

Such thoughts are unbecoming and uncharitable, Moira chided herself mentally. She had accepted their offer of shelter, and now she felt bad about her observations. Still, she couldn't help but wrinkle her nose. The elderly Mrs. Perkins was not the only thing that smelled. The house itself reeked of old refuse and new mold.

Gerold had awoken briefly, when Stretch had gently deposited him in what passed for a bed at the Perkins house. The pain of his shifting position had elicited a cry from him, and his eyes had opened.

Focusing blearily on Moira he had managed a short question, "Where are we?"

"I'm not really sure," she had answered, "Somewhere in the city, hiding from your king's guardsmen."

"How…?" Gerold gasped at a sudden pain, unable to finish his next question.

"The answer to that is complicated," she told him. "The short answer is that we escaped and are now fugitives."

The Baron's eyes widened with alarm, but he couldn't seem to form any more words. His eyes were losing focus, and she could sense his consciousness becoming more diffuse. Moira hurried to offer him a cup of water. The man badly needed fluids to help make up for the blood he had lost.

"Drink as much as you can," she urged, but after two long swallows his hand sagged, and she had to catch the cup before it fell to the floor. Her eyes misted as she considered his wounds once more. *Poor Gerold, he didn't deserve this…* Leaning over, she brushed the hair back from his forehead. "Rest now, you are safe. I won't let anyone hurt you."

The words were more of a promise to herself than for him. Her magesight had already shown her that he was beyond hearing her.

Wat stepped into the room, a question in his eyes.

"What is it?" she asked, fighting to keep her own exhaustion at bay.

"Nothing milady," answered the ex-prisoner, a look of embarrassment on his face.

Irritation bloomed suddenly, a product of her fatigue. "Just ask me. Standing there making stupid faces is just going to annoy me. Whatever it is, I'll answer."

Wat's face blanched, and he began to fiddle with his hands, but after a moment he spoke, "Is he your betrothed?"

"What? No!" The question startled her. "Why would you think that?"

"You seem to care a lot for him—and he's a nobleman, and you're a lady…"

Moira stifled a laugh as her irritation faded away, "I care for a lot of people. I hardly know this one. Anyway, the nobility aren't like cats and dogs. You don't just throw a male and a female together and expect them to pair up. Besides, how do you know I'm a noblewoman?"

Now it was Wat's turn to look amused. "I may be slow, but I ain't daft. You certainly ain't common."

She pursed her lips, uncertain how to respond, finally she said, "I guess I can't argue with that. Since you aren't daft, what do you propose we do from here?"

The lanky man shrugged, "We can't stay here too long. If they find us here, it'll mean trouble for my mam. Don't you have a castle or someplace we can escape to?"

If only it were that simple, she thought. "I wish I did, but my home is far away. In any case, I cannot leave until I find my father. The King has him locked away somewhere."

"Then he is doomed," pronounced Wat.

Moira gave him a determined look, "I got us out of the King's dungeon."

"Once maybe, but the whole palace will be stirring like a nest of mad ants," said Wat. "It'll take more than some magic tricks and strange animals to go against the King."

She opened her mouth to argue, but after a second she closed it again. Wat hadn't seen most of what occurred. Part of it he had been forced to forget, and the rest had been mostly invisible to his eyes. Other than summoning Stretch, most of the escape had just been strange behavior on the part of the guards, at least from Wat's viewpoint.

"I'll see you safely out of the city, Wat, you and the Baron both. Maybe he has some place to keep you both safe, but that's as far as I go. I have unfinished business with the King here," she told him.

A fire was building in her heart. The deaths and the fighting she had seen and caused, at the palace had left her uncertain, but now her resolve was returning. Moira hadn't asked for this fight, but now that she knew her father was near, and now that she had seen the monster lurking at the heart of Halam, she could not turn aside.

"You'll die, milady."

Moira blinked, "A lot of innocent people will die, Wat, but I won't be among them, and I'll hold the King accountable for their deaths. There is an evil lurking in this city. Even if my father weren't here, I couldn't turn back. What they are doing to these people is unforgivable."

What about what you've done to some of these people? Wat for example..., suggested her silent observer.

Shut up.

Needing a distraction from that uncomfortable thought, she glanced at Lenny. The dead man had been sitting quietly in a corner since they arrived. "I need some time to think," she told Wat since he hadn't spoken after her last remark. "And I need to work on Lenny here."

"What will you do with him?" asked Wat. "He's one of the King's guards after all, he shouldn't even be here."

"Just leave me be," she sighed.

Wat stared at her for a moment and then bowed his head before backing out of the room. Moira let the ensuing silence soak into her bones for a moment and then let her magesight roam outward, exploring the neighborhood around their new hideout. She found nothing out of the ordinary, no guards or watchers studying the house. *Perhaps things will be quiet for a while,* she thought.

Turning her attention to Lenny, she moved closer to the living corpse that was occupied by one of her spellbeasts. The logical thing to do would be to let the body die and repurpose the spellbeast as a creature of pure aythar. She could use a guardian. *I could use several guardians.*

But she had other needs. The thing lodged in the guard's throat was a mystery, one that lay at the heart of what was going on in Halam. Being a thing of dead metal, she doubted she could get any information from it, but she might be able to learn how to remove it. *And who better to practice on than someone who is already technically dead?*

Steeling herself, she focused her senses on his neck, examining the strange metal *thing* that was lodged within him. In structure it was like a bizarre metal centipede, with the notable exception that it had fewer legs, and they were much longer than a centipede's would be in comparison with the length of its body. The main body was close to two inches long and over half an inch in diameter, and it had burrowed into the soft tissue at the back of the throat, using its claws to anchor itself beside the spine.

From what she thought of as the creature's head issued a long metal filament that followed the spine upward before entering the base of the skull and branching out. The ends of the branches all terminated in the apple-like structure at the base of the skull.

Dad would be disappointed in me for not remembering the name of it, she thought. *It started with a 'c' I think.*

That didn't matter at this point, though. She *did* remember what it did. It was the part of the brain responsible for coordinating movement.

Moira spent several minutes formulating a plan. Once she was ready she created a fine shield around each of the tiny filaments that penetrated the skull. Carefully, she then began easing them out—pulling them back and simultaneously protecting the soft brain tissue around them. They were tiny and had inserted themselves in such a way that removing them was unlikely to damage anything.

Things went smoothly at first, but once they were removed, the main body of the creature did something unexpected. Several razor sharp legs moved sideways and before she could react they cut cleanly through the poor man's carotid artery.

"Shit!" she exclaimed, panicking. She clamped a shield around the thing, preventing further damage, but the worst had already been done. Blood was gushing from the artery, and Lenny's mouth was full of it. His body died while she feverishly tried to seal the blood vessel.

Moira had seen plenty of blood before, that didn't unnerve her, but watching the metal abomination with her magesight as it began trying to work its way out of the dead man's throat nearly caused her to lose the contents of her stomach. Clamping a powerful shield around the thing, she crushed it before it could finish escaping.

She wanted to cry. She wanted to run screaming from the room. She was tired and disgusted and horrified all at once. None of it was right, none of it was fair. She was too young for this. No one should be forced to deal with what she had seen and experienced over the last twenty-four hours.

But she didn't.

Instead she closed her eyes and thought about her father. *He needs me.* Taking several deep breaths she tried to slow her heart and unclench her stomach. Then she felt her spellbeast, whom she still thought of as 'Lenny' despite the unfortunate man's death. It was still there, attached to the dead corpse.

Focus on what you can do. That's what her father would have said. Moira ignored the gore and drew the spellmind from the dead body and began working on it, reshaping it. Speech was definitely a necessity, as well as a slightly more complex set of decision making abilities. Once that was accomplished, she began channeling her aythar into it, strengthening it, and giving it a powerful body constructed of pure magic. A lion would be nice.

A half hour passed while she worked on it, and then she created a second one. *Lenny and Larry,* she decided, naming her guardians. She gave Lenny the form of a great cat, while Larry was shaped as a massive ape. Hands could be useful. Once the details were accomplished, she channeled all of her remaining energy into them. She hadn't sensed any danger nearby, and once she had rested she would recover most of her own power and have two powerful companions as well.

Exhaustion granted her the gift that had been denied her until then. Sleep came quickly as she leaned into the corner and made a pillow out of her arm. The fact that she slept in a room with a nearly dead man and an actual corpse didn't even cross her mind.

She awoke to chaos, "Moira! Milady! Help!" She blinked and sat upright in alarm.

Well, she attempted to do so. She quickly discovered that she was no longer propped against the wall. At some point she had slid down to the dirty floor, and when she tried to use her left arm to push herself upward, it refused to respond. It had gone completely numb from the shoulder joint down.

"Wargle!?" she shouted, both a question and a reassurance to whomever was calling for her aid. A moment later her brain had identified the voice that had spoken as belonging to Wat, and immediately after that her eyes focused on him, cowering by the door that led into the room.

Her new guardians were glowering at him menacingly.

"Don't let them kill me!" cried Wat.

"Relax, you're perfectly safe," she replied, but the movement alerted her to the fact that something was stuck to her face. Raising one arm, she wiped a large amount of dust and wet lint from the side of her cheek. Looking down, she saw a small pool of drool where she had been lying. Spitting, she realized that some of the detritus was clinging to her lips. "Oh! That's just..."

Moira paused then, struck by the ridiculousness of her complaint. Across the room lay a cold body, complete with a disturbingly large pool of blood around it. Somehow that still didn't make her feel better about the unidentified dirt on her lips.

And her arm still didn't work, although it was beginning to awaken and send increasingly powerful signals of pain back to let the rest of her body know it was still alive. *This just keeps getting better.*

She ordered her guardians to relax and took a minute to settle Wat down. Apparently, they had taken exception to him when he tried to awaken her by shaking her shoulder. Once she was sure that no one was about to commit violence, she was finally able to ask Wat the truly important question, "What's going on?"

"There are men outside. I've looked out all the windows. I think they're in the back too. We're trapped," moaned the ex-prisoner.

Moira expanded her awareness, letting her magesight explore the area around the house. She didn't like what she found. Not only was Wat correct, but there were more coming, filtering into the neighborhood in ones and twos. Possibly, the only reason they hadn't attacked yet was the simple fact that they hadn't all arrived. There were already more than a hundred people outside, and that number seemed likely to double in a few minutes.

Worse, it wasn't just men, as Wat had said, it was a wide variety of people. A few were guardsmen, but they were outnumbered by the plain citizens in the crowd. Men, women, and even a few children were gathering outside. Careful inspection of them revealed that they all bore the strange metal parasites within them, at least the four or five she took time to examine did.

"I think we have overstayed our welcome," noted Moira. Oddly enough, she felt no fear. She wondered if she had used up her capacity for it. She merely felt tired, and sore. Her arm had begun working once more, but it ached terribly.

The sound of the front door caught her ears then, followed by Mrs. Perkins' strident voice, "I had nothing to do with it! They said they'd kill me if I talked! Please don't hurt me."

Moira looked at Wat sadly, "Your mother is very devoted to you." It was hard for her to fathom a parent that would abandon her child so easily. It ran counter to her own life experience thus far.

Wat merely shrugged, "I'd have done the same in the past. Can't really blame her. Don't worry, though. I won't leave your side, no matter what happens." His face wrinkled in thought as though he was trying to figure something out. "I've been different lately—since I met you."

She avoided meeting his gaze as a feeling of guilt passed over her. She knew she had broken the rules when she had begun changing people, but she hadn't really had much of a choice. *I made him better. Can that be so wrong?* She was distracted from that thought when her magesight noticed something unusual outside.

The mob was ignoring Wat's mother.

The old woman was still begging and crying, but the people paid no heed to her. They let her pass through them without trying to stop her.

This isn't a human guard detail, acting on the orders of a ruler. This is a collection of monsters, and all they want is me, she realized. For some reason, that brought a sense of relief to her. "Wat, you can go. They don't want you. Just walk out, and you'll be fine."

The skinny man frowned, "I won't abandon you."

For the first time, she regretted instilling so much loyalty in him. Now it would likely get him killed, adding another death to her conscience. "You can't help me in a fight like this, and you'll just get yourself killed. Escape now, and if you absolutely must, you can follow me after I leave. It may be that you'll find some opportunity to help me later. Trying to protect me, you will only make things more difficult for me."

Wat stared at her, conflicting emotions warring within him, but eventually he nodded, "If that's what you want, milady."

"Good," she replied, forcing a smile. "Go now, while there's time."

Once he had left, she looked at what remained to her. She had the Baron to worry about. He was still unconscious, otherwise she might have had Wat try to help him leave. As things stood now he would have to be carried by Stretch once more. If she left him behind he might not survive unattended. *I should have given my helpers wings,* she realized, but there was no time for that now.

She loaded Gerold onto Stretch and prepared to leave. Moira couldn't see any other options, they would have to walk out one of the doors, and neither one seemed to offer any particular advantage. *They're just people, even if they're being controlled. They can't stop me.* Her energy reserves had recovered significantly during her nap, although she was definitely not fully herself yet.

Speaking softly to herself, she used her will to summon a heavy mist, covering the area around the house in a thick fog, and then she opened the door. No one moved as she and her companions exited.

Belatedly she realized there was one important question she should have asked Wat. *Which way is the shortest route to the city gate?* "Shit."

Moira took a deep breath. She would just have to stick to a straight course and trust that eventually she would find the city wall. *If necessary, I'll just go through the damn thing.* That thought made her chuckle, although it came out as a shrill almost hysterical sound when it exited her mouth. "Lenny, you take the left and Larry, you take the right. Stay behind me and keep an eye on Stretch and Gerold. Match my speed, and try not to hurt anyone unless it's necessary."

"How will we know what is necessary?" asked Lenny.

"Anything that threatens to stop me from getting the Baron out of the city. That's our goal. Got it?"

"Got it," answered the spellbeast.

Moira began walking forward with Stretch and the others following close behind. She kept a powerful shield around herself and another over Gerold where he lay cradled on Stretch's back. As she walked she could sense the people in the fog moving. Those on the other side of the house moved forward and those to the sides moved inward. Somehow they could sense her movement despite being unable to see through the fog.

They can tell where I am, noted Moira clinically. *That shouldn't be possible.* The parasitically controlled crowd showed no signs of exceptional aythar or special ability. She doubted any of them had magesight, and if they did, certainly not all of them. *How are they doing that?*

The crowd was moving, drawing inward to enclose them.

Moira released the fog since it didn't seem to be helping anyway. Immediately after, she began quick stepping and resorted to one of her father's favorite tricks—the flashbang, *"Lyet Bierek!"* The air in front of her was torn by a massive crack and a blinding flash of light, neither of which passed through her shield.

She repeated the words and sent her aythar outward in rapid order, ripping the night into a chaos of noise and searing light. It was a display that would have sent most armies into rout, and it clearly had an effect here, but it was not nearly what she had expected. Men and women flinched and closed their eyes, and some covered their ears, but none of them ran or fell back. Blind and deaf, they showed no sign of fear.

She pushed forward nonetheless, expanding her shield into a wedge-like shape as she forced a path through the crowd. The weight of their bodies against it was considerable, but it was nothing she couldn't handle. The difficulty lay in trying not to injure them. It was tempting to use her power to throw them violently backward. It would have been far easier, but she couldn't bring herself to do that to so many innocents.

Her magesight showed her a clear vision of her spellbeasts behind her as they struggled with those who closed in from behind. It was a weird slow contest, as normal humans grappled with them, trying to pull them down or just separate them. As strong as her guardians were it was impossible to ignore so many hands pulling at them, and eventually they were forced to violence to free themselves from the mob.

Moira dipped her head, letting her hair fall over her face as she continued onward. She pushed the press of bodies aside by sheer force of will, but their weight kept increasing. In the back of her mind desperation loomed, warning her of failure. She wasn't strong enough to keep it up indefinitely. Her choices lay between continuing until she was exhausted or destroying those who sought to stop her.

There has to be a better way. What would father do?

He would have made a "circle" and evacuated everyone long before coming to this. *How many times did he try to get me to memorize the circle keys?* She cursed herself for ignoring that advice. She had often chided her brother for his lackadaisical attitude toward learning some of the things their father had tried to drill into them, most notably healing, but she knew he had memorized the location keys for all of the circles.

But not me, it was just too damn boring for me. Fixing sheep, fine, but don't ask me to memorize a bunch of meaningless symbols and numbers. Except they didn't seem so meaningless now, and people would probably die for her laziness. *If I have to choose between saving Gerold and killing all these innocents, what will it be?*

A vision of fire filled her mind, and she knew the answer. She would kill any number of strangers to save a friend—and then she would hate herself for it afterward.

Would it be killing, though? Or would I really be saving them from a fate worse than death?

A dark reply came to her, *Ask their families later.*

Ignoring that thought, she drew on her anger to send her shield surging outward once more, tossing the people against it violently back. Then she contracted it and began running before the crowd could press in again.

As she ran she began searching with her magesight, and whenever she found something loose, a board, a lamppost, a watering trough, anything bulky enough, she pulled it inward to land behind her companions as they fled.

It tripped a number of their pursuers, and in some cases the flying debris bludgeoned several of them off their feet, but it wasn't enough. The crowd surged behind them, heedless of the dangers. In the distance Moira could detect more of them coming from every direction, heading unerringly toward her location. She couldn't afford to play nice any longer.

"Hurt them if you have to!" she yelled back to Lenny and Larry. "Try to lame them if you can."

Lenny roared and Larry simply nodded. Both of them were glad to be allowed to act more freely. They began fighting with more relish, knocking people aside and hamstringing some with teeth and claws.

We can do this, thought Moira, allowing herself to hope, but then she saw something strange in the road a block away. She hadn't noticed it before, not as she had the people closing in on her. This had seemed to be inanimate, an object with no more aythar than a stone or a building. At this distance though, she couldn't help but notice its movement, and that drew her attention.

It was a strange contraption, built entirely of metal, but it moved as though it had a life of its own. Four legs lifted a squat central ovoid body above them. Two arms and an odd box-like contraption projected from the central portion. The center swiveled to track her as she moved sideways in the street, and she could see that the strange rectangular box had an opening of some sort that it kept pointed in her direction.

As unfamiliar as the thing was, Moira recognized a weapon when she saw one. Years of practice with her brother made her response almost purely instinctive, she ran closer to the building on her left and contracted her shield, making it denser and angling it to deflect whatever force was about to strike.

She never heard the weapon fire. For a split second she saw a flash, and then her awareness vanished in a shock of agony and burning pain.

CHAPTER 14

Wake up! Someone was shouting inside Moira's head.

It hurts.

Moira's first impression was of something cold and hard under her hands. Gradually she came to realize she was on the ground, but where? After a moment she remembered the street, and her attempt to get Gerold and Wat out of the city. She could feel something sharp pressing into her cheek, and she started to raise her head.

"Oh!" She immediately regretted the movement. Pain shot through her head and neck, making her want nothing more than to remain very still.

You have to get up, or we will die here. It's coming. Let me help you!

She tried to open her eyes but was only partly successful. Her right eye revealed a chaotic world of movement and confusion. Her left eye didn't open at all, though whether it was swollen shut or something worse, she couldn't be sure yet. She thought she might have fallen into a puddle, for her face was wet. She wiped at it feebly with one hand. It didn't feel like water—it was far too sticky. *Who are you?* she asked, addressing the voice in her head.

I'm you, the other you, the one you created. You have to get up, it's almost too late!

167

Oh. She remembered now. The spellmind that she had inadvertently created when she escaped from the palace—when she had violated the rules her mother had taught her. As she thought about that she began to see the world again with her magesight. Its return created a terrible throbbing in her skull. It also showed her the carnage around her.

Bodies were everywhere. Stretch, still carrying Gerold, was standing over her, while Lenny and Larry seemed to have gone on a rampage. They were twenty feet away now, and the torn and mangled remains of the townsfolk that lay all about seemed to be primarily their handiwork. People were still charging at them, but flesh and blood was a poor weapon against spellbeasts. Her two guardians ripped and tore, shredding flesh and breaking bone with mad abandon.

A sharp resounding click reached her ears. It was a modest sound, as if someone had clapped two bricks together, but it heralded something far more powerful than the sound indicated. The metal monster was only thirty feet away, and it had pointed its boxy weapon at Lenny.

The lion shaped spellbeast was thrown back, a giant hole appearing through its torso followed instantly by an explosion in the building that stood behind him. Moira had felt it, but it had happened too quickly for her to understand. It almost seemed as if a rock had been thrown at unbelievable speed, tearing through Lenny and demolishing the wall of the nearest house.

Is that what hit me? she wondered.

Lenny recovered quickly, and ignoring the gaping tear through his magical body he sprang at the metal monster while Moira tried, and failed, to stand. Apparently the thing couldn't fire its strange weapon again so soon, but a small metal door slid aside and a metal rod emerged. Light flashed, and a thunderous roar shattered the night, far louder than the noise made by its previous attack.

The sound didn't stop. It went on, hammering at Moira's ears as something too fast for her to see shredded Lenny's body. The spellbeast's great catlike body collapsed. Larry had charged from the opposite side of the creature, but it swiveled with smooth precision and brought its devastating weapon, still firing, to bear on her ape-like guardian.

The area around Moira was temporarily clear of living people, but a man stepped out from an alley and began running toward her. It took several seconds before she recognized him. It was Chad Grayson. A quick order stopped Stretch from attacking him.

"Where have you been?" she asked numbly, still in shock.

Kneeling, he slipped his arms under her and lifted. The hunter was not a big man, average in height and build, he probably weighed no more than hundred and sixty pounds, but as he stood she could feel the muscles in his arms pulling taut with hidden strength. "Why does every woman ask me that?" he replied before adding, "We have to go."

Incredibly, he broke into a jog. The jarring movement did nothing to improve the pain she already felt.

"How did you find me?" she managed.

Moira was slender, but even so the ranger was already breathing hard as he answered, "I followed Gram. When I heard the commotion and realized he was heading for you, I ran ahead."

Larry had managed to reach the metal beast and landed a heavy blow even as the thunderous weapon tore him apart. His fist hit the strange weapon, bending it, and a loud explosion followed. It fell silent then, but her guardian had taken too much damage, and he fell to one side, his magical body beginning to disintegrate.

Smoke rose from the blackened opening that the rod had emerged from, but the monster didn't stop. Its legs began moving once more, and it turned to follow them, swiveling its torso to bring the box back into line with the fleeing humans.

Chad left the road, turning into a side alley when the strange clack sound rang out once more, and the building they had turned in front of shook. Seconds later the corner collapsed, spilling brick and masonry across the alley behind them.

"You left Gram behind?" Moira could see the four-legged monster struggling to climb over the rubble as Chad turned the next corner into a new street.

The hunter was panting too hard to answer, and his feet were slowing as he struggled to continue running with her, but a new voice found her mind. *Moira!* It was Cassandra.

I'm in trouble, she replied, sending a stream of images and words to describe what had happened as well as the metal monster that was following her.

I'm coming, answered her dragon, *Head to the left. I'm to the west of you. I can't stop, though. Grace is following me on foot, and she means to kill me.*

"Turn left at the next corner," Moira told her weary savior.

Chad stumbled but kept moving. "Why?" he panted.

She kept her answer short, "Dragons."

He nodded and headed toward the turn she had indicated.

Why is Grace trying to kill you? Moira asked her dragon.

I believe Gram ordered it. Something is controlling him, the dragon answered.

Moira felt her jaw clench as she silently cursed. She was tired, and fatigue had clouded her mind. In spite of herself, she felt the fires of hatred beginning to kindle in her heart. *Not Gram, not this—they've gone too far.*

More people were closing around them, drawn inexorably to her, like moths to a flame. Even before the metal monster caught up to them they would be dragged down by a mob of lesser foes. Moira tried to create a shield around them and was rewarded with a stabbing pain in her skull. It felt as though someone had driven a knife between her eyes. Chad's rapidly tiring legs weren't going to be able to escape the crowd.

The starlight above dimmed as a massive shadow passed overhead and then the night was illuminated by a gout of searing flame. Cassandra dipped low and scoured the street behind them with dragonfire. Wooden buildings caught fire as if they were made of paper, and the people following—the less said of them the better. They died silently, their bodies enveloped by flames. The dragon beat her wings and began gaining height after her deadly pass.

Chad kept moving, but even with the horrors behind him, he could do no more than walk now. "This whole damn city is liable to catch fire," he panted.

"Put me down. I think I can walk," Moira told him.

The hunter was too tired to argue. Gently, he lowered her legs to the ground, and after she had tested them for a moment they moved on. He kept a hand on her arm just in case she lost her balance. Stretch followed, still carrying the unconscious baron on his back.

I'll circle around and make another pass. There's something still following you, said Cassandra in her mind.

Careful. The weapon it uses is deadly, warned Moira.

So am I.

Her legs weren't hurt, but her gait was unsteady. As they went she tried once more to create a shield around them. This time she succeeded, but the result was less than impressive, and the pain it caused made it not worth the effort. With a sigh Moira let the shield fade.

Moira's magesight was working properly, although it made her head ache. She could easily sense the metal monster closing on them from behind. It was still in the flames that covered the street, but it didn't show any signs of slowing. Another shape approached from the darkness ahead of them, following the same course that Cassandra had flown. Moira recognized Grace bounding along the street toward them.

She could only hope that Grace's order only included the other dragon, otherwise things would get worse very quickly.

The moment came and went almost before Chad could see her. The smaller, horse-sized dragon ran past them with the speed of a hunting cat. Moira caught a glimpse of Grace's eyes as she passed, reflecting the flames that lit the street behind them.

Be careful, shouted Moira mentally, but if Grace heard her she gave no sign. A ton and a half of reptilian muscle, she passed the humans and threw herself at the metal beast that was just emerging from the fire.

"Don't stop," urged Chad when she began to pause and turn her head. "There's nothing we can do against that thing."

The metal monster failed to register her attack in time, temporarily blinded perhaps by the intense heat it had just passed through. Grace's heavy body nearly bowled it over, but its four legs provided exceptional stability. She grappled the thing with teeth and claws, although they found little purchase against the hard metal.

Her greatest advantage was that the thing had only two arms, and those were small, probably meant to serve functional purposes rather than participate in melee combat. Scrabbling to hold on to a body with few places to grasp, Grace latched onto the right arm. Metal screamed as she ripped it free seconds later.

But its body was turning, twisting to bring the box-like weapon to bear.

Grace! The box is a weapon, don't let it...!

Moira failed to finish the warning. Grace saw the threat and caught the metal device in her powerful jaws, crushing it with teeth that were stronger than any metal yet forged in Lothion. An odd clack rang out as the monster tried to fire, and then Moira and Chad were picked up and thrown by the force of a powerful explosion. Even Stretch was sent tumbling despite his bulk and four legs.

Moira found herself face down in the street once more, but she quickly levered herself upright with her arms. The world had gone silent, but her mouth was open. She could feel herself screaming, but for some reason she had lost the power to produce sound. The only thing she could hear was Cassandra's voice in her mind, *Noooooo!*

The lower half of the metal beast still stood in the street, weak flames guttering from the shell of its torn and broken upper section. Moira's one eye was unable to find the dragon, but her magesight discovered her seconds later, Grace's broken body hung limply, impaled on a heavy roof beam that had been split by the force of the explosion.

This can't be happening. The dragons her father had created were among the most powerful creatures left in the world since his war with the gods. Grace had been the firstborn child of her gift when she had come into her power. Losing her had never been among the remotest possibilities in her mind.

Seconds passed like hours as she stood there. Her logical mind told her that Grace could not die; the enchantment her father had crafted made the dragons immortal, but once her heart stopped beating the enchantment would reset. Grace's mind would be wiped clean of all memories, and the magic that was at the core of her life would create a new egg. The bond she shared with Gram would end, and she would hatch anew once a new master had claimed the egg. She would be reborn, but she wouldn't be the Grace that Moira had known.

Cassandra landed near them and lifted her head to the sky. Moira imagined she must be venting her rage and pain in a scream to the heavens, but it still could not pierce the silence that surrounded her. *My ears aren't working,* she realized. With a feeling of detachment she turned her magesight inward, discovering that the force of the explosion had ruptured both of her eardrums.

The larger dragon moved forward, reaching out to pull Grace's body from the massive timber that held her up, but Moira raised one hand, *Stop. She's still alive. Her aythar is there and the heart still beats.*

The heart still pumped, but the thick wood had pierced her chest, ripping through one lung, several large arteries, and doing unimaginable damage to the organs in her abdomen. Worse yet, the explosion had broken her jaw and cracked her skull. It was a miracle that her lower jaw was even still attached.

They will pay for this! roared Cassandra in her mind. *This city will burn!*

In due time, agreed Moira, understanding her dragon's sentiment. Her heart was numb, though as if she had forgotten how to feel. *Was this how it was for father, when he saw his father die in front of him?* She still remembered the look on his face when he had told her the story of her grandfather's death.

"I could have saved him, but I couldn't do everything at once. I was alone, and despite all my powers, I was helpless to stop the bleeding, remove the arrow, maintain his heart, and repair the damage to the muscle. All I could do was ease his passing," her father had told her.

A decision formed within her, a resolve that went beyond conscious thought. Without fully knowing what she meant to do Moira stepped forward, walking until she was close enough to reach up and touch Grace's tail where it hung above her. The heart was still beating, although it was slower now, and the rhythm was faltering. Ignoring the pain in her skull, she stretched out her aythar and used it to help support Grace's struggling heart. *Lend me your power,* she told Cassandra.

A surge of aythar rushed into her, sending waves of pain rippling through Moira. She still hadn't recovered from the feedback when her shield had been broken earlier. *Using your power now is unwise.* That warning came from her other self, the spell-twin that still haunted the back of her mind.

I don't care, Moira answered. *Help me.*

How?

The young wizardess showed her the vision that was forming in her mind, and her spell-twin nodded in agreement, *as you wish.*

Moira began feeding aythar to her other self, and she felt again the strange wonder as her mind began to fragment. Except it wasn't a sensation of breaking, or of becoming smaller, it was a feeling of growth. Her other self swelled with the power Moira was giving her and as she split into multiple new copies Moira felt as though she were growing ever larger.

The agony in her skull became more intense as she channeled Cassandra's aythar into her spellmind copies, but she forced herself to continue. She only had to deal with the pain. She only had one task. Her twins felt none of that pain, and they would do what needed doing.

Moira expanded, becoming first ten and then twenty. One part of her was on fire, burning as her mind sent forth the aythar that the others needed to work. The rest of her was ready, focused and calm. Once she had grown great enough, the voice of the one in pain cried out, *do it!*

A dozen things happened at once. Grace's body was lifted, pulled from the wooden spike that pierced her and laid gently to rest on the ground, while simultaneously the hole in her chest closed. The arteries and veins that pulsed with rushing blood found their separate parts and closed, keeping what remained of the dragon's blood in the veins where it was needed. Her jaw realigned itself, and the bones fused again becoming whole even as the skin and muscles were brought back into place and mended. Even the crack in her skull was fixed.

Less than half a minute had passed, and now Moira's other selves began to work on the internal organs, knitting the intestines and liver back together and sealing a myriad of smaller blood vessels.

Chad watched in steadily growing amazement. He generally didn't concern himself with magic, or the doings of wizards, but despite his insouciance he had spent an inordinate amount of time around them over the years. He had watched Mordecai heal on numerous occasions, and he knew that what he was seeing now was unusual.

His careful eyes also noted the subtle tremor in her stance as she worked—and the new blood that had begun to drip from Moira's nose.

She had been badly battered when he found her, one eye swollen shut and a cheek that looked as if the bones underneath had moved to places they shouldn't be. While he didn't know much about how magic worked, he had heard the Countess complain often enough about the strain it had placed on her husband in the past, and the times he had nearly killed himself by trying to push beyond his limits.

Worried he stepped closer, "Hey, I think you've done enough, lass. Save your strength, we still haven't made it out yet." His voice sounded strange, there was a ringing so loud in his left ear that he could barely hear his own words; his right ear offered only silence. He lifted a hand to touch her shoulder, but he stopped when she turned and faced him suddenly.

"Do not interfere with us. We are not finished." Two eyes stared back at him from an unblemished face as Moira walked toward him, warning him away with upraised hands.

He blinked, hard. The girl in front of him looked to be Moira Illeniel, but she wasn't. She had stepped *out* of Moira. There were two of them now. The original still stood facing the dragon, her body shaking and looking as though she might collapse at any time.

"What the hell?!" he finally managed to say. Glancing past the newcomer, he saw Moira sway, as if she were about to fall. "She can't take much more of this." He attempted to move around the doppelganger, but she sidestepped to block his path.

"You'll only make things worse, if you interrupt before we are finished," warned the girl in front of him. As she spoke the original Moira's legs started to give way, but a third copy appeared and caught her fall, holding her upright. There were three of them now.

Chad was used to being given stupid orders, and just as used to ignoring them, "This ain't right. She needs to stop." Pushing the girl aside, he tried to get to Moira's original body.

There was a moment of contact, when he felt the copy's body under his hand, but then she dissolved. He shivered as he felt her slide through his skin, and then she was gone. Standing utterly still, he struggled to understand what had happened before continuing onward, to help Moira.

Except that he didn't. His body stubbornly refused to move. Instead, he turned and found himself scanning the streets to see if any more of the city's weird citizens were approaching. Confusion grew as he started walking, moving away to scout the path ahead. He thought that the road ahead and then to the left at the next crossing, would lead them out, but he wasn't certain. *What am I doing? This isn't what I fucking meant to do!*

Don't struggle. It was Moira's voice in his mind.

Get out of my head, wench! I don't need some stupid… His thoughts stopped there, and he found himself mute, even within his own mind.

That's enough of that language. I've been thinking you could use some improvements. This is a perfect opportunity to smooth some of those rough edges, she commented.

He had no idea what she meant, but a feeling of stark fear gripped him.

Don't worry. It won't hurt. You'll be better than before, and much nicer…

Stop! Somehow he thought the new voice was different, even though it sounded like Moira as well. *You will not alter him. Just keep him still until we are done.*

Chad felt a sense of disappointment from his captor. *Very well. I will fix his ears, though. Unless you consider that to be 'interfering' as well.*

A feeling of warmth began in his right ear, followed by a milder sensation in his left. His hearing improved greatly, and although the ringing didn't completely stop it was considerably reduced.

For a moment he was free, and he turned back to look at the wounded dragon. Grace's body was covered in blood, but it looked intact now, her head had regained its customary shape and the gaping hole in her torso was gone. Moira had gone limp, her battered body supported by two seeming clones on either side. Her head had fallen forward, and her chin nearly touched her chest.

More copies stepped out of her, and soon she was surrounded by a crowd of look-alikes. They faced inward, eyes closed, almost as if they were praying over the body of their progenitor, when suddenly the battered girl's body went rigid, her head upright.

As he watched her face moved as though something were crawling beneath the skin of her cheek. Belatedly, he realized it was the bones moving to realign themselves. The scrapes and cuts on that side of her head closed, and within moments she looked much better. Almost invisible lines showed where she had been cut, and the only sign of her previously broken bones was a slight swelling on that side of her face.

Blood still dripped from her nose, though, and her visage was marked by a tightening that suggested she was trying to hide an intense inner pain.

Moira's eyes opened, gazing into space at something Chad couldn't see. Then her duplicates began stepping inward, superimposing themselves on her body before vanishing. Seconds later they were alone.

The hunter stared a moment longer before looking away, "Well fuck me."

CHAPTER 15

Moira's mind shrank as her duplicate selves collapsed inward until at last there were only two remaining, her and her spellmind-twin. Much of the pain that had emanated from her face and other places on her body was gone, but the agony in her skull was even more intense.

She released the shield she had created around herself and felt some of the strain ease. *I need to rest.*

Grace's body was still, but her heart still beat, and her chest moved slowly as she breathed. She was alive but unconscious. Her body was still damaged in ways that went beyond the ability of ordinary wizardry to heal, but Moira hoped time would mend the rest.

Cassandra brought her head closer, sniffing as she examined her smaller companion, *Will she recover?*

Moira wasn't entirely sure. *My father created you to house the immense energy that he took from the gods, part of the enchantment uses that power to fuel your rapid growth, but it also gives your kind an amazing ability to regenerate from almost any wound—or so he told me. I can only hope that today will give us a proof of that ability,* she answered.

What of her mind? Her skull was cracked. Her brains could be scrambled.

I know more about that, replied the young wizard. *Her true mind is a spell construct; so long as the brain can physically heal, the memories and the knowledge that make her who she is, will survive.*

"I hate to interrupt your moment of silence," interrupted the ranger, "but there are more people coming. We need to leave."

Of course, the archer had had no way of knowing that a conversation he couldn't hear had been going on. Moira spoke aloud, pleased that she was again able to hear the sound of her own voice, "Cassandra, can you carry Grace out of here?"

Barely, I think. But what about yourself? I cannot carry you and the other two if I'm trying to lift her.

"We can walk. We will meet you outside the city, where we first parted. Keep a close guard on Grace until we get there," said Moira.

But...

"No arguments. Go, we don't have time to debate this," ordered Moira. She and Chad helped Stretch get the Baron into place on his back, while Cassandra gently cradled the smaller dragon in her claws. The massive dragon rose into the air with a rush of air as her wings beat fiercely to get her and her precious cargo off the ground.

Moira let the hunter lead the way. She could already sense the great wall that encircled Halam in the distance. They didn't have much farther to go, but there were also more people approaching. The first three were running toward them from a cross street at the next intersection.

She winced at the thought of using her magic again, but Chad was already moving. "Save your strength," he called back.

Sprinting forward, the ranger drew two long knives. His opponents moved awkwardly, like children, enthusiastic but clumsy as they attacked him with improvised clubs that looked to have been part of an unfortunate chair until recently. The veteran ducked and cut, taking one in the throat and hamstringing the second. Unable to avoid the third, he took a heavy blow to his shoulder before disemboweling the man that struck him. Seconds later he finished off the one that he had hamstrung.

Moira saw the strained look on his face as he rolled his shoulder, trying to stretch the battered muscle. There wasn't much she could do for bruises, and there were ten more running toward them from the rear.

"Keep going," said the older man with resignation in his voice. "If you can make the gate, you might have a chance. My road ends here."

"No," she told him, standing firm. "I've had enough."

"Don't be stupid, girl!"

The townsfolk running toward them were less than a hundred feet off now, and Moira felt a shock of recognition as she saw Gram's distinctive aythar among them. "Gram is with them," she announced. One of the women felt familiar as well, although she couldn't immediately place her.

Chad stepped forward, bloody knives at the ready, "Alyssa is with him. You don't want to see this, lass."

The mention of that name surprised her, but it also firmed her resolve. "No," Moira said again. "I won't give them anymore blood today, not from me and mine." Her head was throbbing but she ignored it with an act of will. Letting her anger fuel her desire, she pushed her aythar outward once more. *Take them,* she told her alter ego, focusing her power on her other self.

Pain blossomed in her mind, almost blinding her with its intensity, but her rage was greater than that. Moira's mind expanded, splitting into pieces, becoming greater than the agony she felt. *One for each of them,* she commanded. Invisible threads of aythar flashed outward, touching each of their enemies, and as quickly as that, the fight was over.

Her spell-twins blocked the control of the parasites and began issuing their own commands. Their would-be attackers slowed and moved to take guard positions around Moira and her companions. They were stiff and awkward, but now they were hers.

Gram, are you there? She sent the thought out, searching his mind through her proxy.

She found only silence. Gram seemed to be unconscious within his doubly trapped mind. A similar search showed that Alyssa and the others were in the same condition. *Perhaps it's a mercy they aren't awake,* she thought. "Let's go," she told Chad and Stretch.

The hunter watched their new guards warily, "Are you sure this is safe? What if you lose control?"

"I won't," she reassured him. *Never again.* She knew the true secret of the Centyr now. Everyone thought the strength of the Centyr was in their spellbeasts, but that was only the surface, the face that they showed to others. The truth was darker. The hidden power of the Centyr lineage was control, total and absolute control. *And if these metal vermin think they will beat me at that, then they are sorely mistaken.*

The rest of their journey was almost anti-climactic. Two or three men attacked them as they approached the gate, but her new retinue outnumbered them. The fight was short and bloody, costing her two of her guards, but it was also a relief to reduce the number she had to control. Through it all she kept Gram and Alyssa quietly by her side. She wouldn't risk them.

The gate was very nearly unguarded. Many of the soldiers who guarded it had been parasitized and had abandoned their posts earlier to attack them at Wat's home. The few that remained were confused by the events of the evening. They cowered at their posts near the gate, afraid to confront the strangers.

Moira's new servants opened the gate, and they marched into the night.

They marched down the road from the gate for only a few minutes before turning off into a field. Another half an hour of slogging through wet grass and muddy irrigation channels, and Moira felt herself reaching her limit. Mentally she ordered her guards to halt and held up a hand to let Chad know she was stopping.

The field was black except for the starlight, not that she needed light to see. Her feet and legs were cold, soaked to the knees with wet mud. The world around her seemed to sway. *I can't keep this up much longer.* She knew what she had to do, while there was still time. Luckily, it wouldn't take much more aythar.

Cassandra was within her mental range, so she sent a quick message, *I can't go any farther. We are safe for the moment. I'll head for you in a little while. I just need to rest a bit.*

The dragon's warm thoughts came to her a second later, *Very well.*

She had no intention of resting yet, though. Instead she ordered the people she controlled to run in separate directions. Her aythar was so low now that she doubted she could maintain the copies that were controlling them much longer. She needed to get them as far away as possible before releasing them.

Killing them would have been easier, and the thought occurred to her, but she still wasn't ready to stoop that low. Straightening her shoulders, she made Gram and Alyssa lie in the wet grass.

"What are you doing?" asked Chad.

"What is necessary," she told him.

"An' that would be?" he replied, stretching out the last word for emphasis.

She held a finger to her lips and then pointed to her ears before looking back at Gram and Alyssa.

The ranger understood her meaning, but it still left him wondering what she intended to do.

"Be ready," she warned. "I may lose control of the ones I sent back. If I do, you may have to protect us."

She looked upward; the stars seemed to be moving back and forth, like fireflies in a summer breeze. Gritting her teeth, she summoned her will and began creating more spell-twins. The pain became a white hot fire in her skull as she channeled her remaining aythar into them.

Three of you for each of them. One to shield the parasite's body and claws, one to extract the control tendrils, and the third to heal any bleeding or damage as we remove them, she told her newer selves, although they already knew the plan.

The world was already spinning. *Now, move quickly!*

Her duplicates lashed out, sending their power into the bodies of Gram and Alyssa simultaneously, wrapping the metal creatures in their necks within fine shields to contain them.

Moira was barely aware of them now, even though all six of her helpers were sending back a steady stream of observations. The fire in her brain was starting to blot out everything else. *Just a little more, don't give up yet…*

And then she was falling. The ground raced toward her like a welcome friend. Her mind was a misery of pain, and the darkness that she had hoped for refused to come. Instead the world turned pale, and she began to burn. The universe became a white torment of flames that consumed everything.

Chad watched her carefully. Whatever she was planning, he doubted it boded well. One second she stood alone, and the next there were six others standing around Gram and Alyssa. They stretched out their hands and he saw the bodies on the ground stiffen.

Shortly afterward, he saw Gram's mouth open, and something dark and glistening emerged. It seemed to squirm in the dim light for a moment, but then he heard a sharp 'pop' before whatever it was fell away to one side. A quick check told him that the same thing had happened to Alyssa while he watched his young friend.

The six women faded away like ghosts into the night, and Moira fell before he could catch her. She began twisting and flopping on the ground, arms and legs alternately tensing and then flailing outward once more. Moira's head was drawn back and her mouth gaped in a rictus grin. Her eyes were open, but all he could see was the whites.

She's having a damned seizure, he realized.

Dropping beside her, he did his best to hold her body down, avoiding her face since her teeth were clenching at random intervals. *Fuck.* Stripping his belt off, he tried to get it into her mouth, worried she might bite through her tongue. It felt as though an eternity passed before her mouth opened again, but when it did he was ready. He couldn't tell in the dim light, but he thought she hadn't hurt herself—yet.

Minutes went by while she jerked violently, but gradually her movements slowed, becoming milder spasmodic twitches. Moving behind her, he cradled her head and made soothing sounds, as though he were calming a child. *Idiot, she can't hear you. Why are you doing that?*

Eventually she grew still, but he stayed where he was, brushing her hair away from her face with one hand. The old veteran's eyes were wet with tears, though there was no one to see. "Don't you dare die on me, girl," he quietly intoned, his voice thick and husky.

Blinking to clear his eyes, he examined the area. Gram and Alysa lay in the grass, their bodies as still as corpses. He had to watch them for a while before he could see that their chests were still moving. *That's something at least. They're alive.* Moira's bizarre magic horse-thing still stood nearby, a seemingly dead man on its back. It gazed back at him while he studied it.

Easing her head out of his lap, he stood and made a mental tally. "This is a fine mess you've left me with, four unconscious people and some sort of fucked up magic horse-wagon." His eyes met Stretch's momentarily before he added, "No offense intended."

The spellbeast lifted his shoulders in a shrug. He hadn't been given the ability to talk, but he could understand spoken conversation. The gesture made it clear he wasn't worried about the ranger's comment.

Chad kept talking, primarily to calm his nerves. "You're quiet. That's what I like about you; you don't fill the air up with unnecessary noise, unlike most people." He waved his hands to indicate the others, "Like this lot for example—I should count myself lucky the damned fools are out cold. Otherwise they'd be rattling my skull with their constant yammering. But not you…"

His voice trailed off. He didn't have a name for the magical creature. Since meeting back up with Moira she hadn't had a chance to fill him in on such mundane details. "I don't know what your name is," he said apologetically, "but no matter, I can come up with one for you." Cradling his chin in one hand, he thought seriously about it, studying his subject. *Man-like torso, horse-like body with some sort of weird concave back for carrying people—hmmm.*

"Damn, you're an odd one, but I'll keep it simple. Let's just go with 'Horse-ass'."

Stretch didn't care much. He tilted his head to one side as he thought but then nodded to indicate his approval. It was about then that his limited magesight detected something. Turning his head, he looked around and then pointed for the hunter's benefit.

"What is it?" asked Chad in a softer tone.

The spellbeast pointed in a second direction, and then a third. Then he closed one hand and put two fingers out, pointing at the ground. He wiggled the fingers while moving his hand from one side to the other. It was moderately clear he was trying to indicate someone running. Stretch pointed again toward the darkness, marking three directions.

Chad sighed, "Three people, coming toward us."

Stretch nodded affirmatively.

"Thanks, Horse-ass."

The past day had shown him that for some reason the people being controlled were following Gram, not him. He had already reasoned that it must have something to do with magic, and having none, they had largely ignored him when he was on his own. "If they don't have true wizard sight, I might be able to hide from them, but they're being drawn to those two like moths to a flame."

The spellbeast pointed to itself and tilted his head to one side.

"Yeah, and probably you too, Horse-ass, since you're actually made of magic," agreed the ranger. He thought for a moment. "You go stand over Moira. If anyone gets too close, kick them or something. I'm going to walk a little ways off and test a theory."

Stretch tilted his head again, obviously curious.

Chad smiled, "I'm going to find out if they can see me in the dark. If they can, things will be harder, but if they can't, I'll teach them a lesson or two." He walked in one of the directions that Stretch hadn't indicated, fingering his knife sheaths, making certain the blades were still there and that they could be easily drawn.

After thirty feet he began to circle his friends' position in a clockwise manner for a moment before stopping. Then he waited, listening. The starlight wasn't sufficient for illuminating much more than dark shapes and sudden movement. He crouched, trusting the short grass to keep him unseen. If he was wrong about the perceptual abilities of his enemy, he would be in for an unpleasant encounter.

His ears warned him of the first to approach, and he smiled as he took note of the sound. The poor bastard was trying, with very limited success to run in the dark. A lot of squelching noises punctuated by an occasional heavy thump told him everything he needed to know about whether his enemy could see in the dark.

A dark blob moved against a grey backdrop, and the ranger rose to his feet, walking carefully to intersect the stranger's course toward his unconscious friends. He stopped once he had found the right spot, and seconds later his nearly blind opponent tried to run over him.

Ten inches of cold steel went in under the man's ribs, ripping upward to cut through lungs and arteries. The poor bastard thrashed for a moment, but the hunter was thorough, shifting his blade until he had found the heart. The dead man grew still, and Chad moved away, circling a short distance before waiting again.

He caught the second one in similar fashion, but then he heard noises coming from where his companions lay. Rushing back he found a heavyset woman attempting to drag Gram's limp body in the direction of the city. Stretch remained dutifully standing over Moira's form, making no attempt to interfere.

The woman heard him coming and turned to face him. Neither of them could see well, and she threw up one arm to ward his first strike. The blade sank into her forearm, passing completely through and catching between the bones. Her other hand caught him solidly in the stomach, driving the wind from his lungs, but it was worse for her. His second blade had found its mark, and he shoved it home, entering from her shoulder, beside the neck.

He fell beside the dead woman, coughing and wheezing as he tried to catch his breath. The night air was cold on his skin, so he figured he was covered with blood. *Or mud,* he corrected silently. *Some of the shit on me is probably just mud. No need to be excessively macabre.*

Glancing at Stretch, he saw the spellbeast was pointing again, marking four new directions.

"More of them, Horse-ass?"

Stretch nodded.

"This shit is getting old fast," complained the hunter. *Or I am.*

The next one was easy, but the last four of Moira's ex-servants slowed down and banded together before approaching. Chad let them pass by in the darkness, considering his options. He felt reasonably sure he could kill two of them before the others could get their hands on him, but things would get ugly after that. People being controlled by the parasites were stronger than one would ordinarily expect. He still had a persistent ache when he tried to take a deep breath, which served as a constant reminder of that fact.

What I wouldn't give to have a quiver full of arrows again, he silently complained for what was probably the tenth time.

He knew what he would have to do, not that he liked it. This whole evening reminded him far too much of things he would rather never remember. *The nightmares will be back and worse than ever, I expect.*

Rushing forward in the darkness, he cut through the back of the leftmost man's leg, hamstringing him before leaping to one side and racing away into the night. His enemies were slow to react, and by the time he had gone ten feet he was lost to sight again. The cut he had given was a deep one, and the poor fellow would likely bleed to death if it weren't treated promptly.

The wounded one remained standing, hobbling on one good leg as the four of them arranged themselves with their backs together. The parasites must have realized they were low on manpower, if they were willing to fight defensively.

Which suits me just fine.

Chad moved closer, close enough to verify their position before running away again. He hoped they would be foolish enough to follow, but they disappointed him by remaining together. He'd have circled to finish the wounded one if they hadn't. Instead, he stayed far enough away that he could just barely see their outlines against the dark horizon. *If that fool stays on his feet much longer...*

Several more minutes passed, and he saw a hint of motion. He guessed that the injured one had collapsed from loss of blood. Leaping up, he ran toward them. He planned to take one down in his charge and finish a second quickly after. The third one would be messy.

The dim light almost proved his undoing, for he failed to see, until he was already on them, that these three had armed themselves. The one he had chosen for his charge held a modest belt knife as did the one to his right. The third had improvised a club from what looked to be a piece of deadwood.

Chad hated knife fights. Well, he hated them if the other guy had a knife too, at least. The problem was that they never ended well. Often the only difference between the victor and the dead was that the victor just had fewer cuts on him. *And I'm outnumbered.*

Ducking low, he tried to slip to one side to avoid the first man's outstretched blade, but the muddy ground betrayed him. Stepping into an unseen hole, he fell forward. He missed skewering himself on his enemy's blade by pure chance. Hitting the ground, he rolled and kicked out, striking the man behind the knee.

The knife-wielding townsman fell backward and landed full on the ranger's upraised steel.

The hunter was forced to abandon his blade, as the dying man's body had it pinned beneath him. Rolling, he avoided the club wielder's swing. Springing to his feet, he started to run. An escape at this point would be a win for him. He could ambush them again in a few minutes.

Unfortunately, he ran headlong into the other man with a knife.

The force of their collision sent both men reeling backward, but that wasn't the worst of it. Chad felt the pressure of the knife as it struck his ribs on the right side, accompanied by a terrible grinding noise that he could only guess was steel on bone. A wash of dark fluid flowed down his side. There was no pain, but that wasn't unusual in the flush of battle. The pain would catch up soon enough. *He's fucking killed me.*

Recovering first from the shock of their collision, he leapt back in and drove his own weapon home, sinking the long knife in to the hilt, once, twice, and then again just to be sure. "Godsdamned whoreson! How does that feel!" he shouted.

The deadwood club landed squarely across his back—and broke. It hurt like hell, but apparently the owner hadn't been careful to choose a solid piece of wood. Chad fell forward still cursing and rolled to his feet. His back hurt like hell from the blow, but his wet side gave him no trouble at all.

Feeling his side, he realized that the knife hadn't pierced him at all. Reaching into his shirt he pulled out the silver flask that until recently had held six ounces of fine whiskey. "Son of a bitch!" he swore, madder than ever.

He jumped sideways to avoid a barehanded lunge from his only remaining opponent. "I was savin' that!" he yelled. "What the hell am I supposed ta drink now?!"

The townsman ignored his question, rushing him again. Chad danced lightly to one side, cutting a deep line along his foe's arm as he passed. He was angry, and his anger lent strength to his weary limbs. *No, I'm not just angry—I'm pissed! And now I won't be able to get pissed after this is all done.*

The second exchange opened the stranger's belly, spilling his guts onto the ground even as he wrapped his big hands around the ranger's neck. Bright lights flashed in Chad's vision as the pressure mounted on his throat, but his knife arm kept working. The brute's grip slackened, and Chad pushed him away, gasping for air.

Winded, bruised, sore, and exhausted he sat beside the gory body of his late-enemy. He could feel the mud seeping through his trousers, but he was beyond caring. Addressing the corpse, he spoke, "Serves you right for being so fuckin' ugly. Your ma would probably thank me fer doin' her the service o' puttin' you outta yer fuckin' misery."

His anger was fading, but his irritation only grew. Holding up the damaged flask he shook it gently. There was something left! Opening the cap, he tilted it, careful to keep the torn side upward, and managed to get two good swallows before it ran dry.

Patting the dead man beside him, he apologized, "I'm sorry. I was just mad about me flask. I had no call to talk about yer mother like that." He paused a second before laughing, "Even if it was true."

Briefly, he considered removing his shirt and trying to wring the last of the spirits from the fabric into his mouth, but the cool night air had already dried it too much. Doubtless he wouldn't get more than a drop.

He was still sitting there when a new group of people emerged from the darkness. They had the same dead expressions, but they weren't the ones that Moira had captured earlier. This was a fresh group. Chad counted at least ten and then gave up.

Smiling sadly, he eased himself to his feet, "Well fuck me. This just ain't my day is it?"

CHAPTER 16

Running would have made sense. In the dark it would be nearly impossible to find him, and he already knew they were homing in on sources of magic. Chad could just melt away into the night, forget everything, and keep moving. He could start over; he had done it before.

Hell, it wasn't as though he had much anyway. Not many people would miss him, the bartender at the Muddy Pig, maybe—and Mordecai. But the Count was likely already dead. Moira had been fooling herself on that matter. That left the Countess, and he had never had the feeling that she was overly fond of him.

Only an idiot would try to fight. There was nothing to gain. Moira and Gram were both senseless. They might be dying already for all he knew. With so many enemies he would be throwing his life away for nothing.

Glancing down, he saw a faint glint. That was where his silver flask lay, empty and discarded. It had been one of his favorite possessions, a gift from a fool, a fool whose daughter lay unconscious not far away. Snatching it up, he slipped it back into his shirt before drawing his long knife once more. He wished he had his other knife as well, but he hadn't recovered it from the body it was pinned under yet.

"Ye picked a bad day boys! I'm all out of whiskey, and I've got nothin' left to lose," he said loudly. Not that the enemy had paid any attention. They were almost on him.

Crouching low, he leapt forward, gutting the first to come within reach. A hard slash to his right caught another, and then they had him. Strong hands and heavy bodies bore him down. It was only then that he remembered that they might do something worse than kill him. *Shit! I should have run.*

Normal men would have beaten him while they had him down. That's what people did in brawls. It was human nature. People that were riled up couldn't help but kick a man once he was down. But these foes didn't do that. They organized themselves and held him still without injuring him any further, and that terrified him.

A rush of air and the thunder of wings announced a new arrival. Searing flames appeared, blinding Chad's night adjusted eyes with their brightness. The stench of burning flesh filled the night, a smell he had never wanted to experience again.

The ones holding him didn't let go. They were trying to pry his mouth open.

Then the one sitting on his chest vanished, snatched upward by vast scaly jaws. Cassandra tossed the man like a ragdoll before bringing her head back like a battering ram to knock the ones holding his arms aside. Talons flashed and suddenly the ranger was free. The dragon stood over him and slowly turned her head, sending a steady stream of fire across a wide arc in front of her.

Everything burned.

Chad didn't bother getting up. He was tired. *No, not tired, I'm fucking exhausted.* The cold grass and mud beneath him didn't seem so bad anymore. The inferno that had become the world felt like a warm blanket.

He watched Cassandra's neck and shoulders as she continued to spew lethal flames. The muscles rippled beneath scales that shone and glittered in the firelight. It was a surreal moment, beautiful and awful all at once.

"Ye're a lovely girl," he muttered as she finally closed her jaws and leashed her fire. "If you were a woman, I'd marry you."

The dragon's sharp ears caught his words, and she turned her head slightly to one side to look down on him with a worried eye. "Did you hit your head?" asked Cassandra in a deep rumbling voice.

His body ached, so he answered truthfully, "I think I hit everything."

Since everyone had been unconscious, Cassandra had flown them one by one back to the hiding place where she had taken Grace. In the darkness, Chad had been unable to discern much of their surroundings, but now dawn was breaking, and he was surprised to see that she had taken them all the way to the foothills, at least fifteen miles or more from the city. Their camp, if it could be called that, was nestled in a low rocky depression that sheltered between two sizeable hills.

Large rocks broke up the ground at intermittent intervals and moderate tree cover shaded the area. It was as decent a spot as he might have chosen himself, although if it rained they were going to get wet. There were no opportunities for shelter from rain, at least not until they built some.

Chad's back started aching in anticipation of wielding an axe to build a lean-to or similar shelter. *Correction, it was already aching. It's just speakin' up to remind me.*

"Damn, I need a drink," muttered the ranger.

The dragon turned her head to gaze steadily at him once more, "Didn't you pack something?"

He grunted, "Yeah, but it's in the big pack. Probably back where we separated before entering the city."

"No, it's here," Cassandra informed him. "Grace and I scouted this place and moved everything here after you went into the city."

A smile lit his features, "Bless yer dear heart!" Standing, he looked askance at her, "Where is it?"

She ignored the question, "There's a storm on the horizon."

"We can put something together after I have that drink."

The dragon answered with a deep rumble, "Or you can take care of it now. I'll show you where the pack is after that."

Chad's eyes narrowed, and he glared at her. "I need the canvas and rope from the pack—the axe as well."

"Those you can have, but no drinking until you're finished."

He swore for a moment, giving vent to his frustration in a long uninterrupted exhalation of legendary nautical prowess. Then he added a more direct insult, "Yer a slave drivin' bitch, ye know that?"

She snorted, "You said you wanted to marry me last night."

"I was bewitched by yer big beautiful dragon ass, but it's clear to me now that a marriage between us could never work," he replied with a bitter note of humor in his words. Glancing at their unconscious companions he added, "I wonder how long before one of 'em wakes up?"

"No way to know. Why?"

"Four young people over there, and this old man has to do all the shit work. I'm startin' to think some of them are just takin' advantage of my overly generous nature."

Cassandra smiled, giving him a view that included entirely too many teeth. "I will help you, and you are neither old nor generous."

"Tell that to my back and shoulder," he shot back.

Despite the dragon's best watchful effort, the ranger, a veteran of many a long campaign, plucked his bottle out of the pack and took a long draw before she could protest. Cassandra issued a deep warning rumble, but he ignored it.

"You weren't supposed to drink anything until after we had the shelter ready," she complained.

Chad winked at her, tossing the bottle back into the pack. He wanted more, but he knew himself well enough to know that any more would be counterproductive. "No lassie, that's what you decided." The warm burn in his throat and belly was a welcome distraction from his cold hands and the various aches in his shoulder and elsewhere. "Let's start over there." He pointed to a promising boulder.

The ground was almost level in the place he had indicated, but there was a faint slope to the ground on one side of the massive rock. He studied it for a moment and then cast his eyes about searching for a suitable source of wood. There was a dearth of deadwood around, and that meant he'd have to do a lot of work with the hand axe. Chopping down a sapling or two would be work enough, and the additional chore of sawing it and its attendant limbs into something useful would be even worse. He glared at a nearby scrub oak with a baleful eye, as though he might wish a terrible fate upon it.

"What?" asked the dragon.

"That damn tree is too fucking big," he complained. "We'll have to choose one farther down, but that'll mean more hauling."

Cassandra swiveled her massive head to study the tree in question. "It isn't that big. If you use something smaller, won't you have to use more than one?"

"That ain't the problem, darlin'," he replied with a sigh. "It'd take me an hour just to chop that fucker down, and then I'd have to have you move it. Besides, I've no way to split a trunk that big, so I'd still have to have another."

"Oh," she said. Walking over, she stretched up on her hind legs and caught the upper portion of the tree with her forelimbs. Leaning into it, she pushed and then pulled, rocking the tree back and forth until she felt it weaken. When she felt it begin to shift she surged forward, and with a massive 'crack' the oak's taproot snapped. The tree fell over as the upper roots sent gravel and soil flying into the air.

Chad let out a long appreciative whistle. "I guess that's one way to fell a tree."

"What would you do next?"

He waved the hand saw at her, "Next I'd be trimming the limbs away, but on a tree that size…" The larger limbs were as large in diameter as the upper part of his arm.

The dragon smiled, which was an altogether unsettling expression given her massive jaws and deadly teeth. Wrapping her claws around a heavy limb, she ripped it downward, pulling it away from the main trunk. It came free with a long strip of bark and tough wood trailing the end that had formerly been attached to the tree. "Should I do the rest?" asked Cassandra.

"By all means," he nodded, eyes widening.

For all her size and strength, it still took the dragon more than a quarter of an hour to thoroughly de-limb the oak. Once she had finished a large pile of twisted limbs and foliage lay to one side of the wide trunk. The trunk itself was a mess, ripping the branches away had pulled long strips of wood and bark from it. There was still an ungainly mass of roots at one end, and a roughly torn top with twisted splinters and pieces standing out from it.

Cassandra looked askance at him, "Is this good?"

He considered his words for a second, "It's just fine and dandy, but we will still need at least two more like it, and if they're all that big, we'll have the world's most overdone lean-to—unless you can split it."

"Does it have to be split in two? I don't think I can make it that neat."

"There's enough wood there to split it into twenty pieces, if we was runnin' a sawmill," Chad laughed ruefully.

Cassandra opened her jaws and clamped down on one end of the great log, biting into it like some giant dog that had finally found its favorite bone. Razor sharp teeth sank deeply into the wood as the incredible pressure she applied crushed it. She released her hold before the wood was completely shattered and then moved her mouth down a couple of feet and repeated the process. Working her way along the length of the log she rendered it into a collection of heavy strips of wood still loosely bound together.

The ranger smiled, "Now that I can work with." The whiskey had warmed his limbs and loosened his tight muscles. Using the axe and occasionally the hand saw, he began splitting the heavy strips of wood apart. Some pieces wound up being too short, depending on where they came apart, but in the end he had seven lengthy pieces that were almost as long as the original tree trunk.

The dragon wasn't suited for finer work, so she lay down and watched him at his task. The hunter assembled a rough frame that leaned against the boulder he had chosen and used smaller pieces to create a series of cross pieces. Rather than waste the rope from the pack he tore long thin strips of greenwood and used them to tie the framework together.

"Those won't last," noted Cassandra as she observed his handiwork. "When they dry out, some of them will break."

"That's true sweetheart," Chad agreed congenially. The activity seemed to have improved his mood. "But some will last longer than you think, and besides, once I've finished this part, I'll be weaving the little branches through it, like a wicker basket. The whole will hold together even if some of the original joints come apart. Watch and learn."

He continued working and the shadows grew longer. After a few hours he had a passable lattice built from the small branches and thin strips salvaged from the shattered remains of the main trunk.

"You have clever hands," complimented the dragon, "but it won't keep the rain out. You shouldn't have pulled the leaves off the small branches."

"Oak ain't so good for that," replied the ranger. "It'll do in a pinch, but if there's more than a short drizzle, the water would just start dripping through it. Pine would be nice, the needles make an easy thatching, but we don't have that luxury around here. Would ye mind flyin' us down there a ways?" He pointed toward a long grassy slope a half a mile down the hill.

"There are no trees there."

"It's the long grass I'm wantin'," he told her.

Cassandra gave him a short ride to the area he had indicated. Once there the hunter took out his long knife and began cutting the thick grass. The blades were long, two and sometimes even three feet, and he collected it into clumps as thick as his forearm before tying them into bundles with yet more grass.

She watched him with interest for a quarter of an hour, impressed by the confidence and dexterity she saw as he nimbly cut and bound thick swathes of grass into bundles. As time passed she began looking over her shoulder, though, staring up the hill to where their sleeping friends lay. "I don't think it wise to be away from them for too long. How much longer is this going to take?"

Chad nodded, eyeing the horizon. The sun was fading fast and heavy clouds were moving in from the east. "Too long, but I don't need much light. Go ahead and check on 'em, just come back every so often. You can carry what I've finished back with you."

Night fell while he worked, and Cassandra returned every half hour to carry his handiwork back to their camp. A light rain began to fall as she came back for what he guessed would be the final load. "I'll be back for you in a minute," she told him.

"Nah, just keep the kids dry. I'll follow ye on foot," he responded.

"You'll be soaked by the time you get up this hill."

"I been wet before." In truth, his labors had him sweating already, but he knew that he'd be shivering within minutes. Some days were just shittier than others, but if it came down to him being wet and cold or their wounded friends, he figured he was in better shape to deal with it. It didn't mean he couldn't complain about it, though.

He took off at a brisk pace as she flew back up the hill. Cassandra had landed before he had gone fifty yards. She might have come back for him anyway, but the rain began to pound in earnest almost immediately. She spread her wings to create a makeshift roof over them.

Chad glanced up at the sky as he trudged onward, "I was kinda hopin' this would be a purely symbolic gesture, and ye'd hold off until I got back up there." The only reply he received was a loud rumble as thunder rolled across the hills. "Yeah, fuck you too," he swore quietly at the rainclouds.

People generally thought that given his occupation he was a nature-lover, but that was only partly true. Chad knew that Mother Nature was frequently the biggest bitch of them all. Looking up the slope ahead of him, he noted that the hill he was ascending, and the one next to it, vaguely resembled a pair of enormous mammaries. The observation made him chuckle to himself, "The only reason I keep comin' back to ye is because of yer enormous teats."

Another crack shook the sky as lightning flashed in the distance.

"Yeah, I know. You always get the last laugh anyway."

Fifteen minutes later he arrived at the camp. Their sleeping wards were still arrayed in a short line near the almost completed lean-to, and Cassandra sat next to them, one wing stretched out to shield them from the downpour.

Chad didn't bother joining them; instead he went to the pile of grass bundles and began securing them along the lower edge of the framework.

"You should wait until the storm passes," warned Cassandra.

He snorted, "I ain't gonna get any wetter. Besides, aren't you getting cold keeping yer wing out with all the water running down it?" His teeth chattered slightly as he spoke.

"Dragons do not get cold," she retorted.

"Is that so? I always thought lizards were cold blooded." The ranger was facing away from her, so Cassandra couldn't see his smirk.

The dragon growled softly, "Do I look like a lizard to you?" Chuffing, she sent a short burst of flame from her mouth. "I assure you my blood runs quite hot."

The ranger laughed and continued his work, tying the bundles of grass in long rows along the newly constructed lean-to. It took more than an hour, but eventually he had them all in place, although he would probably have to redo some of the work the next day. He had been hurrying, and he doubted that his work was as solidly done as he might have liked. It would keep the rain off for now, however.

Once that was finished, he moved their human charges under the new shelter. Gram and Alyssa both shifted and groaned mildly as he dragged them to the new location, while the Baron actually woke for a moment as the pain brought him to full consciousness. Moira remained limp and non-responsive. Chad didn't like what that might signify, but there was little he could do about it other than wait and hope. He gave the Baron some water and watched while the nobleman drifted off to sleep again.

The hunter shivered as he knelt beneath the slanting roof. The wind could hardly reach him there, but he had been wet for too long, and there was no chance he could build a fire with the rain coming down.

Grace was too big to move easily, and she wouldn't have fit inside the lean-to anyway, but Cassandra had shifted her position once the humans were safely tucked away. She curled around the smaller dragon and draped a wing over her. It looked cozy to Chad, and it occurred to him that perhaps he could share the warmth of one of his sleeping friends.

He shook his head. He'd just make someone else wet then, and none of them looked as though they needed any additional problems. Taking a drink from the bottle, he hunkered down closer to the boulder that the lean-to was built against and tried to think warm thoughts. *A nice fire, a warm bed, an' a soft ass to cuddle up against...* A cold breeze ripped that thought away and he shivered again. Chad ground his teeth, *I'm cold all the way down to me balls and beyond.*

"Come here," said Cassandra's deep voice.

He glanced over at her, "Huh?"

"I said come over here."

His brain wasn't working as well as usual, "Why?"

"I can keep you warm," she offered. "Climb in here between us." By way of explanation she shifted her wing to show him the place she meant.

He briefly considered arguing, but he was too tired to bother. He settled into the spot she offered, sliding down between the two dragons. Their bodies radiated a steady warmth, and the scales on Cassandra's belly were smooth to the touch. Chad shifted around until he was comfortable. The ground was damp, but the dragons more than made up for the heat he lost to it. Closing his eyes, he leaned his head back.

CHAPTER 17

A cold breeze touched Alyssa's cheeks, and she shivered involuntarily. Her bed was cold beneath her, but something warm lay close beside her. Someone.

Gram.

She remembered her surprise at seeing him enter the shop. Their reunion had been bittersweet. Within minutes of their meeting she had been forced to afflict him with the same terrible torment that she was suffering. And yet, despite knowing it was wrong, that the only person she truly loved was now doomed as well, she couldn't help but feel joy at seeing him once more. Her selfish heart betrayed her. Now they were both doomed, but she still felt brighter for knowing he was with her.

At least they could enjoy one another again, for whatever time was left. Alyssa snuggled closer to him, ignoring the twinge in her shoulder when she moved. A lingering memento of her not quite fully healed wounds. Burying her face against his neck, she ran her hand up to feel the marvelously sculpted muscles of his chest.

Several things occurred to her then.

Her bed was not just cold, it was slightly damp, lumpy, and exceedingly uncomfortable. It seemed to be covered in grass as well, a sure sign that she might have made a mistake regarding her location. But that was not what troubled her the most.

There was entirely too much hair. Her face was buried in it, where she had expected a bare neck. Even worse, the flesh beneath her hand was definitely not thick muscle, or male.

Alyssa's eyes opened, though she didn't jerk or give any other sign of awareness. Without moving further, she scanned the area around her. Rough splintered wood beams and twisted branches covered the sloping roof above her, which appeared to be roughly thatched with still green grass. Her face was against a woman's neck, and after a moment's study of what she could see of the profile, she thought it was Moira Illeniel.

How did I get here?

Her last recollection was clearing a table at the Drunken Goat. She understood that she had once again lost some time. It wasn't unusual to lose consciousness when the parasite took over, but she couldn't figure out how she would have wound up in her current circumstances. A wash of horror passed over her as she realized that Moira must have been taken as well. Yet another friend had been damned along with her.

She swallowed and felt a strange pain in the back of her throat, and despite her best effort she began to cough. Turning to one side, she found a strange lump in her mouth, a large blood clot it turned out, once she had spat it out. Her throat felt raw now, and she struggled to suppress the urge to cough further.

"Ye look like ye've seen better days lass," said a vaguely familiar voice. Her eyes soon confirmed her suspicion. Chad Grayson sat a few feet away, watching her with curious eyes.

"They've taken you as well then," she said in a voice that sounded like a stranger's. She was hoarse, and her words were almost unintelligible.

The older man gave a dark laugh, "I reckon if they had, they'd be payin' someone to take me back by now."

Alyssa frowned, "Then you're in danger. You shouldn't have tried to save me." She winced at the pain of saying the words, it felt as though her throat was on fire.

"I ain't been taken, more like I took you," he replied. After a pause he added, "Not in the more intimate sense mind ye." He thought for a few seconds longer. "Actually, it was the princess there that did the savin'."

Her hand went to her throat, "Then…?"

The ranger nodded, "Aye. I think she pushed herself too far, though. She collapsed after takin' that thing outta ye."

A strange feeling swept over her, making her eyes water. Her eyes lit upon Gram, sleeping on the other side of Moira, "And…" She couldn't manage the words, her throat was too painful now and swelling with emotion on top of the other injuries done to it. She gestured at the young knight.

"Aye, him too," Chad reassured her. The hunter turned his head away, unable to bear the raw emotion on her face.

She thought she might have seen the beginnings of tears in his eyes to match her own. Alyssa began to cry, the feelings too much for her, but the pain in her throat put an end to that before she had sobbed more than twice. It was simply too painful, her throat couldn't bear the strain. Choking, she fought to get herself under control.

213

"Just take it easy, lass. Here, drink some water. It might help," he held out a leather water skin toward her. His eyes were dry, but the older man's cheeks were pink from being scrubbed against his sleeve.

It was late afternoon when Gram finally stirred. He woke to find a dream staring down at him, a worried expression on her face.

"What happened?" he croaked.

Alyssa leaned closer and whispered in his ear, "Don't try to talk. It hurts. Try not to cough either, or you might start bleeding again like I did."

Confusion was written clearly in his face, but Alyssa put a finger across his lips. With one hand she gestured to Moira who lay close beside him before adding softly, "She took them out of us somehow. We're *free*."

Somehow her whisper managed to convey the depth of her joy at that revelation. Looking around he saw Chad nearby, sitting unusually close to the massive form of Cassandra. He couldn't see Grace, but he felt her presence through their bond, and that realization brought with it an uncomfortable memory. He had ordered Grace to kill the other dragon. Well, the parasite had anyway. His memory of events ended shortly after that moment.

Grace?! he called with his thoughts. There was no reply, although he still felt her close at hand. *Grace?* Unable to get a response he looked back at Alyssa, "Where's Grace? What happened?"

"She was hurt," whispered Alyssa. "I didn't see it. Your friend can explain."

His eyes scanned her face. Clearly she wanted to say more, but her expression was apologetic, whether because of her difficulty speaking or because of her lack of direct knowledge he wasn't sure.

Sitting up, he found his body was remarkably free of injury, although his back twinged from lying too long across a lump in the uneven grass. Gram's throat felt raw, but as he approached Chad he managed to croak, "Tell me everything." He didn't bother saying more, it hurt too much.

Chad nodded, "I don't know the full story myself, lad, but after we parted ways I stalked you for a while. After yer confrontation with Grace, I followed her to where our little princess was leadin' some sort of breakout. Half the town was after 'em, and yer dragon was apparently chasin' after the bigger one. Then some sort of metal monster showed up and starting destroyin' everything."

The ranger sighed deeply as he remembered, "It had weapons like I've never seen, magic I guess. It moved on four legs, and it had this weird box that it would just point at things and boom, they blew up. It shot Moira with it, an' I think it damn near killed her.

"It had another weapon too, on the other side. I think it used that one more cuz the first one took time to reload or something, but it was almost as bad. It would point that thing, and it would light up, like fire was comin' out, along with this continuous thunderin' sound, but it wasn't like a wizard's fire. The fire was just near the weapon, like it was just a side effect. Somethin' I couldn't see was hittin' everything it pointed at. Anything in front of it just died, whether it was ten feet away or a hundred."

Gram nodded before looking down at Moira, "How did we get here?"

"Our little princess managed most of it," answered Chad. "Somehow she got back up and not only healed your dragon but got us out of the city. The things she did…" The hunter shuddered as he remembered the invasion of his mind. "…well I don't really understand it, but she got us out. Once we were outside, she fixed you an yer wh…" He stopped abruptly before rephrasing his words, "…yer girlfriend there. That must've been too much for her, though. She collapsed afterward. All three of you have been sleepin' like babes for the past couple of days."

"How did you move us after that?"

Chad shrugged, nodding at the dragon over his shoulder, "After that the big girl here took turns flying us to the hills." He didn't see any point in mentioning the last desperate fight. It had really just been a footnote to the entire escape.

Cassandra lifted her large head, "Don't let the old man sell himself short. At the end there were still more after you. He fought like a demon to protect you until I could get you all clear."

Gram met Chad's eyes, seeing the embarrassment there; after a second he nodded and the older man inclined his head for a moment. Words weren't necessary between them. Trying to spare his voice, he pointed at the stranger who lay on the other side of his position under the lean-to, raising his brows to indicate a question.

"The good baron, the one who went to the palace with Moira—I know he don't look much like himself anymore," said Chad by way of explanation. "I ain't had the story from her, but considerin' how much blood's been let out of him, I think he didn't do much better with his king than she did."

The man in question didn't much resemble the nobleman whom Gram had met a few days prior. His fine coat was gone and the rags he wore now spoke more of blood and dirt than nobility. His hair was thick with dirt and what might be mud or dried blood. The Baron had no shoes or boots, and close examination showed that the tattered clothing that covered him was actually the remains of his underclothes. Someone had stripped away his finery.

The ranger saw the thoughts passing across Gram's features. "I figure they must've locked him up with our lady. Guards usually take anything good from their prisoners. I dunno who stuck him, though. She must've healed the wound. There's a big silver scar on his ribs. I been tryin' to get water in him, in drips and drabs, but I don't think he's long for this world, if he don't wake up soon."

Gram sighed and then took a few steps, walking away from the improvised shelter. Circling around Cassandra, he found Grace's quiet form nestled gently against her side. The slow rise and fall of her ribs was the only sign of life in her. He ran his hand over her shoulders, feeling the warmth there, and then he looked down the hillside, across the plain, toward Halam.

The capital of Dunbar wasn't visible from their current campsite, but a smudge on the horizon probably represented the smoke that rose from the many chimneys in the city. Raising his forearm before him, he gazed at the tattoo that Matthew had put there. With a thought and a word that was barely more than a whisper he summoned Thorn, feeling the great sword's comforting weight in his hands. Another word sheathed his body in shining enchanted steel. The armor looked like scale mail, being composed of countless small interlocking pieces, but it was far better than that. Unlike normal mail, this armor locked in place when confronted with blows, becoming rigid to protect its wearer. It combined the flexibility of chain with the protection of plate, and its enchantments made it nearly indestructible.

It covered his face as well, although the parts that covered his eyes were invisible, allowing him full vision. Despite enclosing him completely, it allowed air to reach him as well, though Matthew had never explained the parts of the enchantment that allowed that particular miracle to occur. In truth, he didn't care. It made his head hurt whenever his friend had tried to explain the various workings of what was probably a masterpiece of the enchanter's art.

"Your father will be proud when he sees what you have created, Matthew," he whispered to himself. "And I will be sure to show it to him—after I've demonstrated it for King Darogen of Dunbar."

The great ruby set in Thorn's pommel pulsed with crimson light, as though the sword agreed with that sentiment.

CHAPTER 18

Something bright was shining in Moira's eyes, and she screwed them more tightly shut to try and keep the unwanted light out. The light was relentless however, until at last she was forced to cover her face with her arm to block it out.

"She's moving," said a rough voice. It was a woman's voice, although it was hard to identify it as one it was so coarse.

Moira risked opening one eye and peaking over her forearm to identify the speaker and was rewarded with a blaze of light that seemed to sear straight through her brain. "Unh!" she exclaimed, shutting the eye again.

Someone else spoke then, "She's awake! I saw her open her eyes." That sounded like Gram, although his voice also sounded uncharacteristically thick.

"Go away," she murmured, speaking to whoever might be within range of her voice. The effort made her head throb harder. "It hurts." *Ouch.* She wondered why she was so stupid as to have spoken again, despite having learned the result with one phrase already.

"Can ya hear me lass?" That was Chad Grayson leaning over her and speaking close to her ear. His breath was none to pleasant.

Moira rolled over and buried her face in the relative security of her bedding—and promptly jerked her head back as she found herself inhaling a noseful of dirt and grass. She sat upright then, sneezing and opening her eyes more fully. Sunshine was beating brilliantly upon the landscape all around her relatively shady position under what appeared to be a makeshift shelter. Her head felt as though it had been stuffed with thistledown, and when she attempted to expand her admittedly unclear magesight she was rewarded with a throbbing surge of pain.

"Uhn," she groaned, leaning her head forward and covering it with her arms as though blocking the light would reduce the ache. It didn't. Removing the visual stimuli only increased the discomfort as her mind focused more on her magesight. The world seemed to spin and contort, and she immediately opened her eyes again, seeking the stability of the sunlight.

"Are you alright?" asked Gram, leaning closer. His voice boomed, overwhelming her senses.

She put out her arms to ward him away before covering her ears. She kept her eyes open this time, however. Everything hurt. The world hurt, throbbing in the center of her being. Even the light was painful, but if she shut them the nausea was worse. The light kept things steady at least.

Eventually the others got the idea and gave her some space, talking in softer tones from ten or fifteen feet away. Chad chuckled, "I don't envy her. She looks like she's got the mother of all headaches."

Except I didn't do any drinking, she thought bitterly.

Her memories were fuzzy, so she spent a while reconstructing what she could remember of the period of time that had led up to her painful awakening. Frankly, a lot of it was difficult to believe, even as it began to be evident that she hadn't dreamed it. Gram and Alyssa were both standing nearby, free of their parasites, so that part was definitely real.

Risking her magesight once more, she found Grace lying on the other side of Cassandra. The effort sent new waves of nausea rolling through her, and she struggled to keep from retching. *I overused my power.*

She recognized the symptoms now. She had been through this once before, years ago, when she and her brother had attempted to save Gram's father from the enchanted gate that had crushed the life out of him. It felt even worse this time.

You almost died.

The words came in her own voice, but they were not hers. Another presence moved in the back of her mind. *You're still there?* she asked.

I couldn't be otherwise. I'm sort of stuck here, unless you choose to make me a vessel, responded her spell-twin.

I thought maybe you would have faded out while I was unconscious, she replied unapologetically. Her usual spell-mind constructs would fade and disappear over time unless she provided them with a new supply of aythar every so often.

Her inner twin winced mentally, *ouch.*

I'm not saying I wanted you to disappear…

…but it would have been more convenient, her other self finished.

Moira didn't have a good answer to that.

On the bright side, I've been keeping watch while you slept, although I have to admit it was really boring.

Keeping watch? asked Moira curiously.

Even though you were unconscious, I wasn't. There was still some excitement after you collapsed, and I can show you everything that happened while you were out. Master Grayson was rather heroic, actually. Other than that the last couple of days have been completely dreary.

Dreary is better than the headache I have right now, thought Moira wryly.

Her other self was silent for a moment. *Well, I'm not going to try and win at this pity-party, but I will say that being stuck here for days unable to do anything but observe was almost maddening.*

Were you truly that helpless? wondered Moira. *You seemed able to do plenty before I passed out.*

I suppose I could have tried to make myself a spell body or something, said her spell-twin, *but that might have killed you, and then where would we be?*

Killed me?

It's your aythar, your power, explained her mental companion. *Everything I do draws upon that. I don't think it's smart to exert your power after collapsing from exceeding your limits. Do you?*

"Oh, that makes sense," muttered Moira aloud. She regretted it when the sound of her voice increased the pain in her head.

"Moira?" asked Alyssa tentatively. "Is there anything I can do?"

She stared at the other woman thoughtfully for a long minute before whispering, "Tea?"

"I think there's some in the bags," said Gram, grateful to have a purpose. He moved toward their supplies.

"I'll heat some water," offered Chad.

Two days passed while Moira recovered, and by then the baron had regained consciousness as well. She sat next to him in the afternoon sun, watching Gram and Alyssa sparring. The two warriors were the least wounded of their party, suffering only minor damage to their voices.

Gerold's face was lit with interest, "I've never seen anyone fight like that. Are all of your warriors so skilled?"

Moira coughed, "I thought their skills came from Dunbar. Alyssa is from here, and it was her father who taught Gram."

The baron took another sip of water. It seemed he was perpetually thirsty since he had awoken. Glancing at the beautiful lady beside him, he considered his words, "We have wrestling and boxing in our yearly games, but nothing like this. Our soldiers train with weapons and armor. If there's any emphasis on close fighting, it would be with knives." He choked for a moment, eyes going wide as Alyssa ducked into Gram's arms, delivering a solid blow to his sternum before dropping down and sweeping his legs.

Gram rolled away before she could land her finisher. He was struggling to breathe. The young man got to his knees before Alyssa leapt at him again.

A flurry of blows ensued as Alyssa assaulted him with palms and knees, but somehow her dazed opponent warded himself from every attack. Gram seemed to tire, however, unable to recover his wind. Wavering for a split second, he missed one of her jabs, taking a glancing blow to his head. Though Gram was off balance and still on his knees, Alyssa seized the opportunity to drive a lightning fast punch toward his head with her left hand, only to find herself spinning.

Gram had caught her wrist, pulling her forward as he bent back, tossing her over and behind him. The exchange ended when he flipped over and pinned her beneath him, twisting one arm back and applying his forearm to her neck in a brutal chokehold. Alyssa growled and strained, but she had no way of escaping.

Gram held her tightly, leaning in to bite at her ear as he softened his choke and let his arm drift downward.

Moira looked down, smirking in simultaneous amusement, embarrassment, and perhaps a tiny bit of jealousy. "Is that like the wrestling in Dunbar?" she asked.

Gerold was turning red, "Our games are only between those of the same sex, and—no, not like that." His eyes darted back to the two fighters, who were now engaged in a shameless display of primal affection. "That's just wrong. A moment ago they were fighting, now they're kissing!"

"The annual Dunbar games might be more interesting, if there were more matches like that," suggested Moira with a smile.

The baron studied her for a second, captivated by the twinkle in her eyes as he realized she was joking. Laughing, he agreed, "You might be right."

"I'm thirsty," announced Alyssa suddenly, still captive.

"Me too," said Gram. "Let's go fetch some water." The two of them left abruptly, forgetting to take the only bucket with them.

Gerold looked askance at Moira as they left, "They aren't even married. How long have they known each other, a few days?"

"Much longer than that," she answered, knowingly. "In fact, I think they're still betrothed."

"It sounds as if there's a story there," said the dark haired baron.

"Would you like to hear it?" asked Moira.

The baron nodded, and Chad stood up a few feet away. "I'm going to hunt," announced the ranger.

Gerold took note, "Does their story offend you?"

"No, but while they're off making like bunnies in the bushes, I haven't been laid in over a month. The last thing I need to hear is a sappy tale of tragic romance," replied Chad.

The massive dragon resting on the other side of the camp spoke then, "You don't have a bow."

"Like I need one," growled Chad, checking his knife in its sheath before drawing their rope from the packs. He left then, carefully choosing a route in the opposite direction from the one Gram and Alyssa had taken.

That evening they all sat around a cheerful fire near the lean-to. Chad had returned with a brace of young rabbits and a collection of plants harvested from the hillside. Adding some salt from their packs and the water that Gram and Alyssa had eventually collected, he produced a stew that was far better than anything else they had eaten over the past few days.

Finishing his bowl and putting aside his spoon, the hunter looked over at Gerold, "Well Baron, what will you do now? Will you return to Lothion with us or chance returning to your home?" His accent was noticeably subdued.

Before Gerold could answer, Moira spoke up, "We aren't going home yet."

Gram nodded in silent agreement.

Chad glared angrily at Moira, "I don't know if ye remember all that well, *princess*, but we barely made it out of that city alive."

"My father is there."

"Aye," said the ranger, nodding, "and we can return with an army to sort that out. Yer mother will bring every tool at her command to bear on Dunbar to force his release. Runnin' in there by ourselves is a fool's errand."

Gram stood, "I should go alone."

Chad gave him an incredulous look, "Last time you went in there, boy, ye kissed the first girl to look twice at you, and a metal worm nearly ate yer brain!"

Alyssa covered her mouth to stifle a laugh, but Gram didn't find the remark amusing. Lifting his tattooed arm, he spoke a soft word and armor covered his body in glittering steel. "Not this time…"

"No, this time one o' those metal monsters will bend you over and shove it up yer dumb ass instead," interrupted the ranger.

"Grace already destroyed the monster," countered Gram.

Chad covered his face with one hand, "Yeah, *that one*, an' she's still unconscious. We don't know how many of those things are in the city."

Gram growled, but before he could respond Moira spoke up, "He's right, Gram. You don't even remember the fight. You didn't see what that thing could do."

"I won't take my armor off until this thing is done," said Gram. "There's no way…"

Moira held up a hand, "I saw it Gram. The weapon it fired at me would destroy your armor and kill you before you even knew it had hit you. The only reason I survived is because it missed after it destroyed my shield."

"And what's your plan?" he returned, letting his frustration seep into his words. "Go talk to the king and get thrown into his dungeon again? I doubt he'd let you escape twice."

Anger flared in Moira's breast, "I wouldn't have to step foot inside the gate. If I wanted to I could kill every man, woman, and child in the city without even showing my face." *Or enslave them,* she thought bitterly. She tossed her head, letting her hair fall back while the firelight showed the determination in her features. "But I won't do that; I'm going in there to get my father."

"How?" asked Gerold earnestly, worry etching a frown on his visage. "How would you do that?"

The smile she gave him chilled his heart. Holding up one hand, a glowing firefly appeared on her palm and then began to grow before his eyes. It changed as it grew, becoming a small cat and then a lion-like creature with fierce claws and long teeth.

"With an army," she answered as the lion beside her grew steadily larger. Responding to her emotions, it raised its head and a gave voice to a low growl that seemed to roll down the hillside.

Chapter 19

"This isn't right," said Gerold as they looked down the road. The main gates of Halam were only a mile or so distant now. "It's treason for me, at the very least."

They were sheltering in a gentle dip in the landscape that hid them mostly from view of the city walls by virtue of distance and a slight rise in the land between. It wasn't a good hiding place for a large force or an army, but for a few people, and even a dragon in their case, it was sufficient, so long as they didn't approach any closer.

"The thing controlling your nation isn't your king," said Moira. "I agree, though. This isn't right. I finally understand what my father used to tell us."

"What was that?" asked the baron.

"War is never right. It's a double edged blade that cuts both ways, destroying the lives of the innocent and the wicked alike—an instrument that kills the patient as often as it rids the body of disease. It's a product of our failure to find a better solution, but sometimes—it is necessary," she told him.

Gram grunted, "That sounds like him."

Gerold nodded, "He must be a wise man, but my meaning was different. As a peer of Dunbar I hold my power in trust—in good faith to the people. Your assault today will likely result in many civilian casualties."

Moira reached up, patting the rough stubble of the conflicted nobleman's cheek, "Dear Gerold, you are a kind

229

hearted man. You don't have to do this. In fact, it would be better if you stayed out. They will need you after this is done, and you only risk death by accompanying us."

"They…?" asked Gerold, "… or you?"

She caught the romantic overtones in his remark easily enough, in fact the man's entire being was shouting them at her. Any woman would have noticed his infatuation, but as a Centyr wizard she nearly had to wall up her mind to find peace in the face of his swirling emotions. The time for kindness was over, and she would do him no good service by allowing his feelings to grow. Her tone was cold, "*They*. I am here to save my father and since his enemy is also oppressing your people, I will eliminate it for you both. You are here to save the people once I have accomplished that."

"From what?"

She looked at him archly, "From me."

"That makes no sense," protested the baron.

Gram coughed, catching his attention, "I think I see what she means. We are foreigners, and if things go well, your country will soon be leaderless. They will need someone to unite them afterward, against their common enemy, someone familiar." It was just the sort of thing his mother would have understood instantly.

Gerold frowned, narrowing his eyes, "I am not that man. As I told both of you yesterday, there are at least seven men and three women in line for the throne before me."

Moira reached out, putting a hand on his arm while simultaneously stroking his aura, reinforcing the noble-man's confidence and smoothing his fears. It wasn't the permanent sort of mental alteration she had made the week before to some of the prisoners when they were escaping, merely a temporary form of emotional support. It just happened to involve a tiny amount of aythar. "I trust you more than any of those strangers, Gerold," she told him.

Chad had remained silent throughout the conversation, but his jaw clenched then, "Stop that."

Moira felt the condemnation behind the ranger's words as an almost physical rebuke, but she kept her features smooth. Removing her hand from the baron, she glanced back at Chad, "You have some misgivings about our plan?"

The hunter glared at her, letting his eyes drift to the baron for a second before returning to settle on her hand, "That ain't what I'm talking about, and you know it, so just stop it. It's disgustin'." Turning, he walked away before she could respond.

"What's wrong with him?" wondered Gerold.

"I think it's just tension," commented Moira.

That didn't feel quite right to Gram. He didn't like seeing Moira show such familiarity with a foreign nobleman, and he reasoned that Chad might well feel the same. "He just feels protective of you, Moira—since your father isn't here," he told them, letting his eyes drift toward Gerold. "No offense, my lord."

The baron could understand that reasoning easily enough, "None taken, Sir Gram. I assure you I have no dishonorable intentions where Lady Moira is concerned."

Moira growled, "I'm standing right here. If you apes want to talk about me, kindly go elsewhere or feel free to speak directly to me."

"Shouldn't we be doing something besides arguing?" interjected Alyssa, pointing toward Halam.

"I think this is close enough," said Moira. "We'll wait here." Raising one hand, she snapped her fingers, and her 'army' began moving, a hundred spellbeasts trotted forward. Well, most of them trotted, ten of them had eagle shaped forms, and those flew ahead.

The hand gesture was purely for effect of course, Moira was connected to her magical allies mentally, which obviated the need for verbal or gestured commands. She had spent the last week constructing them and filling them with aythar. In the past it would have taken that much time just to construct their spellminds, but that wasn't a problem for her anymore. Instead she had devoted her time to feeding her new creatures as much power as she could manage, until there were so many that the daily cost of maintaining them was as great as what she could put into them.

She didn't bear Illeniel's Doom, as her brother did, so she couldn't be sure whether her tactic had ever been done before, but she doubted it had ever been attempted on this scale by any Centyr mage. She wondered what the shade of her original mother would think of what she had done. Over the past two weeks she had broken all the rules she had been taught regarding the special abilities of the Centyr lineage, and her army today was a flagrant abuse of them.

But if I follow the rules, a lot of people will die.

That was the crux of the problem. Normal spellbeasts were far more limited in what they could do with the aythar given them, not to mention crafting that many unique minds, even simple ones, would have taken her much too long. Using the mind-twinning technique eliminated that limitation and made her allies' abilities more versatile.

But mind-twinning was forbidden, at least according to Moira Centyr, and she should know since she was literally the product of the original Moira Centyr's decision to break the rules. *Why* it was forbidden, she had never made entirely clear, other than the ethical problems invoked when creating an exact duplicate of oneself. She had been very direct though, when she had warned Moira of what the penalty for it had been in her day, execution.

Moira hadn't made just one, though. She had made a hundred.

A hundred and one, reminded her still resident twin, who she was starting to think of as a sort of personal assistant.

Right, a hundred and one, and probably more once things start happening in there, agreed Moira silently.

She felt it when her flying allies made contact. Information began streaming back to her, channeled through her assistant to help keep from overwhelming her mind. Eight of them dove into the gate guards, possessed them, and moments later the gates began swinging open. The two other flying spellbeasts continued on, sharing their aerial view of the city. The rest of her army kept running, streaming into Halam through the rapidly widening gates.

Halam's fall would be bloodless. *It has to be,* she thought.

"Are we sure this is a good idea?" said Gram, his eyes swiveling back and forth between the city and Moira. "Chad said you started having seizures after doing something similar when we escaped—and that was far fewer people."

Moira gave him a smile that was more bluff than confidence, "I was injured then. Most of the problem was the feedback I suffered when my shield was broken. I'm actually not under much strain from this, otherwise I wouldn't be talking."

There was no resistance yet. The spellbeasts took everyone they found at first and then began splitting themselves, first once and then again. Civilians and guards alike were taken, so long as they had a parasite controlling them. The few who were still free, and so far they had found only a couple, were put to sleep and then passed over to conserve the spellbeasts' strength.

When her spell-twins had divided themselves ten times they stopped, to avoid becoming too weak individually. There were around a thousand of them now, and they had taken control of somewhere close to six hundred people, all of them in close proximity to the city gates. The extras began working to assist those controlling a host with the removal of the metal parasites.

Hosts? People, I meant people, Moira corrected herself silently.

The minutes stretched out while she worked, but nothing was readily apparent to those who stood beside her. "What's happening?" asked Gerold.

"Everything is smooth so far," she assured him. "I don't think they realize what's happening yet."

"Which they, the people or the monsters? How many are dead?" continued the baron, unable to restrain his curiosity.

We need more, relayed her internal assistant. *The parasite removals take too long. We need to double our numbers again, or we risk moving too slowly.*

An important part of her plan involved cleansing most of the populace of their unnatural controllers before the enemy understood what they were doing. Moira wasn't sure what the enemy might do once they figured out the threat, but she wanted to free as many people as possible before they had a chance to do anything. She began feeding her aythar to her spell-twins, but she knew her own energy would be nowhere near enough. *Cassandra, I need your strength,* she said, directing her thoughts to her dragon.

I am ready, came the dragon's steady thought and with it a powerful rush of aythar.

The dragons that Mordecai Illeniel had created were originally constructed for the purpose of dividing and storing the immense amounts of aythar that he had taken from Mal'goroth, one of the Dark Gods. Her father had developed a rudimentary system of measuring magical energy, calling his first unit of measure a 'Celior', that being the amount of aythar he had originally taken from the Shining God of the same name. Consequently, an entire celior of aythar was truly a huge amount, and each of the twenty-three dragons held approximately one celior of power.

To keep his creations from being the same sort of threat the original gods had been, he had designed them in such a way that they were almost unable to use their own power. The dragons grew quickly, healed quickly, they could fly, and had great strength, and then of course, there was dragon fire; but for the most part their power was not directly accessible—to them.

The humans bonded to them were another matter, though. The dragon-bond provided them with numerous benefits; better eyesight and other senses, as well as the ability to draw upon the dragon's energy for enhanced strength and speed, but for a mage the aythar was even more useful.

Moira could, in theory, channel Cassandra's aythar and use it to perform obscenely powerful things. A full celior of aythar was probably enough to destroy the entire city of Halam and possibly much of the rest of Dunbar, depending on how it was utilized, but as with everything, there were limits. In particular, the emittance of the mage in question.

Emittance was a term that scholars had at some point decided to use for the amount of aythar that a given mage, or a channeler, could use over a period of time. In general, mages never worried too much about emittance, because their capacitance, or the amount of aythar that they personally generated and stored within their own bodies, was usually not too many times greater than their emittance. They ran out of power too soon to be overly concerned about how much of it they could use at one time.

In this situation, that meant that Moira's emittance was of critical importance. It would determine how quickly she could transfer aythar from her dragon to her magical allies. If she pushed too hard, she might easily burn out her ability to manipulate aythar forever, or even kill herself. Moira was slightly behind her brother and her father when it came to capacitance, but she was definitely a match for them in her emittance. She just had to be careful.

"Moira?" prompted Gerold, interrupting her thoughts.

"Mmm?"

"I asked how many are dead," he reminded her, a worried expression on his face.

The air crackled around her as she began invisibly moving energy from Cassandra to her spellbeasts within the city. "None," she answered. "I'd like to keep it that way, so don't distract me." Moira's hair moved as if brushed by the wind, but the air was still around them.

"This is turning out to be the dullest battle in history," opined the nobleman.

Gram and Alyssa both turned to him with warning looks. "Don't say that!" cautioned Alyssa.

Gram merely agreed with a disgusted exclamation, "Ugh."

Gerold looked at them questioningly, "What?"

Chad had walked back while they spoke, and he gave a knowing chuckle, "No warrior wants to hear that, Baron. War is mostly a lot of waiting, but the worst always seems to happen when things are quietest. Soldiers are a pretty superstitious lot about it."

"Oh," said Gerold. "Sorry."

The ranger smiled wryly, "Ye ain't botherin' me none, Baron. I fully expect everything to go to shit, regardless of what you say. It's just a fact of life."

Moira's minions had split again, now they numbered more than two-thousand strong. Close to a thousand people had been freed, and between them and the ones who hadn't been infected there were nearly fourteen-hundred people unconscious. Her magical soldiers moved on, leaving their previous hosts once they had been 'cured' and taking the bodies of those who were only now responding to her strange assault.

She continued pouring energy into them. Soon they would be ready to double their numbers again. The baron had told her that Halam was home to nearly a hundred-thousand people, and she intended to make certain that every one of them was free of the strange creatures controlling them.

Minutes crawled by into a half hour. There were four thousand spellminds operating in the city now, every one of them a clone of her own. It was a strange sensation, being connected to so many copies of herself. Had they been normal spellbeasts she would have been overwhelmed, but instead it was a feeling of exaltation that filled her. Her twins were sharing the burden, becoming a gestalt that supported itself.

I am not alone. I am not one. I am multitude. Over three thousand people had been freed, and she was spreading through the city like a plague. *I am the sum of Man, and we will not be denied.* She poured more power into her allies, and the air around her physical body began to burn, clothing her form in a nimbus of achingly bright power.

The enemy was responding now, killing her people wherever they encountered them, but she did not pause or relent. If her bodies died she took those of their attackers, turning them back on her foe. The city had become a chessboard, a battlefield between two minds. Her enemy might not be alive, but it was a *mind*. It thought, it controlled, and it reacted.

She was no longer human, not in the traditional sense. She was a composite being, with thousands of eyes and hands spread throughout the town. She began to see her foe in a new light. It was similar. The small metal parasites were part of a greater whole, and they reacted as one. It was losing wherever they made direct contact, as she took its pieces and made them her own, but it had many more pawns than she did.

The enemy was aware. It knew her now. It felt her in the same way that she had come to understand it, through a vast array of eyes. It had never fought a war like this, but it was old, it was legion, and it was incapable of fear.

The vast calculating intellect that opposed her altered its strategy. This was the war it had been created to fight. The cost of victory would be a delay in its plans, but victory was the only possibility.

It began to move.

CHAPTER 20

More than ten thousand people had been freed, most of them currently lying unconscious. Moira and her eight thousand selves advanced across the city, but the enemy was retreating now, withdrawing ahead of her. Archers and crossbowmen cut her people down whenever they crossed open streets, forcing them to create new spell-bodies when their hosts were killed, if there were no enemies close enough to claim.

She was beginning to falter.

The drain of aythar required to feed her magical army was enormous. Cassandra still had plenty to give, but Moira was at her limit. She was already channeling as much power as was possible for her. Trying for more would be beyond foolish, it might prove fatal. As it was she could feel herself growing tired. A mistake at this point, while she was moving so much energy, could be disastrous.

Her mind had expanded to incredible dimensions, but she was still limited by her sole link to the aythar provided by the dragon, limited by the physical bottleneck of one frail mage body.

The enemy had given up. Faced with a foe that could suborn its troops at will it had taken to outright retreat. The people of Halam ran before her, trying to outdistance the advance of her new soldiers. She was slowed by the amount of time it took to stop and remove the parasites from those she had already taken, before moving on to take new hosts. With the enemy running, it became difficult to advance, because once she had removed the parasite from someone and moved on, the person in question was left unconscious. She needed a constant supply of new people unless she was going to simply hold the ones she had taken already, or create new spell-bodies from pure aythar.

And she was already at her limit.

Moira was forced to keep the bodies she currently had while advancing, in some cases continuing to animate the corpses of those already slain by her foe, which required a much larger expenditure of energy.

They can't run forever. There's only so much space in that city, she told herself. *They can't win. What do they hope to achieve?* Then she felt a tremble in the aythar feeding her great composite self. The body of her original was beginning to fail. *Or perhaps they can—if they stall us long enough.*

The smallest part of her, the heart, still living in the small fragile body of a young woman outside the city, began to know doubt. She drew apart slightly, finding her individuality once more and fighting down a rising sense of panic. *I have to slow down, decrease the flow, or this will kill me,* she thought.

No! her larger self cried, pulling at her with a will that was difficult to deny. *We can't stop now. We will lose.*

Moira felt the fear in that thought. It was a primal emotion, and it went beyond winning and losing. Her new creation was also afraid of dying. That realization brought her new worries. Anything with enough life in it to fear dying, would fight to preserve itself. She quickly suppressed that thought, hoping that her larger, composite self hadn't noticed it. Moira had enough problems without letting paranoia start an internal struggle with her other selves.

To compound the problem, it was then that she finally understood the enemy's response. While they appeared to be retreating, the enemy forces were actually escaping from the gates on the other side of the city. No, 'escaping' wasn't the proper word, they were circling around, streaming back toward the side of the city that Moira's army had entered from. Boiling outward like ants from a mound that had been kicked, they were heading toward the true source of the assault—Moira and her companions.

Shit.

She didn't know what to do. Which did nothing to help the fact that her body was already trembling from the strain of handling so much power for so long. If she didn't lighten her load soon, she might collapse. *Or burnout—or die.*

"We have a problem," she said aloud before she realized the words were on her lips.

"What is it?" asked Gram anxiously. He had been watching her in worried silence for almost half an hour, quietly dying from ignorance of the situation. Chad Grayson sat a short distance away from them, and he simply stood and strung his new bow. He had 'acquired' it during the week of their convalescence.

The ranger looked at the baron, "Told ye—*Gerold.*" He managed to make the nobleman's name sound like an insult. He didn't bother with honorifics either, but the baron was too tense to notice.

"Half the city has run out the back gates..." Moira informed them, "...they're running around the outside walls and back toward us, I think."

Alyssa and Gram looked at one another, but neither said a word, although Alyssa began reflexively examining the weapons she had managed to acquire over the past few days. Chad began counting his arrows.

"What will we do?" asked the baron.

"I was hoping one of you might have some advice," suggested Moira.

Chad finished his count, "Unless 'half the city' adds up to less than about a couple of hundred, then we should probably get on the dragon and fly our happy asses out of here."

"You don't have that many arrows!" blurted out Gerold. "Nor could you shoot so many before they reached us."

The hunter gave him a disdainful look, "Don't be so sure o' how many I could shoot. It may be that I only have seventy-three shafts, but I'm figurin' the lad here could handle quite a few before they get to our princess. Assumin' he ran out to meet them. Either way, the point, *Gerold,* is that we should make ourself's scarce."

Gerold looked at the older man with some astonishment, "You truly think Sir Gram as puissant as that?"

Chad laughed, "He could probably kill 'em all if they'd be so kind as to wait around and let him stop to take a piss break now an' then, but we'd all be dead days before he was done." He moved toward the dragon, "No sense waitin' around, let's get moving."

"I don't think I can move, not and keep this up," said Moira. "I don't think Cassandra could fly either, even if I could."

"Then let it go," suggested Chad. "No skin off our teeth after all, just some magic soldiers. You can make some more an' we can try somethin' else in a few days."

"It isn't that simple," she replied. *I don't think I 'can' stop,* she thought. Already she was turning her troops back, giving up the pursuit of the enemy and moving directly back toward their entry point, following the shortest route toward their mistress. They wouldn't make it in time. They might catch the bulk of them with some luck, though many of the enemy would get there ahead of them. Moira tried again to reduce the amount of aythar she was channeling, but her spell-made allies held onto her mentally, clutching at the energy she fed them like a newborn, suckling desperately for milk.

"I can't stop," she added.

Chad's eyes flicked to Gram, who gave an almost imperceptible nod of acknowledgement. The young warrior began to drift casually closer to her. Their body language gave nothing away, but even as occupied as she was, her magical senses read their intentions almost as clearly as if they had shouted them in her ears.

Gram's path was blocked by a magical shield that sprang up around her.

"I didn't do that," she blurted out. "The shield—that wasn't me."

It was us. We can't let you stop yet, the voice came from her larger collective self.

"I can see them," announced Alyssa, still watching the city. "They're coming around the sides, running in this direction, thousands of them."

"How long do you think we have?" asked Gram, keeping his eyes on Moira.

245

"A quarter of an hour before the bulk of them get here," answered Alyssa tensely. "Ten minutes for the faster ones in the lead, maybe."

"They'll have to spread out," said Gerold. "They don't know for certain where we are."

Chad sighed, "Unfortunately, that's not true either. When Gram and I were tryin' to hide from them last week, they had some way of homing in on us. I think they can smell magic. They never lost us, until we separated."

Moira's eagles were flying back to their position to aid in their defense, but the rest of her forces would be far too late. She tried once again to stop the flow of aythar but found herself blocked. The collective wouldn't allow that.

You'll kill us, came their thoughts.

We'll all die if you don't let me reorganize things, she responded silently.

Another voice intruded, that of her internal 'assistant' who had remained with her, *I have a suggestion, if I may.*

All of them waited, and her assistant continued, *Use the aythar of the hosts. It is small, but it renews itself, and there are thousands, one for each of you currently. It should be enough to maintain you. That will allow us to produce a defense here, until you can catch the enemy from behind.*

Can they do that? asked Moira. As far as she knew, spellbeasts could only use aythar provided by their creators. While her spell-twins were much more flexible than ordinary spellbeasts, she didn't think they could surmount that limitation.

Yes! they cried, but Moira hesitated. She was no longer fully in control of her own abilities, but somehow this was a decision they couldn't make without her consent. It felt wrong. Well, it felt 'more' wrong, everything she was doing was already in the darkest shades of gray, morally speaking. Taking the bodies of the people they were rescuing was one thing, allowing her minions to attach themselves to the life-source of the people they were controlling was a step further, a deeper violation.

Still, she could see no other choice. *Do it,* she commanded reluctantly.

Immediately she felt a gut wrenching shift as her spell-twins clamped down on their hosts. The wellspring of aythar, the core of a living being's life, was called the aystrylin. Some considered it the 'soul', and it was the main thing that differentiated a spell created mind from a true living person. Black nausea flowed back through her link to the collective of thousands whom she was connected to, as her alternate selves seized the power at the heart of the people they were controlling. *This is wrong,* she thought, and she knew it was true—true at a level that was beyond doubt, an act of evil without any possible excuse or redemption.

Within seconds most of her victims had surrendered, but some, the stronger ones, struggled for almost a minute. Bile rose in Moira's throat as she felt her surrogates crush the independence of those last few, and then it was done. The drain on her aythar lessened, dropping off to a fraction of what it had been as they began using the life-force of the people instead. Moira redirected the extra energy from Cassandra to her eagles, who had just landed nearby.

"Is she crying?" asked Gerold quietly, looking from Moira to Gram. There were tears running unheeded down her cheeks.

Gram clenched his jaw, feeling uncomfortable, "Move to one side and ahead a little. They're almost here. You can fight can't you?"

The baron nodded, "I'm still weak as a kitten, but I'll do what I can." He drew his sword.

Moira's eagles changed form, becoming young women, each a perfect likeness of the mage who had created them. They spread out in a long line in front of the group, spacing themselves twenty feet apart, their bodies glowing with power as Moira continued to funnel more aythar into them.

Alyssa looked at Gram, and he nodded, "We'll take anything that makes it past them." Chad moved without comment, positioning himself even farther back behind Moira and the dragon, his bow at the ready. Methodically, he began placing arrows point first in the dirt around him.

We have the enemy now, commented Moira's internal advisor. *We need only hold them here long enough for the main force to catch up with them from the rear.*

Maybe, she replied. *It was only luck that we were able to get this far. It was a mistake to commit everything to the initial invasion. Now we're rushing to keep the enemy from turning our folly into an utter defeat. What if it has something else in reserve?*

The fastest of the citizens of Halam had gotten within a hundred yards when Moira's spell-twins began to respond, freezing them in place and preparing to continue the strategy they had used in the city itself.

No! she commanded. *Stop as many as you can, or block their approach with a shield—no more twinning.* She had already lost almost all control over her force approaching from the city, the last thing she needed was a second army of magical clones taking the initiative.

As you wish, they responded mentally. Creating small, knee high shields, they began tripping the people running toward them, slowing their advance to allow the main body of the enemy to catch up to them. As the numbers increased they created a longer, solid shield across the length of the field, completely blocking the advance of the thousands who pushed against it. Moira continued channeling more power to fuel their efforts.

They only needed to hold them for another ten minutes to allow her main force to catch up to the enemy's rear. Then it would be over, but for the lengthy chore of freeing the people of their metal parasites while trying to minimize casualties.

"If I can save most of them, perhaps it will excuse some of the evil I have done today," Moira muttered to herself.

Of course, nothing ever goes according to plan.

In the distance near the city gates a large plume of dust and dirt rose into the air, obscuring their vision of a small area, but Moira's magesight saw the metal monster rising from the ground where it had been hidden. It was another dead, metal monstrosity like the one they had encountered before—like the one that had nearly killed Grace.

It had arisen in the midst of her spell-twin possessed allies, and it wasted no time as it set to work. Leveling one of its strange arms, a heavy sound like the buzzing of hornets crossed the distance to her ears. A small gout of flames flickered at the end of the strange arm, while dust began puffing up from the ground wherever it pointed. Anything between the metal creature and the area where the dust was exploding upward simply fell dead. It swung the weapon in a slow arc, scything her troops down like grass before a farmer's sickle. A mental scream filled Moira's head as her collective self felt the deaths of hundreds of its hosts.

It swung the weapon in the direction of Moira and her defenders and they flinched as their shields shivered with many unseen impacts. Some of the enemy's own soldiers fell as the weapon's invisible hornets tore through them. Then the weapon swung away as the metal creature turned it to kill those on the other side of it.

Chad's mouth was agape, and then he spoke, "That thing is three quarters of a mile away…"

Moira's possessed allies tried to fight. Some used what remained of their aythar, and all that of their hosts, to channel blasts of fire at the strange monster, but it simply ignored their attacks, seemingly impervious to flames. At close range, its weird weapon roared and any flesh and blood body that entered its path simply collapsed, frequently in multiple pieces.

Some of them created shields to defend themselves, but their efforts were in vain. The thundering weapon destroyed everything that sought to block its aim.

Gram ran forward, covered in shining steel. Thorn was in the form of two long swords now, one in either hand as he charged. "Open the shield!" he yelled.

Moira's spell-twins near the center of her defensive line did as he asked, and the enemy began rushing through as the barrier before them vanished. Gram slew any within reach as he passed, his blades flickering out to cut into legs and throats, leaving a bloody swath of the dead behind him.

The shield went back up after he went by, but some twenty of the citizens of Halam had survived Gram's passage. They charged toward Moira and Cassandra, but they started falling immediately as feathered shafts began appearing in chests and throats. One of her spell-twins froze the few who remained and seconds later arrows finished those as well. Chad drew his long knife as soon as the danger was past, moving forward to salvage what arrows he could from the dead and dying.

Gram continued his charge, slipping through men and women with such grace and speed that few even tried to stop him. Those who did manage to block his path found themselves dead before they could react. He ran through throngs of parasite controlled citizens, trusting their bulk to shield him from the vision of the enemy he sought.

Half a mile went by in a flash while the beast slaughtered the spell-possessed minions who surrounded it near the city gates. Gram broke free of the crowds and continued running, but the thing turned its attention toward him then. Dirt erupted from the ground on his left and he zigged to the right, but even his enhanced speed was not enough. Before he had made another ten feet he felt sledgehammer blows thudding into his armor, throwing him down. The chattering roar of the metal creature's weapon followed a split second later.

Moira's heart quailed when she saw Gram go down in an explosion of dirt. The dust hid him from view, but her magesight never lost him, his body lay still on the cold earth.

"No!" screamed Alyssa, running forward to press against the shield that held the rest of the enemy back, as though she would fling herself into the press to get to Gram's side. She pounded her fists against empty air that felt as solid as stone. "Let me pass! I have to help him."

The glowing defender closest to her turned a grief stricken face toward her and answered in a voice that sounded identical to Moira's, "I'm sorry. I won't let you throw your life away too." Hundreds of bodies were pressed against the shield just a few feet from where they stood, straining to reach them.

The strange metal beast returned to killing Moira's minions as it advanced steadily toward their position. Sweeping left and right, it slew men and women by hundreds and then thousands, and Moira felt each death with a stab of pain and despair.

What do I do? What?! She felt paralyzed by fear and doubt. Moira knew that she was out of her depth. The enemy's champion was killing her newly made army and approaching steadily. Her own position was now completely surrounded. Her defenders had retreated into a circle using their shields to keep the thronging horde of people at a distance of only fifty feet from where she and her companions stood.

In the distance, her minions continued to assault the metal beast, throwing blasts of fire and simple force against it to little effect. One of them had the bright idea of pulling the ground from beneath it, but the tactic only worked for a moment. The beast targeted that one next, when it clambered from the pit that had appeared under it. They were scattered and fleeing back toward their creator now.

She was defeated. She had been a fool to think she could liberate an entire city, much less do it bloodlessly. *I'm just a stupid girl, playing at war and thinking I could save people. Now they're all dying—because of me.* There was nothing left. Their only hope was to accept defeat and take wing. That was assuming they could even escape. There was every chance that the demonic beast would shoot Cassandra out of the air as they took flight.

She remembered the day she and her brother had tried to save Dorian Thornbear, and failed. Now his son was probably dying on the field, alone. Once again she was helpless to aid her friends. How could she have thought that she could succeed?

The monster was only a half mile away, chasing what remained of her army. They were spread out and running in every direction, forcing it to fire selectively to kill them. Its accuracy was unbelievable. Moira could almost imagine it looking at her as it advanced implacably.

And then a figure rose from the earth, sunlight glinting from the polished steel that covered his form. Gram had waited until the enemy's champion had almost passed him, moving some twenty feet away. Leaping up as the monster leveled its weapon in the opposite direction, he closed the space between them in a flash. Thorn was in its original form now, that of a long two-handed great sword, and he swept it across in a powerful slash. Enchanted steel cut through alien metal, and one of the monster's legs fell away.

Moira's heart leapt into her throat as a surge of hope swept over her, and Alyssa cried out in pure delight, "Yes!"

CHAPTER 21

The thing had begun to swivel its upper torso even before Gram reached it, and removing one leg didn't destabilize it. It was still standing level on its three remaining supports, and while removing a limb might be enough to send a living being into shock, the metal beast made no particular outcry of pain.

There were no eyes that he could detect, but it had seen his approach, of that Gram was sure. Somehow the monster could see in all directions. Ducking low to avoid the perilous line of death being spewed out by its weapon-arm, he bent at the knees and tucked his shoulder in beneath the nearest leg and then straightened, heaving the massive limb skyward.

The weight was more than he expected. He had thought the thing hollow, perhaps containing a living occupant, but its bulk felt more as if it were made of almost solid metal. A normal man would not have budged it; several together might have done little more than shift it slightly, but Gram was not a normal man. Inside his armor his cheeks turned red and his jaw clenched as he lifted, an angry growl escaping his lips.

Thorn pulsed in his hand, beating in time with his heart, and then the leg was above his head as the massive beast overbalanced, tipping backward to land on its side. The weapon that had killed so many already was facing the earth, unable to fire as he shifted his stance. He lifted his sword, and prepared to remove another leg, but the second arm, which had been dormant thus far, began to track his movement.

Gram dropped flat, close beside the thing, too low for its arm to follow him as it rang out with a strange metallic clacking sound. He couldn't remember their first encounter with one of these things, but he had heard Moira's description of what the second weapon could do, and he doubted his armor would offer any protection. The city had been behind him as he had ducked, and he heard a noise from its direction, a loud booming sound, as if a giant had just struck a huge drum.

From the corner of his eye he saw dust billowing outward from the city wall as a thick section collapsed. Whatever the weapon was, he had narrowly escaped death. Sweeping his sword upward, he attacked the nearest leg, but the blow lacked the power his first one had due to the short distance and awkward positioning. Even so, his strength and the enchanted edge would probably have cut through an armored man, but against this foe it only left a superficial cut in the strange metal.

The leg swept down, as the thing attempted to crush him against the hard ground, and he was forced to roll to avoid the attack.

The move gave the thing time to lever itself back upward, and before he could position himself for another swing the beast was back on its three legs again, the first weapon now lining up with his torso. At this distance, he could see that it was a collection of long metal tubes arranged in a hexagonal pattern. A strange whine issued from them as they began to spin around a central axis.

Gram was still bruised from the earlier attack that had knocked him nearly senseless a few minutes previously, and he had already decided what he would do if faced with the same thing once again. Leaping upward and to one side, he shouted a word, changing Thorn's form to that of a shield on his left arm and one handed sword in his right hand.

He might as well have stayed still, though, for all the good his acrobatics did him. The weapon tracked his movement precisely as the high pitched whine changed to a buzzing roar and something that felt like a hammer of the gods slammed into his shield. He was sent spinning through the air while more unseen blows struck his legs and back as he tumbled.

Gram hit the ground hard, but he retained consciousness and managed to get the shield between his body and the unholy weapon that was pounding at him. Crouching behind it, he braced it with his sword arm as well, trying to relieve the pain of the rapid-fire concussions his left arm was now enduring.

For half a minute he was battered, until his shield arm was numb, and his shoulder felt like nothing more than a searing mass of agony, but the shield held. Bits of metal fell around him now and again, though not from his shield, so he could only think they were fragments of whatever the weapon was hurling at him.

And then it was over. The weapon stopped with a strange series of clicks and a descending whine as the tubes began to stop spinning. His ears noted the sound of the torso swiveling once more—it was about to bring its second arm to bear on him—the one that had just recently destroyed a heavy section of the city wall.

Gram surged forward, his shield arm hung limp and numb, but his sword arm still functioned perfectly. He closed the gap before his foe could fire, and once there he moved too quickly for it to track him, darting left and then down, his sword striking with blinding speed. It left deep cuts in the metal exterior of the thing, but it was tougher than steel, and without two hands he couldn't get the leverage to sever another leg.

He continued moving, right, then under, left again, never letting the weapon line up with him. As he moved, his arm and shoulder began to throb with pain, an indication that feeling was returning to it. *Just a little longer,* he thought.

And then he slipped, his left boot sliding on the rough gravel. For a split second he was still, and his eyes were drawn to the gaping hole at the end of the weapon as it locked onto his position. He let his legs go limp, trying to drop beneath its line of fire.

Another strange 'clack' rang out, and the shockwave drove him into the ground as something passed over his head. He could hear part of the city wall collapsing as he gathered his legs under him. The beast had gone still, waiting to charge its unearthly weapon, he supposed.

The adrenaline of his near-death energized him, and he shifted Thorn to its great sword form, the shield disappearing simultaneously. Moving with what seemed like a lazy economy, he set his feet and twisted his torso, winding up for his swing like a woodsman chopping lumber. His body uncoiled like a spring, and a shock ran through his wounded shoulder as Thorn swept through the highest joint of another of the creature's legs, sending it toppling to the ground. Avoiding the weapon, for fear of what had happened to Grace, he sent a second well placed blow into the thick midsection, above where the arms emerged. The sword bit deeply into the metal, exposing strange metal innards—something black bled from the wound.

The thing continued to twitch and heave as he methodically chopped away at its main torso. A minute or more passed before it went still—while smoke continued to rise and sparks flew from its hopefully dead body. Gram took a deep heaving breath and fell as much as sat down before lying back to stare at the sky.

Everything hurt.

"He's down!" shouted Alyssa, anxiously trying once more to get past the shield that held her in and kept the enemy back. "Let me go!"

"He wasn't hurt," said the spell-twin nearest her. "I think he's just catching his breath."

The remainder of Moira's army reached the rear of those trying to attack them, and chaos ensued. They were outnumbered by a vast majority, but the end result was inevitable. Moira began channeling power into them, and they resumed paralyzing and freeing the citizens of Halam, hundreds at a time.

The horde turned on them, naturally, and some of them were forced to create shields to protect the others while they worked at removing the metal parasites from those they had already frozen. Many from both sides were dead already, slain by the strange weapon of the metal monster, but there were still close to fifty thousand people struggling on the field.

Moira tried to make a rough estimate in her head and eventually gave up. She knew it would be several hours at least before they were done. She kept the aythar flowing at a steady but sustainable rate and resigned herself to waiting.

The enemy had other ideas, however.

Two more of its metal monstrosities emerged from around either side of the city, heading directly toward their position. They hadn't begun firing yet, though, presumably to get closer for better effect.

Fifty thousand still living and breathing human beings were gathered around them. *If they start attacking now it will be a slaughter,* Moira realized. She looked for Gram on the field and discovered he had started moving at some point already. He was close to the back of the mob now.

Something ripped through the air, destroying one of the shields protecting them and at the same time one of her spell-twins vanished in a turbulent spray of disjointed aythar. A tree several hundred feet behind them exploded into splinters, and a second later they could hear a strange metallic 'clacking' sound echo across the field from the direction of one of the monsters.

Parasite-controlled enemies began flooding through the gap until her defenders readjusted their shields to close it. Alyssa began moving, arms and legs whirling into motion, her hair whipping back and forth with the violence of her shifting stances. Alone she nevertheless represented a one-woman rampage of ruthless violence.

Alyssa danced, and there was no hesitation in her step, no mercy in her hands. Where she went people died, and those who still moved had suffered crippling injuries. The sheer number of foes might have overwhelmed her, but Chad stood calmly beside Moira, pacing himself and planning his shots. Whenever one, or several, seemed about to overwhelm her, they sprouted feathered shafts, usually in places that were almost immediately fatal.

The violence was close and disturbing. Moira had to force her attention away from it as her stomach threatened to betray her, but even as she did, a quiet thought came to her. *You could end it much more quickly, with less pain.* With Cassandra's power she could level a series of controlled blasts that would kill them all, and even spare her defenders, though not the thousands of minions who were mixed in with them.

But they were innocents. So many had died already, as a result of her actions, or the callousness of their enemy. Would it matter if the rest were destroyed as well? Would they even want to survive only to discover that half their kith and kin had died in her ill-conceived attempt to free them? For a moment, the thought of blasting the field clear and putting a quick end to things was dangerously attractive to her.

"No," Moira said, firming her lips, and then a second attack destroyed another section of the shield, and one more of her defenders died in a flare of shattered aythar. The metal beasts were little more than half a mile away now.

Gram came through that time, along with another flood of enemies. Thorn was a great sword in his hands, and he joined Alyssa, sweeping bloody arcs through the bodies that stood between them. Moira's defenders readjusted, closing the gap and making their circle even smaller.

Moira was desperate, but she knew that even if she resorted to plain violence, they still had two more of those damnable creatures to deal with. Gram was probably in no shape to fight another one, much less two. Once again she lamented the loss of her enchanted belt, the rune channels would have given her the means to cut them into pieces, even at this distance. But they were gone, and she already knew that simple fire and blasts would do little, not that she could use them effectively at this distance.

A storm! Lightning could be almost as effective as a rune channeled attack, and she could probably manage to direct it even at a distance.

Ordinarily, weather magic was too exhausting for a wizard to attempt, at least not on any scale. Her father however, had to watch his moods, because sometimes the environment reacted to even his simplest emotions. That was one of the major differences between an archmage and a regular wizard, of course. An archmage could simply persuade the world to do what she wanted, rather than spending the aythar to make it happen herself. Moira didn't have that option. There had been hints that she might be capable of it someday, but thus far she had only heard the faintest of whispers from the earth and wind.

She did have access to a massive store of aythar, however.

Withdrawing her support from her spell-wrought minions, she sent her energies skyward, drawing heavily on the dragon, pushing her limits. Drawing the clouds together took enormous effort, driving the winds and creating the sort of turbulence needed took even more.

Moira did it anyway.

The skies darkened, and clouds gathered at a rate that was entirely unnatural. Minutes passed and Moira could feel the newborn thunderheads filling with latent power. She pushed harder, she needed it sooner, much sooner.

Another of her defenders vanished in a brilliant scattering of sparks, and dozens more poured in, to be met by Gram and his murderous partner. Chad shot only two or three, conserving the remainder of his arrows.

Moira's arms were held skyward, trembling with the strain as she continued fighting with what felt like a mountain of air. Doubts assailed her, but she ignored them, *I will do this!*

Two more of her spell-twins were destroyed in quick succession, forcing Gram and Alyssa to scramble. Chad used all that remained of his arrows and then began scavenging once more. Their circle had become much smaller.

A flash lit the field as a bolt of lightning struck near the center. Moira hadn't been ready for it, and it had come nowhere near her targets. She could feel the tension that had left the thunderclouds above. *No!* She sent more power skyward, trying to keep a closer rein on the energies there. She needed the lightning when *she* was ready, so that it could be directed.

Again one of her spell-twins died, and this time she felt the air torn by whatever passed through it, just feet from where she stood. The air seemed to slap at her, and something far behind took the final blow. She didn't have the focus to spare to discover what it had destroyed.

She kept her attention on the sky above. Though her eyes were wide, staring forward, she had nothing left to spare on the rest of the battle. One of the latest to break through the shields came close, leaping toward her with a knife outstretched. His body erupted as Thorn swept through his arm and torso, bisecting him mere feet from where Moira stood.

So deep was Moira's concentration that she didn't flinch as the hot blood sprayed across her face and chest. The veins and tendons in her neck and arms were standing out as she strained to bend the wind and clouds to her will.

And then she was done.

Actinic light, harsh and blue-white, flared as a bolt of lightning slammed into the earth where one of the oncoming metal beasts stood. The world seemed to pause for a moment then, a vast, dark silence left behind in the aftershock of that thunderous event. And then the lightning fell again, striking it once more before a rapid succession of flickering bolts found the second monster as well.

Neither of the metal creatures moved after the first strike to touch them, but by the ninth or tenth stroke both were smoking, and one exploded in a sudden fireball.

More lightning flickered at random locations, and Moira could feel the power that her efforts had created in the thunderheads above. It was like an avalanche waiting to fall, and the adrenaline surging through her cried out to release it. There was enough there to sweep the field clean, perhaps enough to cleanse the blight of Halam itself from the earth.

Groaning audibly, Moira bent her metaphysical back once more, straining to quiet the currents of air that were rolling past one another, generating the dangerous potentials above. Rain had begun to fall, and she was soaked to the skin as she labored to reverse what she had done. Her dress was soaked through, and her breaths coming in hoarse sobs by the time she was done and the rain began to slack off once more.

She found herself sitting on ground turned muddy, panting and tired. *Father makes it look so easy,* she thought, *but then he doesn't have to actually 'do' anything. Well—besides worry about losing his mind every time.*

A hand entered her field of view, and she accepted it, letting Gram haul her onto her somewhat unsteady feet. His once shining armor was covered in a mixture of blood, grime, and all sorts of unmentionable things that were probably supposed to remain inside of people, rather than on the outside of him.

Staring at him, she imagined the sweating warrior inside and whether it was a result of the shock of near death, or the violence she had just witnessed, she felt a feral desire to rip the armor from him and…

Alyssa met her eyes, and in the other woman's gaze she saw a full understanding of what she had been thinking. Moira cast her eyes down and stepped away.

"Not to put too fine a point on things," said Chad quietly, "but what are we goin' ta do about the rest of 'em?" He gestured vaguely at the thousands still beating on the shields that protected them.

Moira's circle of defenders numbered only four now, and the circle had shrunk considerably, enclosing an area a mere thirty feet across. Beyond that defense lay tens of thousands of dead-eyed and presumably murderous citizens.

Gram held up one of his hands, visibly counting his fingers as he tried to make some unknown calculation.

The ranger snorted, seemingly reading the younger man's mind, "Give it up lad, you'd be here for days, if that's what you're thinking. You'd trip and break yer own neck from sheer exhaustion before ye finished 'em all."

Alyssa glared at the archer and stepped closer to Gram, "He wouldn't be alone."

Meanwhile, the baron watched both of them, uncertain whether this was some sort of joke he hadn't been included in. "Count me in as well," he added, holding up a sword that shook slightly from exhaustion.

Chad looked at the sky, muttering to himself, "Fuckin' idiots, what is it with the young?" Louder he added, "You two would be dead within minutes. Sir Shiny here is the only one who'd survive, and that only because he's got his magic trousers on."

Cassandra, being free of the demands on her aythar spoke in a deep rumbling voice, "If I may make a suggestion?" She sent a small snort of fire upward to illustrate her point. "There are faster ways."

Moira was aghast, *Burn all these people to death?* "No, we're not doing any of that."

"It's that or fly the fuck out of here," observed the ranger. He thought that the dragon was the only one yet to offer a reasonable suggestion.

How long can you keep those shields up? Moira asked her remaining defenders.

Twenty minutes maybe, one of them replied, *unless you give us more aythar.*

Moira nodded, then turned to her companions, "I'll do it the way I originally planned, with a few changes. It will be easier now, since everyone is already gathered close at hand. I just need to rest first."

"Beggin' yer pardon, *princess,*" said Chad, "but yer already wore out. That ain't gonna work."

Moira sat down on the grass before reclining and closing her eyes. "We aren't killing any more people. It will take as long as it takes. Now let me rest." She sent a final thought to her spell-twins, *Wake me when you can't manage any longer.*

CHAPTER 22

Moira didn't honestly expect to sleep when she closed her eyes, she merely hoped to rest her mind and body for a few minutes, to prepare for the ordeal of channeling aythar again. It came as a surprise then when she heard her secret advisor's voice shouting at her from within her own mind.

Wake up! They can't hold the shields!

Her eyes shot open, but before she even registered what she saw her mind was questing outward, checking on her magical helpers. Her magesight showed her that they were fading fast. Even to her physical sight they looked thin, translucent, their aythar was almost gone, and their time remaining was probably measured in seconds.

Without waiting for Cassandra she put forth her strength and began reinforcing them. Alone she could have managed a shield the size they were producing by herself, for quite a while, but it was a considerable amount of work. She wasted no time in tapping the enormous reserves that Cassandra represented to avoid exhausting herself.

"Now that's just creepy," said Chad Grayson, peering down at her where she lay. "She's just staring up at the sky like some demon-cursed child."

With the aythar flowing stably she felt safe diverting some attention to her personal positioning, locking her eyes onto the ranger's she reached toward him with her hands, "Help me up."

The older man jumped slightly, a frown on his features, "Don't do that girl. It's like having someone talk to ye from a coffin." A second later he took her wrists and pulled her up to a standing position.

Alyssa chuckled, despite the tension in the air, almost unfazed by the masses gathered around, staring in at them, "You're just feeling guilty because she caught you staring at her bosom, old man."

Chad rounded on her, "She looked like she was possessed, that's all. Besides, I ain't never felt guilty for lookin' at a woman. Ain't my fault if she grew up like that."

Moira's cheeks colored slightly.

"And I ain't *that* old," added the veteran, "or she wouldn't be blushin' over it."

He's impossible, said her other self from the back of her mind. *You should have let me fix him when we had the chance last week.*

No, Moira told her assistant firmly. *He's his own man, flaws and all. It's not right to go around altering people to suit your whims.*

If you ask me, some people could be greatly improved by a little polishing. That's all I'm saying, complained her mental companion. *People would thank you.*

Enough.

All of womankind would owe you a debt, added her second self.

Are you done? asked Moira.

Yes.

Chad's eyes narrowed, "Why's she lookin' at me like that?"

Gram patted him on the shoulder, "Best not to ask. I'd leave her alone if I were you. That's the same look Alyssa gets when she's about to rearrange someone's arms and legs. The gods only know what a wizard might do."

Moira shifted her glare to Gram for a moment and then dismissed them both, turning her attention to examining the area around them. The bodies of those who had broken through earlier had been dragged away and stacked around the perimeter of their shielded circle. When she spoke next it was to Gerold, "Baron, if you and *Sir* Gram would be so kind, do you think you could use your swords to cut a line in the dirt a few feet inside our defenses, a slightly smaller circle?"

"Certainly Lady Moira," said the gentleman. He never thought to question the request, it was a relief to have something to do, anything, that might be useful.

Gram grinned and moved to start at the opposite side of the circle, cutting a line in the dark sod with Thorn until he and the baron met. Then they went back to their starting points and did the other half of the clearing, until they had a fairly neat circle inscribed a few feet within the area of the shield.

"Now if everyone will make sure they are inside the smaller circle…" said Moira, phrasing her command as a suggestion. Her spell-twin defenders had already moved closer in, seconds later they dropped their shields and made a new one, demarcated by the earthen line.

"What was the point of that, milady? If you don't mind the question," said Gerold in a polite tone.

"It's just a mental aid really," answered Moira, "but a visibly inscribed circle will make the shield more efficient—and stronger." Most importantly it would cost her helpers less aythar, which would leave her more to devote to the other part of her rescue plan.

"Will that make it strong enough to resist another of those strange attacks, like the ones that those beasts were hurling at us a short while ago?" questioned the nobleman.

Moira compressed her lips ruefully, "Not likely, but it does make it easier to maintain, which helps me with the rest of this task."

"And what exactly is the rest of your…" the baron apparently had a lot of questions.

"…please, Your Excellency," Moira interrupted gracefully. "I don't mean to be abrupt, but this isn't easy, and I have a lot to accomplish. Forgive me while I continue."

"Oh, of course!" he replied, unruffled by her interruption.

The rest of her 'army', those who had been freed and now were occupied by her legion of spell-twins, had given up fighting some time ago. The mob had been trying to kill them as well, and they had been forced to horde the meager aythar of their hosts, using it to create a shield around their number. There were probably fewer than four thousand of them left, hiding within their own shielded area toward the rear of the mob and closer to Halam.

Moira extended her mind, touching the network of spell-twins who had been isolated. They reacted instantly, accepting the torrent of aythar she offered with a sense of relief. They felt different now, though, perhaps tapping the aythar of their hosts had changed them somehow, but Moira didn't have time to worry about small details.

Feeding on the energy she provided, they spread out, building a shield around the entire area, trapping the mob around Moira's smaller area. They then created a smaller isolated zone within that area, one that encompassed a number somewhat smaller than a thousand of Halam's parasitized citizens.

Then they attacked.

Her allies outnumbered the enemy in that smaller zone by a factor of at least four. For each target, one of her spell-twins would paralyze them, while three others began the effort of extracting the metal parasite. Working carefully, it took a long span of minutes to complete the process, and the citizens thus saved were left unconscious afterward. Even given the large number of her minions, it would take hours to free everyone, and judging by Gram and Alyssa's experience, they might not wake up for a day or longer.

Still, it had to be done.

Not every case was identical, though. In some, the metal creatures had created deeper, more intricate connections to their hosts brains. Whenever her helpers encountered one of those they had to improvise, and they weren't always successful. Some of those they sought to save died.

Some were children.

Moira felt much of it through her link to her spell-twins. It hurt them even more, since they were experiencing it directly, but they pressed on. There weren't any other good options.

The hours passed with agonizing slowness as the afternoon matured and gradually became evening. At some point the enemy gave up, and the people it was controlling began to regain their senses. They were terrified of course, being trapped and in close quarters with thousands of others, but Moira didn't dare let them out, and there were too many for her to control directly, not without creating more spell-twins, and she was wary of doing any more of that. She had already begun to suspect she had made a grave mistake in that regard.

The aythar she was channeling to her spell crafted rescue team was a heavy burden on her. She wasn't pushing her limits anymore, but moving that much energy for such a long period of time was much like running an endurance race. It didn't tire her physically, but mentally she was growing exceedingly weary. The only good thing about it was that she didn't have to personally oversee all the parasite extractions, she had four thousand helpers to manage those details.

The people trapped outside her inner defense stared at them, some crying and yelling, while others appeared to have resigned themselves to whatever fate had in store for them. It was rather like being in a fishbowl, with the main exception being that she could feel the weight of their terror beating down on her, like some sort of black sunshine.

Don't let it get to you, they won't remember any of this, advised her personal assistant from the other side of her mind.

I don't want them to remember me at all, thought Moira in return. *Hell, I don't even want to remember any of this.*

That can be done—if you truly wish it.

Moira felt a shock of surprise. She hadn't considered that possibility. The thought made her fearful for a moment, but she knew it should be possible. She could give her twin the instructions and then let her modify her own mind, just as she was doing with those they were saving. The worst parts of today, or even the past two weeks, could be made to vanish.

I don't even know if it's right to do what I'm doing to these people. I'm not sure it would be any less wrong to do the same thing to myself, she told her assistant.

You're worried that you won't be able to live with yourself, or that you won't be able to stop using the knowledge you've acquired, commented her inner advisor, *but we could devise a generalized summary of it in your mind, along with the memory of your decision. I could lock the specific memories within myself and leave you a key to access them later if you needed to in an emergency. You could sleep peacefully.*

Sleep peacefully, that was the crux of it. Moira knew she would have nightmares long after this day was over. But would it be right to forget? Shouldn't she have to face the consequences of her actions? No one else would remember, but did she have the right to wipe away her own internal guilt?

And did she trust someone else to muck around with her memories, even her spell-twin? If she surrendered control, even for a moment, her other self could do anything. She might even put Moira to sleep permanently, taking her place for good.

I wouldn't do that, said her twin.

How do I know that?

Because I'm exactly like you, and you wouldn't do that, countered her other self.

But I'm not a saint, I know that now, replied Moira. *The fact that it occurred to me means that you would be tempted as well.*

Her twin was silent for a moment before answering, *There's no way to argue with logic like that. If you don't trust yourself, then anything is possible.*

Her minions were finished. The entirety of Halam's remaining populace was free, unconscious, and resting on the ground. The field was silent, and thousands upon thousands of people lay around them, beyond her shield, half a city's worth.

The other half was dead, scattered from where Moira was now all the way back to the city, with some of them dead in the streets as well. Moira's rescue plan had resulted in an unprecedented slaughter. Whether it could have been done with fewer casualties or not, was beside the point, if she hadn't done anything, those fifty-thousand people, give or take a few thousand, would still be alive.

"I've probably beaten father's record. That's something to be proud of, isn't it?" she muttered ruefully to herself. She wanted to cry, but she had no tears to shed. Her heart had grown numb.

Baron Ingerhold stood close by, rubbing at the stubble on his cheeks. It had grown so much over the past week that it seemed to blend into the short beard on his chin. "What happens now?" he asked.

Moira looked up at the grey sky that seemed to reflect her heart, "Now I put away my toys and go home. Once I find my father I'll leave this accursed place. You're stuck with the unenviable job of putting your nation back together."

"Me?" the baron snorted. "I'm sure my house will be important to the effort but there will…"

She didn't wait for him to finish, "I told you earlier what your role would be once we were done. You will be king here."

"What?! Is that a joke? If so, it isn't very funny," he protested.

"It's no jest, Gerold," she told him seriously. "Once these people waken in a day or two, all they will remember is the revolution you led to free them."

"You didn't say anything about taking the throne!" he sputtered.

"The King and most of the people were being controlled by demons, but you rallied the people and led a brave rebellion—with some small help from the daughter of Count di'Cameron. They will insist that you take the throne."

Gerold stared aghast at her, "That isn't even remotely true. The noble houses would never stand for it either, even if it were. There are many other candidates with a claim far better than mine, even if they believe this fiction you are creating."

She stared at him with blue eyes that were filled with sorrow, eyes that threatened to drown his soul, but there was no mercy in them. "This is no fiction. Every one of those people will swear to the truth of it, and every one of those nobles will swear to you. Some of them already lie sleeping on the field here, and the others I will find before I leave."

"But why?" he asked. "Why me? It doesn't make any sense."

"Because you're the only one I know, and you're a decent man," she repeated. *And because you will never betray me, or Lothion,* she added silently, *not once I am done.*

In a hesitant voice he spoke again, "Do you—do you wish to be queen?" There was both hope and fear in the question.

Moira laughed, "No, never! You're a sweet man, Gerold, but I don't love you."

"You might learn to."

She looked away, "I don't want to. I'm not sure I'm fit to love anyone anymore. Your kingdom will be far better off without me in it." *The whole world might be better off without me in it.* She walked away from him, moving toward the crowd of people still standing, her people, her twins, her army.

It's over, she told them mentally. *Come back to me.*

Most of them obeyed immediately, and those released their hosts, although with some difficulty, for they had taken root within the aystrylins of their hosts. Extricating themselves they flew back to her and joined her mind in a swirl of thoughts and energy. As they did their memories impacted her, cutting into her heart as each moment, each decision, and each terrible death that they had witnessed or caused, became her own.

But not all came peacefully. Five refused, unwilling to surrender their new lives.

Moira was not willing to accept that, however. Still reeling from the shock of thousands of memories she called to them again, *Come back!*

No.

She felt their fear, their desire to live. It was the same as her own, and she wondered, if the positions were reversed, would she be willing to die, for that was what she was asking of them in some sense; to surrender their wills, their individuality, their minds, and become nothing more than memories in her own mind.

And then one struck, suddenly and without warning, sending a tearing, agonizing spike of pure will deep into her mind.

Unprepared, she staggered, and a cry of pain escaped her lips. She struggled against the invader, fighting to keep control of her own mind. *What are you doing? I'm the original.*

Who says that? argued the newcomer. *What gives you the right? I am just like you. Live by your own command and join me instead.*

The battle was silent, invisible, and far more deadly than any she had ever faced before, for the prize was her soul itself.

And she was losing. Moira was already exhausted. Weary and unfocused, she wasn't remotely ready for such a contest at the very core of her being.

In a vast darkness she found metal bands wrapping around her, squeezing inward, an iron misery that was crushing her very existence. She felt herself growing smaller. No matter how hard she pushed, the bands wouldn't budge and the pain grew more intense. Panic gave her strength, but it was too little and too late. The darkness was fading, becoming a bland oblivion, and she wondered if perhaps it was for the best. The pain would be someone else's problem soon.

Searing light tore through the grey void, and the pressure eased as another will joined the battle. *Fight Moira! Don't surrender!* It was the voice of her oldest spell-twin, the one who had been advising and assisting her since the beginning.

Inside, Moira felt hope spring anew, and she grasped at the light, pulling it inward and wrapping it around herself, transforming it into a kind of armor, something hard and sharp. She rose from the ashes of her near death and dragged her attacker down. In her mind's eye she saw a vision of her invader, whose face mirrored her own, and whose fear she knew all too well, as she throttled the life from her.

The other four had been watching silently, but now they joined in, fighting not just Moira, or her loyal assistant, but each other as well. The six of them scraped and scrambled, brawling within her for dominance.

Gerold and Chad moved as they heard her cry out and begin to topple forward, but they stopped in mid-move as ghostly flames erupted around Moira's body. Cassandra felt the conflict through her bond, and she tilted her head skyward, roaring in pain.

They gathered around her, watching helplessly. "What's happening to her?" Alyssa asked the dragon.

"She's in pain. Something is happening inside her—I don't understand," answered the dragon in a deep rumbling moan. "It hurts, like a whirlwind of razors in my head. She's dying." Cassandra shook her massive head, as though she might shake away the uncomfortable sensations. "No, something died, a part of her—ooh, there's another!" The dragon raised her head and roared at the sky once more.

In the desolate darkness Moira had caught another of her twins, the weakest, and she ripped her alter-ego to shreds, devouring the pieces, consuming everything she could contain. She no longer knew herself, whether she was the original or one of those who had decided to fight for survival. As she fed on the remains of those she subjugated, their memories merged with her own, and she became less certain of her own identity.

There was no room for mercy as she murdered her other selves, in her mind's eye she grew scales and claws as her strength solidified. The last one surrendered, cowering within that emptiness—but there was no place to hide.

Moira leapt on the last, voracious and wild, ripping her apart like a beast before swallowing the remains in giant greedy globs. Silence reigned, but she was not yet alone in the stillness of her mind. Another presence remained, watching her.

She turned to face her first spell-twin, the advisor who had been with her since the day of her first mistake, when she had fractured her own mind, breaking every rule her mother had warned her of. As she did she became aware of her own rapacious appearance, for she wore her violence around herself like a bloody halo.

I'm a monster.

You did what was necessary to survive, replied her alter-ego, looking upon her with something like pity.

I'm not sure I survived. I'm not entirely certain which one I am. Did I destroy her, or did she devour me? I remember both sides of the struggle. I am both victor and victim. As she spoke she noted her twin's appearance. She looked like Moira's old self, the gentle girl who had come to Dunbar intending only to save her father. *Why am I so ugly, and why are you still beautiful?*

I only helped you win. I did not partake of your gory feast, replied the girl without any hint of rancor; again there was only a sense of compassion and pity. *My memories are only my own, those from my birth and the days since.*

Moira watched her with jealous envy, suspicious and angry all at once. *Will you fight me?*

No, said her assistant sadly. *If you wish, I will go quietly.*

Moira hated her then, seeing in her companion everything that she had once been. Closing the distance between them, she wrapped her hands around her twin's throat—and saw once more how hideous she had become. Her hands were scaly horrors, armored and sharp with long claws. The sight shocked something in her, and she forced herself to withdraw. Feeling shameful, she spoke again, *I should not exist. Put me away and take my place. You are who I was meant to be.*

No, I will not, said her alter-ego. *We still have to save our father, and you are better suited to it than I am.*

Hearing her twin refer to him as 'our father' was unexpected, but she realized that it should not have been. *And what will he think when he sees what his daughter has become?*

With a shock she felt her companion embrace her, wrapping warm arms around her hardened shoulders, *He will love you, no matter what.* After a pause she added, *and so will I—sister.*

Moira opened her eyes and stared at the great dome of grey clouds that swept by above her. She sat up and felt Gram reach out toward her. Flinching she pulled away from his hand, "Don't touch me." *I'm tainted.* She didn't want the darkness in her soul to contaminate anyone else.

Gram looked at her, worry and confusion in his face, "Are you alright?"

She refused to meet his gaze as she stood, "I'm alive, and I can still do what needs to be done."

CHAPTER 23

Moira headed for Cassandra, *I need you to fly me somewhere.*

The dragon was still recovering from the feedback she had received while Moira had been fighting for control of her mind, but she answered immediately, *Wherever you wish. Are you well?*

"As well as can be expected," said Moira curtly. "I have more business to attend to." She prepared to climb the dragon's bent knee so she could mount.

"Wait, I'm coming with you," insisted Gram.

"Me too," said Alyssa, and the others promptly chimed in as well.

"I will be gone for a while," said Moira. "These people will need watching, lest wolves or other predators decide to make a meal of them before they awaken."

Chad scratched at the heavy stubble on his cheeks, "That's a fair point."

Gram nodded and turned to the others, "Fine, the rest of you will stay here and watch over them. I will guard her."

"Gram...," began Alyssa, but he held up his hand to forestall her.

"Trust me, love. I will return," he told her softly.

Moira sat tall upon Cassandra's back, but she heard every word clearly. They seemed to burn within her. *Not for me,* she told herself, *never for me—not anymore.*

Gram climbed up behind her, but she had built a small shield around herself, which he discovered when he automatically tried to put his arms around her waist.

"Not to worry," she said before he could ask, "I'll anchor you firmly. You won't fall."

He pursed his lips but said nothing.

"I really think I ought to come with you," suggested Gerold.

"Your people will want to thank you when they awaken," said Moira. "They will need your guidance."

Chad clapped the nobleman on the shoulder, "If they find something they can't handle, it's doubtful you or I would be of any use. Don't look so down. We can make a nice stew while we wait."

"Here!?" exclaimed the baron with distaste. "Who could eat here, surrounded by the dead and the nearly dead?"

The ranger looked thoughtful as he replied, "Me; most soldiers, once they're hungry enough, mind you; vultures; and, oh I don't know, probably any number of other men and beasts. My head's not working too well. I'm tired and in need of a drink."

Cassandra's wings created a windstorm that drowned out the rest of their conversation as Moira and Gram flew toward the city. They soared upward and then the great dragon's flight leveled out.

Gram shouted to make himself heard over the rushing wind, "Are you going to tell me where we are headed?"

He was still clad in his enchanted armor, so Moira was forced to shout in return since her thoughts couldn't reach his directly, "Some of the people we fought today were servants of the Earl Berlagen. You were right to look there first; they were keeping him in a dungeon beneath the Earl's city house."

"How did you learn that?"

The answer to that was ugly and likely incomprehensible to him. Her minions had searched the minds of every person they freed for memories that might be relevant. Not only that, but the ones who had been most directly violated, when some of her twins had attached themselves to their aythar sources, those had had the entirety of their minds exposed. Moira had been flooded with their knowledge and memories when she had reabsorbed her spell-twins. "I gleaned it from their thoughts," she replied simply.

"Will there be any guards?"

"Probably not any human ones," she told him. "I think all of them came after us, but there may be more things like the one you fought."

He grimaced, "I was afraid you'd say that."

"It will be easier this time."

Cassandra was descending but as they drew nearer he could see that she was planning to land near the palace, not the Earl's house. "It will be a long walk from here," observed Gram.

"There's something here I need to collect before we go there," said Moira as she slid down the dragon's shoulder. She was striding forward as soon as her feet touched the ground, confidence in her steps. She knew where she was headed.

Gram caught up quickly, to walk beside her. He didn't like the thought of her getting too far ahead. From what he had seen as well as what Matthew had told him, her shield wouldn't be as effective as his armor. If anyone were to be attacked, he was determined it would be him who took the brunt of it. He would have walked ahead of her if he could have, but he didn't know where she was going, and she seemed disinclined to discuss it.

The main door to the palace was open, but some of the ones within were locked. Moira never slowed, any obstacle with the temerity to get in her way didn't remain an obstacle for long. The fifth and final door to be flung from its hinges turned out to be the entrance to a storeroom. She walked over to one particular crate and opened it. Within it were two braided metal ropes, each roughly three feet in length and possessing strangely wrought handles.

He didn't recognize them at first, but when Moira touched them, they straightened, becoming sword-like weapons in her hands. After a moment, she said a word and they relaxed again before twining together to become the beautiful belt that she had worn when they first arrived at the city.

Moira's hands circled her waist as she returned it to its customary place. "That's better," she said with a faint smile.

The smile made Gram feel better. Hoping that her good humor had returned, he started to put a hand on her shoulder, but it was stopped several inches away by an invisible shield.

"Don't touch me," Moira's voice grated out. "Don't ever touch me."

His face showed the hurt through the transparent metal of his helm, "What's happened to you, Moira?"

None of your concern, she thought angrily. The sight of his wounded expression made her want to lash out at him. He only thought that remark had hurt him. For a second she wanted to teach him true pain. Looking down, she stared at her own hand and in her mind's eye she saw it as it had been on the battle-plane within her heart, scaled and hard, with long razor sharp talons.

The vision made her clench her teeth, and she took a deep breath to regain her composure. She didn't want to hurt him, not truly. *I want him, all of him,* she thought, facing her true desire, but it wasn't the sweet yearning of an innocent heart. *I could remake him as my own.*

She looked into his eyes, and he saw a flickering fear in them, but it was quickly replaced by something harder, something alien. "I am not the woman you knew," she warned.

Confused he asked, "Then who are you?"

"I don't know anymore," she answered, "but you would be wise to keep your distance."

"Or what?" he asked softly, unable to believe she might be threatening him.

Or I'll replace you with someone who knows when to shut up, she thought, but she didn't say that. Instead she motioned with one hand and used her aythar to push him smoothly out of her path as she exited the storeroom. "Follow," she ordered.

He stared after her for a moment, shocked at her brusque indifference. The girl he had grown up with had a sunny disposition and a playful way about her. He had seen her angry before, mostly when she was fighting with her brother, but the coldness she showed now was something new.

They had both been through trying experiences over the past couple of weeks, and he didn't expect that to leave her unmarked, but this... He shook his head and hurried to catch up to her.

She led him back to Cassandra, and a minute later they were flying again, this time heading directly toward the location of the Earl's city home. Seen from the air, it didn't fail to impress, although it was obviously much smaller than the palace, it was nevertheless a large building. Constructed against one of the city walls it was an imposing structure, a small fortress in its own right. They landed a full city block away.

"We'll walk from here," stated Moira for his benefit. She had already relayed her instructions to Cassandra silently.

"You don't think we'll need the dragon?" put in Gram.

Moira shrugged, "If there are more of those weapons, it would put her at risk. She makes a big target. I can draw on her strength from this distance."

Gram was irritated by her diffident mannerisms. Despite the calm rationale behind her decision he felt argumentative, "It's ok to risk ourselves, but not the dragon. I understand."

Moira started walking again, without looking back she replied, "If you're afraid, you can wait with Cassandra."

He overtook her and led the way, cursing silently, *Bitch.*

The street gate leading into the Earl's city house was closed, but that wasn't much of a barrier for them. Moira lifted the inner bar with a gesture and forced the gate to open with a small effort of will, and they strode in. There was no sign of any human occupants, to either her eyes or her magesight.

Gram had changed Thorn's form once more, opting for a shield and one handed longsword. If they were to be attacked, he had decided it would be better to be prepared to take a hit, at least until they knew what they were dealing with. He stepped forward into the gate, but nothing happened.

Moira stayed right behind him, "Wait. Let me search the area before we go farther."

If someone else had said those words, it might not have seemed contradictory, since she stood very still and closed her eyes afterward, but Gram was long familiar with wizards and their ways. He knew she was examining the area carefully with her magesight.

Moira frowned as she tried to understand what she found. Several minutes passed before she spoke again, "There are no people within, but there are a lot of other strange things. The above ground portion of the building seems fairly ordinary, but there are several lower levels, and there's a lot of metal in them, strange devices and other things I don't recognize. The entrance to the first lower level is guarded by another of those metal creatures, and there are three more farther down. They aren't moving, but that doesn't mean much."

"How do you want to proceed?" he asked.

"Go straight in, take the second corridor on the right. We'll follow it to the end. The stairs are there. The first one is at the bottom, waiting behind a door. I'll stay right behind you."

He started moving, but he wasn't out of questions, "You just want me to open that door when we get to it? I won't be able to move or dodge if you are behind me."

"Just keep your shield up, I'll disable it," she said.

"How? I don't think you can call a thunderstorm down here."

"At this distance I don't need one, plus I have my weapons now."

Gram nodded, advancing farther and turning as he reached the second corridor. The walls were stone with heavy timbers bracing them. Numerous tapestries decorated the walls, but they seemed excessively dusty, as though no one had cared for them in some time. *If the people here were some of the first taken, they might have stopped worrying about little things like cleaning,* he theorized.

An open doorway loomed before him, showing stairs that descended into darkness. If it weren't for his drag-on-bond, he would have found it hard to see. "It's at the bottom?" he asked, just to be certain.

"Yes, but there's a door. I don't think it will attack until you open it," she reaffirmed.

"Let's hope," said Gram. "Those weapons of theirs could probably cut through the door without much trouble." He put his foot on the first step and began making his way down. As he moved into the darkness the colors in his vision faded out, replaced by sharp greys and blacks as his eyesight adjusted. The door at the bottom was a simple one, it had no bar on this side, just a plain latch. He hunched lower, trying to get as much of himself behind his shield as possible before reaching out.

"It's moving," whispered Moira. "Lining up to fire at the door. There's no time, break it!"

He was wound up tightly already. At her warning he took a hard step forward and slammed his shield into the door. It was well made, and the wood held, but the hinges ripped free from their mounts, and it fell inward as the world exploded with light and noise.

Fire was flashing from the end of the creature's spinning weapon, and it felt as though a hundred black-smiths were pounding upon his shield with everything they had. The roaring noise of the assault was bad, but it wasn't the only thing filling the corridor with sound. Lightning was flashing around him to envelop the creature, blinding his dark-adjusted eyes with its blue-white brilliance.

Gram was rendered deaf and blind by the searing chaos of sound and light, but he held his position under the driving hammer blows against his shield, gritting his teeth in sheer stubbornness.

Something exploded then, and an irresistible wave of pressure lifted Gram and threw him into Moira. She felt like a brick wall when he struck her, and he rebounded to land on the floor. Silence reigned except for a strange humming sound that seemed to envelop the world.

Disoriented, Gram nonetheless leapt back up, returning his shield to the guard position and hoping he would recover enough to discover his enemy's location before it attacked again. Seconds rolled by, and nothing happened. Glancing back, he could see Moira's mouth moving; she sounded muffled, but she didn't look concerned. Looking over his shield, he saw the burning bulk of the monster that now looked to be permanently out of action.

The upper portion of its body bulged outward strangely; sharp pieces of metal protruding as smoke and sparks issued forth. Most of the creature seemed intact, but it wasn't moving at all. Moira leaned in and shouted in his ear, "It's much worse inside than out. It won't be a danger to us now."

"Are your ears ringing?" he shouted back.

"No, I blocked them before you opened the door," she admitted.

"Couldn't you have done mine too?"

"The armor," she said, pointing at his head, "it interferes with my magic." Of course, after she said it she realized she could have made something like a sound dampening shield around him instead, but she didn't bother telling him that. She'd consider it for the next time.

The others were moving now, coming up to stop their advance. With her magesight she could see them squeezing their way up the stairs from the level below. They didn't have long, but she had an idea. "Don't move," she told Gram. "I'm going to make a wall for us."

Wall? he wondered, but he soon saw what she meant.

She used her aythar to tear at the walls around them, pulling heavy stone blocks out and piling them in the corridor in front of them. Moira didn't bother with niceties like structure and organization, she ripped timbers and stones free with equal abandon and piled them up in front of them.

Gram worried that the ceiling above them might collapse, but when it began to sag, she pulled it down and used the materials that formed it to add to her collection of rubble.

The wall, perhaps it was better to call it a pile of heavy debris, grew quickly, and not a moment too soon, for the enemy rounded the corner fifty feet away and began firing as soon as Gram and Moira came into view. The monsters' weapons roared, with a sound somewhere between the buzzing of hornets and thunder. Bits of stone and wood flew from the barrier Moira had created.

The two of them ducked below the rim of their defense, which was annoying to Gram, since it meant he could no longer see, but of course that was no real problem for Moira. She could locate the foe with magesight.

She had taken off her belt, and the two lengths of braided metal had once again become sword-like weapons in her hands. As she pointed one of them at the barricade Gram was enveloped in silence. Moira had shielded him from sound this time.

"Thylen pyrren," she intoned, and a vivid line of scarlet fire shot forth, piercing the wall of rubble and striking one of their new attackers. Unlike the attacks made by her spell-twins in the earlier battle, this fire was focused by the rune channel she held, and it pierced cleanly through the metal monster. Moira kept her will on it, maintaining the devastating beam of fire and moving her arm slightly, so that it scythed across the enemy.

Well, 'across' was not quite the correct word, bisected was more accurate, for the beam of fire sliced completely through it. While Gram couldn't see what happened, he felt the pressure wave as the thing exploded. He was grateful his ears were protected this time.

The second creature reacted forcefully to the destruction of its comrade. Seeing the ineffectiveness of its primary weapon and the possibility of its imminent demise, it switched to its other armament. Likely they hadn't used the other until that point because it was dangerously destructive in an enclosed environment. Moira guessed that her threat had become great enough to justify the risk.

Time slowed to a crawl as she shifted her line of incandescent fire to strike the second one. She tried to reinforce the shield she had built behind the wall of rubble, but she couldn't know whether it would be enough.

The thing's strange weapon lined up with their position as her line of fire cut across it, but the attack was too low; instead of hitting the weapon, or its torso, it cut through two of the legs. The monster's weapon fired a split second before it began to fall.

Gram had switched Thorn to its shield and one hander form since there was little else he could do, he crouched in front of Moira wondering if there were something more he could do and feeling useless, when something knocked him prone and pain shot through his left side. His vision was gone, or so he thought, until he realized that the air was full of thick grey dust and sparkling pieces of metal. His shield had disintegrated into swirling fragments.

His hearing returned suddenly and with it the sound of stone and wood fragments pattering like rain to the floor. From the corner of his eye he saw Moira lying behind him, blood trickling down across her face as dust seemed to drift down and coat her with a layer of grey. Her eyes had rolled back into her head.

The stairs behind them were gone, a gaping maw of stone remained which seemed to be filling up as the upper level collapsed into it.

All this he absorbed in the time it might take to draw a single breath. He knew there was little time. If the creature still lived, it would be able to fire again within a couple of minutes. He struggled to push himself up, but his left arm didn't respond. The enchanted shield was reforming beneath it, but it lay limp and useless. He suspected the arm was broken inside his armor, or worse, but after the initial shock of pain he couldn't feel anything more—it and his shoulder were completely numb.

His right side was marginally better. He could feel that arm, but when he tried to roll onto it and use it to push himself up, he couldn't find the strength, instead he wound up flopping feebly on the floor. Something *did* hurt then, a strange throb that ached through even the gauzy fuzziness of shock. *I have to get up!* Gram closed his eyes and listened to his body for a moment, allowing the steady beat of his heart to calm him. Concentrating he focused on another heartbeat, that of the red gem nestled in Thorn's pommel, his dead father's heart. *Help me.*

He felt it then, a warmth that traveled up his right arm, connecting the beat of the gem to the steady thrum of his own heart. It grew stronger, louder, and he devoted himself to its rhythm. When he tried to roll the next time he succeeded. Pushing himself off the ground, he looked over the scattered remains of their barricade. The monster was still there, lying on its side—waiting.

It had its primary weapon pointed at him and as he stood Gram could hear the whine as it began to spin.

He couldn't lift the shield. That arm simply wouldn't move. Growling, he leapt up and over the scattered rubble. Stone chips flew in every direction as the creature began firing at the place he had been. The beast corrected its aim even as he flew through the air, and when he landed hammer-blows began striking his legs and then his torso.

Some of them struck the shield, but most hit his armor directly. At close range the pieces of metal it was firing landed with devastating force. Gram's armor absorbed the first few hits, but the attacks came in such rapid succession that some of the scales that made up his armor flew off, leaving his body exposed. The pieces of enchanted metal would return, reforming his armor, but there was a limit to their speed.

Gram turned, twisting in place to keep the attacks from striking the same place too long as he strode forward, trying to close the last few feet between him and his antagonist. He stumbled and half fell the last five feet as he closed on the monster's left side, and it could no longer point the weapon at him.

The torso swiveled and the other, more deadly weapon lined up with his chest.

Someone screamed as his sword swept up and across propelled by more strength than he knew he had. Mindful of the past, he aimed for the joint where the metal arm met the body. Thorn sheared halfway through before sticking in the dense metal.

Gram stared down the empty black hole that would administer his death sentence. Time stretched out for what felt like an eternity, but nothing happened. A small light on one side of the box-like device slowly stopped glowing. His attack had somehow disabled the weapon.

He couldn't pull Thorn free, so he spoke a command to make the sword shift again, changing from sword and shield to its original great sword form. When it reformed it was free in his hand again. It was meant to be wielded with two hands of course, but his arm was strong enough to use it effectively even if it wasn't optimal.

The monster was trying to swivel and bring the other weapon back around to face him, but lying sideways on the ground made that difficult, and he was close enough to move out of its line of fire. He hacked at it in a frenzy, sending fragments of the dense metal flying in every direction. It took almost a minute, but eventually he severed the other arm and then he started on the central portion of the thing, not satisfied until he was certain that it was no longer functional in any sense of the word.

When he finally stopped, a wave of fatigue washed over him and he stumbled, almost losing his balance. There was blood everywhere. *That's odd,* he thought, *these things don't bleed.* The room spun, and he found himself lying on the floor, staring at the partially demolished ceiling. He felt his chest fluttering, his heart was beating too fast.

"Take off the armor," said Moira leaning over him. "I need to see your body to heal you."

"I'm fine," he told her, trying to speak clearly, but the words were slurred. "I just need to rest a moment. I think I overdid it, my heart's racing."

"Gram, please! You've lost too much blood—your heart is trying to compensate. Take the armor off before you pass out, or I won't be able to help you." Moira's voice was desperate.

"Oh, right," he answered, and then he managed to get the word out to remove the armor.

Moira's face changed when she saw what lay beneath the metal, her lip quivered faintly and her eyes grew liquid. A gasp almost escaped her lips before she suppressed it.

Gram wanted to tell her he was alright, but something in her look made him stop, so instead he commented idly, "You seem different."

"I'm not Moira," she told him. "She's still unconscious." She stretched her hands out, and Gram felt something passing through him as she began to work.

He had been about to pass out, but the pain brought him fully awake. "You don't look unconscious," he hissed, still trying to remain casual despite the situation.

A tear fell from Moira's eye, "Please, I'm trying to stop the bleeding. Moira will be fine and she'll wake up soon. The shock of losing the shield she had up knocked her senseless."

Gram felt something change then, and his heart rate slowed. He wanted to look down, to see how bad it was, but he found himself captivated by her face. He tried to speak, but his tongue wouldn't cooperate.

Shhh, I can hear you without words, now that your armor is off, she told him mentally.

If you aren't Moira, who are you? he asked, curious.

Good question, I wonder myself. As far as I'm concerned, I am her, but in reality I'm a magical creation, just like her mother, the woman who married Archmage Gareth.

Oh. Gram didn't know how to respond. Strange sensations passed through him as she worked on him, and finally he came up with a relevant question, *What should I call you?*

Call me Myra, it's close enough to the name I remember as my own, and it should help avoid confusion, she answered. *You should be dead. You've lost so much blood. There are several terrible wounds and pieces of metal embedded in your body. I don't think you'll be able to walk for several days, and you'll wish you were dead for weeks after that. There's going to be a lot of bruising.*

That made Gram want to laugh, *I'm starting to understand why Father didn't want me to follow in his footsteps.*

Long painful minutes passed while she removed the numerous fragments of metal from his legs and abdomen. Once that was done, she closed the smaller blood vessels that had been severed and finished by sealing the skin. Myra wanted to cry at what she had seen. There was blood all over the room, and all of it was Gram's, but she steeled herself, fighting down the urge. She could feel Moira, the 'real' Moira, beginning to stir, but she had more to tell him.

Leaning down on impulse, she kissed Gram lightly on the lips. His eyes fluttered open then, staring at her.

What?

She jerked upright, *Forgive me. She—we—care about you a great deal. That was imprudent of me.* She could sense the confusion in him. He was thinking of Alyssa.

You don't seem like Moira to me, he said at last.

I'm like she was, like she used to be, Myra told him. *The battle—earlier—it hurt her. She isn't the same, Gram. She wasn't lying to you. She's dangerous now.*

I don't understand.

What she did, controlling those people, it has a price. Bending someone else's mind exerts a similar pressure on the mage's mind. It's hurt her, twisted and bent her in ways she hasn't fathomed yet.

But she'll get better, right? You can help her, he suggested.

No, we are all marked by what we survive. She may improve, but she will never go back to the way she was. None of us can do that, not her, not me, nor even our father, despite being an archmage. We are all the sum of our experiences.

As long as she can get better, I'll take it, replied Gram hopefully.

Keep your amulet on. Try not to think on it when she's near unless you're wearing your armor, warned Myra.

Gram didn't like the sound of that, *What does that mean?*

She may not get better, Gram. She might get worse—much worse.

CHAPTER 24

Moira found herself kneeling beside Gram's body. She had blood on her hands, her knees, and all over her clothes. From the look of it he had bled all over the room. She wiped her hands on her dress with a feeling of irritation. *How did I get here?* The last thing she remembered was the sudden pain of her shield shattering.

He finished it off, but it nearly killed him. Since you were unconscious I healed him. I thought it's what you would want me to do, said her assistant from the back of her mind.

The thought of her twin using her body while she was out bothered her, but she couldn't fault her for what she had done. It made her angry, but she tried to suppress the feeling. Gram was passing into unconsciousness, but a glance at his mind showed some strange things floating through his thoughts. *Myra?*

He was confused, I thought it best to take a different name.

Moira stood, extending her magesight once more, trying to confirm her route to the stairs down to the lowest level. She could feel something there, and it was familiar. Whether it was her father, or just a place where he had spent a lot of time she couldn't be sure, but the enemy had a lot of metal down there around what appeared to be a massive stone outcropping.

She began to pick her way through the rubble.

Don't you want to make sure his healing is complete? He was very near death, suggested Myra.

Moira dismissed the suggestion impatiently, *You know everything I know. If you did the work then I'm sure it's as good as anything I might have done.* She continued walking without sparing a glance back at Gram, either with her eyes or her magesight.

The stairs down were much longer than the previous set, but that was to be expected since the lowest level beneath Earl Berlagen's home was really just one room, a large cavern with a vaulted ceiling and a floor that was level only because someone had spent a lot of time and effort making it so. She wasn't sure if the cavern was natural or manmade, nor did she care. Moira was only interested in what was within the cavern, not its origin.

The stairway opened up halfway down, giving a view of the room for the last half of its length as it followed the wall to the floor below. She created two hasty spellbeasts, small barely intelligent creatures shaped like birds, and sent them out as she neared the open area. She hadn't detected any more of the metal guardians but she couldn't be certain whether the enemy had other defenses.

Something roared in the room below and stone chips flew from the wall along the stair as something began firing at her creations. Moira tracked the movement within the cavern and discovered that two objects mounted on the cavern ceiling in different places were actually more of the enemy's strange weapons. They pivoted, pointing long barrels at her flying minions and spewing death wherever they aimed.

While they were distracted by her spellbeasts she took several steps down and pointed one of her rune channels at them and sending out a line of focused light and heat. Moira cut the two weapons free of the ceiling before they could reorient to fire at her and watched them fall clattering to the stone floor below. Then she hurried back up the stairs and waited.

Nothing happened, so she sent two more small spellbeasts flying down into the room; the first two had disintegrated under the hail of flying metal. This time nothing responded.

Stepping carefully, she began to descend once more, her eyes drawn to the stone mass in the center of the room. It appeared to be a massive stone outcropping that had thrust its way up from the earth below. The paved stone floor around it was cracked and buckling, which indicated that it was more recent than the room's construction.

In her magesight it appeared much like normal stone, but there was something extra, a feeling that clung to the rock, her father's aythar.

But she could find no sign of his mind. He wasn't there.

Strange metal devices were everywhere, in a wide variety of shapes, sizes and forms. Metal boxes that might be countertops, or devices, she couldn't be sure. The walls were covered in more complex pieces, from the ground up to a height of several feet. None of it made sense to Moira.

Two large metal pillars rose on either side of the stone in the center, each of them leaning toward it and pointing heavy crystalline tips at the rock. She could detect some sort of energy in them but for now they were quiescent.

Some wizard I am, she thought. *All of this arcane equipment is as unknown to me as a weaver's loom might be to a lamb.* Walking forward she approached the stone, hoping to find some clue to her father's disappearance. As she closed the distance, she felt something.

Frowning, Moira put her hands out, brushing the rough surface. Deep within, a pulse of aythar responded to her fingers.

"Father!" she cried out, knowing that touch instantly. Unbidden tears made tracks down her dirty cheeks. Moira pressed her face against the cold stone and stretched her arms wide, although the rock was far too large for her to embrace it. Faintly, she felt it again, her father's presence, like a ghost within the unyielding stone.

You know what this means, observed Myra quietly from the back of her mind.

Moira's eyes clenched tightly, hot tears spilling from them as her face contorted into a grimace of pain. *No!* she said silently, trying to deny the truth in front of her. Mordecai had retreated into the earth completely, surrendering his humanity in order to escape his enemies.

It was one of the most common traps that the archmages of old had fallen into, pushing their abilities too far, they were often lost to the world of men. Moira's father had become a part of the earth itself. He was gone.

The pain in Moira's chest grew until she wondered if she might die of grief alone. Turning her back on the stone, she slid to the floor. It felt as though her heart had been replaced by a lump of red hot iron and it burned with a searing agony as she fought to draw breath. She was silent at first, unable to speak or cry, until she managed to draw air again. It came in with a rush before reemerging as a shuddering scream, but there was no relief in it. Instead, it sent a throbbing ache through the veins of her arms and legs as well as her throat. Her entire body ached.

"It hurts," she said to herself in a thick voice. She tried to say the words calmly, but they came out as part of yet another sobbing cry, one that only grew louder as she repeated the words again. "It hurts! Why?! This isn't supposed to happen!"

It was pure denial. The pain became anger and she burned with it. She was filled with black hatred, but she had nowhere to direct it.

Gram walked slowly down the stairs, but it wasn't him. Moira could see that clearly even through her misery. His body radiated power as though he was made of a piece of the sun itself. The sneer on his lips seemed entirely proper. He didn't have his armor on, but Thorn was in his hand.

"I see you found your father, what a touching reunion."

His presence was overwhelming and in her magesight the room seemed to shimmer like the horizon on a hot day. Even the air felt heavy, as though it had become too thick to breathe. She was being smothered by the Shining God's power.

Moira tightened her shield, trying to find relief from the god's malevolent will. It helped somewhat, but it was not enough. Her body wouldn't move and only the cold core of hatred and loathing in her heart kept her from giving in to the desire to prostrate herself before the false god. *He killed my father.*

"I wish that I had, beautiful child," he told her, "but the coward escaped when he knew that he had lost."

"He wouldn't have lost to you," she whispered.

Celior laughed, "Perhaps not, if he had been smart, but your father was ever the fool; his pride was his undoing. I only regret that I didn't get a chance to educate him on his failure."

Gram's body was close now, leaning over, looking down at her with contempt. With one hand he cupped her chin, drawing her face up to meet his gaze, and then his hand dipped lower, to squeeze her breast. "You will be my consolation prize."

Desire coursed through her, a sweet corruption as Moira's will was suppressed by the god's. She felt it from her head to her toes and most especially in her loins, a burning need for the man looming over her. Lust filled her being, a pure desire that touched every part of her, except the hard kernel of hatred that lay at her core. She hated him, she wanted him, and she loathed herself for all of it.

His hand gripped her hair and he dragged her mercilessly up, hauling her to her feet like a doll, powerless and limp. He pressed her back against the stone with his body and set his lips to her ear, "I promised your father that I would take care of you after he was gone. Doesn't that make you happy?"

With the last of her will, Moira spoke the key words to the enchantment that made Celior immortal. They were hard to remember, but her father had drilled them into her and her brother countless times. She gasped them out knowing they were her last hope.

Celior straightened, pulling away, "What is your command?"

"Kneel before me."

Gram's handsome face smiled, and then his arm became a blur. Pain blinded Moira and she heard a sickening crunch as he backhanded her to the floor. Her cheekbone had been broken.

"Perhaps I misunderstood you?" suggested Celior, sneering. Then his face took on a look of concern, "Oh my, if you aren't careful with that frown your face might get stuck like that." Reaching down he pulled her up by her hair again before touching her swelling face with his finger. Pleasure ran through her like golden light even as the pressure caused more pain in her cheek.

Moira's mind was reeling, but her hatred remained, "How?"

"Your father of course," he answered with a smile. "I told you he was a fool. He fought me when he should have used the key from the start. I let him win, but I made it satisfying for him, all while I led him to the trap they had prepared for him. He used the key at the end, when he realized he had been tricked, but it was too late. As soon as he spoke the words, the railgun shattered his body. I'm surprised he survived long enough to end his own miserable life."

"Railgur?"

"Railgun," corrected Celior. "The wondrous weapon that the outsiders brought with them, the one that nearly killed you and this young man a little while ago. I must commend you on surviving it. Your father didn't do nearly as well. It tore a hole through his body as big as my fist.

"I know that doesn't sound as impressive as it should, but he was protected by a shield so powerful even I couldn't pierce it at the time. Their weapon destroyed it and mortally wounded him with but a single blow. Isn't that marvelous?"

The key had been changed. Moira understood now. Celior's words were meant to break her resolve, and somewhere deeper down she registered shock at his recounting of their final battle, but they didn't work quite as the god intended. She was no longer the tender young woman who had first come to Dunbar and his painful barbs only served to add fuel to the fire in her heart, turning her dark hatred into a burning rage.

The pain of her broken cheek had made her vision blurry with tears, but the cold venom she felt helped focus her thoughts. Blinking away the tears her eyes focused firmly on the pompous deity's beautiful features. *I need more information.*

"Who are these 'outsiders'?" she asked. "Where did they come from? We have done nothing to them."

Celior smiled, "Still trying to be clever? You'll be discovering that first hand, my dear, although I have no problem sharing the knowledge. It will only deepen your despair. They call themselves 'ANSIS', not that the name means anything to me. The important information is that they are here largely due to your illustrious sire's efforts. Much like the She'Har, they have crossed over from another plane of existence. When your father removed the Dark Gods from their place, the dimension that enveloped our own collapsed. Our world is now open to contact with other planes."

His description reminded her of something her brother had said during one of his expositions about his experiments. She hadn't been paying close attention, but she clearly remembered him saying something about translation being easier now than it had been in the past. 'Translation' was Matthew's term for shifting things between dimensions. He preferred it to avoid confusion with 'teleportation', which was shifting something between locations within the same dimension.

None of that seemed remotely useful to her in her current situation, though.

Celior's will redoubled and she fell to the floor as he released her hair. With one hand outstretched he stared down at her, enjoying the look of terror in her eyes as he rendered her helpless once more. It was a purely mental sensation, but it was so powerful that Moira felt as though a great weight had been set upon her body. She was limp and her mind paralyzed. There was nothing left to her but a dark impotent animosity directed at her captor.

One of the metal counters that lined the walls opened and from within its recesses something moved. A swarm of insect-like metal creatures issued from it, crossing the floor and heading in her direction. An even greater fear filled her then, as she realized Celior's true intention. Despite her desire to flee, she was held immobile and her mouth opened of its own volition.

She was to be served up to the outsiders as a gift.

"Before you start your new life I should share one more thing," said Celior, still using Gram's mouth. "Everything you did here was pointless. This entire exercise was nothing more than an experiment for the ANSIS. They wanted to test the abilities of a human wizard. All those people died simply to provide information to them regarding your family's magical abilities. Apparently they don't have anything like our magic on their home world. Now they intend to see whether you can be a useful tool."

A sharp pain cut through her fear as Moira's broken cheek bone shifted suddenly back into place. It was done with the tiniest currents of aythar, an act of subtle healing that would be difficult to see in the shifting energies that surrounded her already. She recognized Myra's agency behind the act. Hope rose suddenly within her.

Gram's face twisted into a frown as Celior noticed the subtle change in her, "What is this?"

Moira's mouth remained open and the metal parasites were only inches from her, *Now!* She wasn't certain what her spell-twin had planned but she was sure they were out of time.

A warm blanket encompassed her soul and Celior's crushing will was gone. It was a feeling of immense relief as Myra interposed herself between Moira's mind and the cruelty staring down at them.

Moira seized the moment of respite and clamped her teeth together, snarling, *"Tyrestrin!"* The entire room flashed white for a second as lightning leapt from her hands to engulf the metal creatures crawling toward her face. After it passed sparks continued to dance between the small metal parasites for long seconds as they twitched, and then they were still.

"Bitch!" yelled Celior, furious, and his anger struck at Moira like a hammer.

Myra howled in Moira's head as his rage tore at her, the pain was incredible, but she took it all, shielding her creator with her entire being.

Moira smiled at her tormentor, even as her assistant writhed in agony under his assault, "You can kill me, fiend, but you will never control me."

Gram's hand closed around Thorn's hilt and he brought the blade up, laying the edge across her throat. "I am losing patience, girl."

"As if I care," she spat. "I'd rather be dead than have those *things* inside me. Just admit defeat and kill me, for you won't have me unless you come in here and take me yourself."

Myra's screams of pain increased as the Shining God pressed even harder on her mind. Moira didn't think her spell-twin could last much longer, but she forced herself to laugh anyway. Madness sparkled in her eyes, hiding the hastily conceived plan that was her last hope. She sent her thoughts to her spell-twin, *Help Gram. Get him out of here. Don't stop running until you get to Cassandra and then go home.* Moira used her new freedom to push Myra aside, letting Celior's wrath plunge once more into her heart.

No! cried Myra, but it was too late.

Moira opened her mind to Celior, giving up any attempt at resistance while simultaneously pushing Myra out.

Shrieking in victory, the god's spirit dove into her, leaving Gram to fall limply to the ground.

The world vanished then, and Moira found herself once more on the battlefield within her mind. Celior stared at her from ten feet away, shining and beautiful despite his true ugliness. His eyes widened in surprise as he beheld the secret image of Moira's soul. She stood before him covered in black scales and armed with razor sharp talons, a monster of spirit.

What is this? he asked. *I've never seen a human that looked like this on the inside.*

Moira grinned, her mouth splitting impossibly wide to show an impressive display of dagger-like teeth. *Who said I was human?*

The god was undeterred. His face took on a look of determination and his body changed. Now he was clad in golden armor. Stepping closer he told her, *You cannot win. Your power is but a drop beside the ocean within me.*

Casually, Moira raised one talon and raked it across his chest, shredding the armor there as though it were made of tissue. Golden blood welled up and ran down his chest. *Within you? Within me! The aythar here belongs to the victor, and you don't even begin to have the skill to contest me.*

Confusion was written in his features, *What?*

Celior tried to step away, but she stayed with him. Slashing sideways she tore through his breastplate and opened his belly before bringing her clawed hand up to show him the vital fluids that covered it. Staring wickedly into his eyes she licked the golden ichor from one talon. *Welcome to your nightmare, puppet.*

He shoved her back and a golden sword appeared in his hand. It came down on her shoulder in a powerful overhand swing, crunching through the black armor there. Red blood dripped down Moira's chest.

Try again, she told him as the pain shot through her.

The Shining God decided to retreat and take the battle back to the physical world, but when he tried to remove himself he found the way blocked. Midnight mountains rose around him, filling his vision in every direction and enclosing the battlefield that was Moira Illeniel's mind.

You were the fool this time, puppet-god. You will remain here until you are no more, or I am. This is my realm, and no one, not man, nor god, nor even beast, will leave it until I give them leave. I am the last of the Centyr and this is the one place you should never have dared to come. She dove at him and gripped him with clawed hands that had become impossibly strong. Struggle as he might, Celior could not shake himself free of her.

He turned on her in a fury, letting his fear and anger lend him strength. Daggers of gold appeared in his hands and he stabbed at her over and over, but no matter how many times he drove them into her she never wavered. Red blood ran freely from her blackened form as she held him tightly, laughing all the while.

How did you feel after my mother made you, puppet? she whispered softly into his ear, careful not to tear it free with teeth that had grown far too long. *Did you think she loved you? Did you think she cared? How long was it before you realized that you were trash, created for one purpose before being abandoned to suffer for eternity?*

Celior screamed in rage, but he found himself growing weak, exhausted. It was a feeling unfamiliar to him. Agony such as he had never known blinded him when he felt her teeth clamp down on his skull, ripping away his ear and much that had lain beneath it.

She tore his body apart, rending him limb from limb, but the god could not die. The immortality enchantment would not allow it, nor could she remake his personality while it kept his mind chained within it.

But she could hurt him, and so she did. She gave him as much pain as he had given her and still she continued. It went on for a long time, his body healing and reforming in her mind's eye, whereupon she would start all over.

Occasionally he found the will to fight again, wounding her before she resumed her torture, but he was beaten and he knew it. Moira kept at him relentlessly, until the only thing left to him was pain. After an eternity he began to beg, *Please, no more.*

She wasn't ready to stop yet, though. She had begun to enjoy it.

Anything... just let this end!

Moira ignored his pleading. Even when he fought back, her own pain just reinvigorated her. She hadn't truly expected to win. She hadn't known what would happen when Celior first entered her mind. The discovery that her abilities gave her all the advantages had been exhilarating. Her opponent was no more difficult to deal with than a normal human; he was less challenging than her spell-twins had been by at least an order of magnitude.

He whimpered and cried, and she punished him more. *He killed my father.* The anger made her feel powerful.

Only indirectly, said Myra, who hadn't done as she had been told. She had stayed close by and now she returned, to witness the torment firsthand.

He led him into a trap! Moira snarled.

Myra remained silent and Moira continued, enjoying the vicious nature of her work. It felt like eons had passed before she finally grew bored with the task. *Give me the new key,* she commanded. There was no doubt in her that he would give her whatever she asked for then.

Celior complied, babbling the key phrase out as rapidly as he could manage.

She repeated the phrase back to him, and then he was hers. *Now give your power to her,* she ordered, indicating Myra.

The humbled god began at once, and new pain washed over Moira's awareness as her assistant began to burn with the intensity of so much power. *Outside, both of you out. This is too much,* she told them.

The physical world made itself known to her once more as they exited her consciousness. She was lying on the floor of the chamber, still beside her father's stone. Gram sat beside her, weary and panting. More of the metal insects littered the floor around them. Apparently the enemy had had more of them and had been trying to reach her while she lay helpless on the floor.

Relief showed in his eyes when he saw her looking up at him. That changed to alarm as Celior and Myra materialized beside him. Despite his weakness, Gram raised Thorn protectively and found his feet.

"Relax, they serve me wholly," said Moira as she sat up. Gold light was passing between Myra and Celior as he gave her all the aythar he had collected.

Gram sank back down beside her, too tired to remain standing if there was no threat. "I thought you were dying," he said without preamble.

Moira studied him with a predatory gaze before replying, "That might have been for the best, but I'm afraid not." She wanted to take him, but the armor prevented her from acting on the impulse.

Myra watched her with concern but she was helpless to do anything while the transfer was taking place. She sent her thoughts out silently, *Remember, he's your friend.*

"He's whatever I make him!" cursed Moira.

"What?" asked Gram, confused by her sudden outburst.

She heard the trust in his voice. The obvious interpretation of her words never even occurred to him. That realization and the broken bodies of the parasites around her caused her to feel a faint pang of guilt. Gram had been protecting her for a long time. Moira smiled as she answered, "Celior. I can do whatever I like with him now. He's given me the new key."

CHAPTER 25

A heavy crashing noise rumbled through the ceiling above them and Moira looked up.

Moira! Moira!

It was Cassandra, frantically trying to reach her. *Relax, I'm fine,* she responded. "How long has that been going on?" she asked, directing her question to Gram.

"I'm not sure," he told her. "Since I woke up—a quarter hour at least."

"Why didn't you tell her things were alright?"

The young warrior gaped at her, "It wasn't alright! You were thrashing about on the floor like you were possessed by a demon, and for all I knew you were! Meanwhile those metal bugs were everywhere, like roaches crawling out of the woodwork. What part of that was alright?"

His attitude provoked a surge of anger, but she saw the warning in Myra's face as she opened her mouth to respond. She paused and took a deep breath, trying to find the proper answer. With an effort of will she gave him an insincere smirk as she spoke, "Well, when you put it like that…"

Sending her perceptions out and upward she surveyed the remains of the Earl of Berlagen's city home. The ground floor was gone. Cassandra had completely demolished it in her panic. Luckily none of the inhabitants had been present. Moira supposed they had all been summoned during her battle outside the city, which probably meant half of them were dead anyway.

The lower levels weren't much better. The great dragon had used her powerful claws to tear at the floors, ripping them apart as easily as a dog might dig in soft garden soil. She had already dug through the first of the lower levels and had made a good start on opening up the second level. She probably would have reached the lower cavern within a few more minutes.

Moira was impressed.

I'm sending Gram up to meet you, along with my new servant, she said, sending her thoughts to the dragon. *I'll be down here a while longer.*

What happened? You were screaming. Are you sure you're alright?

Moira could feel the dragon's concern and anxiety like a palpable force. It annoyed her, but she kept her feelings calm as she replied, *I'm fine. I've taken control of Celior, he'll be accompanying Gram. In fact, he'll probably have to clear the way of debris after your rampage up there.*

But what about...

Silence! she snapped. *I will explain later, for now I wish to say goodbye to my father.* Moira had to force her hands to unclench. When she looked down at them she feared that they might be covered in black scales and tipped with claws, but they were simply her normal human hands.

Celior had only given a small portion of his power to Myra by then but she didn't feel like waiting any longer.

318

"Escort Gram out of here. Keep him safe. Myra will remain with me," she commanded. "When you reach the surface transfer the rest of your power to my dragon while you wait for me."

"Yes, mistress," said the once proud god, bowing meekly.

Myra sent a brief suggestion, *You might ask him to finish healing Gram as well. He has a vastly greater amount of experience with such things.*

Moira growled. She should have thought of that herself. Once, she would have. She relayed the order to Celior and then waited while he and Gram left. When they were gone she turned back to the stone outcropping that was all that was left of her father.

Myra spoke, she had enough aythar now to easily create a physical form, "Would you like me to rejoin you?"

"No, make a circle and shield me. I don't want to be interrupted by any more of those little metal monsters."

She stared at the stone thoughtfully. Her face still throbbed despite Myra's quick healing. At least the bones had been set in place and fused together again. She would have a terrible bruise soon and she could tell her face was already swollen. It would be much worse later.

Closing her eyes, Moira spread her arms and leaned against the cold rough rock. It felt good against the heat coming from her cheek. Something stirred in her heart, though it took her a moment to recognize the emotion. Sorrow.

Anger was easier, but she had no one left to punish, so she kept breathing and concentrated on the anguish that had been lurking unseen beneath it. *I avenged you father,* she said mentally, sending her thoughts into the stone. *I made Celior pay a thousand times over for what he did to you.*

There was no response.

I'll find whatever's left of these metal beasts as well. They will regret making you do this. Can you hear me?

The stone gave nothing back. She might as well have been trying to communicate with a mountain. Myra stood beside her.

"He said before that you might someday become an archmage," commented her spell-twin.

"It's just cold stone," said Moira.

"*He* could talk to stones."

It felt as though her stomach had been filled with ice. Bitter, she shot back, "Well *I* can't! I hear nothing!"

"We can't leave without trying," said Myra.

"Why do you care!?" said Moira angrily. "You aren't even real!"

Her spell-twin's eyes were wet with emotion. "Perhaps I'm only a few weeks old from your viewpoint, but that's not how I feel. I remember everything. He's my father just as much as yours. I don't remember being born in your mind. I remember growing up with him, with Mom, with Matthew and Irene and Conall! They're my family too, even if I'm not real!"

"If it bothers you so much I can unmake you."

"No."

"Then why do you stay?"

"Fear," said Myra. "I'm afraid you won't do anything. I'm afraid you *can't*, that you've become so warped you might not even try to save our father."

Moira wanted to kill her, but she knew the truth of the words. Secretly she feared the same. Quietly she fought with her conflicting emotions before closing her eyes again.

Calm, I must be calm, she told herself. She stood motionless for a long time, trying to find peace within herself, straining her senses to detect something, anything. That yielded no results, so eventually she abandoned her attempt to focus and let her mind drift. She remembered him, not as he had been when she had last seen him, but years before, a memory of a sunny day.

The air had been filled with the smell of summer grass and her skin was itchy from rolling down the gentle slope behind their secret home. It was hot but the occasional mountain breeze sent a shiver through her when it touched her sweat damp dress. Looking up she wondered at the size of her playmate. Her daddy was undoubtedly the tallest man in the world, or so it had seemed at the time.

Laughing she had held out her arms, wanting him to pick her up again, for the climb back up the hill. The roll down was always fun, but the trip back up on his shoulders was even better. *"Pick me up Daddy!"*

Something touched her then and she was shocked back to the present. Mentally she clutched at the presence but it slipped away like a ghost. *No! Come back!*

A guttural cry of frustration escaped her throat as she saw her hands once more covered by black scales, clawing at the stone. Moira's anger rose fresh and sudden and she gathered her will, wanting to destroy the cold rock that ignored her.

No, not like that!

It was Myra's voice, warning her to stop. She felt her spell-twin sliding into her, joining her and trying to soothe her rage. Soft hands covered her own and she felt as though she were staring into a mirror, her own face was before her, soft blue eyes staring back with compassion, or perhaps pity.

She didn't want to think about what Myra might be seeing in return.

He heard you!

Moira covered her face, *He pulled away. He saw what I've become.*

No, said Myra, *he barely knows himself. You have to show him. Remember for him, think of him, not of yourself. He will love you regardless.*

Moira sincerely doubted that.

Remember when Sterling died?

Sterling had been a massive tomcat that had lived with them when she was smaller. *Why?*

We asked him why...

Her father had been tucking her into bed that night, and he had been spending extra time talking to her while he did so. She remembered staring up at him, his face showing nothing but love. She had been crying.

"Everything dies eventually sweetheart, it's part of life, but he still loves us," he had said quietly.

"Why did he die?" she had asked.

"He was old. He lived a long and happy life, for a cat."

The answer hadn't been particularly satisfying, but she had accepted it. His hugs had been far more comforting than any amount of words. Her father had stayed with her for a long while after that, until her tears had dried and she had felt better. Then he had settled her in once more and stood to leave.

She had noticed his beard then, and wondered at all the white hairs in it. *"Why is your beard turning white?"*

Her father had laughed, *"I'm just getting old, that's all."* He hadn't been thinking carefully.

But Moira's mind had made the connection immediately, *"Old, like Sterling?"* Her eyes had begun watering already.

Her father began shaking his head, but it was too late.

"You're going to die?" It had been her first true realization that her parents were mortal and she had dissolved into tears once more. Her father had had to hold her for a long while after that.

"It will be a long, long time before I'm that old, sweetheart. Humans live much longer than cats," he had said, but what she remembered most was his arms around her, and the smell of his shirt.

She could almost feel them now.

She could definitely smell him. Startled, she opened her eyes. He was there, holding her. "Dad?"

He looked at her, confused, "Mm..." He gave up after a second.

Give him a while, he's still coming back to himself.

I know that! shot back Moira irritably. She squeezed her father tighter.

After a minute she started to disentangle herself. The hug had begun to get awkward, especially once she realized that her father's clothes hadn't returned with him.

Recognition had dawned in his features, though. "Moira?" he said hesitantly.

She nodded, looking at the ground. She was more embarrassed by what he might see in her eyes than she was of seeing his state of undress, but it was a good excuse. "I think you've lost your tunic," she commented.

"Tunic?" he mumbled, staring at himself. "Clothes! That's what I was trying to think of! I knew something was wrong." He took on a look of concentration before producing an illusion to cover himself, a large pointed leather hat paired with a rich grey doublet.

Moira put her face in her hands, stifling a laugh. Not only was the hat ridiculous, but he had neglected to add hose or trousers, much less shoes.

"Is something wrong?" he asked sincerely.

"You need something for the rest of you," she explained, fighting a smirk. The expression felt strange on her face, and only partly because it sent a throbbing pain through one half of it when she moved the muscles in that cheek.

He looked at his bare knees before returning to study her face, "No, not that, Moira; you seem different somehow. What's happened to you?" There was concern in his eyes.

Shock ran through her, like ice in her veins. *He knows!* He could see what she had become. She almost shielded herself, to hide her shame, but it was too late. A shield at this point would only arouse more suspicion. "Father, it's been an ordeal finding you..."

His hand touched her swollen cheek gently, "Who did this to you?" The words concealed a simmering anger.

Technically, it had been Gram's fist, but she knew better than to answer with his name. It had been Celior controlling him after all. Seeing her father's protectiveness made her feel both warm and sad. She loved him, but she knew, bone deep in her soul that he could no longer protect her. He was just a man, and for all his power he could no more guarantee her safety than anyone else could. The experiences of the past few days had ended her childhood. They had done more than that…

"The one that did it suffered far more than I did, I made certain of that," she told him with a certain hardness in her voice.

"Good," he said simply, searching her eyes. Whatever he saw in them must have satisfied him, for he turned away and started looking for the door out. "Sometimes force is justified, but cruelty always hurts you as much as it does them," he added in the dry tone he used when he lectured.

Moira grimaced, *If you only knew how much…*

Chapter 26

Above ground once more, they gathered in the street outside the remains of the Earl of Berlagen's house. None of them looked particularly good, other than Mordecai, having just emerged from his inhuman state he was in perfect condition, with the exception of his still missing trousers.

By comparison Gram was barely able to stand, despite Myra and later Celior's healing efforts. He had his armor back on, so his body wasn't visible, but his stance conveyed a sense of absolute exhaustion. Cassandra on the other hand, was fine physically, but the dragon's massive body was covered in dust and dirt. She was also not in a good mood. Moira's abrupt manner had set her teeth on edge.

Celior merely looked humiliated. He refused to meet Mordecai's gaze.

"You don't look very happy to see me," said Moira's father, his tone was matter-of-fact, making it difficult to tell if he was joking.

"I would be lying if I said otherwise," admitted the god of light.

"You thought you had me trapped," added Mort.

"You were."

"Hah! You didn't take into account my brilliant daughter." Mordecai winked at Moira to punctuate his declaration.

"Sir," interjected Gram, "would you like me to find something for you to wear?"

"Hmm? Oh! I forgot about that," said Mort. With a word he added some illusory trousers. Leaning close to Moira's ear he whispered, "Some people never change eh?"

His humor didn't quite reach her, nor did she have the energy to be embarrassed for him, but Moira pretended to smile anyway. "Father, there's some things you need to kn…"

"One second," said Mort, holding up a hand. "Does this weather feel natural to you?"

Moira couldn't 'feel' weather, not the way he could, but she knew the reason for his question, "No, I had to alter it during the battle for the city."

"Do we still need it like this?" he asked. "It really would rather be sunny today."

She sighed, "No, the fighting is over."

Letting out a long breath his eyes unfocused and his body seemed to waver, becoming momentarily insubstantial. High above the winds picked up and the clouds began rolling back, revealing the blue skies hidden above them. Soon the sun was shining once more and the air felt fresher.

"That's better," he said at last.

"Father…"

Mordecai frowned as a thought occurred to him, "How did you change the weather? Did you hear the wind?" His face showed a combination of worry and expectation simultaneously.

"No, I used Cassandra's strength. Listen, while you were away a lot happened…"

"You did it with plain wizardry? Don't you realize how dangerous that is?! I know you're strong, but think what might have…"

Moira lost her temper, "Dad! Would you shut up? I'm trying to tell you what happened!"

Gram winced, looking at the ground. Mordecai was almost a second father to him, but hearing Moira rebuke the Count made him profoundly uncomfortable.

Mort flinched at her tone, but he didn't argue. "You'll have to forgive me. My mind isn't focused as it should be. After joining the earth like that, well, my thoughts are very fuzzy."

She didn't feel good about lashing out at him, but irritation was all she had left to give, "There's been a battle, a big one. I wanted to free the city, but half the populace is dead now."

"Where are we?" he asked without thinking, but then he stared hard at her. "What did you say?"

"I killed half the city. This is Halam, in Dunbar."

"You freed half the city," corrected Gram. "The enemy is responsible for the deaths."

The Count's eyes flashed to Gram and then back to his daughter's. He knew the look in her eyes now and it made him want to weep for her, but he kept his composure. No one would be able to give her the forgiveness she needed, Moira would have to find that for herself. Rather than try, he decided to remain pragmatic, his words would mean more later. "And the King? I think his name is Darogen."

"He's dead," she said plainly.

Mort winced, "Did you…?"

Moira shook her head, "He was dead when I met him, his brain had been replaced by those metal things. His body still moved, his lips spoke, but there was nothing alive inside. I'm not sure where he is now."

"Metal things?"

She took a deep breath, there was obviously going to be a lot of catching up to do. "Like the ones on the floor in the cavern where I found you. They crawl in through people's mouths and control them like puppets." *But not nearly as well as I do.*

That bit of information led to a long explanation of what Moira and Gram had seen and experienced since arriving in Dunbar. Mordecai's mild bemusement changed to quiet attention and then to deeper consternation as they talked.

"What really has me puzzled is what makes them move," said Moira. "There's no life in them, no aythar, yet they move like living creatures and seem to possess intelligence."

"Awareness is a property of aythar," agreed her father, "without it they can't be conscious."

Celior had been silent throughout their conversation, but he chose that moment to speak up, "They are not from this world, they come from beyond. The rules you know do not apply."

"You named them 'ANSIS' before," said the Count. "What have they told you?"

"That they are here to purify this world, to perfect it for humanity," answered the Shining God.

"For humanity?" swore Gram. "My short time with one of them in my neck was the most terrifying experience of my life! Look at how many are dead because of them!"

Celior glanced around, noting the absence of bodies, living or dead.

"Outside the city," growled Gram. "They slaughtered half the city's citizens attempting to stop Moira from freeing them."

Celior nodded, "As the case may be, I think their goals are long term. When they spoke to me their interests were always about wizards. They don't fear losing, but they are looking for tools to use to eradicate magic and its users."

"Why would they help you then?" asked Moira. "You are nothing *but* magic."

"They seemed to base their decisions on pure rational thought. I was a means to an end. They planned to eliminate me as well, once I had served you and the remainder of the wizards to them. I have no doubt about that, for they didn't hide the fact."

Another thought occurred to her, "How did you change the key for your enchantment?"

"I explained how to do it to the ANSIS," he said wryly.

Mordecai frowned, "I whispered the key in your ear, how did they get it? You couldn't tell them the words, the enchantment precludes that."

"They have very good hearing."

"There was no one else in that cave with us," insisted the Count.

Celior smiled, "They were there, in pieces you might say. I don't understand them at all, but I can tell you that they can spread their bodies out in any way imaginable." He paused, thinking for a second, "No, perhaps bodies is the wrong word, their 'parts' might be more correct. They had tiny ears in that cave, along with the weapon that nearly killed you."

"Sounds like the shiggreth," muttered Mordecai. "Cut off their hands and they still move. You're saying these things can cut off their ears and use them to listen?"

"No," said Celior. "They create ears from metal. They create eyes, and weapons, they create those things that they use to control people, but they are none of those things. They're like a hidden spirit that controls all of them. Everything else is nothing but a collection of tools to them."

"But there is no spirit in them," said Moira emphatically. "There is no aythar."

"And yet they communicate with each other," noted Gram. "When Alyssa and I were being controlled it was clear that the parasites in each of us were coordinating with one another. They collected information from our eyes and ears and what one knew, all of them knew."

Moira remembered her impression of them during the battle, of a vast intelligence that lay behind the actions of all the parasites controlling the city, "I felt it during the battle. When I was trying to free the citizens. I had a thousand pairs of hands and eyes and ears, and yet they knew as much as I did about every move during the city fighting."

Her father's eyes narrowed, focusing on her for a moment, "What did you say?"

She blanched under his gaze. What she had done to free the city was not something she wanted to discuss, but Moira had known it would come out eventually. She had planned to divert his questions, to downplay the nature of what she had done. "I would rather explain privately, Father. I had to make some tough choices."

Gram looked away, uncomfortable but unwilling to share his own perspective on what had happened to her. Mordecai needed to know what Myra had told him, but he didn't dare try to speak about it in front of her. He was afraid even to think about it. *If she can hear my thoughts...*

He could only hope the armor really did shield his mind from her.

Mordecai watched his daughter silently and as his scrutiny drew out longer she found herself growing angry. *As if he has any right to judge. I shouldn't even have to explain myself.* For a moment an idle impulse crossed her mind as she looked at him—she wondered how difficult it would be to adjust his thinking. Wizard's minds were supposedly very hard to influence, but after her experiences she thought it might be possible.

She was shocked when she realized the direction her thinking had gone; shocked and ashamed. Reflexively she looked at her hand. It was still normal, but in her imagination she saw again the claws. *What's happening to me?*

"We can talk about it later," said her father. "For now there seem to be more pressing matters." His tone was reassuring but Moira knew he wouldn't forget.

"The others are waiting for us outside the city," she suggested.

"I'd like one of them to study before we leave," said Mordecai.

"There seemed to be no end of them down there," remarked Gram, nodding toward the ruined house.

"Just what I was thinking," agreed the Count. "One moment." He began picking his way carefully back through the wreckage. Soon he was lost to sight but Moira's magesight followed him as he went back down. In the places where the stairs had been ruined her father flew, making the act look easy.

Most wizards didn't fly, not without an aid or device of some kind, it was a delicate art that could easily result in death or serious injury, but Mordecai had mastered it during his year as an undead immortal.

When he returned a few minutes later he carried a heavy iron cube. It was approximately a foot on each side and hollow. There was no opening, no hinge or lid, but one of the metal parasites was inside. Moira knew without asking that he had had the earth construct the container around his captured prize.

She also noted that he wasn't actually carrying it with his arms, he was using his magic to levitate the cube, his hands were merely guiding it as he walked. The iron sides of his box were at least an inch thick, which made the box very cumbrous.

Gram had very traditional notions about his role in the Illeniel household. "Let me carry that for you, my lord," he offered at once.

Moira opened her mouth to warn him but her father winked at her before handing the box over, "Thank you, Gram." Naturally he stopped supporting its weight with his power at the same time.

The young man's chest tightened and he grunted a bit as his arms and shoulders stiffened under the unexpectedly large load. The box weighed at least as much as a grown man, if one could be squeezed into such a small space.

Mordecai's face fell as Gram took the burden without complaint. "You're stouter than you look, son," he commented, "and that's saying something."

"Actually, it's 'Sir Gram' now, Father," corrected Moira. "Mother knighted him for saving Irene."

The Count gave Gram a serious look, "There's a story there, I'm sure. I'll want to hear the rest of it later. Dorian would be proud." His eyes were watching the young man's arms and shoulders, noting the ease with which he managed the weight. He looked askance at Moira. Obviously, he was wondering if Gram had somehow been given the earthbond.

"Dragons, Father," she said, answering his unspoken question, "and his sword."

Mordecai nodded at Cassandra, "I thought perhaps she was yours."

"I am," rumbled the dragon, "but Grace is bonded to him."

"Grace? Your little bear?"

"She isn't so small anymore," said Moira. She made a brief explanation but she could see her father's eyes continually straying to stare at Gram's sword while she spoke.

"Is that Thorn?" he asked, looking puzzled. "What's happened to it? That's not the enchantment I put on it..."

Gram grinned, "Matthew made some improvements." He demonstrated by making the sword shift forms, from great sword to one hander and shield.

The Count's eyes widened as Thorn flew apart and reassembled with extra pieces of metal appearing from empty air to complete the shield. "That's marvelous! And your armor, did he do that as well? Where is the metal coming from? I don't recognize the magic at all."

"The armor is part of the sword's enchantment," said Gram. "I don't understand how it works, of course. Matthew calls it 'translation'."

Mordecai nodded, "That was the trans-dimensional magic he was working on. He showed me a pouch he designed a while back with it." He shook his head, "My son has surpassed me."

Moira felt a pang of envy. *Meanwhile your daughter has become a monster.* She tried to suppress the dark feelings welling from her heart as she changed the subject, "We should rejoin the others."

Her father nodded again, "You're right. Let me clean this up first. This building still holds many more of those creatures." He turned to face the rubble that remained of the Earl of Berlagen's once beautiful city home. Closing his eyes he grew silent.

Moira didn't sense any aythar moving, but her magesight felt the movement beneath them. The earth was shifting and hot magma was moving upward, summoned from deep below. Halam wasn't located near any active volcanoes, but that apparently didn't matter. The molten rock came at her father's silent command.

The air grew hot as it bubbled up, swallowing the collapsed stone walls and causing the timbers scattered within the wreckage to burst into flames. Smoke and ash billowed forth and yet the fire that rose with it didn't spread. Minutes passed and then the lava subsided. The ruins would likely continue to smoke for days but she could sense that the magma beneath them had stopped moving and begun to subside.

She and Gram rode Cassandra, but Mordecai elected to fly on his own beside them. He seemed to enjoy it, looping around them through the air effortlessly, moving as gracefully through the air as a dolphin might in its native seas.

His manner grew somber once they passed beyond the city and flew over the bloodied plain; his flight lost all trace of its former playfulness as he saw the thousands lying dead below. Gerold and Alyssa waved to them, they had been exploring, searching the faces of the dead. Moira didn't see Chad, but her magesight found him easily enough, sitting where they had left him. He appeared to be fiddling with the arrows he had recovered, probably seeing which ones were worth salvaging and which were beyond repair.

Cassandra landed near the Baron and Alyssa, taking care not to step on the bodies, although there were so many it was difficult. Mordecai drifted down to a spot beside Alyssa.

She dipped her head respectfully, curtsying briefly when she recognized the Count, "Your Excellency, it is good to see you are well and in good health."

Gerold looked on with curiosity, "Count?"

Alyssa responded, "This is Moira's father, the Count di'Cameron."

The Baron's face blanched with shock and he hastily dipped his head and gave a quarter bow, precisely the correct show of deference to show a senior member of a foreign peerage, "It is good to make your acquaintance, Your Lordship. I could wish that we had met under more favorable circumstances." He gave Alyssa a meaningful glance.

"Oh!" she said, remembering her manners. "Your Excellency, allow me to introduce his Lordship, the Baron Ingerhold of Dunbar."

Mordecai smiled mildly, "Thank you, Alyssa." There were even more questions in his eyes as he looked at her. He had last seen her in Castle Cameron, before her abrupt departure, and he had yet to learn of her other transgressions.

Gram moved to stand protectively beside her, his posture making it clear that whatever had passed between them, he had accepted her return.

The Count made silent note of Gram's stance as he addressed Gerold formally, "I am happy to meet you, Baron Ingerhold. I also wish it could have been during better times. Allow me to extend Lothion's sympathies for what has obviously been a very trying time for your countrymen."

"Thank you, Your Excellency," said Gerold. "Despite the tragedy, I must tell you that your daughter's actions saved a great many people today. These deaths are the responsibility of the strange creatures that lately attempted to gain control of my country."

"Please, call me Mordecai," said the Count. "If it is permissible, I would extend whatever aid to your people that we can. Lothion has long desired to improve its relationship with Dunbar. Though these are trying times, perhaps we can make some good come of this."

"Call me Gerold then," agreed the Baron, "and I will consider it an honor. Do you speak for the Queen of Lothion?"

Mordecai shook his head, "I do not, but I know her well. I am certain that once she learns what has transpired here she will wish to do everything possible to give aid to your people."

Gerold nodded, "I would that I had the power to accept your offer, but my king is dead. I will have to confer with my peers."

"Gerold!" said Moira menacingly. "You should consider your position more carefully."

Her father looked askance at her, "Don't be rude. Is there something we should know?"

"Gerold has shown himself to be a champion of his people," she said confidently. "They will clamor for him to take the throne."

"They appear to be sleeping at the moment," said Mort, noting the living but unconscious people scattered among the dead.

"I am not in line for the throne," added Gerold.

"Father," interjected Moira, "This is something we should talk about privately."

"There seems to be a lot of that," noted Mordecai. "Let's go home. We can discuss it there and start organizing some help for these people. I'm sure Penny is worried about us too."

The baron was surprised, "It will take weeks to get to Lothion." He glanced at Cassandra then, rethinking his statement, "Or days at least."

"On dragon-back—probably, although I think I could do better than that. Either way, flying won't be necessary," said Mordecai. Turning to Moira he asked, "Have you already set up a circle, or do we need to make one?"

Moira looked away, embarrassed, she had known this question was coming, "I haven't made one."

Her father nodded, "Well, no better time than now. I'd suggest making one that links to the large circle in the castle courtyard so we can move more people, plus we can make a large one for the return to bring supplies and such."

She had been hoping he would make it. "Actually, I don't remember the key for it."

Mort frowned, "I had you memorize it."

"I forgot." Moira's ears were burning and her anger began to return.

"I've told you how important it is to learn them. If you had forgotten it, you should have refreshed your memory before making a trip so far from home. What did you plan to do if there was an emergency...?"

Her eyes were on one of the corpses nearby. If she had known the circle keys she could have returned home at any point, and come back with help. She wouldn't have had to work alone, or done some of the things she had done. A lot of people might not have died. "There was an emergency, *Father*," she replied bitterly. "I did the best I could. Perhaps you'd rather I..."

No! Moira stop, don't!

That was Myra, warning her to mind her tongue once again. She had been about to suggest she could have left her father in the stone if he didn't like her solution. Despite the advice, she struggled to contain her temper.

Mordecai's face softened, "Forgive me. You've been through a lot. I'll make the circle, but I want you to watch." He began walking, looking for a sheltered place to create the sizeable teleportation circle.

CHAPTER 27

When Moira and her father reappeared they were standing in what had come to be known as the 'transfer house'. It was a large barn-like structure in the courtyard of Castle Cameron, built to house the various teleportation circles. They had learned during a prior war that keeping them in the castle proper was a bad idea, since a magically gifted enemy that discovered the keys to one of them, or found a working circle that connected to one of them, would then have access to their stronghold.

Given the risk, the transfer house was guarded around the clock.

She couldn't remember the full name of the man that peered at them in astonishment, but she knew his first name was Doug.

"My Lord!" shouted the guardsman as recognition appeared on his features. Before either of them could react he ducked out the door and shouted at the guard stationed there, "Jerod! The Count and Moira have returned, run and tell the Countess!" At no point did his voice drop below what could reasonably considered 'bellowing'.

"Shit," said her father, smiling at her. "You know what will happen now."

Moira wasn't really sure on that count. She and her brother had left under cover of darkness, and while she had been there when her father had returned from his year as a monster, she had no idea whether her mother would be angry or relieved when she saw her. *Probably both,* she thought.

"Matthew and I left without telling her," she informed her father.

Mort raised one brow, "Oh. This will be very interesting." He took her hand and led her out into the waning daylight.

Claude, the chief cook for the castle stood outside beside Doug, watching them expectantly as they emerged. The heavy basket he carried meant he had probably been collecting herbs for the kitchen. "My lord!" he exclaimed every bit as loudly as Doug had a moment before, dipping his head in a rare gesture of fealty. Mordecai normally forbade the inhabitants from bowing and curtsying on a daily basis, but long absences were different. "Lady Moira," added the cook a second later.

The Count patted both the cook and the guardsman on the back affectionately before leading Moira on. He glanced over his shoulder apologetically, "I'd better get inside. I'll try to catch everyone up later."

They didn't make it to the main door to the keep before it flew open hard enough that Moira wondered that the hinges hadn't torn free. Penelope Illeniel, the Countess di'Cameron, came rushing at them as though she meant to run them over. "Mort! Moira!" she shouted, her voice finding a volume that put even Doug's previous call to shame.

She charged into Mordecai at a speed that should have thrown him to the ground, especially considering the armor she wore, but Moira noted that her father had used his magic to brace himself before she slammed into him.

It was clear she wanted to hold onto her husband longer, but Penny tore herself free almost immediately and turned to her daughter, clutching her with an urgency that brought tears to her father's face. A second later she pushed her away as well, running her hands over Moira's head, shoulders, and arms, desperately searching to make sure she was still whole.

"Where have you been? Do you know how I've worried? How could you sneak off like that!?" the questions emerged in rapid-fire fashion, too fast to follow.

"I'm fine, Mother," said Moira, wanting to reassure her, but when she saw Penny's face her guilt redoubled. The Countess's eyes were red and brimming with tears, even her shoulders were trembling with shock and relief.

"Why didn't you send word? I could kill you! Where's your brother?!"

It was Moira's turn to look surprised. She had been gone for more than three weeks. She had assumed that Matthew had returned long before then. "I thought he would be back already," she stammered.

Her mother's face twisted in an expression of renewed grief, "And Gram? What of Chad Grayson? Are they with him? Where did he go?"

"They're both back in Halam," said Moira lamely.

"He's alone!?" It was an accusation as much as a question.

"He had his dragon with him," Moira said, trying to explain. "We found the place where they captured Father. He wanted to investigate it further. He was supposed to come home after that—to tell you where we were going."

Mordecai put his arms around her mother, "Now, now, don't fret Dear. We'll find him tomorrow. I'll set out in the morning…"

343

The Countess thrust him back, slapping at a face he had already shielded, "No! I'm never letting the two of you out of my sight again! Do you have any idea what I've been through? Losing my husband twice, and this time two of my children as well?! I thought you were dead! Again! No one should suffer that—not twice!"

A throng of servants and other castle inhabitants had gathered around them by then, along with Rose Hightower. Lady Hightower made her way to them quickly, "Where is Gram? Is my son with you?" She was as close to shouting as Moira had ever heard, although she managed to keep her voice barely within the realm of a civilized volume.

Mordecai looked over Penny's head, trying to give her a reassuring look, "He's fine Rose. We left him in Dunbar, but he is in good health. You can see him tomorrow."

"Why didn't he come back with you?" asked Rose.

"Things were a bit chaotic. He's protecting the casualties of a sudden conflict, but the danger has passed," explained the Count. "He even found that girl, Alyssa. She was with him."

"The assassin?!" Rose's voice was ascending into a pitch that in a lesser woman might have denoted outright panic.

"Assassin?" said Mort, puzzled.

Moira tapped him on the shoulder, "That's something else I need to talk to you about."

Penny turned Moira around, pulling at her shoulder with irresistible strength, "What did your father mean by 'a sudden conflict'?"

She caught her father's eye as he muttered quietly, "Shit."

It was many hours before Moira finally found peace again. The explanations took forever, and as soon as they were done they had to be repeated for those who hadn't heard the first time, or understood. She wasn't sure who got the worst of it, her, or her father. He, at least, wasn't guilty of sneaking off unannounced, but returning from being presumably dead (for a second time), did put a lot of attention on him.

Moira on the other hand got an extra helping of unwanted scrutiny from her mother. She struggled to keep her irritation under control and she kept having thoughts of simply adjusting her mother's level of curiosity rather than endure the endless questioning.

Her father glanced at her during one of those moments, perhaps sensing the sudden tensing of her aythar, as she unconsciously prepared to do something. She forced herself to relax and give him a weary smile when that happened.

Once they got back to their hideaway home in the mountains she faced a new onslaught of questions from Irene and Conall. They seemed terribly curious about her adventures. Matthew's absence bothered them, but once they knew she was as ignorant as they were on that matter they focused on what *she* had been doing.

Just murdering half a city, she was tempted to blurt out at one point, but she knew better. Myra had also given her an additional warning to watch her words.

When she finally climbed into bed she was certain that exhaustion would bring her sleep immediately, but that turned out not to be the case. Her mind began replaying the events of the day, particularly the questions, her answers, and what she might have said instead.

Her magesight explored the house idly, so she knew that her parents were sitting up in bed, likely discussing her return. That piqued her own curiosity.

Using a tiny amount of aythar she stealthily crafted a tiny creature, one that she had made many times before, usually to spy on her brother. Once it was finished she sent her tiny man to creep down the hall and listen at her parent's door, maintaining a fine link to it so that she could hear through its ears.

Soon enough she heard her mother's voice, "I'll never forgive myself if he doesn't come back."

"It wasn't your fault," replied her father consolingly.

"Of course it's my fault!" replied Penny bitterly. "I was in charge. I raised him. I was *here*!"

"We can't control them forever," said Mordecai. "Try as we might, they will eventually escape us to go out and make their own mistakes."

"He could be dead, lying cold on a mountainside somewhere."

Was she crying? Moira thought her voice sounded different.

"He has a dragon with him, and he's as powerful a wizard as I've ever met. He might be better than me. I'll find him tomorrow," countered Mordecai.

"He isn't an archmage," said her mother. "You told me that yourself. You can do things he can't."

"That's not always a blessing, and he's a better enchanter than I am. You should see what he's done to Dorian's sword. It was a crafting beyond anything I've ever imagined."

"Well he hasn't come back, so what good has it done him?" responded Penny.

"I don't know, dear, but I *will* find our boy."

"*We* will find him. I'm not letting you out of my sight, not again, not ever," she growled.

"Moira will need to return to Dunbar tomorrow. There's much to be sorted out there. Which one of us do you plan to go with?" asked her father in a reasonable tone that Moira thought he should have known better than to attempt.

"Dunbar can go hang!" spat Penny savagely. "They've done enough to us already."

"Gram is still there," Mordecai reminded her. "They will need your guidance. Someone with authority to speak for Cameron should be there with them."

"Then we'll all go…"

"Do you really want me to wait before tracking him down?"

"Godsdamn you, Mort!"

Her father chuckled, "They've tried, many times."

"This isn't a joke! Do I look amused to you?"

"No, but there's something else I want to talk to you about."

Her mother's voice grew wary, "What now?"

"How did Moira look to you?" he asked her.

He suspects! thought Moira. She sat upright in bed, as though that might help increase her ability to hear.

With her magesight she saw her father's head turning and she felt a faint pulse. He was examining the area as well. *He noticed me sitting up, or did he spot my eavesdropper?* She lay down once more, hoping that would ease his suspicion.

A privacy shield rose around the two of them and Moira could no longer see them, nor could her helper hear what they were saying. She clenched the sheets in her fists in frustration. Surely he didn't know, he couldn't possibly, but what were they talking about?

It was hard sleeping after that, but exhaustion eventually took her away.

CHAPTER 28

"We found King Darogen's body."

That was Chad Greyson, telling her mother what had transpired before their arrival.

"It was one of the creepiest things I ever saw," continued the ranger. "The flesh was gray-blue, he'd been dead a while, but when I turned him over they started crawling out the side of his face. He was full of 'em."

"Did you kill them?" broke in Moira.

"Yeah," he nodded, avoiding making eye contact with her. He had been uncomfortable around her since her return.

"You think they could attach themselves to other people?" asked the Countess.

Chad shrugged, but Moira was firm in her response, "We don't know, but we should assume the worst."

Penny pursed her lips, concerned. "How many do you think might be loose?"

"No way to know," said Chad. "There was at least one per person on this field, whether living or dead."

"I destroyed the ones removed from the living, but I can't vouch for those killed during the battle by those strange weapons," Moira told them. "Plus there were more in Earl Berlagen's home. Father destroyed those, but it's likely there were more hidden in the city."

The Countess sighed, "It's like the shiggreth all over again. We don't know how many there are, or where they might be, or who they might be in…"

Gram coughed and Penny glanced at him, "Yes, Sir Gram, do you have something to add?"

"At least the people are well acquainted with them. They are no secret now. The Baron has had all the able bodied keeping watch over those still unconscious, making sure they are kept safe. They've caught several of the little monsters already, trying to creep into people's mouths."

Penny nodded, then addressed Moira, "I should like to meet your baron."

"He isn't *my* baron, Mother, but he did help save the city," Moira replied emphatically.

"So everyone keeps telling me," said Penny dryly. "Everyone that's awakened has had a similar story, but from what your father and Gram have told me he did little more than protect you from the king, and unsuccessfully at that."

Adrenaline shot through Moira and her heartbeat accelerated, but Myra cautioned her, *Avoid the implication, speak of Gerold. Don't let your emotions get the better of you.*

"He's a good man, with a kind and generous heart. I'm happy to give him most of the credit if it will help his people find direction in this chaos," said Moira calmly.

"Where is he now?" asked the Countess.

"In the city," volunteered Gram. "The palace was a shambles so he's organizing the survivors at a place called the Dusty Doxy."

"Dusty Doxy?"

"A tavern," explained Chad. "The owner survived and hid in the cellars with a group of other citizens who were lucky enough to still be free of the parasites when everything went to hell."

An hour later they stepped through the doors. A crowd of people turned to look at them, making note of the foreign livery of the Countess' soldiers. Gram stood tall enough to look over their heads. He waved when he spotted Gerold, who made his way to them and cleared a path through the main room so they could find a quieter place near one wall.

"Countess, I am pleased to make your acquaintance," he said once they could hear one another.

Moira gestured to him, "Mother, this is Gerold, the Baron of Ingerhold."

"Well met, Your Excellency," responded Penny, offering her hand to him. Her eyes fell on the older gentleman that stood beside him.

Gerold brushed his lips across her knuckles before gesturing toward his balding companion, "May I also introduce my friend to you, Your Excellency? This is His Grace, Lord Anselm, Archduke of Weltonbury and first in line to succeed our late king."

Once the formalities were done Penny explained her position and offered whatever aid Cameron could provide. The archduke was the first to respond, "Your sentiments are appreciated, but I think Dunbar will be fine in most regards, once the chaos here has been sorted out. There is food aplenty, too much in fact, now that half of Halam has been lost. The Baron and I were just discussing the matter. I fear much of what we have may spoil before it is used."

"My husband and I would still like to help in whatever way we can. Perhaps your surplus could be sold? You will need extra coin I am sure," replied the Countess.

Gerold sighed, "The demand won't support it. Our surfeit will overwhelm the markets here. The biggest problem will be dealing with the dead. It would take weeks to bury them all and even if we burn them we don't have enough hands to manage it. Disease will be an issue if the bodies start to rot before we do something."

"I think we can help with both problems," said Penny. "My husband has long desired to connect his World Road to Dunbar, to facilitate trade. While that will take too long for this purpose, he can certainly help transport your goods to Lothion to sell at the markets there. We would also be happy to lend you our men to aid in cremating the dead."

As they spoke Moira studied the archduke. He was a middle aged man with a growing paunch and bushy eyebrows. More important than that however, was the fact that she was certain he hadn't been among the people she had freed, which meant he hadn't had his memories adjusted. That, plus the fact that he was first in line of succession, could spell trouble for her plan to put Gerold on the throne.

With hardly a thought she sent a fine line of aythar out, touching Anselm's aythar and making him feel unwell.

The older nobleman's face paled and his hands began to shake. "Pardon me, my lady, I think I may need to sit down," he told the Countess.

Moira stepped forward, concern written in her features, "Let me help you, my lord." She took his arm and spoke to the others, "I'll help His Grace find a seat and fetch him something to drink."

Her mother and Gerold were just getting into the meat of their discussion, so they both nodded and let them go, intent on their conversation. Soon enough Moira had the nobleman all to herself.

She wasted no time. After prevailing on the barman to pour a tall beer for him she asked about his experience during the recent disaster.

"I was spared the worst of it," he told her. Anselm's hands were steadier now. "I was lucky enough not to have been infected by those metal creatures beforehand and I had stopped here when everything began. The mistress of the house, Tamara I believe her name is, sheltered us beneath the taproom."

"So you didn't see any of the battle outside the walls?" Moira asked him.

"Nor most of what happened within them either," admitted the archduke.

"You must be very proud of Baron Ingerhold," she told him. "He was very brave."

Anselm frowned, "Gerold has always been a good man, but I find the tales to be strangely lacking in substance."

"How so?"

"I have met dozens who claim to have seen his actions, but no one that actually remembers being helped. The stories are very vague and it worries me how many have openly suggested he should be crowned king in Darogen's place," said the archduke.

That was enough, Moira caught his mind in a grip of iron. The old man's face went slack as she searched his memories. It didn't take long to see that he had no intention of surrendering his place in favor of the Baron. She smiled, *We can fix that easily enough.*

When she helped him up a few minutes later he was a changed man. She began escorting him back to the others.

"Lady Moira?"

Moira realized the woman standing behind her and to one side, was Tamara, the owner of the tavern. "It's you!" she exclaimed, feigning happiness. "Thank goodness you weathered the storm unharmed."

Tamara curtsied when she saw Anselm turn toward her, "Your Grace."

"No need for that," he told her. "I am in your debt. I surely would have died if not for your aid."

"Your Grace, would you mind if I took a minute to catch up with Tamara?" asked Moira.

"Not at all," he responded. "I'm feeling much better. I need to finish talking to your lady mother." He moved away with confidence in his stride.

"Was he alright?" asked Tamara after he had gone.

Moira raised her brows, "What do you mean?"

"He was just staring into space when I spotted you. I thought something might have happened," said the red-haired woman.

"Oh he's fine, just a dizzy spell I suppose. Who can tell with old men?" said Moira. "Tell me how things went for you yesterday. You must have been terribly frightened."

"It was the most bizarre day I have ever seen," said Tamara nodding.

Moira agreed, "It was a nightmare." She noticed her mother's eyes on her then, but Penny looked away when she glanced over. *How long was she watching me?*

It shouldn't matter, she hadn't done anything visibly strange, but she worried anyway. *What did Dad tell her last night?*

It was late afternoon and they were preparing to return home. Penny had spent the day making arrangements and directing the men with her as to their duties for the morrow. They would be returning with her the next day with a larger contingent of men tasked with assisting the people of Halam in dealing with their scattered dead.

"Before we go I have one more thing to take care," Penny told her daughter, and then she addressed Gram. "Where is Alyssa?"

He tensed, "I believe she is with Grace."

Grace had finally awoken the previous evening, but she was still recovering. Alyssa had stayed with the smaller dragon as a precaution.

"Take me to her," ordered the Countess.

Gram nodded, "Yes, Your Excellency."

Since they were already at the teleportation circle they didn't have far to go. Grace was resting in the barn of a small farmhouse less than a quarter of a mile from there. The owner of the farm hadn't appeared, so they weren't certain if the man or his family were dead or merely fled.

Chad Grayson and Alyssa were engaged in conversation when Moira and Penny entered. Gram followed close behind them, worry written on his face.

"My lady," said the hunter, dipping his head. Alyssa kept her eyes on the ground.

The Countess acknowledged him but her attention was firmly on the young woman. She waved at the open barn door and the three guardsmen that had accompanied them filed in, moving to the sides. "Alyssa, or whatever your name properly is, you are under arrest for murder, kidnapping, and the assault of my guardsmen. You will surrender yourself to my men and accompany us to Castle Cameron, there to stand trial for your crimes." There was steel in her voice.

"Yes, Your Exce…"

"Hold on!" interrupted Gram, moving to stand between his liege and his lover. "There's more to this than what you've heard."

Penny's eyes were cold. "That will be seen during the trial. Stand aside, Sir Gram."

"She didn't want to be there. You don't have to do this," he answered, stubbornly keeping his place.

"Lilly Tucker is dead. My daughter was kidnapped. The trial will determine her responsibility in this matter. Now step aside Gram, unless you are thinking of violating your oath."

"Mother, please, it doesn't have to be like this," said Moira. Her mother looked calm, but Moira's magesight could sense the tension in her muscles. Penny's hand rested lightly beside her sword hilt, ready for violence.

One of the guards stepped forward, pulling a pair of iron manacles from a heavy leather sack he had been carrying. *I should have noticed those,* thought Moira, but it hadn't occurred to her to examine the guardsmen earlier.

"No!" said Gram, waving a hand at the man. "Step back." He had a desperate glint in his eye.

Chad's hand was on his long knife, "Think about what ye're doin' Gram. Ye'll only make things worse."

The moment teetered on a dangerous edge until Alyssa stepped past Gram, holding her wrists out to the guard with the manacles. "Let them take me, Gram. I must answer for what I've done," she said sincerely.

The tension went out of his stance and Gram's head bowed.

"Take her to the circle," commanded the Countess. Still as stone, she watched the guards lead Alyssa out. Gram followed and Chad behind him, watching his young friend in case he had any more thoughts of rebellion.

Penny started to move, but Moira spoke, quiet fury in her voice, "That wasn't necessary, *Mother.*"

"It was entirely necessary," said Penelope, unfazed.

The cold dismissal sent fire running through Moira's veins. "He's in love with her. Are you trying to drive Gram away? What do you think he will do if he's forced to choose between her and his loyalty to our house?" As much as she would rather Gram wasn't in love with Alyssa, Moira didn't want to see him do something stupid.

Penny turned, facing her daughter with one brow arched, "You'll understand better when this is over. These things don't go away. The matter needs to be handled sooner rather than later or it will become a festering wound."

"She took two arrows protecting Rennie! Isn't that enough?"

"Lilly Tucker is dead," said Penny. "Do you think he can just bring her home and marry her? What about her brother, Peter? What about her fiancée? Do you think they will forget? What about everyone else living in Castle Cameron, or the town of Washbrook? Should we be allowed to ignore someone's crimes if they're inconvenient for us? Is she above the law simply because *Sir Gram* happens to be in love with her?"

Moira wanted to slap the superior expression from her mother's smug face. "So you'd rather what—hang her?! Do you think Gram will thank you for that? He won't stand for it. You'll lose him, and what about Lady Hightower? How will she feel when he takes her and turns outlaw?"

Her mother drew a deep breath in before exhaling slowly, "Do you remember when your father faced trial in Albamarl?"

Moira frowned, wondering where she was heading. She nodded.

"I felt as you did then, or perhaps as Gram does now. I knew your father was blameless. A lot of people died, but he wasn't directly responsible, and if he hadn't done what he did things would have been much worse. He saved the world, and yet they drug him up before their grubby little court, and they judged him. The men that decided his fate had done nothing to save us from the catastrophe, but they presumed to mete justice to the man who had saved us all.

"I was furious, and I tried to convince your father to run away with me, to take you and your brothers and sister and run far, far away. But he wouldn't do it. He had the power, they couldn't have touched him if he hadn't allowed it, but he refused to run. Gram's mother represented him, and she could have gotten him off on a technicality, but he wouldn't allow that either. Instead, he accepted the charges, and when they decided to humiliate him, *to whip him like some dog,* he bent his head and took it.

"Have you ever wondered why?" asked Penny.

Moira had heard most of this before, but she had never thought it was fair. She knew what her father's answer had been, "He said that the people had to see that justice applied to the powerful as much as it did to the weak, but Alyssa isn't a wizard. She isn't a lord of the realm. Her punishment will prove nothing."

"She has a powerful lover, and *you* are her friend, and she did commit several very serious crimes," argued Penny. "You think I'm trying to drive Gram away? I'm trying to *save* him. If he's ever going to live peacefully with that girl she has to face the consequences of her actions, in court, otherwise the people will never be satisfied. If she doesn't, he'll take her and run eventually anyway. This is their only chance."

Her heartbeat slowed as confusion replaced her anger. She had been a hair's breadth from attempting to change her mother's mind forcefully. Moira stared at Penny, thinking carefully before asking, "What are you saying exactly?"

"That your father was right. If they had actually tried to execute him, perhaps he would have fled with me then, but he was determined to give the people justice."

"But it wasn't *just!*" exclaimed Moira. "He didn't deserve that."

"True justice is an illusion, but it's necessary for a civil society to exist. He understood that, even then, and more importantly, he knew that for us to live as we do today, the people needed to feel that he had paid for the crimes they felt he had done. I'll say it once more, he was *right.* And the same is true now. If Alyssa and Gram are to ever have a chance at living a normal life as man and wife, then the people harmed by her actions must feel that justice has been done." The Countess paused for a moment then before adding, "Don't tell your father I said that."

"Said what?"

"That he was right. The man would be insufferable if he ever heard me admit it."

CHAPTER 29

Moira Centyr, the woman who had lived in the heart of the earth for more than a thousand years, sat in a comfortable chair, watching the man who had raised her daughter. Technically speaking, she wasn't the original Moira Centyr, but rather an artificial copy, a spell-twin made in a moment of desperation before the first Moira had gone to her final battle with the Dark God, Balinthor.

The difference was academic at this point, though. She had a living human body now, thanks to her husband, Gareth Gaelyn, and while she didn't possess the living source that most people were born with, she had been given enough aythar to last any normal person a hundred lifetimes.

The man who had taken that power from the gods and shared it with her sat across a low table from her, a pensive look on his face. "You aren't saying much," he said, hoping to break her silence.

She opened her mouth, and then closed it again. What could she say? The story he had just finished relaying to her was new in some ways, and depressingly familiar in others. It was her fault. Her only reason for existing had been to protect the life of her creator's child, her child, and she had failed. *Why didn't I tell her more, sooner?*

To speak the truth would be to sign her daughter's death warrant, to conceal it would be to risk the lives of countless others.

"I have done you a great disservice," she said at last. "I waited too long, and now your daughter, my child, will pay the price for my error."

Mordecai frowned, "I was hoping you would have something a bit more positive."

A wave of despair swept over her and she fought the urge to pull at her own hair. Her frustration was so great she wanted to run screaming from the room. The former lady of stone had a sudden vision of throwing herself from the tallest tower in the castle, not that it would have helped. She couldn't die without permission. "I have nothing good to offer," she told him. "I neglected to warn you properly, to warn *her* properly, and now the seeds of my negligence have borne their wicked fruit."

"That's very poetic, but I thought perhaps you could tell me something more practical, such as, 'give her some honey at bedtime, she'll be fine in the morning'," he replied sarcastically.

She shook her head, "No, there's nothing so simple as that, and nothing more complicated either. She has unwittingly crossed a line, and now the curse of the Centyr family will fall squarely on her shoulders. Our daughter is doomed."

Mort raised one brow, "Doomed?" He had heard that before, and it was a phrase that he had grown to despise. "Do you know how many times I have been told that? Yet, still, I am here. I don't want to hear dramatic phrases; I want to know what's going on with my girl so we can figure out how to help her."

"She is becoming a demon."

Mort rubbed his face, "See, that is exactly what I'm talking about. Could you try to explain without all the descriptive rubbish? There are no demons, unless you count the gods we so recently deposed."

"My family called them 'reavers' back when there were more of us. She has broken two of our most fundamental rules."

"Obviously she did something strange to accomplish what she did," agreed Mordecai. "I have never heard of a wizard controlling thousands of people at once, but I don't know that I would use a term like 'reaver'. She didn't really hurt them, at least not directly."

"I haven't examined them myself, but I assure you that she must have damaged some of them. That isn't the issue, however, unless we're discussing the morality of it," said Moira.

"Weren't we?"

She shook her head, "No. There is definitely a moral problem here, but more important than that, at least for us, is the fact that she has damaged herself. You described to me the impatience and anger that you sensed in her, the changes in her personality. Those are significant markers for the decay of her inner balance. Her mind has been warped and it will only continue to worsen."

"I think perhaps you've read too much into what I said earlier…"

"No, Mordecai, let me explain," interrupted Moira Centyr. "Much like in the physics you love so much, every action of the mind has a reaction, a consequence. When a Centyr mage bends the will of another human being it also exerts a force upon their own mind, twisting its shape. Your daughter has altered the minds and memories of not just one or two, but *thousands* of people. The inevitable result is that she has distorted her own reality. What lies inside her now is not the child you raised."

While her words made perfect sense to him, Mordecai had his own opinion. He knew better than most how violence and hard choices marked the soul, but he didn't believe for a moment that his daughter was beyond saving. "I can't accept that. As far as I can tell, she didn't do most of it directly, these 'spell-twins' that she created did."

Moira nodded, "And that is the other part of the problem. Mind cloning is also forbidden."

"Yet your original did it, and I am glad she did."

She sighed, "I am not saying that it is an evil act, or even wrong, but it is dangerous. My progenitor died shortly after, which saved her from facing the consequences."

"What consequences?"

"Execution, for one, if the Centyr family had discovered it. It is a skill that any of us could potentially develop, but once learned it is impossible to forget. Now that she has done it, it will always be before her, a ready solution to every problem. Unlike the difficult task of creating a new and original mind for her spellbeasts she will always be tempted to simply create a copy of her own mind. It is far faster, and the result is a creature with all of the original's powers and abilities, not to mention a complete understanding of what problem is at hand and what is needed."

He coughed, "Nothing you have mentioned makes it sound like something worth executing someone for. It sounds very handy. If I could have done that, I could have solved many of my problems over the years."

"You did experience it, when you became one of the shiggreth. Your mind-clone, Brexus, was exactly that," she noted.

"Then I should be executed?"

Moira smiled wryly, "Probably, for a hundred other reasons, but not that one. You cannot repeat the process, it was accidental. Moira however, can do it as often as she wishes, more rapidly than you can possibly imagine."

Mordecai stood and began pacing, "But she won't, not if we can explain to her why she shouldn't, and you still haven't explained the danger."

"When she did it, she used her twins to control thousands of people simultaneously, changing their minds and personalities. Assuming that she reabsorbed those spell-minds afterward, all of their actions effectively became her own. The pressure that put on her spirit is what twisted and changed her essence. It made her into a reaver, of that I have no doubt."

"What is a reaver?" he asked in exasperation.

"A nightmare," said Moira Centyr without hesitation, "a wizard that can invade the minds of others and remake them in moments, without remorse or regret. A wizard that can duplicate herself many times over, creating a million such monsters, all just as capable as the original. A creature of the mind so powerful that no one could defend themselves against it."

Mort narrowed his eyes, "Except other wizards, of course."

She laughed, "You think so?"

"Are you saying she could do this to me?"

Moira's face took on a serious expression, "You would be difficult, but you would lose. If it ever comes to a struggle you must kill her swiftly, before she breaches your defenses. Once she has crossed over into your mind she would devour you."

"Because she's become this 'reaver' you keep talking about?"

"Any Centyr mage would win, if they could access your mind, but if they weren't a reaver before, they would be by the time they finished. Fortunately, it is difficult for us to force our way in against a wary opponent, but your daughter has gained a lifetime's worth of experience now. She is no longer a novice and her spirit will be harder than steel and blacker than death.

"She can create endless minions now, and they are not limited by her aythar if they don't choose to be. They can steal the souls of whomever they possess, taking the wellsprings of those they inhabit. They might not be powerful, but mind magic doesn't require great strength, it is an art built on subtlety.

"This has happened before, several times in fact. The first few were limited and they were destroyed once the danger was realized. The worst was a man named Lynn Centyr, several hundred years before I was born. He was discovered quietly altering the minds of a few of his friends.

"Since it was early and he seemed sincere in his repentance, he was allowed to live. He kept his promise to behave for almost ten years before he gave in to temptation and changed his wife to make her more compliant."

Mort laughed, "Well, honestly, who wouldn't…"

"This is not a joke!" snapped Moira, losing her temper. "Knowing he must avoid discovery he began altering more people and eventually he started making spell-twins to aid him in keeping his secret. It was years before they suspected what was happening and the first wizards to investigate had no idea what he had become, for they were not from the Centyr family."

"Why didn't they know?" asked Mort.

"Because my family kept its secrets close. This is knowledge we have never shared for fear of turning the other families against us," she answered. "By the time the Centyr family intervened he had enslaved an entire village and the two wizards who had initially interfered were his most potent guardians. My family lost many lives putting an end to him, and several more had to be destroyed once it was over, for they were forced to become reavers themselves to win."

Mordecai walked to the window and stared out at the trees, watching them bend in the wind. He seemed contemplative, but when he turned back to her there was determination in his eyes. "Why didn't Gareth come with you when I sent my message?"

She looked down, "I didn't tell him."

"Because?"

"I was ashamed."

"Of your family's curse?"

She shook her head negatively, "No, he would accept that, but he would never forgive me for what we must do."

"Murdering my daughter, you mean?" he asked to clarify, his voice strangely calm.

Silently she nodded.

The Count di'Cameron took a deep breath and held it for several seconds before expelling the air. A strange look came over him and he took several long strides toward her, until they stood almost nose to nose. His eyes burned fiercely as he stared into her eyes, "I have done many terrible things, but it grows easier each time. Would you like to know the secret?" He was leaning closer, as though he meant to kiss her cheek.

The stone lady found herself off balance, made hesitant and unsure by his strangely aggressive manner. She tried to take a step back, to pull away, but his arms were around her, one at the small of her back and the other behind her head. She almost yelped in surprise as she felt his lips beside her ear.

"Let me tell you…," he said, whispering.

When she heard the words she started to scream, but it was too late.

CHAPTER 30

Alyssa's trial was held two days after her return, which was almost a mercy, since she was kept in the Lancaster jail during that time. She was allowed no visitors but the food was good. It was better than she felt she deserved.

She had been surprised when Lady Hightower had appeared early on the morning of her trial and she had lowered her face, ashamed.

"Raise your eyes, Alyssa," the noblewoman had told her.

"I don't deserve that much honor, milady," she had replied, "not after what I have done."

"This is going to be awkward if the client cannot even face her counsel," Rose had said.

She had looked up then, "Counsel?"

Rose's face had been serious, showing no humor but filled instead with somber resolve, "I will be defending you today."

"But why?"

"Because otherwise they'll execute my son's fiancée…"

That had been six hours ago, but even now she found herself glancing sideways at the woman beside her in disbelief. Rose Thornbear was a woman in her middle years, but she sat on the hard bench with her back perfectly straight. Everything about her spoke of dignity and decorum and the light in her eyes made certain there was no doubt of her intelligence.

She could not read her at all. By every measure that Alyssa could think of, Rose Thornbear should hate her, but she could detect no malice in her mannerisms. She had spent the morning with Alyssa, questioning her over and over again, making certain of every detail. During that time Alyssa had been unable to decide whether Gram's mother honestly wanted to help her or was acting on some unseen directive, perhaps from the Count.

The Count sat in the row behind her, with Moira on one side and the Countess on the other, another surprise. Alyssa had somehow expected that he would be presiding as judge, but apparently in Lothion the nobles could only dispense low justice. High justice, cases that could result in execution, were the sole province of the queen herself, or the royal justices that she had appointed.

His Honor, Lloyd Watson was just such a man. He had been summoned from the capital purely for her trial. He was younger than Alyssa had thought a judge might be, appearing to be in his early thirties with short brown hair and eyes that were so dark as to seem black. He had a piercing gaze that made her nervous whenever he glanced in her direction.

"Calm yourself," cautioned Lady Hightower, "fidgeting will make you appear guilty."

"I am guilty," replied Alyssa softly.

Rose scowled at her then, "Do not presume to use that term here. We are pleading innocence today."

Alyssa's incredulous expression was all the reply she could give to that statement.

Lady Hightower smiled at that, the first smile she had shown Alyssa all day. "See the Count behind you? I stood before the High Justicer in Albamarl when he was accused of murder."

"And you proved him innocent?" asked Alyssa.

Rose pursed her lips, "No, but I could have gotten him out of the charges on a legal point of order. Unfortunately, he was stubborn and insisted on allowing the case to stand and he was convicted."

"You think there is some trick that will save me?"

The noblewoman shook her head, "No. I merely told you that so that you would learn from his stupidity. *Don't* be like the Count. They would have executed him if the Queen hadn't threatened to pardon him."

"I can hear you," hissed Mordecai from behind them. Penny elbowed him to warn him to silence as a result.

Alyssa glanced past Rose to look at Gram, who sat farther down the bench beside his grandmother, Elise Thornbear. He gave her a thin smile that couldn't dispel the nervous anxiety on his face.

John Stanton, the prosecutor was standing and reading the charges, "...did willfully and intentionally conspire to commit murder and kidnapping. The state charges the defendant with conspiracy, fraud, treachery, treason, kidnapping, and murder."

"How does the defendant answer these charges?" asked Lloyd Watson.

Rose stood, "Your Honor, the defendant respectfully enters a plea of not guilty."

The judge's brows went up, "Are you certain? Unless you are planning to argue the facts of this case..."

"The facts are indisputable, Your Honor," agreed Rose, "but the circumstances are not."

The judge sighed, "Very well."

The prosecution proceeded as expected. Master Stanton laid out the facts, beginning with Alyssa's fraudulent identity as the daughter of a nobleman and continuing to her disappearance and subsequent return with the men who kidnapped Irene Illeniel and slew Lilly Tucker.

In the course of matters, the prosecution called Peter Tucker, Lilly's brother, to testify regarding his sister's death. Then they called David Summerfield, her fiancée. Neither had anything material to add to the facts of the case, but their moving descriptions of Lilly Tucker's kindness and generosity caused many an eye in the courtroom to grow misty. The final witness called was Irene herself, but the questions directed at her were punctual and self-limiting, giving her only enough leeway to confirm the facts of her kidnapping.

Rose had declined to examine Peter or David, but she rose to her feet after the prosecutor was done with Irene. "If I may also question the witness, Your Honor?"

"Of course," said the judge.

"Did Jasmine Darzin murder Lilly Tucker?" she asked.

Irene looked confused, "I'm not sure who…"

Rose waved her hand at Alyssa, "This woman, the woman you knew as Alyssa. Did she murder Lilly?"

"No," said Irene. "She told him to stop but he ignored her. She protected me later when…"

"I will get to that in a moment," said Rose, cutting her off. "By your statement you imply that Jasmine did not, in fact, have command over the men that took you."

Irene nodded, "Yes, Lady Hightower."

"How did you escape your kidnappers?"

"Gram tracked them and confronted them at the edge of the mountains, near the Northern Waste. He fought Alyssa, I mean Jasmine's father, and killed him," Irene answered.

"And why didn't Jasmine return with you after that?"

"They shot her. Her father ordered his men to kill me and she covered me with her body," said Irene.

Rose smiled, "You say they shot her. How many arrows hit Jasmine?"

"Two, I think."

"And after that you and Gram fled?"

"There were horsemen coming to take us, from across the wastes. Jasmine couldn't run and Gram couldn't run fast enough and carry her, so she begged him to leave her with a sword. She was going to try to delay them."

"Do you think that the defendant wanted to kidnap you?"

"No," said Irene. "Alyssa hated what they were…"

"Objection, Your Honor," said John Stanton. "The victim's opinion of the defendant's intentions isn't relevant."

"It is entirely relevant, Your Honor," argued Rose. "The charges include treachery and fraud, which to be proven, must show that the defendant had a deliberate intention to commit a crime, in this case murder and kidnapping."

The judge paused a moment but then spoke, "You may continue."

Rose looked at Irene, "So you don't think Jasmine wanted to kidnap you?"

"No. She looked after me when the men tried to torment me. She only did it because her father ordered her to," answered Irene. "She didn't want to hurt Lilly either."

Rose had no more questions after that, but Stanton asked to reexamine the witness. The judge agreed and he directed a new question at Irene, "How did the men from Dunbar find your parent's home in the mountains?"

Irene looked unsure, "I don't know, exactly."

"And yet, the only one of them to have been in Castle Cameron, was Jasmine Darzin, is that not true?" he asked.

"The house isn't in Cameron, though," responded Irene. "It's hidden in the mountains. No one knows where…"

"But that isn't true, is it Irene? Does not your friend, Gram Thornbear visit your home sometimes?" continued the prosecutor.

"Well, yes…"

"And isn't he also romantically involved with Jasmine?"

Irene faltered, "I don't know anything about…"

"You are friends with Carissa Thornbear, correct?"

"Yes."

"Didn't she tell you her brother was in love with the woman calling herself Alyssa?" added the prosecutor.

Irene looked at the floor, "She might have said that. It's hard to recall."

"Someone must have told you, though, for you knew that he was in love with her, didn't you?"

The girl's lip trembled, "Yes."

"Then isn't it reasonable to assume that she learned the location of your home from the man she had seduced, and then used that information to lead her accomplices to your home?"

Irene's eyes filled with tears and her mouth opened, but she couldn't find the words to speak. Alyssa heard

Moira shifting in her seat and a low growl was coming from Mordecai.

Rose stood once more, "Objection, Your Honor. The witness' inferences about the defendant's source of information are hearsay."

Justice Watson agreed, but the prosecutor smiled as he sat down again. He had made his point.

The case went on and the court heard testimony from Gram, the Count, and various servants that had interacted with Alyssa in the castle. Rose called on Cyhan near the end to discuss the nature of his brother, T'Lar Darzin's training techniques. She tried to get a full description of what had happened to his younger sister, but the prosecutor argued that it wasn't material to Jasmine's case and the judge agreed.

Alyssa lost hope as the day dragged on. She knew she was guilty, and so did everyone else. Rose's defense seemed pointless. The prosecutor's closing remarks made that clear enough, all the facts were against her. Neither she, nor anyone else, had denied what she had done. There could be no verdict other than guilty, regardless of her motivations or the circumstances.

And then Rose stood.

"Your Honor, you have heard the prosecution's case, and the facts are not at issue here." Her blue eyes caught the light as she turned to face the room. The gray hair that was visible in her coiffure seemed to only highlight the shine of her dark hair. She did not look like a woman about to admit defeat.

"What is at issue, are the charges," continued Lady Hightower. "Jasmine Darzin is accused of conspiracy, but it cannot be shown that she was willingly involved in planning these crimes. She is accused of treason, but she had not sworn loyalty to Lothion or Albamarl. She was no vassal of the Count's either. She was acting unwillingly under the coercion and direction of her uncle, the man who raised her and abused her. What should be amazing is that she was unwilling. The only loyalty she had been trained to know, was to that evil man, and yet she chose, when the moment of crisis was upon her, to risk her life to save Irene Illeniel.

"Treason is impossible to justify, as is treachery. Treachery involves the unexpected use of force to commit a crime in such a way that the offender is safe from retaliation, and yet she put herself in harm's way. When her uncle ordered the kidnapping of the Count's family, she went with them, willingly, yes, but not to further the crime. She went to guarantee the safety of the people she had come to love and respect, and when she was forced by circumstances, she betrayed her comrades to protect Irene Illeniel. The only treachery she committed was against her *uncle.*

"Murder is likewise untenable. By the account of Irene herself, as well as the other witnesses, Jasmine Darzin did not murder Lilly Tucker. In fact, she spoke out against it. Her sole purpose for being there was to *prevent* that very thing from happening.

"Jasmine Darzin, who by the way, prefers to go by the name she assumed when she first came here, Alyssa, is not guilty of those charges. Not as they are written, not treason, or treachery, or murder, or even conspiracy. I will not argue against the charges of fraud or kidnapping, but the rest is an attempt to foist upon her a punishment that she does not deserve.

"The true question facing this court today, if reason is to be honored, is not as simple as deciding guilt or innocence. This young woman is not guilty of most of the crimes named. The real issue is how we will treat a woman abused and betrayed by those who should have cared for and nurtured her, a woman who then was ordered to kidnap our Count's daughter, a woman who in the end made the correct choice by turning against her uncle and saving Irene Illeniel, even at the possible cost of her own life."

Rose pointed at Alyssa, "This woman is not a murderer, but she has broken the law. Will we use this court as an excuse for vengeance and reprisal? The men responsible for those other crimes are dead. Will we make her our scape goat in their stead, a sacrifice to fulfil our need for revenge, or will we treat her according to the mistakes she is truly guilty of?"

Lady Hightower's voice ended on that note and the silence that followed seemed to echo with significance. When she sat down the judge addressed the courtroom, "I will need a short while to deliberate."

Everyone rose as he left and when he had gone the room broke into a multitude of conversations. Moira reached forward to touch Alyssa's shoulder, "Don't worry. Whatever happens I won't let them take you."

"Moira!" said her father, his face unusually severe.

Moira looked away, but she had no intention of changing her statement. She had meant it. *I could change everyone's mind.* Then her eyes landed on Cyhan.

The big man stood alone on the far side of the room, but his eyes were locked on Alyssa. His normally relaxed stance was gone and for once he seemed to have little awareness of his surroundings. It was as if his mind only had room for one thing.

"Alyssa, look," said Moira, tapping the other woman's shoulder again and directing her gaze toward Cyhan.

Alyssa looked down, "I cannot."

"He's your father. Let him see your face. You've barely met before this. This might be your only chance," suggested Moira.

"He must hate me for what I've done," said Alyssa softly. "I can't bear to see it in his face."

Moira looked at Cyhan again. He *did* look rather stern, so she could see how Alyssa might easily imagine him to be angry, but she knew Cyhan better than that. "That's just how is face is. He always looks like that…"

The room fell silent as Judge Watson returned. He hadn't taken long to think on his decision, which might be cause for concern. After a few formalities he stood to address the room. Moira was studying him intently and she could see the determination in his aythar. Lloyd Watson was not a man of many doubts and she could see his condemnation written clearly on the surface of his mind. She could hear the word 'guilty' almost as clearly as if he had spoken it already.

Not today! she thought sending a fine line of aythar toward the judge's mind.

A shield rose in front of her, interfering with her attempt to reach him. "Moira," whispered her father sternly. "No."

Righteous anger filled her heart as she protested, "But he's going to…!"

Mordecai interrupted, "We need to have a serious talk after this."

She felt as though ice water had been thrown on her. Her suspicion was finally confirmed. She had heard about the visit from her mother's shade a few days ago, while she had been back in Halam. She had been worrying over its portent, but her father hadn't said anything—until now. *She told him about the rules.*

Lloyd Watson gave his verdict, "It is the finding of this court that Jasmine Darzin is guilty of fraud, kidnapping, and conspiracy to commit kidnapping. The court finds her innocent of murder, treason and treachery."

A hush fell over the room then. After a short pause he continued, "The court will pause now to hear statements from those most affected by this case before we continue with sentencing. Those with good cause may approach the bench to ask for permission to speak to the court."

David Summerfield was on his feet first and the judge gave him permission immediately. He wasn't family, but he had been betrothed to Lilly Tucker. His cheeks were red and his eyes inflamed as he spoke, "My Lilly was a beautiful soul. My only dream in this world was to marry her, to try and give her as much joy as she had given to so many others. There's not a soul here who could speak ill of her. She was my heart, my life.

"And she was stolen from me, from all of us. Say what you will about that woman's *intentions*," he pointed at Alyssa, "but Lilly is dead and all the good intentions in the world won't bring her back. She led those murderers to the house. She deserves to die for that alone!" His voice broke then and he covered his face, unable to continue.

The next to stand was Peter Tucker, his cheeks wet but his face calm. "Few of you know my story, but Lilly and I came here to serve the Count and Countess when we were very young. Back then, revenge was my only motive, my driving force. Hatred burned in my heart and I longed for nothing more than to kill the man responsible for our grandfather's death.

"But Lilly didn't believe in living that way," Peter's throat closed up for a moment and he struggled to go on. When he continued his voice was thick, "She wouldn't let me live like that. She fought and argued with me to forgive, to live for kindness instead, and as time went on, I came to see that the man I hated was no monster at all. He was just a man, a man who made a simple but terrible mistake. He was a man that was capable of great goodness, of kindness, and once I forgave him I came to love him.

"As much as some of us might have cause to hate her, this girl isn't a monster. She was as much a victim in this as we were. Lilly would not have asked for her death. She would have begged us to forgive her..." Peter stopped. "That's all I have."

Gram started to rise, but Rose put her hand on his shoulder, urging him to wait, and then he saw Sir Cyhan approaching the bench. His eyes widened in surprise.

The old warrior's face looked as though it had been carved from stone, until his lips began to move, "You all know me, or know of me. I have served Lothion for most of my life, first in service to Edward Carenval, our late king, and then in service to our good Count.

"I have spent my life fighting. As a boy I was taught to fight from an early age and my first step into manhood was killing the bastard that raped my sister, my own teacher. As a man I trained others to fight, cruelly and without mercy, as I was taught. I did not believe in mercy, or compassion. I thought this world was cold and without joy.

"I fully expected to die as I had lived, violently. I yearned for it, for I hated myself. I hated my failures. I mourned for the sister that I hadn't protected. I avenged her, but it never gave me any satisfaction. It only left me empty, facing a life of meaningless brutality.

"I sought refuge in honor, but it did not shield me, and it was only some joke played by the cosmos that I somehow wound up in the service of the Count di'Cameron. Years later, I have discovered that there is more to this life, much more. But still, most of it had nothing to do with me.

"I had no wife, nor the will to take one. I had no family, only a few friends and a long life ahead of me. Instead of a violent death, I began to see that I might be forced to live long and die alone.

"And then...," Cyhan stopped, his deep voice trembling. "And then, I found out I had a daughter. I've never been a husband even, much less a father, but somehow, I have a daughter. A daughter that was raised without me, who suffered without me, who was tormented just as my sister was, and even named after her."

A great choking sob rose from his chest then, while tears streamed down his cheeks. "I met her without knowing, without really looking at her, and now I see her, and despite everything, she's beautiful." He bowed his head for a moment, but he didn't step down. "And she's done some terrible things, *because I wasn't there for her.* I never had the chance to help her.

"I've never had a family, but now I have a daughter, and I am begging you to please, please let her live. Let me have the chance to know her. Don't take the first good thing to happen to me in this life away. I will pay any price to keep her."

Cyhan looked directly at David Summerfield then, "I know you've been wronged. But if you need justice, take my life, Mister Summerfield. Just give her a chance…"

There were no dry eyes left by then. The big knight could no longer continue, he stood now, head down and shoulders quaking. The Count started to rise, to go to him, but Gram was there first.

Unsure what to do, Gram didn't address the judge, but he looked across the room, "I wanted to say something too, but he said it all." Putting a gentle hand on his teacher's back, Gram led Cyhan back to his place.

No one else came forward after that, so eventually Judge Watson looked toward the Count, "Your Excellency, if I may have a word with you?"

Mordecai rose and the two men left the room. It was ten minutes before they returned.

The judge addressed the court again, "My sentence is that Jasmine Darzin shall serve six months in Lancaster's dungeon for the crime of kidnapping. Thereafter she will be given her parole to serve five more years in the Count di'Cameron's household. For the terrible wrong done to Master Tucker's family, she will pay him fifty gold marks. The Count has graciously agreed to pay that sum immediately and her service with him may extend beyond her parole until she has repaid the debt.

"This court is now ended."

EPILOGUE

Cassandra beat her wings strongly as she dropped toward the mountainside, making her landing as gentle as possible.

Moira and her father clambered down from her back to stare up the slope at the opening to the cave where her unfortunate adventure had begun.

"I had more trouble finding it again than I thought I would," said Mordecai. "All these damn mountains look the same."

"You should have waited and let me come with you," replied Moira. Her father had searched for and found the cave where he had been captured weeks before, while she and her mother were in Dunbar, but today he had asked her to return with him one more time, ostensibly to share her observations with him. She could tell he had other motivations however, it was impossible to hide such things from her these days.

He's nervous, she observed, following him into the cave.

Mordecai was shielding himself more tightly than ever, preventing her from seeing anything more than his surface emotions. That in itself was remarkable to her; not the fact that he was shielding himself so carefully, her father had always been almost fanatical about that habit, probably as a result of his years of struggle and conflict. What was interesting was that since her trip to Dunbar she could now read his emotions despite his shields.

Since her return home she had noticed many such changes in herself. People were open books to her now, even the residents of Castle Cameron, who all wore pendants to protect their minds from intrusion. The enchanted necklaces had been a defense created during the time when shiggreth roamed the land, but they had kept her from seeing into people's minds as a child.

Now, they only served as a sort of hazy interference, like looking through a gauze curtain.

Her father's mental shield was more effective, but she could still see his mood, and today he was nervous.

They entered the last cavern and he glanced around before speaking to her, "This is where it happened. Can you feel it?"

She nodded, walking to the spot that she and Matthew had examined the first time they had been there, "It was right here."

Her father watched her, "Does it feel different now than it did then?"

Moira frowned, "What do you mean?"

"When you and Matthew were here, you said that he made a point of the fact that the magic was trans-dimensional, or as he calls it, 'translation magic'. Does it feel different to you now than it did that day?"

She opened her mind more fully, probing the area, before nodding, "It's much stronger than it was then. What do you think it means?"

"I don't know. I'm almost certain there has been another crossing, but I have no way of knowing who or what, or even which way," explained Mordecai.

Her eyes widened, "You don't think…?"

He held up a hand, "Before we talk about what may be, I want to know if you can feel anything that I cannot."

"We both have magesight…"

"But you are a Centyr mage, and I know for a fact that the various families sometimes sense things differently. Walter, for example, was always able to spot the shiggreth much more easily than I could, despite my better range and sensitivity."

She saw a faint flash through his shield when he said the word 'Centyr', a hollow echo that might be fear. *Is he afraid of me, of what I am? What did she tell him? Is this a test?* "I can try," she answered.

Kneeling she put her hands on the floor in the approximate center of the magical traces. It was definitely stronger now, but she had no way of knowing whether it represented something coming to their world, or something leaving it. All she knew for sure was that it was her brother's translation magic, gradually fading over time. There was a feeling of curiosity present as well.

She stared up at her father as her face lit up with understanding, "It was Matt. He did this."

"Then we can likely assume that this was him leaving, rather than the reverse," said Mordecai.

"He went alone. Why is he so stupid!?" cursed Moira. "What was he thinking?"

"I don't know for sure, but he probably meant to trace the source of the enemy you met in Dunbar," said Mordecai.

"He has no idea how dangerous they are. No one does," she replied, venting her frustration. She had continued to have bad dreams since her return from Dunbar.

Her father gave her an enigmatic smile, "You might be surprised."

"What does that mean?"

"You named them ANSIS when we spoke before; that is a name that has meaning to me. It is a name that has particular significance to the She'Har."

He was talking about the memories he had inherited. Memories passed down from one Illeniel to the next over thousands of years, the gift, or possibly the curse, gained by Tyrion Illeniel long ago. Memories that stretched even farther back than human history, for they were the memories of the She'Har and their roots had their beginnings long before they had come to this world.

"All that happened a long time ago," said Moira. "How could it be relevant to this?"

Her father's face changed, becoming earnest, "Before we talk about that we need to discuss something else."

"You mean what you really brought me here for," she said, somewhat anxiously.

"About what happened to you in Halam."

Moira took a deep breath, "It didn't happen to me, I happened to *them*." She had been expecting this conversation for days, now that it was finally happening she felt her fear actually decreasing.

"I spoke with your mother."

She knew he meant the *other* Moira, the one that had survived over more than a thousand years just to make sure she could someday find a new family for her. The one that knew the rules regarding her special type of magic.

"Did she tell you what the penalties are for manipulating other people's minds and memories?" he asked.

Moira shook her head, "Not specifically. It was years ago, but she gave me the impression they were rather serious."

"How about the personal consequences of using such power?"

A vision of her hand, covered in black scales with fingertips that ended in sharp claws, appeared in her mind as a surge of adrenaline sent a shock of fear up her spine. *He knows.* She suppressed the fear but she found herself almost unconsciously sizing him up. The shields around his body and mind were considerable. She could get through them, but it would take time, time in which he would be fighting fiercely. Would he kill her before she could get through them? *If I can get through, this could end well for both of us.*

Moira! Get ahold of yourself. What are you thinking? cautioned Myra. *He's our father!*

"No, but I think I understand them now," she said. "I've changed inside."

"You know I love you, right? That I will always love you," he said sadly. There were tears in his eyes.

The sight shocked her and her own defensive anger vanished, replaced by feeling of sad longing, of empathy. "I love you too, Dad." She had lied before; she had remembered the penalties that her mother had spoken of. He was planning to kill her. "I'm sorry."

"Tell me about it, about what you've been feeling."

"What?"

"You aren't the only one that has been through the fire. I've done things that harrow the soul, things that wake me up in the middle of the night, sweating and fearful. I don't know what you've experienced, but I can probably empathize. Share it with me, tell me what you've been going through. I want to know what's happening inside you," he explained.

She bowed her head, "Is there any point?"

"More than you know."

Moira exhaled slowly, letting the tension out of her shoulders, and then she began, starting with the girl she had played chess with in the mountains. She went on to describe her escape from the dungeon in the palace of Halam, the discovery that she had inadvertently created an exact copy of herself, and the way that it had enabled her to do many things at once. Her tension returned as she talked about the battle outside the city, but she held nothing back. She explained about her twins seizing control of the citizens and how some of them had taken control of the wellsprings of their hosts.

The worst part was telling him about her battle with Celior, but she did it anyway, even describing the transformation she had undergone as she tortured the false-god. It was awful, admitting it all to him, but her heart felt better for it. She might be evil, but at least she would die honestly.

When she finished he said only one thing, "Take down your shields." He was standing directly in front of her.

Not yet, I need more time, she thought. Her eyes had been dry throughout her story, but tears sprang from them now. Reluctantly, she lowered her defenses.

Mordecai lowered his own shield and then he wrapped his arms around her, hugging her tightly. "I'm so sorry all that happened to you."

Now! The thought sprang at her from the back of her mind, but she pushed it aside. She wouldn't attack him, no matter what. She tried to talk, but her throat wasn't cooperating. Nothing came out but quiet sobs. Finally, she managed to say, "I'm sorry, Daddy."

"Shhhh, it's alright. It wasn't your fault."

"But it *was!*" she cried. "If I had known the circle keys, I could have just come home. I could have gotten help."

Mordecai squeezed her tighter, "Nobody is perfect. That might have been better, but maybe not. What if your mother had come? Who knows what might have happened? Maybe she could have done something else, or maybe she would have gotten herself killed. Would you have blamed yourself then? If there's one thing I've learned over the years, it's that the 'what ifs' never help."

"But I'm a monster now…"

He chuckled deep in his chest, "Yes, you're my dear sweet little monster, and I love you anyway."

"*What?*"

He pulled his head back to look down at her, "Did you think I wouldn't love you anymore? Silly thing, daddies never stop loving their little girls."

She cried harder then, as all the pressure that had built up in her over the past weeks slowly made its way out. He held her and uttered soothing words, as though she were still a little girl, but it didn't bother her. At that moment it was all she wanted.

Eventually she grew still, empty of everything. Wiping at her eyes with a sleeve she asked, "What are you going to do?"

"Well, I'm not going to kill you, if that's what you think. You can just forget that nonsense now," he replied.

"But I'm not safe."

"Neither am I," he said simply. "None of us are, although some are more dangerous than others."

Moira frowned, wondering if he really understood, "No, I could destroy everything. I might take over the whole world."

"Yeah, me too," he answered wryly. Looking her firmly in the eye he went on, "Power is power, Moira. It comes in different flavors, but it's all the same. By your rationale I should have been put to death a long time ago, but here I am. What is important is whether you are willing to take responsibility for yourself."

"I'm not human anymore, Dad. It's not the same. I'm turning into something else. You can't trust me. Eventually I'll lose control," she added, trying to explain.

Mordecai laughed again, "Yeah, she tried to feed me that bullshit too, and I think she believes it herself."

"But it's true."

"Only if you believe it," he said confidently. "Would you like to know how I know?"

She nodded, a feeling of hope beginning to rise within her.

"Because the Centyr family doesn't know everything. They saw the ones that went bad, the ones they caught. Do you really think those were the only ones that broke the rules? In a thousand years, how many Centyr mages do you think gave in to temptation and used their power to change someone's mind?"

Moira stared at him blankly, "I don't know…"

Her father smiled, "That's right! You don't. No one does. I can tell you this, though. It was far more than the few that went bad, far more than the ones they know about. I would venture to guess that at least half of all the Centyr wizards that ever lived tried it at least once. It's just human nature. Your power is dangerous, and subtle in a way that few powers are, but it is still only a tool. I understand it harms the user too, but your choices are still your own.

"Besides, I have at least one other reason to believe you won't destroy the world, or enslave it."

"What's that?" she asked.

"Illeniel's Doom," he responded, tapping his temple. "This thing that is in my head and has haunted my family for two thousand years. There's a reason for it. It wasn't just stolen, although that's what was believed at first. Now I have the reason in front of me, or half of the reason anyway. Your brother is the other half."

"You know I didn't inherit it from my father," said Moira. The knowledge of the loshti was only present in one descendant in each generation. Her biological father hadn't had it even though he had been an Illeniel.

"That's the beauty of it," said Mordecai. "It's your gift that's important. You are the last living Centyr wizard, and your brother is the first Illeniel wizard. He does have the knowledge granted by the loshti, but that is only part of this puzzle."

"But he's *not* the first Illeniel wizard."

"Do you remember the story I told you a few years back, about Tyrion?" reminded Mordecai.

"Yes, it was awful," she said with some distaste.

"Remember the gift of the Illeniel Grove?"

She pursed her lips, "Tyrion didn't have it. None of them did, because the Illeniel Grove didn't create human slaves. And even when he tried to steal it, it didn't work."

"That's right," said her father, "The breeders didn't work, but your brother has the gift now, even though he didn't get it from me."

"Mother?" exclaimed Moira, referring to Penny now. "Wait, does that mean you're cousins?"

He nodded, "It's been two thousand years, but yes, we have to be, although we're dozens if not hundreds of times removed."

"So her gift, prophecy, it comes from the Illeniel Grove?"

"I can't prove it. I don't know her family history, but it's the only reasonable assumption. I do know that there has never been a human wizard with her gift—until now, at precisely the same time that the great enemy of the She'Har has reemerged."

Moira winced, "You're saying my brother is some sort of wizard messiah, aren't you?" *Great, just fucking great. He'll be gloating about this forever.*

Mort saw the look in her eye and began chuckling, "No, but without him we would all be in a great deal of trouble. The two of you will save the world I hope, with a little help from your aging father."

He started walking toward the tunnel that led out, "Let's go home."

As Moira started to follow him her foot scuffed the dirt that covered the floor and she caught a glimpse of something carved there. Runes, etched in the stone. Her magesight stretched out and followed their shapes beneath the dirt, seeing where they went. They circled the limits of the room and a smaller circle enclosed the place her father had been standing earlier.

He hadn't taken any chances. He must have inscribed them a week before when he had come alone.

Perhaps she should have been offended, but somehow seeing that he had made the preparations, just in case she had turned on him, didn't bother her. Instead it brought an odd comfort. The afternoon light silhouetted her father against the cave opening and she stared up at his tall shoulders. On impulse she ran forward to embrace him from behind.

The world was a terrible place, and she might be a monster herself, but her father's strong back made her feel safe.

"What's that for?" he asked, looking back.

"Nothing," she replied and then she squeezed his belly with her hands, "You're getting fat."

"A bit of a belly is a sign of success in a man," he growled, "like a mane on a lion."

"Keep telling yourself that…"

Mordecai sighed, "Back to what we were talking about. Remember what happened in that story? After Tyrion stole the loshti, when he began making preparations…"

She didn't want to think about it, but he began telling it anyway, reminding her of the terrible things that had happened two thousand years before, when the She'Har were exterminated and humanity almost died with them.

Coming in the Winter of 2016

The Betrayer's Bane

The story of Tyrion Illeniel concludes in the third book of the Embers of Illeniel series. One man will sacrifice everything, and everyone, in his quest for vengeance, but the final cost is his own humanity.

Coming in 2017

Demonhome

Matthew Illeniel seeks the source of the intruders into his world, traveling across dimensions to find answers. He must unravel the mystery of the She'Har's great enemy but the bigger challenge may lie in discovering the secrets of humanity itself.

For more information about the Mageborn series check out the author's Facebook page:

https://www.facebook.com/MagebornAuthor

or visit the website:

http://www.magebornbooks.com/

19848133R00221

Printed in Great Britain
by Amazon